DESPATCHES FROM THE DEEP

TABLE OF CONTENTS

CHAPTER ONE

Goe'ma'goe
(16th C, trad arr.)

Wid gall'ans crack and boswain's groan
Ye gallant 'ere dae goe
For in those bow'ells of whit'some foam
Slumbers ole Goe'ma'goe

He's 'ere a damn'd foe to thee
So steer me good and wide
For in that callous'd grin of he
The diville do'st reside

More mariner hast thee within
Those hulkin' gruntin' guts
And more mariner hast thee than sin
'Ere those blinkin' eyelid shuts

The dag that sleeps is't better more
So harken thee my rhyme
The double rocks off Selyvan's shore
Art Goe'ma'goe's not thine

Cornwall, England 2013

The Billy Ruffian bobbed peacefully on the gentle swells off the Lizard peninsula. Despite its fighting talk the Billy Ruffian was a pleasure boat - painted a gloss white and lined with a blue entwined Celtic trim. A sailor would admire her - 30-feet long and equipped with a Bermuda rig. The purist might disapprove of the outboard motor bolted to its stern, for chugging her out of trouble (and frequently relied on by its inexpert crew).

From the prow of the Billy Ruffian, the town of Penzance twinkled with a thousand fairy lights – its homes fastened against the winter chill. The reverse view was no less spectacular, from the shoreline the Billy Ruffian was silhouetted against a great moon, hanging low above the sea. The moon's shattered face rippled across the icy waters of the English Channel. On her sails the sea-spray was already beginning to freeze with the insidious creep of mould on summer strawberries.

Three men sat below deck in a cosy cabin. The small party were reclined, each on their own bed. A fourth bunk lay empty, the neat, pressed linen in contrast to the strewn sheets of the others. A framed photograph of a man on his wedding day is positioned on the vacant pillow. A Post It note stuck to the silver frame said: "RIP Badger 1968-1990". Badger was at home with his wife and three children. Badger could only join them every third year, "that was the deal".

In the middle of the cabin, separating the beds, was a small camping table, hinged in the centre and never quite stable no matter how many beer-mats it rested upon. Two empty wine bottles tottered in the swell, occasionally threatening to fall when a higher wave lifted the bow. Six empty beer bottles sat gathered around a bottle of powerful Argentinian red, half-full and weeping a stigmatic tear. The Queen of Hearts' head bulged freakishly under its green glass, a bloody stain across her smirking mouth. There were three rules pinned to a board above the bunks: the first rule of boat club is you do not talk about work, the second rule of boat club is you do not talk about work, the third rule of boat club is Quentin will not talk about literature. It was printed out in Comic Sans, 36pt. The traces of last year's Blue Tac at the corners, the joke still got a laugh from two of the shipmates.

Two men were laughing more heartily and with less abandon than the third. This pair wore ill-advised jeans and pastel polo shirts with Italian names stitched prominently on the left breast. Both men wore yellow gold rings but know the penalties for mentioning the W-word at sea. The third man had no ring. He wore a collarless white linen shirt, which he will gladly recount was bought from a local market in Tolosa, 'that's in the Basque country' he will add. It has stained at the cuffs from red mortar where he rebuilt the wall outside his Breton getaway. A red neckerchief was tied tight around his neck beneath the sprouting stubble. As the other two men stared intently at their hands, his own cards lay face down on the bunk. Instead, he gazed through brass porthole window, transfixed by the navy clouds that raced across the moon.

"Who said the moon was a ghostly galleon tossed upon cloudy seas?"

The two men looked up from their cards and shot each other a look of resignation. Neither bit, and the question was left to hang.

"Come on, even you two should know this one. It's practically doggerel."

"Quentin, you know the rules," one of the men said and pointed at the sign. "No literature … and don't think I missed your Hemmingway reference on deck earlier."

"Keats," said the other, snapping across his friend with assurance.

"Don't encourage him," the first man stabbed his finger with greater emphasis at the rules.

Quentin leant back on his bed, letting out a sigh as he dropped back, sinking into the pillow.

"It's not literature, it's just a question, a pop quiz," Quentin said. "And the winner gets..."

He paused to consider a worthy motivation for his unwilling grunts. Inspiration struck.

"The winner gets to see the picture of Rosana on my phone."

It worked and the second man screamed out three incorrect answers like a daytime quiz contestant. The first man kept quiet and waited patiently for his flustered friend to finish before delivering his coup de grace.

The wind was a torrent of darkness upon the gusty trees,
The moon was a ghostly galleon tossed upon cloudy seas.

Alfred Noyes, The Highwayman. Your phone please, good sir."

Quentin laughed and made to hand over his phone but snatched it back just as it tickled the palm of his friend.

"If I had pictures on here, which I don't, do you really think I'd share them around like a dog-eared Razzle in the dorm."

The rightful winner wasn't convinced.

"Come on, don't be sour," he said. "You're not even with Rosana anymore, who is it now - the Russian?"

"It's Manca," said Quentin sternly. "And she's Slovenian, besides I decided we shouldn't see each other so often."

"Manky," the second man said with a guffaw.
 "She was gorgeous," said the first ruefully.

Quentin jarred with his old friends, but they were forgiving. He liked a drink, he played off scratch (despite never having visited a pro) and dated a string of exotic women but never married, so he was their unspoken hero - and he loved nothing more than to be idolised. The four, with absent Badger included, were Wellington old boys who cajoled one another into this annual trip and cajoled themselves with the subtlety of the press gang to enjoy it, even if it killed them. Quentin enjoyed to rising above their boorishness and adopted an aloofness he never aired with the Tuscan set but the mentality of the dormitory died hard. Quentin tossed a sock he found in his bed in retaliation to the 'manky' remark. It found its mark on his friend's shoulder who threw it away with as much alarm as though it had been a deadly snake.

"Your prize," he said with a satisfied smirk and gazed back out of the porthole at the moon.

"It's your hand," his friends said in unison, trying to chivvy along the faltering game. Quentin was absent, he had been struck by a moment of poetry.

"It's beautiful, I'm going out on deck to get a photo."

"You're crazy? It's freezing out there," said his friend. "And they're not exactly regulation uniform, sailor."

He pointed at the red stiletto heels Quentin tottered in precariously across the cabin, the forfeit for a controversial reference to a yachting incident in the Alexandria Quartet. Quentin had argued that relevance should dictate the rules, not rules the relevance. He lost the argument on a vote of two to one.

"Nonsense, I'm as steady as a mountain goat in these things," he said with unfortunate timing as he lost his balance and grabbed for the support of his bunk.

"Come on, don't be a hero. I'm not fishing you out of the drink tonight."

"A bet's a bet," said Quentin decisively. "Later when you lose at Gin Jenga - and lose you will - I shall insist you honour your debts. I ask no less of myself."

4

Quentin could not be dissuaded and climbed the steps to the deck, leaving his two friends, still shaking their heads, to get back to the wine, cards and predictable jokes.

The night was invigoratingly cold, and the sea spray stung his thin, whiskery cheeks. He struggled to find his footing on the deck but knew to heed his friends' sage advice meant defeat in some unspoken game. Instead of retreat he clicked the camera into life with a whir and a glow. Quentin liked to get his travel photos enlarged and printed on canvasses to present as gifts to his polite friends. A little smile tickled his lips as he imagined the satisfaction in gifting his two friends the very shot they had counselled against. But first he had to get the shot. The unsteady boat, the finger-numbing cold, the bright moon against the dark sea were irritating factors with which to contend. Quentin had made the snobbish declaration that 'auto mode was for Facebook snapshots' on so many occasions that he felt compelled to shoot in manual even in the secrecy of his own company. Under ideal conditions he generally struggled to find the correct settings, but with his fingers atrophied by the icy air and his brain fogged with Malbec, the results were woeful. He flicked the dial to auto, nobody needs ever know.

But before he could shoot his attention was distracted by a noise across the water. It came from the direction of the shore, low and mournful. Quentin recognised it instantly as human. Over the gentle lapping of waves against the hull floated long, musical syllables. He strained his ear to the sound, its volume increasing and decreasing with the strength of the wind that carried it. The distance was so great that he could not even be certain of the language, but he knew it was neither English, French nor Italian. There was something eerie about this indistinguishable chant that made Quentin suddenly wish to be below deck with his friends and he hastily began to pack the camera into its travel jacket. With the camera tucked away Quentin was aware the mantra had stopped, it had not reached a recognisable conclusion and had drifted away to silence as casually as it had first arrived. With nothing but the sound of the waves once again, the fear that had boiled over moments before felt foolish and he began to doubt whether he had even heard the noises.

Quentin's attention was now arrested by a bubbling churn from the sea, below where he stood. He stared down at the foaming brine, his eyes unable to pierce the inky black sea. The sea all about the yacht became a violent cauldron as though a great turbine stirred the waters beneath. Then, with an explosive crack which rent the blasted air, a great plume of water rocketed into the night sky. Then there was silence. Quentin looked around; his breathing was heavy as his heart pounded painfully inside. He clutched at his chest.

"Not now," he said. "Not here."

His attack had come three years previously, but he had since transformed his life. He sold his business, began exercising, and six months ago he finished the Burford-to-Banbury Burner in under three-and-a-half hours. A complacency had set in but the dizzying, constrictive pain of his stuttering heart returned the terror of that first arrest. With his hands gripped tight against the railings he began to make slow progress back to the cabin. The pain stole his voice and his cries for help came in hoarse whispers. 'The stilettos' he thought to himself as his legs bandied under his toppling weight. 'What a ridiculous way to die.'

Quentin had nearly reached the cabin when he was struck across his shoulders and neck by a terrible weight, knocking his senses with an icy pounding. The water thrown up by the blast now thundered down across the deck. The shock restored some strength in his failing muscles and he was forced to grasp the railings until his fingers whitened to prevent being swept overboard by the force of the deluge. Eventually the plunging water ceased and he lay panting with his face pressed to the deck as the final drops fell like fine sleet around him. Quentin forced himself with the final vapours of his stamina back onto his feet.

Below deck the two men rose to their feet in terror as the crashing water beat itself against the boards above. One of them in his clumsy panic, upended the camping table skittling wine and beer bottles that splintered in toothy shards. When the last blows had drummed, a silence descended and the two men stared at one another with gaping mouths. The single dim bulb swung overhead, lighting one face and then the other.

"What was that?"

But before the other could answer the stillness was pierced as the impact of a shock wave, felt more from the guts to the spine than in the ears, surged out from the sea and petrified both men where they stood. An alien shriek – booming low but with a high-pitched core - sounded and left their senses deafened and stupefied. Each man clasped both hands to his ears, but the sound was inescapable. A shriek like a battle cry, a shriek with a pulse, an organic shriek, a shriek that could never be forgotten, that seared itself as a perpetual echo within the dark caverns of their brains. And then, as suddenly as it had erupted, it was over.

The lightbulb above them burst and plunged the cabin into blindness. The boat shook and rattled, iron pans clattered, mugs smashed, and the men fell back onto their bunks. The yacht pitched in unseen swells and both men were thrown from their beds down onto the floor, prickly and bloody from the broken glass. The cabin had been snug but became chilled with a preternatural cold that iced the moisture from the eyes. The quaking prised boards from their decking in pained twangs. At any second it felt as though the entire structure might fail with implosive destruction. Through the cabin portholes lightning flashed, illuminating its chaos in frozen strobes of wild terror. Bloody hands clutched for stability. Teeth in the blue light gnashed in dumb animal fear. Eyes, wide and horrible, stared through nebulous, red tributaries at catastrophe. And then it stopped.

It was several minutes before either man could speak. They lay like startled mice, refusing to move until danger had passed beyond doubt. A lighter sparked. The second man found the torch. Both stared at one another without speaking, neither certain how to break the oppressive tension.

"My God, Quentin's still out there."

With the blind bravery which only comradeship can inject in fear-frozen limbs, they both clambered the steps to the deck in clumsy haste. In the cold, night air they found themselves alone. They hurried to every side of the yacht, leaning out over the railings into the gentle sea.

"Look."

His friend grasped him and pointed with a steady hand at a break in the railings where there were also two gouges in the deck planks each two-feet long and deep enough to splinter the hard wood.

CHAPTER TWO

East London, two days earlier

Drizzle driven by a cold wind, even the puddles flinched. It swirled in loops so it both stung the eyes and tickled the back of the neck. The weather had turned from a balmy October into a bleak November as suddenly as the calendar page flipped. It was not a day to be outside.

Gordon was ill-prepared. The metal spine of his cheap umbrella had snapped. It had lasted 40 minutes, bought at London Bridge station for loose change. Still Gordon clung to this token through the squall and stretched the limp nylon before him like a shield. His suit was sodden and his brown brogues had rain-stained to a mahogany. He cast them a rueful look. 'They will have to be stuffed with newspaper and left to dry slowly overnight,' he thought. He knew impatient placement on a radiator would surely crack the leather. His Church's shoes were Gordon's prized possessions and only indulgence. The rest of his wardrobe bore the brunt of economy and cultivated an unintentional bohemian raffishness. His suit sat snug where it ought to have hung and sagged where it ought to have nipped. The three ties he owned were bought in one careless swoop in a £15 station deal. Even his super-sized supermarket shirts billowed like a sail.

On days like this Gordon felt too old. The colleagues with whom he had risen through the ranks had already turned off the news reporter's road. While he splashed through the puddles in the cold shadow of a Plaistow tower block they were feathering nests as correspondents, comfortably covering their speciality from the safety of the office. Correspondents with their bylines, their tea-rounds and sponsorship forms for a weekend marathon. Gordon had just passed thirty and blamed the white hairs which sprouted from his chin like an old dog's muzzle on his employer, Associated News. But then he blamed everything on Associated News.

Gordon had been walking for 15 minutes, he ought to be there by now. He looked vainly for a street name. The soggy map he'd printed had transformed into a purple Rorschach test, it was useless. He spun like a radar sweep looking for inspiration. Grimy kebab shops, forbidding tower blocks and a flat roof pub called the Half Moon but there, at the crossroads, he spotted the street he needed. Gordon was exigent and walked with such haste that he stumbled over his own long legs. He could not waste a minute; he knew rival journalists were already on their way. He was lucky, he had stolen a march thanks to a whispered tip from a matey DI. Gordon's first news editor at the Fenland Mercury had gifted him one piece of advice: "Always take your local bobby a Terry's Chocolate Orange." It had not failed him yet.

With a sense of foreboding, he arrived at the address he was seeking, number 14d Byrne House. He took a deep breath. He felt the need for a spiritual lift and fumbled through his jacket pockets. In one swift movement he popped a lint-coated date in his mouth and behind his right cheek like a hamster. Growing up, his father had not liked to indulge him with chocolate and so it was from within a forgotten box of Christmas dates, fished from the recesses of a kitchen cupboard, Gordon first discovered saccharine pleasure. The date's restorative powers fired through the dismal damp and he felt ready for the death knock.

Gordon stooped to check his reflection in a car mirror. 'Omnia vanitas', he heard his father's voice tut, as his cold fingers smoothed and parted his black, bedraggled hair that had stuck in wet strands to his forehead. 'It's not vanity', Gordon said arguing with himself, 'It's professionalism'. But it was vanity; in the reflection he saw his youth fading and he didn't like it. Lines around the eyes, once faint as lemon ink, had deepened. 'I'm getting old,' he thought. A postman startled him from his gloomy introspection with a wolf whistle.

"Looking gorgeous," he said with a smirk.

Gordon straightened himself, prickled with embarrassment. He waited as the postman ambled away down the road, he dragged a tatty trolley that wobbled in its axles like a drunk. Gordon checked himself once more, strode confidently to the door and rang the bell. It was met with vicious barking and savage howls as some semi-domesticated Cerberus lashed itself against the frosted glass. 'Will it hold?' Gordon retreated a step. Inside he heard panicked scurrying as the furious dog was dragged roughly away by its scruff, still thrashing for the fight.

With the creature locked away, the door opened, and a middle-aged woman stood at her entrance. Gordon was knocked back, from behind the door of 14d Byrne House rushed a wave of stale humidity combining the smell of wet dog, fags and cooking oil. The woman surveyed Gordon suspiciously from behind puffy, red eyes. She wore a pastel-pink fleece with grubby sleeves and a faded black T-shirt with the image of a wolf baying at the moon. Her sallow face was pimpled in patches with warts and her thin, greasy hair revealed the yellowing of yeast infection at its parting. It was days like this Gordon hated, but he hadn't forgotten the buzz.

"Is it Mrs McKenzie?" he said.

"Are you from the council?"

"No. My name is Gordon Athelney. I'm from Associated News."

She looked bewildered at the statement.

"I'm a journalist," he said, with the hint of apology. "Can I just say how sorry I am to hear about your boy."

She slammed the door in his face. Then, from behind the frosted glass, she said: "I'm not speaking to the press and if you knock again, it will be my Pilot answering." The dog resumed his frenzied barking at the mention of his name.

Gordon was not dissuaded by the knock back; he already knew she was going to speak to the press. She had to; the story was too good. Jimmy, a 15-year-old football prodigy, trials with West Ham, just about to sit his GCSEs, white, with no police record, brutally murdered for displaying a rare chivalry. The teenager was returning from the cinema with his pretty childhood sweetheart. Enter stage right, a hooded gang of local ne'er-do-wells shouting lewd sexual threats at his girlfriend. In the noblest tradition of the troubadour, he defended her honour. To save face the gang stabbed him six times - one severing an artery in the thigh. He stumbled away to safety before collapsing into the long grass where he bled to death in the arms of his young love. The passion played out in Plaistow.

All Gordon needed was a school photograph... better still photo of Jimmy in all his youth and vitality, in his football strip holding aloft a plasticky cup. Then it was just a quick fact check and a bit of tear-stained colour for the Sundays. He had hopes for a front page on at least three of the less-respected nationals. All of these hopes were locked behind the door that had been slammed in his face, Gordon needed to open it.

"I know you must be terribly upset, Mrs McKenzie," he said. "I promise not to keep you for long."

"Go away."

Many reporters would have left the grieving mother to herself at this stage, any further entreaties could be considered harassment. Gordon had a tenacity that frequently straddled an ethical line. He knew his news editors might not approve, but they wanted the story as much as he did and they were sitting dry at their desks and he was at the threshold. Gordon knew how to unlock the door; he poked an index finger to raise the letterbox.

"I completely understand," he said. "I just wanted to check Jamie's age."

He waited in silence, counting down from five in his head. The door swung open.

"How dare you! It's Jimmy you bloody idiot."

Gordon looked aghast and flicked through his notebook.

"I'm so sorry Mrs McKenzie. They're useless in the press office, the police put out a statement calling him Jamie."

He held out the page of scrawls in his shorthand. It was unintelligible even if you knew T-line but impressed on Mrs McKenzie a professional gravity.

"If they've got that wrong, can I just check a couple of the other facts," he said, thumbing for a blank page. "It would be really awful if the tributes in the papers went out incorrectly."

Mrs McKenzie's face melted and from its sickly, grief-stricken gloom welled pride and dignity. She had resolved to do this and stiffened her trembling lip through the pain. She would do it for Jimmy. She glanced up at the darkening clouds.

"You'd better come in," she said and closed the door behind him.

The deception was not all ghoulish. Gordon sat with Sheila McKenzie for nearly an hour talking about Jimmy. She even laughed herself to tears looking through an old album. It was the first time she had laughed since his death. Gordon played his role, he nodded, he looked solemn, he made notes and even took two brave gulps of the sugary, albino tea Sheila served. 'No sugar and just the tiniest drop of skimmed milk, if you have it' is what he had asked for.

Gordon pointed to a photograph of Jimmy in his football strip holding aloft a plasticky trophy.

"Can I make a copy of this?"

Sheila looked concerned.

"I just need to take it to the office to scan. It will be biked back this afternoon. It's a lovely picture."

Sheila nodded and Gordon had everything he needed. He thanked her for her time and once more expressed his deepest sympathies, promising to write a fitting tribute. But Gordon was never satisfied with a partial victory. As he was leaving, he spun dramatically on his heels, as though struck by the remembrance of a sudden horror.

"Sheila, I really shouldn't say but..."

"What is it?"

Her face wrinkled in concern.

"If a journalist from National News calls just be a bit careful, they're a bit fast and loose if you know what I mean."

She nodded.

"It's just that they've lost a few photos in the past and yours are so precious. I know it's all you've got to remember Jimmy by."

"Thank you," she said. "I'll set Pilot on them if they come knocking."
Gordon nodded in agreement.

"Take care, Shiela."

"Thank you, darling."

He walked from the 14d Byrne House with everything he wanted and Shiela McKenzie closed the door with a warm smile that her happy recollections had provoked. Gordon's glee was short-lived, he checked his mobile to discover 14 missed calls, 13 of which were from Croaker, his news editor. Worse still, they were from Croaker's mobile. This meant not only a bollocking but a backroom bollocking, the most unreasonable kind because invariably Croaker was in some way culpable.

He racked his brains for possible errors in copy, or worse still potential libels. If a mistake went out on the wire to all their customers, it could not be withdrawn. Another version of the story had to be sent with a large CORRECTED REPETITION at the top of the page. It was a wailing siren to announce the reporter had made a complete pig's ear of the original story. Worse still, it was saved on the search engines for perpetuity. A mistake made in a single newspaper was bad, but when a news agency made a mistake every paper in the country might repeat it. When newspaper editors receive phone calls from pedantic readers to enlighten them on their error, it was always a frostier call they make to Associated News to complain. And it was frostier still when Croaker finally caught the reporter responsible. But dallying lost Gordon the initiative and his phone flashed to life with an incoming call, it was Croaker again.

"Where the fuckin' 'ell are you?"

Croaker had a thick Yorkshire accent that he piled on all the thicker when he was angry.

"I'm just about to file, I've got some gold on the McKenzie kid stabbing and a collect."

"You were supposed to be watching for a verdict at the DaCosta trial in Southwark."

Gordon panicked. He ran through potential worst-case scenarios in his head. Had the jury returned a verdict already? That was unlikely, it had been a six-week murder trial starring a minibus full of witnesses and the jury were only dismissed three hours ago. Besides he had that eventuality covered. He had cautiously left David - the work-experience boy he had been reluctantly saddled with that morning - with one simple instruction: "Call me if anything happens".

Unfortunately, as Gordon discovered from Croaker, David had taken his duties a little too seriously. He had sat watch like a sentry in the empty courtroom, taking notes and double-checking times against his two synchronised watches. David's day livened up when the judge summoned the jury at midday to dismiss them for lunch. It was the routine speech where he warned them not discuss anything they have heard in the courtroom and then to reconvene at 1.30. But David, over-spilling with nerves and responsibility, panicked. He whipped out his mobile phone and took a photo of the jury. The camera made a loud electronic snap and the judge's neck spun through 180 degrees, fixing the quivering work-experience boy with a death stare of medieval malice. An already shaky jury - sitting through one of the decade's most grisly murder trials - were understandably concerned by the mysterious young stranger who suddenly photographed their faces. For what purpose? Retribution? A fate worse than retribution?

"Right," said Gordon with sinking hope. "What happened?"

"What do you think happened? It was Hangman Hughes. He called it contempt of court and threatened to throw the lad into a cell. He's called him back this afternoon to explain his actions. The stupid, little bastard's in bloody pieces."

Gordon was trying to assess his precise allocation of blame. It did not look promising. Croaker let the silence hang for a minute before continuing.

"Luckily his old man's got some influence and made a call to Hughes."

"Good."

"Not good for you. His old man is Sir Trevor Stark."

Gordon bit his lip. Sir Trevor was a bit of joke in the office, but he was also Chief Executive of Associated News. Croaker laughed darkly at Gordon's silence.

"So, you didn't ask your young apprentice what his dad does then? Well Sir Trevor wants to know why I sent his 16-year-old son to cover the biggest murder trial of the year... on his own. So what am I going to tell him? In fact, what are you going to tell him because this stinking ball of shit is rolling downhill and as far as I'm concerned you're right at the fuckin' bottom."

Croaker hung up and Gordon screwed shut his eyes, tossed back his head and let the rain fall into his open mouth.

"Comest the hour for objurgation," Gordon said.

CHAPTER THREE

Gordon was troubled on the long Tube journey back to the office. He repeated, dissected, and analysed Croaker's words, seeking for a chink in the armour, a loophole for defence. It was no use. He tried to distract himself with the plight of those worse off than he, opening a dog-eared paperback of Thucydides' Peloponnesian Wars. But just like Demosthenes' night attack on Epipolae, any attempt at diversion fell off the face of a cliff. The bright light of democracy trampled in defeat by the tyranny of martial oligarchs. Gordon sympathised with the Athenians right then.

His paranoia multiplied like a bacterial infection. So, when he passed Debbie, the bird-like receptionist who subsisted on nothing more than seeds and chamomile tea, he thought he detected a smile of pity. 'Did Debbie know what I'd done?' he thought. 'Does the entire office know?' He pushed the button for the second floor reluctantly.

The lift pinged at its destination and with heavy steps Gordon walked out onto the news floor. He was met by silence; the televisions were muted, and phones were left to ring creating an air of suspended dread. Gordon saw the backs of his colleagues huddled in a crowd. A meeting was taking place and Gordon jostled himself into the mix. In the middle of the ring stood the Associated News' chief executive Sir Trevor Starkey. For a moment, Gordon wondered if his humiliation was to be made public like a hanging at old Tyburn. Croaker was stood next to Starkey, hands folded, head bowed, looking solemn and respectful... until he caught Gordon's eye and then he glowered. Gordon turned away.

"What's going on?" he asked Murray, the rugged reporter from Edinburgh with beady eyes, a taste for beer and an incurably obstreperous nature. He was cynical about everything; - all except for Norway, because for a reason nobody had quite discovered, he rather liked Norwegians.

"It's some bollocks about a new initiative," said Murray. "We're going to start telling the news to the 2.0 generation or whatever the fuck that means."

"Click news," said Starkey as Gordon tuned in to his frequency. "That's what we're calling it. It's multimedia, it's instant and it's compulsive. Every story you produce, ask yourself - what makes me click? Think outside the newsprint. Push the envelope of creativity beyond the blue sky. Say to yourself, will a graphic enhance my story? If so, we'll make one. Does this story work best as a photo slide-show. Speak to Gary Hewitt. Can we get some video? We'll do it. The attention span online is milliseconds. They either click or they don't. That's the future and this is the Click News revolution. Now go forth and gather... and be 'click' about it."

His peroration returned an excruciatingly feeble applause which died in the air. The crowds parted and Sir Trevor strolled through with imperial pomp. He glowed with pride as he headed back to the sixth floor with its Nespresso coffee machine and the penthouse crash pad he used after the frequent industry jollies.

Gordon felt a hand on his shoulder, there was no need to guess to whom it belonged.

"With me," said Croaker.

Gordon followed silently with the feet-dragging gait of the condemned. He popped a date behind his cheek - a little sweet to temper the bitterness.

Croaker's office was opposite the reporters' desks. He usually kept the door wide open so he could bark orders without having to leave his desk. His small office smelt like a hospital, largely due to the disinfectant wipes with which he fastidiously polished the end of his phone. But this was the only nod to sanitation. A soupy humidity hung in the air like morning fog. It was the sort of unhealthy room where germs thrived or tropical diseases might mutate into apocalyptic pandemics. The papers strewn across the desk were curled from constant shuffling to find the required sheet, filing cabinets spilled their contents onto the worn carpet with its weave still blackened in places from the days when smoking in offices was allowed and a dropped fag-end was not a big deal.

Croaker sat himself behind the desk and stretched lazily, he wasn't going to rush this. A low, afternoon sun had finally broken through the gloom but only made everywhere look more dank and dirty. After knocking out the crumbs from his filthy keyboard Croaker finally looked up at Gordon, who stood patiently affecting his best display of British phlegm.

Croaker glowered. He was a powerfully built man and often hinted at a successful rugby career cut short by injury. His bushy eyebrows sunk under the weight of his scowl and his tiny, black eyes sat deep within the skull like arrow slits in a castle keep.

"Close the door, this is between you and I," he said.

Gordon cringed at the instruction but obeyed. Despite his wordy profession, Croaker was prone to clumsy solecisms. He suspected - quite rightly - that the reporters had compiled a shared list on the server of some of his best clangers. Gordon sucked hard on his date to prevent himself from smirking at the memory.

"Well, are you going to stand there ruminating like a fucking sheep or are you going to explain?"

Gordon returned a dumb stare.

"Your latest fuck up?" said Croaker. "You see, I've got a vested interest in this one since you saw fit to dump your shit on my doorstep. Well?"

"But surely the collect from the McKenzie stabbing was more important. I had a lead."

Gordon pleaded but Croaker was deaf, lost in the thrill of autocratic power. Gordon knew a second official warning would result in a disciplinary hearing and he knew Croaker wanted this. Breaking protocol on the Royal Rota last month was his yellow card. Gordon just couldn't bring himself to effect the genteel oiliness of the national royal correspondents. But it was a career-limiting move, the Associated News toadied up to Clarence House and the veiled threat of omission from the Prince's next charity engagement had not sat well with senior management. Croaker had his own axe to grind with Gordon. He was secretly afraid of his intelligence and talent, and this manifested itself in jealousy and bullying. Gordon, for his part, unwisely provoked Croaker and could never let a falsehood stand uncorrected.

"Irregardless of whatever you've done on the McKenzie stabbing," said Croaker. "This mess is thicker. So now I'll tell you what we're going to do. First up, you're going to e-mail Sir Trevor and give him the humblest, most heart-wringing apology he's ever heard. In it, you might explain why you thought it fit to leave his only son alone in the traumatic environment of a crown court murder trial. And you're going to copy me in. And you're going to say in future you're planning to keep the news desk informed of your movements at all times, so they can prevent this sort of fucking disaster from happening again.

"For your sake - not mine - you might also furnish Sir Trevor with an explanation. Perhaps if he knows what was so fucking important for you to go tearing off into the heart of darkness, he'll feel a bit more charitably inclined.

"I don't care who dies or who gets caught in bed with who, you're writing this e-mail as priority. Understood?"

Gordon nodded.

"Just don't take too long over it. I want your first page on POLICE Boy out within the hour."

Gordon accepted, pleased he had gotten away so lightly. Whatever a hash he made of things, he was still the best general reporter Associated News had. Croaker, on the other hand, was worried he had sounded too amicable and dismissed Gordon with a rebalancing gruffness.

"Now fuck off," he said.

Gordon spotted a photo of Croaker's alsatian on his desk. The frame was covered in paw prints and said: "What do you mean the postman wants his leg back?"

"How's your dog?" Gordon asked casually.

It was well aimed. Last week one of the sub-editors had been walking his Norfolk terrier through Richmond Park and spotted Croaker and Captain Virgil. The little ginger terrier went bounding playfully up to beefy Captain Virgil. But catching sight of the incoming pup the Alsatian had rolled submissively onto its back and ejected a fountain of piss. Croaker, recognising his colleague, had whitened and gave his timid dog a kick to its feet. In the office, Croaker referred to Captain Virgil as his "land shark."

Croaker's face flickered with rage, he could not be certain if the sub-editor had betrayed him. Gordon had a talent for invidiousness.

"Go and write your e-mail to Sir Trevor."

Gordon left work with a spring in his step. He had bested Croaker, filed front-page news and avoided a disciplinary hearing. Fortunately for Gordon, Sir Trevor was a forgiving man and sent Gordon a short reply telling him not to mention the incident again and that it was all happily resolved. Sir Trevor knew what a liability his son could be and did not want the entire office knowing it too. But Gordon ought to have known Croaker was unlikely to forgive and forget so easily, particularly after his final riposte concerning Captain Virgil. So it was, while Gordon spent the evening sipping gin and tonic, penning notes in the margin of Herodotus for his long-planned historical novel, and listening to the unfolding test from Australia, Croaker's brain was hatching an egg of misery and he planned to serve it to Gordon for breakfast.

The following morning a bleary-eyed Gordon was summoned to Croaker's office. Croaker nodded at a news cutting on his desk, silently inviting Gordon to read it. It was an article from the Cornish Chronicle, carelessly torn so that the final word in the column was missing. Gordon scanned through it.

"TOURIST DISCOVERS DOLPHIN DEATHS

By Max Nash

A HOLIDAYMAKER was "shocked" to discover 15 dead dolphins on Selyvan beach last week.

Roy Harrison, 49, found the dolphins on an early morning walk with his dog.

"At first I thought they were fishing nets," he said. "But Boogaloo was going wild, straining at the lead and barking.

"I was shocked. It's my first time to the area and I didn't know who to call or what to do."

He said the dolphins were "clearly dead" and tightly grouped, as their pod might travel in the water.

He added: "The smell was intense, it clung to my jacket. I ended my holiday early."

Professor Ruben Burroughs, a professor in marine biology from St Austell University said it was "extremely rare and disturbing" for this number to wash ashore in a "single incident."

Last month, nine dolphins were discovered on beaches across the Lizard peninsula.

Tomasz Ludrinzki, 27, a waiter at the nearby Cragg Hotel, claimed he heard strange noises the previous night.

"I heard what was like an animal screaming in pain from the beach," he said.

Ludrinzki reported the noises to the police but heard no more noises for the rest of the night.

Devon and Cornwall police said it was not currently conducting any ..."

Gordon read it through again to make sure he was armed. He could not see where Croaker was going with this one, but he did not like the look of it. He shifted awkwardly in his damp socks, clearly the newspaper stuffed into his damp Church's had failed to do the trick.

"One for Emma?" Gordon said breezily. "Sounds like a job for our environment correspondent."

"You know Emma's seven-months pregnant; you're not slithering out of this one."

"You think it's a story?"

"You tell me? There might be military testing, we might be able to blame the French, there might be a sewage pipe spitting shit into the Channel. You tell me, you're the reporter."

"OK fine," said Gordon, resigned to his fate. "I'll make a few calls, do a bit of digging and try to stand something up. What do you reckon, seven pars?"

But Croaker wasn't listening, he was looking at his computer. He sucked the air between his teeth and chuckled.

"It's nippy down there this weekend, and there's a storm front closing in. Lovely weather for a beach holiday."

Gordon looked askance.

"You're not sending me all the way down there?"

"Oh, I think so," said Croaker. "You can't do all your journalism in a warm office down a phone line you know."

Gordon resented this.
 "But can't the Bristol office send somebody?"

Croaker shook his head.

"Cardiff?"

This time Croaker's face turned serious.

"You're on a final warning Athelney, so we need some decent copy out of this to justify the expense of the trip. Do you hear?"

'So, this is it', thought Gordon, 'This is how they snare you. A wild goose chase to Cornwall.'

"I've had travel Shirley book you six tickets to Penzance."

"Six?"

"You want to come back, don't you?"

"And the other four?"

"This is era of Click News, remember?" said Croaker with a cynical smile. "I'm sending Clara, it might make some good pictures."

Clara had been the Associated News' superstar snapper. In her first week she had won awards for a photo of a haughty City trader striding past a baying mob of G20 protesters - their faces hidden behind black and red bandanas. In the same week she caught the moment when a Met police officer in riot gear mistakenly truncheoned a South Korean university student. She caught the blow, frozen in time, which shattered his glasses and sent his medical textbooks flying. The photo went global. It led to the officer's dismissal and forced the Met Chief to stand down. The next day, she just happened to be there when anti-capitalist protesters pelted the Prince of Wales with eggs on his way to a private charity supper in Mayfair. She caught the look of haughty indignation on his face and it made every front page.

But after this explosive start, she had plateaued. A barren patch lasting three years. The other London photographers - who were convinced she was "just lucky" and never "tack sharp" - were quietly smug. What was more, she refused to shoot with the heavy, foot-long zoom lenses, only ever using a fast 50mm for every job. Her artistic eye and aphorism "I zoom with my legs" only served to rankle and alienate her colleagues. The truth was she hated to carry a heavy bag of lenses, after tearing her shoulder muscles in a skiing prang. Clara was slim and her careful diet did little to improve her muscle mass. In the last six months she had taken over a fortnight off work with shoulder strains and, Gary Hewitt, the photo editor, was beginning to wonder if she was fit for purpose. She had charmed him at interview and her storming start justified his gamble but lately she had begun to grumble when she was sent to bread and butter shoots - press conferences, court arrivals, red carpets. She hated the press pack and the clamour; she liked her own time and space to "find some art". But the papers were not looking for art. Instead, they wanted a clean, sharp shot with some manoeuvre for crops.

Clara stood out for more than her professional methodology. The pack was almost exclusively male, middle-aged and practically scruffy. She stood out, with her black leggings worn under Hunter boots, her fitted wax jacket and Yasser Arafat scarf. She stood out with her long, curly hair that fell in ringlets with 16 shades of blonde tied back in a loose scrunchie. She stood out because she was a woman and she was beautiful.

So when Croaker suggested to Gary Hewitt (he was never just Gary) that Clara joined Gordon for a weekend in Cornwall for a Click News trial piece he jumped at the idea. Gordon was in two minds about Clara joining him. On one hand she fascinated him, and he would steal secret looks at her as she strode across the news floor with her camera swinging at her hip. On the other hand, Clara shared a flat with his ex-fiancee Zara and - although the two colleagues had never discussed it - she had probably heard a tome of terrible tales about him.

"But that's four, what about the other two tickets?" said Gordon.

"Young Master David of course. I think Sir Trevor wanted to show you there were no hard feelings. And no doubt Mr and Mrs Sir Trevor will enjoy a quiet house for the weekend. Just don't go losing him this time."

"Touche," said Gordon, as he walked from the office with a grim fatalism.
But Croaker wasn't going to let Gordon get the last word today.

"By the way," he said. "Your copy from yesterday, POLICE Boy."

Croaker picked up the sheet from his tasters pile and scanned for the sentence. He read it aloud to Gordon.

"The 'crepuscular gang'! I had to fucking look it up just to make sure you weren't taking the piss. You're not writing for the OED you're writing for AN. Remember that down in Cornwall, won't you Wordsworth."

CHAPTER FOUR

The consensus among the general reporters was that Gordon had bagged himself a weekend jolly. He was less certain; Croaker had tied a Damoclean sword above his head. The party of three were booked on an afternoon train to Penzance and Gordon had been given the rest of the morning off to pack and prepare. He hated packing so travelled light, but there was the small matter of the impending visit of Dr Alfred Athelney - Gordon's father - to contend with. Dr Athelney was due to stay for the weekend because the second Friday in November was the annual Friends of the Wake dinner in Holborn.

This was the single entry in Dr Athelney's social calendar and the highlight of his year. Every year he dug out his old dinner jacket, so dusty he looked like one of the exhibits from his museum. Every year Gordon would find his father shifting impatiently outside his flat off the Archway Road. Every year he hurriedly entered with only the briefest greeting. He dropped off his bags, changed and splashed his face and neck first with cold water then Old Spice. Every year at six on the dot, and despite Gordon's insistence he should at least stay for a cup of tea, Dr Athelney left to catch the Tube. Every year he would arrive 45 minutes early and pace nervously outside the doors of Endeavour House until the first guest arrived. And every year the first guest was always Dr Simmonis, Dr Athelney's oldest and dearest friend, despite the fact they only met once a year and could only communicate in nods, hums, and little bursts of awkward laughter.

But this year Gordon was breaking protocol, he had to catch the 16:32 from Paddington to Penzance. This meant his father would have to meet him at the station to collect the keys. Dr Athelney was a man of routine and flustered by change.

Dr Athelney was the founder and curator of the Hereward the Wake Museum, a ramshackle collection of rust, shards and rotten stumps. It bore the unenviable rating as Crowland's third-best tourist attraction on Trip Advisor - placed behind both the municipal park and a caravan showroom. Most of its visitors had to hatch daring escape plans to evade the incessant lectures of Dr Athelney. He once caused a coach of monolingual Japanese tourists to miss their onward flight because they stumbled upon his museum and were subjected to a four-hour lecture on the Anglo-Saxon hearth - only three words of which they understood. Dr Athelney never let museum matters interfere with his true raison d'etre, his Grail-like search for Hereward the Wake's grave.

Dr Alfred Athelney was Gordon's only family. He had not seen his Parisian mother since she abandoned him as a toddler, running off to Cairo with a handsome Egyptian exporter. He never blamed her and knew full well his father was a testing man. She had first met Alfred at Oxford University, then he had represented a living symbol for her Anglo-adventure. He was eccentric, clumsily charming, highly intelligent and with a strange beauty - like a malnourished cherub. The spell soon broke and, after she had heard how Penda had withstood the cross at Maserfield for the fifth time, love thawed; leaving only a puddle of infuriation. Dr Athelney rarely spoke about her to Gordon and if he did, she was always "the Capetian".

When Gordon arrived at Paddington, he found Dr Athelney already nervously pacing the concourse. He was pleased to see the old man. Gordon watched how the stooped figure of his father burned with such nervous energy. Dr Athelney was ageless; he could pass for a decrepit 50 or a sprightly 70. Gordon cared for him deeply, but he was such a source of strife and embarrassment it was often hard for him to mask with patience his constant annoyance.

Gordon wanted a quick exchange of keys with his father before packing him off on the Circle line. He realised he did not want Clara to meet, or even see, his father. Dr Athelney's quirks made him appear anti-social, even unstable. It was the first time Gordon realised his subconscious desire to impress Clara.

Gordon was out of luck. As chance had it, both were standing next to one another at the station and both spotted Gordon at precisely the same moment. They waved in unison, noticed the other, and laughed at the coincidence. Gordon would have to make the introductions.

"This is Clara," he said to his father.

"Lovely to meet you," Dr Athelney said with an outstretched hand. "Clara...?"

Gordon scowled at his father; he knew where this was leading. Dr Athelney had a passion for surnames and their heritage.

"Clara Devowe," she said sweetly.

"That's an interesting name. Where does it come from?"
"Just leave it!" Gordon said firmly.

"It's OK," said Clara, "I don't mind. It's French originally - De Viau I think. We were Huguenots, dad used to say it meant we had huge noses."

"Fascinating," said Dr Athelney, making calculations in his brain, establishing a sweeping tribal descent traced down from the volkerwanderung.

"And where in France?"

"Lyon, I think," she said. "But ages ago, you know."

Clara had swallowed his hook and Dr Athelney was ready to reel her up from the depths of the dark ages until she lay spluttering on his dingy, begging to be clubbed to end the misery.

"Burgundy," he said. "Barely France really. The Nibelung - you'll know from Wagner's opera no doubt. Germanic, naturally, but..."

"That's enough," said Gordon, slamming the door of the conversation shut. "You need to get back for the dinner."

Gordon stoked his father's irrational fears of tardiness and it worked. Dr Athelney attempted a farewell, but his sentences always hung unfinished like a missing punchline and his eye-contact lingered when it ought to shift. Gordon felt a pang of guilt as his father walked away in the wrong direction, only to return seconds later correcting his mistake and with another awkward goodbye. He also had Norman Wisdom's gift, but not intent, for the perfectly timed comedy trip.

"Ooh, is he ok?" said Clara as Dr Athelney stumbled over a wheelie case.

"I'm so sorry," Gordon said. "I had to give him my keys, he's staying with me and..."

"Don't be silly," she said warmly. "He seemed nice. He's like a character in a book."

Clara wore her trademark leggings and scarf, but also a leather biker-jacket and knee-high boots. Only the camera bag, perched precariously on her case, betrayed her profession. Gordon eyed her bulging case towering over his own feeble bag with self-doubt, Clara had packed thoroughly, what had he forgotten. Despite having had a morning to prepare, Gordon's amateurishness shone through. He had found an old gym bag in the back of a cupboard; it still contained his cricket box from school. He had casually stuffed it with a few pairs of socks, pants, and the most essential toiletries. The bag had still looked cavernous, so he dampened the echoes with a set of cotton pyjamas.

A gaggle of women cackled off the Reading train dressed in pink sashes and fairy wings. The leader held aloft an inflatable penis balloon like the Imperial Eagle and the Old Guard loyally followed, Soho-bound. Gordon felt ready to be leaving London, Clara seemed less sure. Within minutes she had made it quite clear the weekend jolly was a tiresome inconvenience. She delivered her gripes with the slightest hint that Gordon had contrived the whole affair.

Clara's mood brightened when she spotted David at the far end of the platform. He was lumbering up the stairs from the Underground. He dragged a suitcase large enough to smuggle a hippo out of Africa and, from the way his tiny frame strained, it might well have contained one. David wore a suit three sizes too big for him and he had managed to tuck a left trouser leg into his Superman socks. His thin hair was gelled, the ploughed strands locked with a paste only a steaming hot shower could dissolve. Like a mouse David moved in ill-considered darts with a furtive twitchiness.

"It looks like his first day at Hogwarts," Clara said.

David spotted Gordon and his pale face beamed. He bounded over, his giant case rumbling behind like Juggernaut.

"You're very well prepared," said Clara, nodding at his case.

David took this as a compliment and proudly saluted her, Clara snuck Gordon a "bless" look.

"We've got five minutes before our train leaves; shall I grab a coffee?" Gordon said.

Clara scanned her options on the concourse.
"If you're going to Cafe Bella, I'll have a Moroccochino - do you need some cash?"

Gordon declined. He was inherently tight but wanted to impress her. He went to leave but Clara stopped him.

"What about David?"

"Of course," said Gordon with a pained smile. "I nearly forgot."

Without hesitation David ordered a cappuccino super-ante. It had to be a super-ante. He always had a super-ante.

"Right, so that's one cappuccino "super ante" and one mochachino."

"Moroccochino," Clara corrected.

"Morocco-chino? They don't grow coffee in Morocco."

26

Gordon could not help himself; the pedant came naturally but he blamed the accuracy required by his profession.

"God, you're such a bore," said Clara. "It's got cinnamon in it. They grow that in Morocco, right?"

Gordon shrugged; he felt the fool.

The train had barely pulled away from Paddington before Gordon was ready to strangle David. Three seats had been reserved - two at the front of the carriage and one towards the rear. He was hoping to spend the evening in breezy conversation with Clara with David tucked safely away in aisle four. But like the puppy playfully bounding onto the lovers' bed, David scuppered the best-laid plans. He took the double seat for himself and wilfully insisted Gordon sat with him. Clara readily assented to take the single, she planned to clamp on the headphones and snooze.

Just outside Maidenhead, David confessed to Gordon he often felt travel sick - once with terrible consequences for a Dutch tourist on the TGV to Avignon. The final straw came when David grasped under the seat with wild impulse for what he believed to be a pound coin. He upset his tray table and sent a scolding pint of cappuccino lurching towards Gordon's lap. Gordon only just managed to leap to safety. His lap was saved a scorching, but his newly polished Church's were covered in sticky milk with a sprinkle of chocolate; and for the second time that day he was holding a soggy sock under a hand dryer. When Gordon returned from the train toilet, the coffee was snaking its way down the central gangway like the Amazon basin. David bashed away at his phone, oblivious.

As so often in his darkest hours, Gordon dipped into Herodotus for succour. It was true, King Croesus the fabulously rich King of Lydia had things far worse. He had sought the employment of the best fortune tellers in the ancient world. Croesus even hatched an ingenious job interview to ensure he got the cream of the crop. His lackeys were sent off to every oracle from Libya to Miletus and, on the hundredth day after leaving Sardis, they were told to ask their oracle a single question: "What was King Croesus doing right now?" To make it a bit tougher, Croesus did the unthinkable and boiled a tortoise in a bronze pot. The Pythia in Delphi answered correctly and so enjoyed the King's patronage. Concerned about the rapid rise of Persia under Cyrus, Croesus' next question to the oracle was less trivial. If he attacked the Persians, would he conquer? The answer was pleasing: "Attack and a mighty empire will fall." Already spending Susa's treasures in his head, Croesus launched an offensive and a mighty empire fell, his own. Gordon always felt a soft spot for old Croesus; the IT department had once played a similar linguistic trick on him with their literalisms and shibboleth. At least he only had a Google toolbar de-installed and not an Empire disbanded.

After this auspicious start the rest of the journey passed pleasantly. Most of the capital's commuters had left by Swindon and so Gordon bought a couple of Earl Greys and went to sit with Clara. David sat in the glow of his phone playing Knight's Lore IV, the rules of which he had begun to explain to Gordon before he beat a tactical retreat.

CHAPTER FIVE

It was late when the train rolled into Penzance. As Gordon stepped out from the heated carriage the cold night air tightened his lungs and provoked a tickly cough. It began to dawn on him how ill-prepared he was with nothing more than a suit and a light cagoule to stave off the chill. Travel Shirley, the woman who organised tickets and accommodation for the newsroom, had booked a hotel in Selyvan, or more accurately the only hotel in Selyvan. It was 15 miles down the coast from Penzance, so the plan was to take a cab from the station.

They made their way from the platform to the taxi rank. A wind blew in from the sea and Clara hooked her scarf over her nose for warmth. There were two taxis waiting, their drivers nervously eyeing the state of the kebab shop crowd over the road. The first driver, pleased at the sight of three heavily burdened travellers from the London train, sprang into action and chivalrously snatched Clara's case as she walked.

"Get in out of the cold," he said, and they happily assented while he loaded their bags into the boot.

"So where to?" he said cheerily.

"The Cragg Hotel in Selyvan," said Gordon. He'd taken the front seat and assumed leadership. Clara was happy to sit in the back shivering and hugging her camera bag for comfort.

"Selyvan?"

The driver's face dropped and betrayed the briefest flicker of fear.

"The thing is, it's my last job of the night and it's in totally the wrong direction for me. I can't take you there I'm afraid."

"But it's late and cold," Gordon said.

"I won't get a return fare from Selyvan."
"We'll pay you double then," said Clara from behind, "Just write us a receipt."

"I'm really sorry," said the driver remorsefully. "There's nothing I can do."

"Come on," said Gordon, piqued. "We'll take the next one."

The driver felt guilty and helped unload their luggage but warned they wouldn't find a cab to Selyvan at that hour. His advice was to stop the night in Penzance at a bed and breakfast and to catch the morning bus to Selyvan. To prove his worth, he even accompanied them to the second cab and waited while his colleague also rebuffed the journey.

"Look," said the driver, his palms held flat. "It's a cold night and I know a decent guest house on the Newlyn road. I reckon they'll have rooms. I'll drive you there, free of charge, and make sure you've got somewhere to stay."

Gordon felt scammed but he did not have a lot of choice. The wind had worked its way through the weave in his suit and chilled his wheezing chest. Ten years ago, his first in London, he had spent a fortnight in bed with bronchitis and the cold always tickled the old scars. Gordon agreed to try the guest house. Clara shifted grumpily and David was silent at last, he was suffering the monumental crash from a second super-ante cappuccino, the comedown of eight espresso shots.

The Gull's Nest guest house was aptly named with two evil-eyed birds glaring from the roof at the new arrivals. The house sat on an enviable perch at the top of a steep hill away from the harbour. The house was run by Mr Voorstampt, an old Belgian batchelor who had moved to England in the 1970s. His house was empty that weekend so he said some company on a cold Friday night would be "just the ticket". The taxi driver looked relieved at his passengers' satisfaction.

Mr Voorstampt was a neat, chubby man with white hair combed in a tidy parting and an immaculately ironed shirt. To weary travellers from London he was a welcome sight. Even more so when he tossed two meaty logs onto the fire's glowing embers. They caught in an instant and were soon crackling. Clara warmed her hands at the fireside. It was all serene until David stepped on a snoozing Jack Russell's tail and narrowly avoided a retributory gnashing.

Mr Voorstampt brought Gordon and Clara a sweet sherry and David a milky tea. He was excited to have three reporters from London arrive so unexpectedly and was keen to sit up chatting, nodding earnestly as Gordon explained the mission. He heard how the taxi drivers had refused a fare to Selyvan.

"It does not surprise me," he said. "Even in the summer they don't like to go, but on a night like tonight it's a no-chancer."

"Why's that?" Gordon asked.

Mr Voorstampt shrugged.

"I don't know Selyvan well. It keeps itself at the length of an arm from us in Penzance. Most of my guests are wanting to visit Mousehole. Now that is a pretty village, you ought to visit that instead. Not Selyvan, no. I don't hear nice things."

Gordon looked puzzled.

"But I don't know," the old man said with a smile. "I never go."

There was a gentle music in his voice and Gordon could have peacefully drifted off after the sherry. Mr Voorstampt asked if they would like to watch a video. He had a documentary about Cornwall, produced by the Tourist Board in the 1980s. He showed them the cover, it promised tin mining, fishing and legend. Gordon politely declined on behalf of the group. Their host was not dissuaded and held up a finger with sudden inspiration.

"I know what you will like," he said.

He rummaged through his cabinet and retrieved a Tommy Cooper video.

"Just like that," he said, with an impersonation that required a Tommy Cooper video in his hand to understand. "He's really the best. Very funny."

Gordon found this suggestion harder to deflect. He wanted peace and quiet, a warm fire and bed. But Mr Voorstampt's charm was infectious and Gordon was losing the battle of resistance. Perhaps just 15 minutes, he found himself saying. Fortunately, Clara saved him by interrupting.

"Come and look at this," she said, beckoning excitedly. She summoned the small party to the large bay window overlooking town. A full moon hung low and bled into the black sea, fragmenting on the waves. The orange lights of town leaked their own long reflections, warm kisses across the cold sea. Off the coast a pyramid of dimmer lights revealed St Michael's Mount and out across the cloudless sky the spattered stars twinkled.

"It's beautiful," she said. "I have to get a shot from the shore. Are you coming, Gordon?"

"Can't you take it from up here?" Gordon said.

Clara looked incredulous, annoyed the question had even been considered.

"You go," said Mr Voorstampt. "We can watch Tommy Cooper in the morning. I'm off to bed, so take my key."

David had fallen sound asleep on the sofa, a miracle considering the amount of caffeine he had consumed. The Jack Russell had forgiven him for his earlier outrage and was curled neatly in his lap.

So Gordon braved the night once again. He followed sullenly behind Clara as they took the steep path down to the beach. Clara was suffering less from the cold than Gordon because she had a purpose to distract her. She insisted, despite Gordon's gentle doubts, that the photograph was necessary.

"It's great for file," she argued. Clara loved the idea of perpetuity and to think of her photos sitting in a vast image library, called upon in years to come to illustrate some glossy feature in a weekend supplement.

The beach was deserted and perilously dark. Gordon suggested heading back on safety grounds, then Clara clicked on a torch. Its beam was weak and narrow, but he was glad for it. Storms could batter this coastline in November and waves would atomise themselves against harbour walls, but not that night. Breakers hushed the beach to sleep and the wet stones shone like jewels in the moonlight.

Gordon inhaled deeply; the air smelt good. He had been pent up too long in the city and it felt good to be free. The salty spray against his skin seemed to cleanse the grime from the long journey and nestled as dew in his hair. Clara was busy scanning the beach for inspiration. A line of great granite rocks formed a crude breakwater and stretched 30 feet out into the sea. This was where she would take her shot. She heaved her heavy bag back onto her shoulders and pulled herself up.

Gordon looked at the wet rocks, glistening in the night. The angles were jagged and unfavourable and alarm bells rang in his head.

"Is it a good idea to go out there?" said Gordon.

"Don't be soft. I'm only going out to the fourth or fifth rock. I have to, for the perspective."

Gordon did not like the idea but took the lead. Clara held the torch and shone a safe path as he stepped carefully from rock to rock. The footing was slippery, but the crunchy barnacles afforded grip for his leather soles. No risk assessment would ever rubber-stamp this mission. After several clumsy bounds Gordon reached a large table-top rock with enough room to accommodate them both. Next it was Clara's turn. She balanced the torch on a rock so her hands were free. She slung her camera around her neck and it cracked her hip as she leapt. Despite her burden she leapt confidently and gracefully, making Gordon's endeavours look all the more pathetic.

"It's hard with leather soles," he said.

The sea was relatively calm, but the occasional wave carried enough strength to crest the plinth and lick their ankles. Gordon took a sorry look down at his Church's – salt stains would be added to the coffee, and it seemed they were destined never to be dry again. Clara was more concerned about her camera, cupping the lens to protect it from the spray. It felt strange to Gordon to be stood with Clara out in the sea and under the stars. He was away from London, away from his father arriving home tipsy and excitable, away from Associated News, and away from Croaker. Six months ago, Clara discovered her new room-mate Zara was Gordon's former fiancée; it was awkward for her. She had broached the subject gingerly by the coffee machine, she had not wanted to embarrass Gordon in case he had learned of it through other channels. She hoped it was not a problem and promised she would never have chosen Zara if she had known. It was difficult though; contracts were signed and it was unfair to cancel. Gordon was embarrassed but had assured Clara it did not matter. She would find out soon enough about Zara, just as he had.

Suddenly the peace of the night was shattered by a heart-stopping sound. They could not identify it, so violently and unexpectedly had it arrived. It came and went without echo or memory. It was powerful and dangerous, like the sound of an oak beam rent with fury, cracking to a sawdust shower. They both stood frozen, waiting for another clue. Gordon's fingers curled deep into his palms until the nails bit sharply. The pair both felt vulnerable and exposed.

"What was that?" said Clara.

Gordon pricked his ears and screwed his eyes in concentration but heard nothing.

"A boat, perhaps? It was a boat in the harbour, I think," he said, lying to himself.

Clara too knew it had not come from the harbour; it came from the blackness of the sea. Gordon took Clara's wrist and urged her back to the beach. She nodded, there were going to be no prizes for bravery that night. But before they reached the sand, it sounded again, duller this time but more discernible. Shrill and brutal, with the blunt-edged trauma of the aftermath of a hammer blow five fathoms deep. It was alien and incomprehensible.

"Should we call the coast guard?" said Gordon. He had no intention of doing so but wanted to hear the sound of a human voice, even if it was his own. He wanted to hear reason. The awful sound produced no echo but it resounded in both of their heads. They stood in silence frozen to the rock. Still they waited, not a word spoken. A wave struck the rock on a rebound and sent an icy jet rushing up Clara's leg. She started, her breath taken away. Then, from the darkness, movement. The moonlight, glinting against the frothy peaks of the waves gave form to the water. It appeared to contour and undulate, running down through itself, concave and hollow. The sea was swallowing itself.

"What is it? Can you get a photo?"

Clara was awoken by a sense of duty and clicked into the gloom. It was a forlorn hope, even eyes sensitised to the dark failed to discern the phenomenon. Dark and surreal it deceived. 'Was it an illusion brought on by tiredness, the cold night and the waves?' they both asked themselves this question.

The alien noise sounded once again, duller still and less penetrating but Clara stopped shooting, lowering her camera. She stood as rigid and frozen as Gordon besides her, feeling just as exposed. Then the sea fastened itself. A tower of water shot high into the air as the vortex snapped and when the final droplets had fallen back into the sea all was still once again. Even the waves maintained their respectful hush.

'Now,' Gordon thought. 'Now is the time to break for the beach'. But Clara held his sleeve and motioned with the faintest nod out to sea. There was a shape blinking through the blackness. A light. It bobbed on the waves, and made steady progress towards the shore. Clara raised her camera but could not bring herself to depress the shutter. The light drew nearer and the silvery bow of a small rowing boat highlighted itself against the moon. A solitary figure pulled at the oars, his strokes powerful and unhurried against the tide. Something uncanny prickled Gordon and he shrank to his knees, pulling Clara with him. The boat was then less than 30 feet from their rock and every stroke pulled it closer.

"Should we say something?" Clara said in a hiss.

Gordon shook his head; he did not want to open a channel of communication. What he really wanted was to lie face down into the rocks, to become invisible, or to be back at the Gull's Nest by the fire. The boat suddenly changed its course and steered away, heading towards the far end of the beach where the headland rose steeply. Over there the sand giving way to coves, caves and sheer cliffs. As the boat swung in the waters, so did the oarsman, and he faced them then. It was undeniable, he plainly saw them both. Even with the distance and darkness there was the stab of recognition as pupil met pupil. His face, lit then by the moon, was blank and expressionless, it betrayed neither surprise nor interest. Neither did his arms hesitate at their stroke, but strained with cold, mechanical purpose to steer the boat to shore.

The pair watched the small rowing boat round the headland. They held their breath in the suspension of fear. When they no longer heard the oars beating against the water, they turned to look at one another, still too afraid to speak. All was silent except for the hushed susurrus of the waves.

Suddenly Gordon's chest vibrated and his breast pocket glowed green, The Flight of the Valkyries played. He fumbled to answer his phone.

"Hello?"

"Gordon, it's your father. The alarm I can't make it stop."

"I told you," said Gordon lowering his voice. "It's the fall of the Roman Empire."

"476. I tried that, it doesn't work."

"I'm not having this argument now. The Empire did not fall with Odoacer, it fell to the Turks."

"1453? You're not still promoting this fallacy."

"Just enter the code and the alarm will stop. I can't talk now."

Gordon hung up, agitated. His father's call had helped him forget his fears. Clara stared back at Gordon in surprise.

"He does it on purpose," he said. "He won't accept anybody else's idea."

Clara shook her head and nodded to the beach.

"Come on," she said. "Let's head back."

There was less care taken on the return journey and they leapt across the rocks hastily. Gordon's felt happier with his feet back on the coarse sand and he had to restrain himself from running all the way back to the Gull's Nest. Instead, they walked back silently. Neither Gordon nor Clara wanted to be the first to review the events. Even back in the safety of the warm house with his feet drying by the fire Gordon preferred not to mention what had happened. 'But what had happened?' he asked himself. Away from the beach, Gordon began to doubt not only his eyes but also his courage - his eagerness to leave the beach may have seemed cowardly to Clara. And yet there was something uncanny about the night's events.

Eventually Clara turned to Gordon.

"Are you going to file anything from tonight?"

He shook his head.

"Are you going to send any of the photos?"

She shook her head. They retired to bed without mentioning it again.

CHAPTER SIX

Gordon woke up refreshed and with his confidence restored. The fears of the previous night were down to tiredness, he convinced himself. Clara too seemed keen to have forgotten and when Mr Voorstampt asked over breakfast if she had got a "nice picture" she shook her head. Gordon accepted a slice of toast but declined anything more substantial, he was always a reticent guest. David, on the other hand, was oblivious to his new surroundings and chomped his way through two bowls of sugary Corn Flakes followed by three rounds of toast dripping with strawberry jam. 'Where did it all go?' Gordon wondered with mild disgust at his greed.

Croaker had chosen not to provide Gordon with a brief but wanted his first copy filing by Saturday afternoon. Gordon hoped the story could be slapped together without a fuss. Any loose ends could be tied up on Sunday morning to leave the afternoon free to read and relax by the sea. The beached dolphin story sounded straightforward but Gordon guessed Croaker was sniffing for some clandestine military culpability. Secret weapon testing; nuclear submarines; next generation sonar - Croaker had been embattled in a long feud with the Ministry of Defence press office, stretching back over a decade from his days as a senior reporter. Croaker had filed the wrong name of a British rifleman killed in Iraq. It went out on the newswire and was picked up everywhere before the mistake was spotted. When the soldier's pregnant wife saw her husband's name leading the 10 o'clock news she was so overcome with grief she miscarried... or so the story went. Gordon was certain it had undergone some embellishment, an unavoidable consequence of working in an office full of journalists.

A miscarriage was not the sort of mistake a corrected repetition or even a humbling apology could put right. The MoD blamed Croaker and he blamed the MoD. Senior management waded in to seek a resolution, but both parties baffled and befuddled with Byzantine guile. The result was indecisive.

He excused himself from the breakfast table, he had some work to do. His first call of the day was to Devon and Cornwall police. He needed to check if there had been any overnight reports. There had been 37 precisely. PC Hollins at Penzance station reeled off the list with the robotic monotony of a jaded teacher reading the morning register. Four dolphins had been discovered beached in Penzance alone, a further six up the coast towards Mousehole.
"Bloody lemmings," the policeman said.

He saw his hopes for a quiet weekend at the station with cups of tea, crumpets and Soccer Saturday disappearing. PC Hollins was frustrated - why was this even a police matter?

"They need a bloody vet not a set of handcuffs," he said.

Gordon received the news optimistically. The story - which he'd always regarded as a non-starter - was showing some promise. It might even make a few pars in the nationals, he pondered, especially if Clara could shoot a pretty picture. If only he could point a subtle finger at somebody unpopular, he thought.

On the train to Penzance Gordon had scrawled down a list of numbers for some comment or guidance. First up was the RSPCA, but the press officer was snotty and non-plussed. 'Why she was even being asked for a comment?' she sniffed. 'Obviously' she thought it was 'terrible', but 'obviously' she repeated. Gordon only stoked her ire when he told her it was fine if she did not wish to comment. 'But of course' she would comment, she 'wasn't saying that'. She just 'didn't know what he wanted her to say'.

"I don't want you to say anything," Gordon pleaded. But she was fuming, and the conversation could not be salvaged.

Next, he called the Ministry of Defence. The press officer was equally nonplussed.

"Dead dolphins? What's that got to do with the MoD?"

Perhaps he should try DEFRA, they helpfully passed the hot potato.

His final call was to the local council. He was looking for a steer, but it was comment and conjecture he received by the bucket load. Gordon was landed with a barmy councillor with a natural inclination for hysteria. Councillor Stewart made a less than delicate hint that the EU fishing policy was to blame.

The ring round had been fruitless. He still had to stand up the story, so he tried Professor Burroughs, whose name he had seen in the Cornish Chronicle cutting. The Professor was terse and irritable. He read out a pre-prepared press statement and refused to be drawn into conjecture or speculation. He cut short Gordon's questions with snorts of derision. Finally, the Professor excused himself because, as Gordon "could probably appreciate, he was a very busy man." Professor Burroughs hung up without a goodbye.

At last, Gordon tried the Cornish Cetacean Society. He had not held out much hope, its website looked like a GCSE project and the number for the press office was the same as the secretary, the head of fund-raising and the manager. A well-spoken but nervous woman called Jeanette Winters-Harris answered, her voice trembled at the edges when she learned she was speaking to a journalist. However, she answered every question Gordon asked. The beached dolphins were Common and Bottlenose, mostly, with a rare Risso's Dolphins too. Mass beachings were not uncommon, but they were worrying all the same. She remembered similar cases in the area, including one in 2002 when 26 dolphins were discovered dead in the shallows around Falmouth. She could not say why it happened, but her theory was that because dolphins hunt as a pod, they could sometimes find themselves caught out by the shallow waters in the heat of the chase. What about sonar? Gordon pressed. Or military testing? Jeannette sighed.

"I'm reluctant to say what I think," she said. "I've been working with dolphins for 20 years and you learn so much about them, the way they think and react. They're such social animals, they respond to a threat as a pod."

"Threat?"

Jeannette paused again, choosing her words carefully. She asked if she could speak off the record. Gordon agreed.

"I've seen what happens with sonar, with offshore wind farms - they're confused, they're lost, they're in distress but this is different. It sounds silly to say it out loud.

"When I was in Penzance last week, after I got the call from the police to supervise, there was one dolphin still alive. A desperate creature, it broke your heart to look at him. I could see in his eyes the fog of terror as clearly as you could see a cataract. Black and oily, stabbing like a wild dagger in its desperation. It looked hopeless and we had to act quickly. We supported its body and six of us tried to carry him back to the sea. But as we approached the water he thrashed with a strength and savage violence I had never before seen. The four policemen managed to restrain him, they pinned him to the beach to try to calm him. But you know he thrashed and flailed with such a burning energy that he died right there on the sand.

"I've worked with dolphins for over 20 years and I've never seen anything like it before. He was afraid of the sea. He had escaped the water and would rather die than return. Please, this is strictly off the record, but I believe he'd beached himself deliberately."

She had spoken as though it were a form of therapy, Gordon thought, as though she was haunted by her suspicions. Had he not spooked himself on the beach the night before it was unlikely that he would have placed much stock in her words. Gordon's London cynicism would have dismissed her and her well-meaning charity as just another "nutter". But now he felt less willing to cast the first stone.

"Would you go on record with this?" he asked politely.

But she was not willing, even with softer paraphrasing. She had spoken honestly but worried her words could discredit the already cash-strapped Cornish Cetacean Society. Instead, Jeanette gave Gordon a more formal comment if he needed it and also her mobile number with the assurance he could call whenever he needed.

An hour on the phone had yielded, at most, three lines of printable copy, the bleeding obvious, a no comment and a fascinating personal account he had sworn not to print. Gordon decided to phone a few pars through to the news desk just to get the ball rolling. But what to call it? At the Associated News every story that went out on the wire had to have a topic and a keyword. The topic was broad, the keyword identified the specific story. Deciding on the topic was always the hardest part. POLICE Dolphin implied a crime had been committed, ENVIRONMENT Dolphin implied a toxic waste dump, DEFENCE Dolphin was as good as pointing the finger at the military. NATURE might have sufficed, except that NATURE stories were automatically uploaded as soft, fluffy news to the Internet Service Provider's homepages. They wanted baby polar bears, skateboarding ducks and life-saving dogs - a skip full of dolphin carcasses did not sit pretty. Gordon settled on SEA Dolphins. At least it had a certain mystery.

Gordon scrawled his copy quickly in an old notepad.

SEA Dolphins

By Gordon Athelny, Associated News reporter

THE deaths of 25 beached dolphins needed "immediate investigation", marine experts said today.

Police confirmed 10 more dolphins were discovered on beaches in Cornwall this morning, adding to the 15 found last week.

Devon and Cornwall Police said it was not conducting an investigation but was "monitoring developments."

Marine biologist Professor Ruben Burroughs of St Austell University said: "It is a rare and upsetting trend which requires immediate investigation."

The founder of a local dolphin preservation society said human influences were sometimes the cause of mass beachings.

"The use of sonar or the turbines from offshore windfarms can be blamed," said Jeanette Winters-Harris from the Cornish Cetacean Society.

Dolphins use echos - ten times higher than the adult human's upper limit - to navigate underwater.

The sounds are transmitted to its middle ear through a fat-filled cavity in the lower jaw, conservationists believe turbines and sonar can affect this ability.

Dolphins are found across the world, mostly in the shallower seas of the continental shelves. They are carnivores - eating mostly fish and squid.

mfl"

The mfl signalled "more to follow later". Something to whet the appetite of the news desks. Unlike other agencies - even more modest operations - Associated News' reporters still had to phone through their copy. There were no laptops or 3G cards, instead they had a call centre outside Hull staffed by a patient team of copy takers who wanted every name spelled out using the phonetic alphabet - including the reporter's own. Golf Oscar Romeo Delta Oscar November. It was painful, slow and allowed rival reporters to bend a prying ear and listen to what Associated News was filing.

After he had filed Gordon panicked, had the final paragraph sounded too much like the Wikipedia page he had borrowed it from? He wished he had not used the phrase 'continental shelves'. Gordon phoned the news desk to confirm he had filed. The weekend editors were Jon and John. To make it more confusing they both came from Bradford. Gordon made a special art of mixing them up.

"Associated News, Jon speaking."

"Plummers?"

"No it's bloody Trevors, Athers."

Jon Trevors... John Plumstead.

"Sorry," Gordon said. "You sound exactly the same on the phone."

"Cos we're both from Yorkshire? That's racist. I could do you for that. There's no aitch in my name."

"Well perhaps you should spell your name when you answer the phone then."

"That's rich, what next? Should we wear a badge saying "northerner" you racist bastard."

It was all good-humoured. They both liked Gordon because he pulled his weight on the tea-rounds. John Plumstead was very particular about his coffee. First the granules went in, then the full fat milk, it had to be frothed up into a mousse and then and only then could the water be added - three minutes after the kettle has clicked and even then very slowly, stirring all the while. Gordon dubbed it the Bradford cappuccino, "the racist bastard".

With his first pars filed and the phone calls out of the way, it was time to venture out and try some old-fashioned journalism. Clara had already been down to the beach. She bagged the basics, police tape, a lonely young officer standing guard at a respectful distance and the four dolphins hidden from view under tarpaulin where they were

41

waiting for collection by the University. She asked Mr Voorstampt what his neighbour's dog was called - she had heard it yapping earlier. It was Brandybrook. She typed the name into the locked network and got lucky with their Wi-Fi password. She had become expert at finding free internet.

The only bus to Selyvan was leaving in half an hour and if they did not want to another night stranded in Penzance they had to hurry.

CHAPTER SEVEN

The bus was waiting in the market square when they arrived. Clara had to stop a ruddy-faced old man to ask for directions, he wore a flat-cap low over his eyes against the elements. He was surprised she was heading to Selyvan.

"There's nothing much there you know," he had told her. "You'll be better visiting the seal sanctuary in Gweek."

"I've got to go, I'm working."

He looked unconvinced.

"Those seals are happy enough in this weather. Doesn't bother them a bit. In fact, I think they rather like it. You should go and see for yourself. Gweek it is."

She thanked him and ran to catch up with Gordon and David who had spotted the bus without help.

It was a tatty coach bearing the pockmarks of a hard life, lashed by the sea. The old diesel motor chugged agriculturally and it seemed full of loose bolts. Occasionally, it missed a beat but always fired back into life with a cough and dirty cloud of black oil from its tarred innards. In faded yellow letters was painted "Trevellyan's of Selyvan". It was not an appealing ride, but it was their only option. The council-run bus service - with its modern, roadworthy fleet - ran only as far as Mousehole, and it was another six miles down the coast to Selyvan. The driver looked surprised when the three passengers appeared at his door asking for three singles.

"To Selyvan?" he said suspiciously.

Gordon confirmed and the driver returned him a languid shrug.

"That's £1.75, then."

"£1.75!" said Gordon, it seemed remarkable value. "For all three of us?"

The driver mistook his meaning and his eyes darkened at the suggestion he was trying to cheat them.

"70 pence for the two singles and I've put him down as a child's fare - 35 pence. That's £1.75."

The driver was a strange beast, with an appearance that particularly unsettled Clara. His movements were listless but with the hint of a reptilian hidden reserve. The barest patch of ginger hair clung to his greasy, freckled head. Despite the baldness, his pallid skin was youthful and unwrinkled and pulled tightly around the eyes causing them to pop. He wore a pair of thick, tortoiseshell glasses without a hint of irony but would have made him King Cool in Shoreditch. His quilted, powder-blue cardigan jacket had been rubbed to a sheen at the elbows where his lazy arms rested. He tutted loudly when Gordon handed him a tenner and fumbled through his pocket for loose change, raising his crotch disturbingly while he dug. Gordon shuddered at the touch from the driver's clammy hand and the warmth of the money from his inside leg. The driver noticed and Gordon felt bad.

"So are you the Trevellyan of Selyvan," he said, eager to restore a friendlier tone.

"I'm Trevellyan, my father was Trevellyan and so was my grandfather."

"But not your great grandfather?" said Gordon playfully.

The driver sighed, he lost patience quickly.

"Yes, he was Trevellyan. No, he didn't drive busses."

"It's lucky, with your name," Gordon said, he was babbling. "Trevellyan of Selyvan"

The driver looked back blankly.

"It rhymes," Gordon said with a hint of frustration.

"It's our name," Trevellyan said and turned his back on Gordon to ring the bell, signalling both his intention to leave and also to end the conversation.

The three found seats towards the rear of the bus. They were the only passengers but did not care to sit too close to the driver.

"Slick talk with the locals," said Clara punching Gordon on the leg. "Why did you have to take the piss?"

"I wasn't," Gordon protested.

"He's creepy," said David far too loudly and Clara hushed him with a firm stare.

The morning had started with some promise, a cold winter sun had broken low and blinding but it was short-lived. A grey blanket of cloud had extinguished any cheer. An increasingly choppy sea swirled in violent squalls. Gordon peered out through the filthy window which had already resigned its gleam to a fine, creeping moss. They pulled away.

The road rose sharply out of Penzance and there was little traffic. In high season it could be gridlocked until nightfall but the chugs of smoke from the chimney pots was evidence enough where the smart folk were spending their Saturday. The direct road to Selyvan ran along the coast, through the fishing villages of Newlyn and Mousehole but the driver quickly turned off the main road and headed inland. Gordon had looked at a map that morning and wondered what route they might be taking. The driver most likely avoided the steep and narrow route through the villages, he reasoned.

"Have you been to Cornwall before?" Clara asked Gordon.

"Once, to Mousehole, a few years back. I went with Zara."

Gordon stopped short at the mention of Zara's name. He did not want to talk about her, and especially not with Clara. But she had a natural curiosity and a playful, teasing manner. Clara noticed how Gordon had pulled up so suddenly. He was her horse refusing to jump - he needed a little rib kick from the stirrups.
"So did you two have a nice holiday?" she asked innocently.

Gordon shrugged. They had chosen the three wet days in July and Zara had been out of temper. Although she had agreed that bracing coastal walks would be "lovely" in London, even buying a new pair of hiking boots especially, when faced with the prospect of a drizzly clifftop trudge she refused.

"But you've bought the boots," Gordon had pleaded. "It will be fun."

But she did not know it was going to be raining when she had bought them.

"They're waterproof!"

Further appeals had soured the atmosphere irrecoverably. Instead, they joined the long queues at the Eden Project and both sloped stoically through the hothouses with a grim determination not to enjoy it. The only time she had laughed all week was when the seagull attacked Gordon and he dropped his 99er with a splatter.

"It was all right," Gordon answered eventually.

Clara smiled, she was feeling mischievous.

"She doesn't know I'm here with you now, I thought that was best."

"I agree."

"Not that she would mind." Clara stressed. "I mean, this is just work."

"Precisely," Gordon said. "But you know how she can be sometimes?"

Clara raised her eyebrows. She did, but was not going to betray sisterhood with admittance.

"Perhaps you don't," said Gordon, turning to look out of the window.

Low-hanging trees tickled the tinny roof as the bus jostled down the narrow country lanes.

"I think she's nice," Clara said after too long a pause.

Gordon had thought so too once. In essence Zara was not a bad person, she was very assured, determined and cunning. She had found Gordon fascinating and believed he could fit her schemes. When it became clear he lacked the necessary rigidity, always collapsing around her foundations like the house made of straw, she should have walked away. Instead, Zara ploughed her energy into trying to make Gordon function properly. They both ought to have recognised the inevitability but Zara's obstinance was met with Gordon's sentimentality and so they could never quite achieve the ultimate split. When she did finally pack her bags and move out Gordon did not realise for three days. He was all consumed at the time with coverage of the Rawlinson Inquiry. This piqued. It was true he had taken the separation more gracefully than she had, but a nagging guilt still lingered. He maintained a chivalrous silence but when she understood he was not going to beg for her back, she launched a smear campaign to blacken his name. And then she moved in with Clara, and this is why Gordon preferred not to talk about her.

"What are you two talking about?" said David, popping up from behind the seat in front.

"Nothing," said Gordon with finality. "Have you finished your level yet?"

He was tossing the stick of diversion to the bothersome dog. David had been stuck with Darkbane, the seventh dragon of the Silver Seal. Gordon knew all of this because he had received a long lecture about Night's Lore IV on the train. He quickly found a way to secrete away his mind while David jabbered on.

46

On the train to Cornwall David asked Gordon if he played Night's Lore.

"Of course, "said Gordon.

"What level?"

"Level 10."

"That's nothing," said David. "I'm a high-elf mage. So what character are you then?"

"The shop fitter."

"Liar, there isn't a shop fitter."

"Yes there is. But he only appears on Level 10."

"I'm on level 74."

"Then you weren't looking hard enough. The shop fitter is the most powerful character in the game - he arranges the dungeon for a more appealing consumer experience."

"You're lying," said David after a moment's thought. But he still could not accept Gordon was completely fibbing and continued to speak about it with references only the initiated would understand. David swung from spells of unrelenting garrulousness to monastic silence, albeit inspired by the less divine quest of Night's Lore IV.

The bus approached a bleak crossroads marked by a squat and gnarly oak tree. The perfect spot for a hanging, Gordon thought. A weather-worn signpost to Selyvan had dropped from its rusted nail and pointed down, it was a mile and a quarter away. Gordon knew little about Selyvan. Its online presence was limited to a few negative reviews and a fragment of a Wikipedia entry. A linked reference to the infamous Selyvan sinking of 1815 had been deleted recently but Gordon could find no other traces of it online. He made a mental note to ring his father, he was certain to know. Even the OS map Gordon had spread out at the Gull's Nest was little use. Selyvan seemed devoid of any of the usual signs of civilisation - church, post office, campsite, school. The map showed a single road running into the village and down to the harbour and that was all. The only symbol of life was the Cragg hotel which, the contour lines revealed, was perched on a bluff overlooking the village, and the Ship Inn.

After the crossroads, the condition of the road deteriorated. The bus plunged with a decrepit crunch into potholes and lumbered breathlessly out. The driver had to steer sharply around ruts that threatened to scrape the belly of the bus. Gordon sympathised with the old bus and forgave its tatty state.

He surveyed the countryside, it was a dismal, storm-battered wasteland. The rocky soil had clearly never ever accepted a plough and only a several derelict cottages were evidence a few hardy farmers had once tried and once failed. The only sign of agriculture was a large orchard. Dumped by the roadside were a season's worth of apples, piled in a mound and sheltered by a loose tarpaulin.

Half a mile from Selyvan, a long avenue of elms was the first hint of civility. They ran along the roadside and joined an ornate wrought iron gate. The great stone gate posts leaned slightly so that one of the gates dug into the earth under its own weight. The green stone globe that had capped the left-hand post had fallen with a thud, half burying itself in the soft, wet earth. The elms followed a pebble driveway into the distance, it dog legged, and Gordon could not see the grand mansion the grand driveway hinted at. Above the gate it was still possible to read 'Mortain, 1850' chipped more than a century ago into the stone.

The bus bumped into Selyvan, a worn sign announcing their arrival. The low-and-lean row of granite houses leading into the village were packed as tightly as penguins braced for the storm. The scantle slate roofs hung heavy with great furrowed brows. Every home had an air of desuetude about it, cool and forbidding. Their squat proportions and greyness displayed a hardiness not found in the lime-washed, powder pink postcard villages up the coast. Ragged blue fishing nets hung from many of the cottages, their weedy innards dripping fresh brine. The bus driver slowed to a crawl as he entered town. Gordon was agog.

The roughly paved road descended sharply towards the harbour. The houses on this incline were locked together even more densely, gripping one another with their ageing lime mortar. Only occasionally did a shopfront break the grey residential monotony. But even these commercial beacons did little to lighten Selyvan's sombreness. The entire town seemed to have grown like fungus under the dirty, subfusc light.

Gordon looked out at a dimly lit grocery, which displayed bunches of brown bananas and shrivelled lettuce in its spartan stalls. A women's clothing shop looked equally bleak with its amber sun filter peeling back away from the glass at its corners, and the frumpy floral print dresses on mutilated mannequins. There were few people about the town and those Gordon saw hurried along furtively with their heads stooped and their eyes to the ground. With a chilly wind rising and the drizzle thickening to rain, Gordon could hardly blame the townsfolk for staying indoors.

As the harbour approached the road widened and the slope levelled, it opened out into a small square. The houses became grander with stately Doric arches built from the polished Serpentine stone, hewn from local quarries 150 years ago. The largest of the houses in the square had the appearance of a civic building, Georgian in its Palladian pomposity. The rarer, red Serpentine cornice work twisted and twirled with a high degree of craftsmanship, evident still through the chips and disrepair. As Gordon followed the flowing lines toward the central pediment, he realised the masonry portrayed a snaking sea creature. It was intertwined and entangled to a gargoyle-esque centre which bore the striking resemblance to a scabrous whale. The date of the building was 1854 and it bore the name Mortain. A brass plaque screwed at street level announced it was the town hall. Gordon scanned the other grand buildings in the square, there was an old Masonic Hall, a library, and a trade exchange. All were built in the 1860s and all bore the Mortain name in the stonework above their entrances.

The bus pulled to a stop with a remarkable jerk considering how slowly it had been travelling. The driver turned and sneered to indicate they had reached their destination. Bumping with suitcases down the narrow aisle Gordon thanked the driver but only received a grunt in response.

"Do you know where we can find the Cragg Hotel, please?" Clara asked.

The driver did not reply but nodded his head to a rocky bluff overlooking the town. From where Clara stood, her camera bag digging into a stiffening shoulder and with the cold, damp air beading on her face, the hotel looked inaccessible. She turned in appeal to the driver but he had already guessed her question, stopping her dead.

"There's no road up there even if I could take you. You've got to take the coast path. Everybody has to take it."

Clara was irked. She had grown accustomed to a low-level chivalry, even if she did not expect it. The driver's lack of concern annoyed her, and she turned her back to him with a goodbye.

"Well, this town looks nice," she said to Gordon huffily and in such a way he knew it was best not to respond, but he rallied all the same.

"Let me take your case, I've hardly got anything in my bag. It's not far and we'll check in, warm up and get a cup of tea."

She smiled, annoyed at herself for snapping. They were all in it together this weekend. Gordon led the way.

CHAPTER EIGHT

Gordon slipped in his leather-soled brogues, first across the wet cobbles in Selyvan's main square and then along the steep path to the Cragg. The route was perilous and dizzying as it hugged the cliff edge, rising steeply from a small car park hollowed from the base of the cliff. A longer, winding path meandered away to the right. This alternative route was gentle enough for a golf buggy to ferry linen, food, and essentials to the hotel. Gordon opted for the direct route.

The footpath was only held together by a few hardy pines, whose thick roots created natural steps but also the possibility to trip and plummet to the toothy rocks below. Gordon stopped regularly to check Clara and David were still safely behind him. His career already teetered on the allegorical cliff's edge, if the chief executive's son stumbled off a non-allegorical cliff it would be more than another yellow card. Gordon was heavily laden with Clara's bag and nearly met disaster on three separate occasions. The other two puffed soldierly in the rear but never once lost their footing.

The Cragg was a statement of sublimity, thrust arrogantly on a wild and unforgiving location. It also possessed neither charm nor warmth. The great, grey granite blocks were imposing and glistened, despite the gloom, from the quartz contained in the rock. The arched windows and entrance were neatly finished in the similar burnished Serpentine stone Gordon had seen in the town, but this time in the more common green. Perched high on the cliff-top the stone had an even more impressive effect with its mottled patterning glowing in the faint light.

A monochrome sign for the Cragg Hotel hung on a black chain outside the entrance. It was bordered by the same intertwined sea snake Gordon has seen on the town hall, a heraldic emblem. Gordon had a romantic inclination and imagined crusader knights setting off from Selyvan's port, heeding Pope Urban's call to arms. With just a little effort he saw this serpent emblazoned on the shields and standards at Antioch under a burning Levantine sun. He pointed it out to David who glanced up half-heartedly.

"Looks like Hagon," he said.

Gordon looked puzzled.

"Hagon, Doom of the Deep, destroyer of Atlantopolis," said David impatiently. "You'd know that if you were really level 10."

'For somebody who spends half their life immersed in a fantasy kingdom, David really does lack imagination,' Gordon thought. He was not especially dull, but his talents were woefully misplaced. Gordon noticed how David had a search engine's ability for recall. Just that morning he had astounded Gordon by reeling off the spec-list for dozens of assault rifles. He knew calibres, muzzle velocities, dates of manufacture, country of origin, actions seen. All this without previously having shown any interest in weaponry - with the exception of Elven blacksmithery. His mind was a magnet for trivia. Gordon, whose own brain leaked from all angles, chided him with a secret jealousy.

'Don't clog up your brain with all that hoarding', he had said. 'Information can always be found if you know where to look. It's the ordering and reasoning of the assorted facts that really requires the brain's processor speed.'

Inside the Cragg hotel was all wood panelling, worn red carpets and unremarkable oil portraits. Paintings which straddled the line somewhere between the jaded professional and the enthusiastic amateur were hung carelessly in ugly golden frames. Behind reception, room keys with weighty brass fobs were lined up on hooks. Judging by the number of occupied hooks it was not a busy week at the Cragg. 'That's good,' Gordon thought. 'They'll be pleased to see us.'

He rang the reception bell but service nobody came. The place had a resinous, tarry smell which was neither sickly nor particularly pleasant, like the inside of a medicine cabinet. Gordon recalled it from school, he remembered chapel - the woodstain and the dust mixed with the faintest drop of damp.

"It smells a bit doesn't it," he said to Clara.

"Hello," said a voice behind reception.

A thin man slipped from the shadows, legs first. He wore a blue blazer and red tie. His grey hair was swept back and his long eyebrows cast spidery shadows. His forehead was ploughed deep from a lifetime of frowning. He had a neatly trimmed white moustache which yellowed at its extremities from a ten-a-day Cafe Creme habit. His stained teeth sank at angles into his gums, scarcely covered by his thin, dry lips. Beneath his unpleasant mouth swung unsightly dewlaps, once fat but ravaged thin by sudden illness.

"Can I help you? I'm Mr Lychgate," he paused before adding solemnly. "The proprietor."

Gordon cursed his bad timing with the comment about the smell, Lychgate had evidently heard.

"We've got a reservation," he said. "Three rooms. It's in my name I think, Athelney."

51

Mr Lychgate arched a brow imperiously and slowly checked his diary. He took such a time over it that Gordon began to wonder if Sheila had mistakenly booked a different hotel. In truth, he half hoped she had. Gordon glanced awkwardly at Clara who shrugged fatalistically.

"That's right," said Lychgate lazily and without looking up. "I was expecting you last night."

Gordon explained the situation about the late arrival and the taxis. He apologised for not phoning, but nothing could sweeten Lychgate's sour mood.

"Well, I shall have to charge you."

"That's fine."

But the hotelier was not willing to cut the argument short even if Gordon shirked sport.

"I've no choice but to charge you," he continued. "I could have let those rooms out. Although even if you had telephoned, I'd have still had to charge you. Taxis, trains or otherwise, that's not my business. It states clearly at the time you book; all cancellations must be made at least 24 hours in advance. But I'm not saying a call last night wouldn't have been welcome. Indeed, it would have saved us sitting up until the small hours. You can probably imagine that's NOT how we choose to spend our evenings after a long day. Although had you turned up at THAT time of night, you'd have been disappointed. I lock the doors at 10pm unless a prior arrangement has been made, which it hadn't. You could have knocked all you like; I wouldn't have stirred. I might run a hotel, but I've got a life to lead as well."

A slow grin formed on Lychgate's face as he imagined his cold, wet guests knocking on the heavy oak door with no answer. Gordon grew tired of the monologue; he was keen to dump his bag and head down to the beach.

"Well, I'm sorry for the inconvenience," he said politically. "Just charge the extra night to our bill. If we could just take the three rooms for tonight, please?"

"Three? I've got two here."

"No, it should be three."

"Well, I've got down two." Lychgate was becoming increasingly waspish.

Gordon had not booked the rooms so was in no position to argue. It was common for travel Sheila to make administrative errors.

"Well perhaps there was a mistake, I'm sorry. Please can we take three rooms for tonight?"

Lychgate reached once again for his diary and thumbed it pensively, shaking his head.

"No, I can't help you I'm afraid."

Gordon glanced at the bulging rack of keys on the wall and Lychgate's narrowing eyes understood his meaning.

"Two rooms are the best I can do," he said firmly.

Gordon looked helplessly at his mobile phone, half-wondering about calling Sheila to double-check. She would not like him calling her on a weekend, she had an indignant work-to-rule attitude. On the other hand, the prospect of sharing a room with David convinced him to try - except he had no reception on his mobile. Signal at the hotel was patchy at the best of times, but in the great reception hall with its thick, stone walls it was a permanent blackhole.

"Clara, do you have any bars?"
She checked, no signal either, or David.

Lychgate gave a derisive snort, if he had been a camel he would have spat.

"You won't get any reception out here," he said with smug cheer.

Gordon looked at Clara and she shrugged once again; she was staying out of this one.

"Well, we'll have to take the two," Gordon said, resigned to defeat.

He would just have to share with David. Gordon took the keys that Lychgate had dumped grumpily on the counter. When Gordon wondered if he needed to leave a credit-card deposit, he received another of Lychgate's pointed speeches; he ran a hotel where they trusted and respected their guests, his only rule was they returned him the same civility. Gordon wanted to point out a few of the other rules he had already heard but thought better of it and retreated.

After dumping his bags in the room Gordon headed out. David was satisfied to lay across his bed with Knight's Lore IV - which Gordon learned then had the pretentious subtitle 'Perdition's Enmity'. Clara wanted to shower first before heading down to join him, so he set out alone.

Fortunately, Lychgate was not still behind reception when Gordon left so he was spared another sparring. If the climb up to the hotel had been treacherous the descent was even more so. At points Gordon was forced to walk crab fashion, he only had one suit did not want it caked in mud on the first day.

The weather had not improved while Gordon was indoors and he was unsurprised to find Selyvan's small, sandy beach deserted. 'Why didn't I pack a pair of trainers,' Gordon berated himself. The wet sand would destroy his Church's. His footwear was not Gordon's only concern - his notepad was empty. There on a deserted beach on the very edge of England, he realised how hopeless his situation was. He had a career-saving story to deliver, and progress was stalling. The 'mfl' he had written at the bottom of his first copy was beginning to look optimistic. What did he have? A bleak beach. The cold bleak sea. Miles upon miles of bleakness. 'No wonder the dolphins were beaching themselves,' he thought. 'Why not a bleak death to end a bleak existence.'
Gordon felt a sudden clasp on his shoulder.

"The famous Gordon Athelney I presume?" a strange voice said.

CHAPTER NINE

Gordon spun around in surprise. He saw a ruddy-faced man beaming back at him. He looked like an illustration of a farmer from a children's book. Gordon stood in open-mouthed surprise, eventually he managed to splutter out a hello.

"I knew it," said the man. "I knew you were the famous Mr Athelney from the moment I spied you."

Gordon could say nothing, so the man continued.

"'But how did he guess?' You're wondering. Go on then, I'll let you into the secret. It was the notepad. We can spot one another from a mile away,"

The man winked and patted his own notepad, curled tightly into his breast pocket along with a quiver full of biros. Gordon smiled again, unsure of what to make of the stranger.

"But how did you know my name?" Gordon said eventually.

The stranger laughed loudly and bent double before slapping Gordon's arm

"You're a sharp one. I knew you would be. Another secret, eh? It's all right, you can owe me. I saw it flash on the wires this morning. I thought: 'Now that is something, an Associated News man out in Cornwall'. Yes, that is something, but I knew I'd find you. But how rude, where are my manners. Introductions, introductions. I'm the famous Max Nash of the Cornish Chronicle."

Max held out his hand and Gordon accepted but it was Max who did most of the shaking.

"I read your copy too," said Gordon. "In fact, my editor gave me your story. That's why they sent me down here."

"Now you're teasing. My copy? In the Associated News? I can see it in the editor's hands now. What a picture. And in London too? Honestly, I'm tickled pink by that. But now I'm sure you're teasing."

Max was perpetually jovial and had the smile-ironed creases to prove it. He bore an avuncular jollity and his plumped face was cocked to laugh at a moment's notice. His laughter gurgled from his guts like a geyser. He had worked his little patch in Cornwall for 40 years and could think of no better life. Max had no ambition to rise to higher-editorial echelons. His greatest pleasure in life was in new acquaintances and he was never shy of an introduction. His curly hair might have whitened but he still had the energy of youth. A loose-fitting khaki gilet and blue-striped short-sleeved shirt partly hid his porcine aspect and his bare arms were proof of his immunity the winter chill.

Max was a journalist in control of his happy little patch. Gordon saw he did not possess the neurosis that infects most in his profession, an illness most can only medicate with drink.

"Who'd have thought it? The famous Gordon Athelney here in Selyvan. I bet you'll be wanting to know about last night's beachings? Well, I was the first one at the scene. Even got some photos," he said patting a tatty compact camera that dangled from his belt.

"Handy things these digitals. This one was a present from my daughter five years back. I expect you've got a much better one than this."

"I don't," said Gordon.

"No doubt you know best," Max said. "I do all my own pictures now, since the cutbacks. A few years back we moved from a bi-weekly to weekly. I saw some friends go then."

Talk of the axe reminded Gordon of his own precarious career, his neck on the chopping block. He steered the conversation back to the job in hand.

"You said you were first on the scene, what did you see?"

Max laughed again and hopped a little jig, he could have hugged Gordon.
"Yes, yes, yes," he said. "A proper journalist. I knew it. Straight in there. The scent of blood in the nostrils, you old news hound. I smell it too. What a famous pair are we, eh?"

Max gave a bloodhound's howl, tossing back his head. He put a hand on Gordon's shoulder and led him down the beach. Max filled the gaps in the scant police statement, plumping and speculating while Gordon jotted it down hungrily. By the time Gordon had arrived there was little to see on the beach, the dolphins' carcasses had already been removed. Footprints the only evidence of earlier activity. Max showed Gordon where the dolphins had been found, a puddle of foamy brine had pooled in the trench where they had lain. A connection formed and Gordon

56

remembered the events of the previous night, the fear he had felt returned. The sharp echo of that alien noise resounded, and a chill ran painfully down his spine. Gordon had to shake himself back to his reality.

"You said you had some photos. Please could I see?" he said.

Max gave a chuckle of delight, only too happy to share. 'He was a funny fish,' Gordon thought. Most reporters are fiercely secretive; their careers hinge on knowing a single fact their rivals have yet to discover. The pressure of the scoop is not such a concern for an agency journalist, time is their first obsession. An agency always has to be first. But never at the expense of accuracy - and there was the rub. Gordon lived in mortal fear of the corrected repetition. All the best journalists were neurotics, but apparently not the famous Max Nash, who was struggling to bring up the thumbnails on his camera screen, stabbing at buttons aimlessly like a chimp with a TV remote.

"Can I try?" Gordon said, just seconds before Max deleted his entire morning's work.

"Please, please," said Max, handing him the camera. "Not sure what's wrong with the old girl."

Gordon was not particularly tech-savvy himself, but was more fluent than Max. A few taps and he was cycling through the snapshots. 'What would Clara say?' Gordon couldn't help wondering as he worked through the collection of missing heads and blurred faces. One man reappeared many times and Gordon soon recognised him. He was tall and towered from the periphery, sometimes directing the proceedings or ordering grumpy police officers around. He wore a long trench coat with a crimson neck scarf. He cut a striking figure with his long, thin nose and pitchy hair which had grown two white badger stripes either side of the crest.
"Who's that?" Gordon asked.

"The nutty professor, that's what I call him. Ruben Burroughs from over at St Austell University. Handsome man?"

Gordon looked surprised and Max laughed.

"He certainly thinks so. He's my age but he's still a terror for the ladies. I pride myself on getting along with everybody, but I draw the line with him. Not that I'm going to speak badly of the man, but he hates journalists and lets it be known."

"I had the pleasure myself this morning," said Gordon, remembering the frost phone interview.

"And?"

Gordon lifted his eyebrows and nodded in agreement. Max erupted in laughter.

"I knew it. I can always spot them and so can you. He's a fox with a natural fear of the hounds, eh?"

Gordon recognised Max could be an invaluable contact and asked for his contact details. Max bristled with pride as he handed Gordon his business card and, in return, received Gordon's with all the pomp and ceremony of a royal diplomatic gift.

"What do you make of all of this?" Gordon asked Max, waving his hand across the empty beach. Max had been covering this patch for so long there could be little that surprised him.

"I don't know, it's odd," he said with uncharacteristic gravity. "I've never seen anything like this before. Certainly, we get the odd dolphin here and there. I've even seen a whale, once or twice. The ones that create the biggest sensations are the cows washed to sea in freak storms - all the local folklore and superstition comes bubbling to the surface then.

"But so many dolphins in such a short space of time, I don't know; it just doesn't seem right. Having said that, you should take what you hear with a hint of salt, especially in Selyvan. If the locals think they've got a soft foreign ear to bend they'll spin you some yarns. Remember it's a remote spot out here and I don't care to visit unless I have to. I'm not saying the Selyvan folk are bad, but they take some warming to. Be warned, they're quick to point the finger and just as quick to exploit. For what it's worth, I'd speak to old Guddy. He knows these waters like no other. He's a quiet chap, not like some of the others but, if you can get him talking, you'll learn more from him than from all the village gossip-peddlers combined. If there's something happening, he's your man."

"Guddy?"

"That's right, the famous Gudbjartotur Olaffson. Just don't ask me to spell you his name," Max said, noticing how Gordon was scrawling down everything he said in his notepad. "He's our Icelandic fisherman but he's been here longer than most of the locals. His is a sad story really; but shouldn't every lonely fisherman have a reason to take to sea? He came to Cornwall for love. He was a different man back then. But you how life has its own plans?"

Max trailed off lugubriously as he stared out to sea.

"Where does he live?" Gordon asked, snapping Max from his silence.

"I bet if you head to the Ship Inn you'll find Guddy there. He's only ever in two places - the sea or the pub and there's a storm blowing in."

"You think he'll be able to help?"

Max shrugged.

"Who can say? But 12 years ago, dolphins started beaching, not so many as this, but enough to get the paper's interest. It wasn't long after Guddy's wife had died and he was in a bad way. I asked if he could take me out in his boat, to take his mind off things more than anything. I had no idea what I was looking for but we'd got maybe six miles off the coast when I saw a big battleship. I'd never seen anything so large in these waters before and I asked Guddy to sail closer to see if we could see what was happening. We didn't get within a mile of the ship before a gunboat buzzed over and ordered us away, non-too polite either. I never did find out why the Royal Navy was there. Anyway, I need to rush back to the office in Penzance. I could stand here all day chatting with a fellow hound."

Gordon thanked him for his help. He watched the strange journalist hurry away down the beach with a lopsided trot. Gordon wondered if he could trust him. He was right about one thing, a storm was blowing in. Above, the blue grey sky was darkening and the billowing cumulus were backlit with a luminous richness. Gordon looked down at the card Max had given him, it read: "The famous Max Nash: newspaper man... man and boy". Gordon laughed; it was impossible not to like Max. He assumed such an immediate intimacy that it always felt as though you had known him for years. Gordon wished he had Max's natural confidence and self-assurance in social situations, he always found himself becoming the person he thought the other person wanted him to be. He hated himself for it.

From a distance, Gordon spotted Clara, she was striding down the beach. Her silhouette was unmistakable, and her long hair was blown horizontal in the developing gale. From her light steps Gordon could tell she was much revived; he had sensed earlier she was losing humour. He did not blame her.

A strange sensation struck Gordon as he watched Clara approach. It was almost like déjà vu, almost uncanny. There - striding against the coming storm - Clara looked to him like a flaxen Gothic shieldmaiden - Hervor or Brynhild. She was a heroine of legend. Her cheeks were plump, whitened against the cold, her nose had reddened slightly at the tip. She was strength and health, she was beautiful. His feelings made him feel suddenly wretched in contrast, but he felt a maddening desire to kiss her. Just to grab her and kiss her. Her cold nose against his hot blood. Just to see what would happen. She might slap him. There would be awkwardness. She might report him to HR. That would be the last straw.

"All right?" asked Clara, wondering at the unusual expression Gordon wore.

The moment passed and Gordon writhed in his own cowardice. The breeze caught Clara's perfume and Gordon caught a whiff.

"You smell nice," he said instinctively, the first words after awakening from a dream. From the look of embarrassment on her face he sensed he had overstepped a mark.
"You look nice too," he added.

Clara's eyebrows arched. She was puzzled, caught off-guard and lost for a retort.

"Thanks," she said eventually and with a dash of incredulity. "What have you been up to?"

"I met a local journalist called Max Nash. He was quite a character. He's given me a lead. He even had some photos of the dolphins here this morning."

"Did you get a frame?"

"A what?"

"Did you ask if he could give you a photo... as a favour."

Gordon screwed the right side of his face and Clara knew he had not.

"Next time I'm taking photos and I hear a good story I'll keep it to myself, shall I?"

Gordon realised his mistake. He knew Clara was in the same sinking boat, and, rather than bailing, he had just added another bucket of brine. She would never say so, but Clara was as worried about her own job as Gordon was for his. Perhaps the situation was even worse for the snappers. Senior management could spend £400 on a DSLR camera and hand it to a journalist - the axe man's dream - instantly the company has saved the wage of a full-time member of staff. The journalists get to call themselves photojournalists - which sounded much more exotic when they were trying to impress in bars - and the photographer can go forth to click all their creativity away on much worthier projects.

"And besides there's loads of money doing weddings," management would say to assuage their guilt.

"Sorry."

It was all Gordon could think to say.

In the madness of a storm comes a sudden clarity. There they were stood on a lonely beach together chasing a wild goose around darkest Cornwall. Suddenly, it all seemed like insanity to Gordon. But he understood then that he would have to work more closely with Clara. After all, his story was nothing without her photographs - especially not in Sir Trevor's new age of Click! News. His motivation returned.

"I'm heading to the Ship Inn," said Gordon.

"Bit early to start, isn't it?"

"There's somebody I want to see there."

"Well keep me posted. I need to get some shots of the beach, just in case the desk needs them, which they won't."

CHAPTER TEN

Clara watched Gordon as he tramped along the beach back into town. His shoes left a perfect impression in the sodden sand into which salty water flowed. Clara saw there was a wretchedness in Gordon's walk. He was tall but self-conscious and it caused him to stoop. She wondered if she had been too hard on him for forgetting to ask for a frame from Max Nash. He had looked so pained when she chided him. Clara knew she had reacted more harshly than usual; she had wanted to break the strange tension. There was an expression on Gordon's face she had never seen, and there was an unusual awkwardness and a clumsiness in his words. It had caught her off-guard and Clara hated to be off-guard.

She waited until Gordon had rounded the bend of the harbour wall and disappeared out of sight. With Gordon gone she could concentrate on the task in hand. She pulled her scarf over her nose against the cold and swapped her leather gloves for the woollen, fingerless pair she wore on winter shoots. On her own, the beach felt forbidding and hostile. Her eyes scanned the sand looking for anything of interest. The grey skies flattened everything. There were no shadows, no tone, no range. She pulled her camera up to her face in forlorn hope, sometimes inspiration would magically crystallize between the lens and the eye, but not then.

She slung the camera dejectedly over her shoulder and walked aimlessly along the empty beach. She knew she must not think negatively, it was counter-productive to feel sorry for herself, but it was hard to stay positive. She felt like she was being swallowed in quicksand, already waist-deep and clawing at the loose earth around. There could be no art without passion, but no passion without energy. She stopped fast, steeling herself into action. She took a deep breath, gave her cheeks a double-sided slap and blinked out her negativity.

"Right Clara," she said, puffing out her cheeks and exhaling. "Let's do this."

The beach yawned impressively, a mile long. It was a large area for Clara to cover so she needed a plan. She guessed the beach closest to the harbour was more likely to have been explored, instead she headed further from town to the narrower fringes. She strode with new purpose, and it was not long before Selyvan was lost behind the shallow curve of the cliff face. The cliffs became taller and steeper away from town. The beach too became increasingly pebbly until the sand had given way to rocks and bleached driftwood. Before long Clara was bounding across shallow rock pools, teeming with limpets and the red suckers she had never dared to touch as a child, despite her father's encouragement.

The cliffs to her left loomed like a fortress wall. Clara admired its strength, standing firm against the sea. The two great forces had been snarling at one another for thousands, perhaps millions of years. The dead weight of rock against the vastness of the sea, dashing its inexhaustible power against in a billion bitter lashes. With her neck craned to the cliffs, she spotted something dark shift above her at its edge. Instinctively she reached for her camera but by the time she had raised it to her right eye whatever had been there was gone.

'Another miss,' Clara thought gloomily.

The beach tightened to an arrowhead, caught between the sheer cliff and the sea. Clara noticed a prominent rock that jutted at the very extremity of the beach, she knew by instinct this was her destination and headed for it. The closer she got to this distant rock the more hazardous the going got; waves tossed themselves more violently, the footing became slippery and the route more uncertain. At several points Clara lost her balance between bounds and landed with a cold thud on her hands or knees. Her camera was always her first concern, and she was prepared to suffer a bruise in order to cradle it during a fall. Despite the knocks, she continued and eventually reached her extreme destination. With great satisfaction she stood looking out over the sea with one knee bent and romantically imagining herself as Friedrich's Wanderer Above the Sea Fog. Even on a grey day there was something elemental about the light that stirred Clara. Her eyes sharpened and she began mapping her surroundings for inspiration.

From where she stood on the rock Clara could once again see the town of Selyvan, drab and cheerless. A mist rolled over the harbour walls and was creeping up into town. Clara's eyes traced the narrow path to the Cragg hotel, which stood grim at the pinnacle like a Victorian prison. She followed the route she had taken down to the beach and saw before her the snaking expanse of sodden sand. But in the foreground the rocks were glistening in the sharp spray, offering the faintest sparkle in the dismal landscape. There was nothing to photograph. The light was flat, the vision bleak. The only activity on the beach that day had been much earlier and Clara had missed it.

She returned to the rockpool where the red suckers thrived, and partly to justify having lugged her camera the length of the beach she fired off a few snapshots. It was fruitless, the light was too low for macro work but as Clara was focusing she spotted something at the edge of her frame. There, sparkling on a silvery rock, was a high-heeled shoe covered in red diamante studs. The shoe was so incongruous, brine-drenched and filled with a fine sand but otherwise undamaged. It sat in an awkward shadow, so Clara lifted it to the top of the rock to make use of the best available light. With a bit of off-camera flash on its left side she hoped to bring a sparkle to the shoe but also to capture the sea and the beach blurring away into the distance. She fired a few test shots and adjusted her exposure. She had a steady hand and not many photographers could get as many usable shots as she could at one twenty fifth of a second. Clara wanted the shoe to pop out of the shot, sharp and defined against the bokeh. She opened her iris all the way and fired another test. 'Almost, almost,' she said to herself. A few more twists, up the ISO, lengthen the exposure and she fired again, checking the sharpness of each shot after every burst.

As Clara looked through her shots, she noticed something strange, a dark spot within the blurred background. At first she thought she had moisture on her lens but checked and it was clean. As she flicked through the thumbnails the dark spot grew larger and more defined. Closer and closer it came. Then in her final frame she saw, it was unmistakable, the dark spot was the figure of a man, and he was approaching.

"Hello," said a deep voice above her. Clara leapt back startled and let out a breathy gasp.

A man stood five feet above her on the rock. He was reaching the last years of middle-age and was tall, besides the advantage, and Clara had to crane her neck to see his face. She felt foolish for having jumped with such shock, she had been engrossed she had not sensed his arrival.

"I'm sorry, you startled me," she said.

"Not my intention, I have the gait of a deer stalker so they tell me."

Clara smiled but it was forced. She felt deeply uncomfortable. It was obvious to her the stranger was not a dog walker who would pass by with a friendly 'how-do-you-do'. The man climbed down from the rock to where Clara was standing. He wore black ankle boots and, encumbered by his long, black trench coat, his descent was less elegant than his vanity would have liked. He leapt the final foot without grace and landed in a shallow pool besides Clara. He dusted himself down from the exertion. Clara realised then how tall the man was, he towered over her by at least a foot. His height was further exaggerated by his proximity. His presence was so unannounced and intimate that Clara felt compelled to address it.

"Can I help with anything?" she said, but he ignored her and stared at the red high-heeled shoe.

"What's this, a fashion shoot?"

"A shoe I found on the rocks," she said, picking up the shoe protectively.

"It's not yours?" he said.

Clara shook her head and the man looked thoughtful, before he suddenly reached out and seized the shoe. Clara was speechless and could only watch in silence as he stuffed it in the large pocket of his trench coat with its six-inch heel protruding.

"It's best not to leave litter on the beach," he said.

64

Clara wanted to protest but reasoned otherwise. The photographs were not of any real importance and she was desperate to get away from the stranger so she could only smile weakly. The man stood with his hands buried deep in his trouser pockets and his thrusting hips created an unnatural hinge between his two halves. What unsettled Clara the most were his dark eyes which were glazed with an eerie, faraway haze but then flickered capriciously with sparks of sudden intensity. The man's bottom jaw hung slightly ajar, as though at any moment he might speak but never did. Clara tingled. She wished she could run but did not want to break this uneasy standoff.

"Well, I need to get back," she said eventually. "Good afternoon."

But as she made to leave the man grabbed her wrist. Clara looked up, her face betrayed fear which the stranger recognised and he softened his grip.

"I'm sorry," he said. "I hadn't expected to find anybody out here. I was just taking a stroll."

He released his grip and instead held out his hand to shake.

"But I didn't introduce myself. Professor Ruben Burroughs."

Clara cast a suspicious glance at his outstretched hand. She did not accept it, but the Professor nodded his insistence. Eventually she shook it weakly and pulled away when his fingers began to tighten around hers.

"Well Professor..." she said.

"Ruben," he said, talking over her. "I'm always Ruben, to my friends."

Clara was uneasy but was keen not to betray any fear and spoke again slowly and confidently.

"Well Ruben, it is nice to meet you, but I must be heading back."

She smiled again and turned to clamber up the rock and away to safety. The small basin in which they both stood felt like a gladiatorial pit and she wanted to be far away. As Clara raised her arms to find a solid hold from which to pull herself free, she found herself once again under his control. The Professor placed two flat hands against the rock on either side of her waist which pressed her flat. He pulled his body tightly against hers and she could feel his hot breath on the side of her head. Clara stood motionless; she was uncertain of her next move. She still did not want to risk provocation until she was convinced of the danger.

"That looks like an expensive camera," he said. "It looks very professional."

Clara nodded.

"And are you?"

Clara could feel his heavy breathing as his chest rose and fell against her back. She considered screaming but with the rising wind, the crashing waves and the abandoned beach it would be better to save her breath.

"Am I what?" she said in a nervous burst.

"A pro."

"Yes."

"I see," said the Professor, each word timed with his measured breathing.

"Do you want to see my photos?"

He exhaled a long breath into her hair and finally pushed himself clear, releasing Clara. She spun around to face him, her face flushed.

"I've been sent to shoot the dolphins, dead ones, the ones that beached, that is," she spoke garrulously with the adrenaline.

'Am I over-reacting?' she asked herself. 'Perhaps he's just a randy, old kook - no harm. You live in Brixton, for God's sake.'

"Photographing dolphins?" said the Professor pointedly. "And I'm guessing you're not from the local paper."

"Associated News. It's an agency. A national news agency."

"Is that so? A funny story for a national agency to cover."

"I think we're leaving soon. There isn't really much of a story."

66

"I suspect you're probably right," he said, taking another step closer to Clara. He looked at her with the thoroughness of inspection and lifted a ringlet of her blonde hair that had fallen across her face.

"You're a lot prettier than most of the photographers I've ever seen."

Clara tried to step back but met resistance, she was already fast against the rock. She pulled herself tighter like a limpet away from the Professor, but he only took another half step closer. His nose was inches from her own and she could smell his sour breath, like three-day old wine but with the rancid spice of tobacco. He did not speak, he only breathed. He raised his arms, putting one and then the other against the rock so Clara was once again his prisoner, only this time she faced him. This was the moment of crisis, she told herself, this was when she had to act but her brain flushed itself dry in its terror. Her mobile phone rang, shrill and piercing through the cool air. She pounced like a cat and answered it.

"Hello, Clara speaking."

The Professor quickly dropped his arms and casually shifted a step back.

"Something bad has happened," said David, his voice was tinny but panicked. "I can't make the water stop."

"What water?"

"From the radiator. It's all over the carpet."

"Well go and tell reception, they'll fix it."

"I can't," he said, his voice breaking with emotion.

"Why not?"

"Because the radiator fell off the wall."

Clara looked up at the Professor who shifted impatiently. He stared at her, his eyes were wide and sinister. She had not forgotten the danger.

"Wait, come and find me," she said. "I'm at the far end of the beach. You're only a minute away. We'll go there together."

"Where are you?" said David.

"Ok I'll see you in a one minute."

"But where are you?"

Clara hung up.

"Sorry about that, it was just my assistant David," she said apologetically and with all the reserves of confidence she could muster. "He's a bit dim but built like a bison so he's handy for lugging my gear around. He'll be here in a minute. I'd better go and find him."

The Professor looked thoughtfully out across the empty beach; he was making calculations. His face darkened with defeat, but he quickly caught his emotions and returned to Clara with a gracious smile.

"Of course," he said. "We can't stay here chin-wagging all day and it wouldn't look good if anybody should catch the two of us. Go, go."

He scooted her away.

"I hope I shall see you again soon," he added as she pulled herself away, she could feel his eyes burning into her back.

Once she was free Clara hopped and jogged back to the sandy beach and safety without ever once looking back. Even when she was within sprinting distance of the harbour she still maintained her pace and her heart pounded from the exertion. Then, from behind the harbour wall, David appeared. Clara recognised his hunched shoulders and shuffling gait and was never happier to see anybody in her life. She could have picked him up and hugged him.

"Do you think Gordon's going to be angry?" David said immediately, as though the question had been troubling him for some time.

"What?" said Clara, struggling to focus on his words in her relief.
"Well the water went mostly over his bag," said David. "I think his clothes are wet."

"Come on, let's go and have a look then," she said, and playfully took David's hand as they headed back to the Cragg. Only then did Clara dare to look back but the beach was empty, there was no sign of the Professor.

CHAPTER ELEVEN

Gordon trudged through wet sand back to Selyvan. The local fishing fleet bobbed on the swells, tethered on frayed ropes in the harbour. Some less seaworthy vessels were beached, their hulls scorched by crude blowtorch scars.

Selyvan was not one of Cornwall's postcard villages, roughly hewn and weather-beaten, a fishing town where the fish were not biting. The stocks had been in decline for years and a good catch only existed in the maudlin yarns spun in the Ship Inn. The fish that bit were young, too small for market. The local fishermen blamed the 'locusts in Spain' and some still flew Canadian flags on the boats, they never forgot the Turbot wars.

Gordon made his way up the steep hill, from the harbour into town. Selyvan was small and finding the Ship Inn wasn't difficult. The pub was nestled between a boarded-up Post Office and a dusty tearoom that looked as if it had last served sandwiches in 1945. The Ship Inn was equally tatty with its grimy windows misted with condensation. A dull yellow light shone from within, and dim silhouettes shuffled behind the glass, it was the faint pulse in that decaying cadaver.

Gordon popped a date behind his cheek and braced himself. He entered, clutching his notepad like a life raft. Every eye in the pub was trained at the entrance as he noisily banged the door shut. Inside a smog hung over the bar like river mist; there was not a smoking ban in Selyvan. The Ship existed in a perpetual dusk, everything inside was stained in the pale, blue half-light. The weather-worn regulars sipped dark beer through stained beards and clutched pints with powerful fingers where nails grew squat and brittle in their swollen, chapped housings. Noses were raw and blistered and cheeks were webbed with burst veins. The drinkers turned to wonder at the stranger in the suit and tie. They gazed listlessly through hooded, watery eyes but their languor was contagious and most quickly returned to their beer and gentle murmuring.

Gordon tried to stroll confidently to the bar. The brassy beer taps had grown a glaucous mould and the pint glasses behind the bar were dusty and speckled with greasy fingerprints. The last thing Gordon wanted was a drink but he could hardly order a herbal tea.

"All right, mate," Gordon said, and his date popped loose from his cheek and landed on the bar. Gordon grabbed it and stuffed it in his pocket. The landlord looked at him blankly.

"A pint of Boatswain's Bounty, please, mate," Gordon said, putting on the awkward Estuary accent he adopted when he felt awkwardly middle-class.

The bearish landlord did not acknowledge Gordon's order, it would take three years of regular drinking before a patron was awarded that first honour. He grabbed a dirty glass and strained at the pump. The tap coughed, spluttered and finally and vomited a frothy, treacly beer into the glass. Gordon didn't have change so had to pay with a twenty. The bar man turned the note doubtfully between his fingers and then, to Gordon's mortification, shouted over to a table of regulars for change to break it. Once more, every eye in the Ship was fixed on Gordon who felt himself reddening. Change was found and Gordon was weighed down a pocketful of coins. Gordon asked - as casually as he could muster - if Guddy was about. The barman did not answer but nodded ill-temperedly to a glum shadowy figure in a sombre corner.

Two ruddy drinkers at the bar eyed Gordon with interest. Their collection of smeared glasses was evidence of a long session, and the drink had given them a sense of bravado.

"You're not from around here, are you?" the first man slurred.

"Of course he's not," the second interjected.

"I'm not," added Gordon.

"On holiday?" said the first.

"He's lost," said the second.

"I'm working," added Gordon.

"For the government?" said the first.

"The government's never cared about us before," said the second.
"I'm a journalist. I'm writing a story about the dolphin beachings."

Both men nodded clumsily, swaying in their stools in a hazy dizziness.

"You should go and interview the jellyfish," said the first and he exploded in phlegmy laughter at the force of his own wit.

"He should find the fish witches," said the second earnestly.

"The fish witches?" said Gordon.

The first man punched his companion in the arm, momentarily evaporating the fog of drunkenness.

"Never you mind," said the first man gravely. "You wouldn't understand."

Silence once more descended and Gordon felt the prickly nettle rash of self-consciousness returning. He looked over to where the landlord had pointed out Guddy. In the far corner he saw a saturnine figure sitting alone. Gordon approached nervously. Guddy looked up with eyes that were beginning to lose their focus in the smoke and gloom. He had a timeless, almost boyish, appearance. His skin was tanned and cured by the sea spray, and the hairs on his unshaven chin were somewhere between aspen and blonde. The creases above his cheeks joined like a thousand tributaries to blue eyes which stared stern and sorrowful. Seven empty glasses crowded the table.

"Are you Guddy?" said Gordon, for want of any better introduction.

Guddy nodded as he picked up a black cap from the bench beside him and pulled it down firmly on his thin blonde hair. Gordon looked shyly at the empty seat and waited for Guddy, but the offer never came.

"You're a fisherman, right?"

Gordon tried again, but the locals on the next table laughed and Gordon prickled in embarrassment. Guddy smiled at them, as the grumpy barman carried over a clear spirit to the table in a schooner. The smell of alcohol was overpowering, even from where Gordon was standing. The barman waited while Guddy drained the glass joylessly.

"See you tomorrow," the barman said and Guddy nodded firmly.

With his drinking done Guddy rose, his chair screeching on the tiled floor. He looked intently at Gordon, who stood awkwardly before him. For a moment both men were fixed in silence. Gordon felt as though a great weight was bearing on his chest and his mind raced desperately for some key to open the conversation. His mind was blank.

"Excuse me," Guddy said eventually.

Gordon quickly stepped aside and Guddy walked with purpose to the door and left. Gordon was left standing, pint in hand, facing the empty corner of the Ship Inn where Guddy had been sat. For a moment he was unsure what to do and a great wave of shame washed over him. Gordon collected himself, put his pint down and chased out after Guddy.

Gordon caught up with him half-way along a steep street lined with grim, terraced houses. Guddy walked quickly, even by Gordon's standards who followed half a pace behind. Guddy pulled up at a house, ramshackle even by the standards of the street. He fumbled with his key for some time before realising the door had not been locked. Guddy either ignored Gordon or was unaware he had followed him from the pub, he looked around in shock when Gordon spoke.

"Please could you spare me five minutes?"

Guddy's eyes blinked for focus but when they finally settled on Gordon they fixed with a frown of concentration.

"What do you want, Whiting?" Guddy said.

"It's about the dolphins, I'm a reporter and I need some help."

Guddy stared at him again, he was processing the words - panning them like gold for their sense. Gordon shifted, he wanted to break the intensity of the gaze, but Guddy maintained.

"Come in," he said eventually and to Gordon's surprise.

The iron number seven swung on a single rusty nail as Guddy fastened the rain swollen door behind him with a shoulder and a shove. It felt colder inside the house than it had outside. The old carpet was more thread than weave and Gordon guessed it was not necessary to remove his shoes, but he did so all the same. He hurried after Guddy but took a wrong turn into the downstairs toilet. The cistern head was missing and Gordon thought he saw something bobbing. Curiosity conquered and he peered in, but gasped at the sight. Two giant pieces of fish floating in the tank.

"It's this way, Whiting," said Guddy from behind. His voice was gentle with only the thinnest trace of an accent.

Gordon turned, his mouth still agape. Guddy laughed and his eyes softened, revealing the kindness he kept buried. Guddy reached past Gordon and pulled the chain to flush the water. Gordon watched the cistern fill and the fish bob back to the surface.

"They're rehydrating," Guddy said, still smiling. "It's salt cod - this is the best way to do it."

Gordon followed him through to the kitchen, it was as Spartan as the rest of his house. There was no fridge, no microwave, no appliances and, aside from a clumsily hewn loaf of bread, nothing Gordon could identify as food. A black frying pan, which looked as though it had been cast by a medieval blacksmith from pig iron, contained congealed butter and fish bones. Hanging from all available space on the walls were giant slabs of salted cod looking like fossilised relics. It could have been the grotto of some grizzled troll were it not for a faded wedding photograph on a sideboard. Guddy looked young and happy. He wore a neck scarf, tunic and a Wee Willy Winkie hat. His wife was beautiful. The only art in the kitchen - and indeed the house - was a crude watercolour sitting alone on an empty shelf - fittingly of a fish. Guddy noticed Gordon staring at it.

"We all have our passion," he said. "Mine is cod. My wife painted it for me as an anniversary present. She said cod was my first love."

Gordon turned and looked at him, but Guddy was staring at the painting.

"You think it's strange to be passionate about a fish?"

"Well..." said Gordon, trying to think of a polite answer.

"Well, I'm passionate. I can see its flesh, the whitest thing I've ever seen. It is purity. Even when it sits in a puddle of melted butter, a thick, salty little puddle, the flesh is still white. It almost glows it is so pure. I don't use herbs or seasoning; it doesn't need it. But when my fork sticks and it flakes, oh Whiting, you should see it, like layers of an onion, the flesh beneath is purer still, like the snow on a mountain in the midday sun."

Guddy took out a cigarette and lit it, offering Gordon one who declined. Guddy's accent became more pronounced as he began to speak more passionately. It had the music of Russian to Gordon's ears, but without the harshness. Letters rolled or elongated and hit stresses an English tongue would never detect. With smoke from the unfiltered cigarette already hanging heavy in the air, Guddy continued.

"Every day I have eaten cod. Back home - that's Iceland - we would butter it like bread and snack on it between meals. Nothing was wasted back then. You know we used to soak the bones in milk until they softened and eat them too. Half a century with that fish and I am still in love."

"There's a chip shop in Crouch End that does a nice piece of cod," Gordon said, trying to understand.

"Fish and chips, your country makes me laugh. You know, cod and chips was your national dish. Then when there is no more cod left to catch, what do you do? Haddock and chips, overnight. Like there was no difference.

"This fish - that you forgot so casually - this fish built your empire. Your love of tobacco, tea and sugar. Three of the most labour-intensive crops and you British wanted all three. Well, your poor slaves weren't breaking their backs for potatoes and beef steaks. It was salt cod, only cod, that kept them working."

"I'm sorry," said Gordon.
"What are you sorry for, Whiting?" Guddy stared at him with a sudden intensity and Gordon's blood chilled. There was something uncanny in the face. A memory bobbed back to the surface like the cod in the cistern and Gordon made the connection.

"We saw you, last night. Off the coast of Penzance, in the rowing boat. I didn't recognise you at first but now I see it."

"You saw me and I saw you right back, what of it?"

"But we heard noises. Noises like nothing on earth."

"I heard nothing," said Guddy.

"It was like thunder but deep beneath the waves."

Guddy took a long drag on his cigarette, its end crinkling in the heat and the paper crackling as it burnt. He did not blink; he did not flinch. His eyes were fixed on Gordon, calculating a foe before a strike. A feint to the right and a jab from the left. Gordon expected him to spring like a pouncing cat at any moment, but still Guddy waited. The fogginess of the alcohol had burned away and his eyes sharpened. Gordon would use silence during a difficult interview. He would ask the killer question and wait. Let the interviewee laugh awkwardly, let them stammer out a half-response and wait. Wait in perfect silence. Compelled by the tension they would start blabbering, mostly mindless, but occasionally revealing. Now Gordon had to resist breaking the silence himself as Guddy stared back at him. There was a look in his eyes that unsettled Gordon, and when his mouth eventually curled to speak it was long considered.

"What are you here for?"

"I told you," said Gordon firmly. "I was sent here to report on the dolphins. Do you know anything about it?"

Again, Guddy drew on his cigarette without a reply. As a child Gordon had been taken to Banham zoo. A crocodile sat at the bottom of a concrete pit, still as a statue. Gordon had not believed it was real and threw a coin at the crocodile, hitting it squarely on the snout but still it did not flinch. Gordon went to throw another penny but before he could release it the crocodile blinked and he dropped the missile in horror. There existed an invisible string between the boy and the crocodile. There existed an invisible string in Guddy's kitchen.

"Dolphins," said Guddy. "Do I know anything?"

"Max Nash said it might be something to do with the military..."

"He probably did, but as with so many things, Whiting, the famous Max Nash is wrong."

"He said there was a similar occurrence twelve years ago and that you both took out a boat and saw Navy ships."

"We did. But the military are not responsible, not now and not then. They were there because something else was."

"Submarines?"

"I won't repeat myself, Whiting, forget the military. It's impossible to talk to people sometimes. But when you've lived a life on the sea you learn about the other things - it's in your bones and your blood and it reveals itself so slowly that you're never fully conscious it is with you."

"What do you mean things?"

"You are a journalist, Whiting. You will see as you please to see. A dolphin no sooner chooses to beach itself than you choose to leap into the ocean. The dolphins run; they are scared. Something is being provoked. It's terror, it's their terror that makes them do it. They're not so stupid. But you're not here for that, you've already decided it's the military, haven't you? And now you're going to leave and write the story you want to write."

"You're wrong," Gordon said. "If I see something I report it. I work for Associated News, we've got no bias or politics. You can tell me, you can show me and I will report the truth."

Guddy clapped.
"That's a pretty nice speech, huh? Well, I'll tell you. Ask in Selyvan where all the fish have gone and they'll blame the Spanish and they'll curse them and spit and swear and you won't hear anything more for twenty minutes. It's easy to blame the Spanish, why not? There's no fish, it's the Spanish. There's a storm, it's the Spanish. They're

idiots in Selyvan. They don't care about fishing, not anymore. They want profit, that's all. They forget we're hunters, they forget that.

"I can tell you what I feel sometimes when I'm out in my boat alone. On winter nights when the sea spray freezes to the main sail and drops like white sheets onto the deck. Just as you might look to the stars and wonder, I look down, staring into the black. But you cannot understand the mystery until you have felt it."

"Felt what?"

"In Grindavik, our fathers would frighten us with stories of the Kraken which would drag us to the ocean floor with a long tentacle if we played by the sea at night. It's healthy to give your children a fear of the sea, I think. The sea is our unknown, Whiting. We must fear the unknown. It's good for our survival, you think too? So why must we try to understand the unknown. When there's so much air and light in this world, why should we poke into the blackest holes. Why disturb it?"

Guddy's voice had reached a crescendo and the intensity had been left to hang in the silence as he flicked free another cigarette and lit it. He poured a vodka from the bottle on the table and shook it as an offering at Gordon who put up a hand in refusal.

"I think I might have misunderstood you," said Gordon. "You're not telling me the Kraken is chasing the dolphins."

Guddy knocked back his vodka and laughed. Gordon felt foolish at the absurdity of his own question.

"When the fish stopped biting, I wondered too. Of course, I did. I might have even blamed the Spanish once or twice. It's the easiest thing, right? But I knew it wasn't the Spanish. I could feel the waters stirring and changing, as real as you see the autumn leaves turn red and fall from the trees. The seas were changing. Patterns through the waves I had come to sense, as natural as the breath in my body, were suddenly different. Sometimes I would let a hand sweep through the water as I sailed and it felt cold, icy cold, the chill of waters that had never felt the sun. Water so cold that my ribs would shrink into my lungs.

"It's not my business to pry but I can't help what I see. On those cold nights, nights like last night. Those are the nights when the ocean speaks and great holes open in the water, open up like a door. On those nights, I have seen him. Down in the coves I didn't even know existed, standing silent against the night like a ghost."

"Who?" Gordon said. "What do you mean?"

Guddy shrugged again and lifted himself wearily. He walked over to his wedding photograph, keeping his back to Gordon.

"I think I miss her more and more each day."

Gordon was not sure how to progress. He did not want to interrupt Guddy as he reminisced about his wife. On the other hand, he wanted to learn more. Who was Guddy talking about? The old fisherman let out a long sigh and turned to face Gordon.

"Too much drink, I need some sleep, forgive me. Please, let yourself out."

He left the room leaving Gordon alone. He sat puzzled for a minute, unsure if he was the victim of a practical joke. Max had warned him about superstitious locals but then Max had also pointed him towards Guddy. Either way, Gordon felt uncomfortable in the strange house and as he rose to leave, he noticed a scrap of paper where Guddy had been sat. He had not noticed it during their conversation. His curiosity burned. 'Had he left it here for me to find?' he wondered. Gordon picked it up and saw scrawled in bold letters the word: "MORTAIN".

CHAPTER TWELVE

Gordon stared at the paper as he wandered aimlessly from Guddy's house, the single word MORTAIN stared back at him. 'What did it mean?' Gordon asked himself. He knew he had seen the word before and fished for a sprat of memory. Mortain was a name, Gordon was certain of that. He was bad at recalling names, it was a regular source of professional embarrassment.

"Mortain," Gordon repeated it aloud in the hope of triggering inspiration.

His brain raced but at a breakneck pace that made recall impossible. It was moments like this Gordon wished he smoked a pipe. He had romantic notions of tackling life's great mysteries with a smoking jacket and a brandy. 'If only,' he thought. 'I could approach my problems as rationally and phlegmatically as a Victorian gentleman.' Gordon often wished he had been born a century and a half earlier.

Gordon paced Selyvan's market square like a caged leopard, he burnt himself out with nervous energy. It was better to sit so he forced himself down onto one of the wooden benches. He could not have chosen a better spot. Across from where he sat it was there, the name Mortain chiselled in the white stone above the door to the local library. Gordon cursed his forgetfulness, of course, he had seen the name from the window of the bus as it pulled into town. It was everywhere, above the Masonic Hall, and then on the trade exchange, the village hall. 'But what was the significance?' Gordon wondered.

He rummaged through his pockets and plucked out Max Nash's business card. Gordon might not have known Max for very long but well enough to know Max would have the answer. He was not wrong. At the sound of Gordon's voice Max bubbled over with facts, snippets, opinions and gossip like an unwatched pan. Mortain could only mean Colonel Mortain of Selyvan Hall, Max was certain. The family had sat watch above Selyvan for long centuries and were responsible for most of the town's development. As the fortunes of Selyvan sagged, when steam-powered trawlers off Grimsby were delivering ten times the profit of the local fleet, so did the Mortain's interest.

"Colonel Mortain is a funny fish," Max said with the music of a great story-teller. "His father was a navy man, his grandfather too, and his great grandfather. But I'm underselling it as usual, his great, great, great grandfather steered the Temeraire alongside Nelson at Trafalgar - and haven't we all tired of that story by now.

"I suppose it must have been a bit of a blow to the line when the Colonel refused to follow the family tradition. There are no sea legs on that one. He joined the army instead, a compromise of sorts. The Colonel has a paralysing fear of the sea, that's what they say. As a toddler, he'd bawl like a banshee when he was taken to bathe at the beach, that's what I've heard.

"Well, I suppose the army's done him no harm. He spent most of his youth in one foreign clime or another, rather exciting, no doubt, but I can't help thinking I'd miss home too much to galivant.

"When his father died - it must have been twenty years back - he put the soldiering behind him and moved back to Selyvan Hall permanently. Of course, he'd always flit between the Hall and his London clubs. I suppose his bones could never quite settle after so many years away. But, having said that, he's always very generous with his time and money. Whenever I've needed anything for a story, he's always been perfectly charming. When the library needed a new roof he dipped into his pockets, without a word or worry."

"Could I call on the Colonel?" Gordon asked.

"Certainly," Max replied. "He's the perfect host. But I'm not sure what he'll have to say. I can't think why Guddy would have steered you in his direction."

Max paused in thought, he knew Guddy as well as anybody and respected his honesty. Guddy was never one for intrigue, he was blunt and spoke openly. Scrawled notes left on a table seemed out of character. Long silences were rare for Max, but he was trawling his memory for an explanation. Max was a treasure chest of local life and gossip, but his internal filing was haphazard, so he often struggled to make the connections. Suddenly he remembered, barking in excitement at his triumph before he steadied himself for the tale.

"This was all years ago, I'd almost forgotten. Now you didn't hear this from me... and I'm not saying there's a bad bone in Guddy's body because there's not, but he and the Colonel have never liked one another. Not that they see one another too often, of course. You won't see the Colonel down the Ship on a Saturday night, if you know what I mean. But there was a time when Lizzie spent a lot of time in the Colonel's company."

"Lizzie?"

"Sorry, Lizzie, that's Guddy's wife. Elisabeth. This was just after the Colonel returned from the Army. I think he was trying to establish some sort of artistic movement in the town, something like that, I certainly wasn't invited into the circle. He might have put on a few exhibitions at the Hall, there might have been a performance or two. Well, that sort of thing always appealed to Lizzie and the Colonel's quite the patron. I don't know what happened

80

precisely, and I don't like to speculate, but at one time he and Guddy had words over Lizzie, and it all turned rather ugly. Plain for all to see, right in the market square. Well after that the Colonel tucked himself away for a few weeks and didn't come back into town - not Selyvan, not Penzance. He holed himself up like a prisoner. But Sue Coleman, who used to do a bit of cleaning up at the Hall, said she saw him with a fat lip the size of a seal. But that's just local gossip. There's probably nothing in it, I'm sure. Lizzie drowned a few years later and I suppose with her gone, Guddy had no more reason to quarrel with the Colonel, but I guess animosity can leave scars where we can't see it."

Gordon thanked Max again for his generosity. Max's story had pricked Gordon's interest and he resolved to visit the Colonel before returning to the Cragg. He could remember passing Selyvan Hall on the bus journey earlier that morning and guessed he could walk there in twenty minutes with a brisk stride.

It was already mid-afternoon and the rain was falling harder as Gordon left Selyvan in the direction of Selyvan Hall. Only on foot did he realise how steeply the road climbed away from the coast, but he trudged on with the forlorn stoop of a retreating army. Gordon's jacket was beginning to dampen and cling. 'One day,' he promised himself, 'I'm going to buy myself a Gore-tex hiking jacket'. He pulled his flimsy cotton jacket over his head like a hood.

Out of town the coastal landscape soon became moorland and the lingering smell of the sea dissipated, making way for wet countryside. Only prickly grasses grew on the moor, and these were blasted, broken-backed by the frequent gales. The temperature dropped with the elevation and thin glazings of ice formed on the surfaces of the pot-hole puddles along the unloved road. A few sheep looked back at Gordon from behind a crumbling dry stone wall, their mouths cycling clumps of the sickly, withered grass.

Gordon reached the elm-lined drive of Selyvan Hall, many of the trees had succumbed to disease and lay rotten and hollow where they had fallen. Ahead the hall loomed ugly and unabashed. It was built at the pinnacle of the family's fortune on the foundations of a much older and even more brutally forbidding seat. The Mortain's apex narrowly missed the refined, classicism of the Regency but coincided with all the pomp and pretension of the Victorian Ruskinian Gothic revival. Red bricks, imported at considerable cost from outside the county, gave Selyvan Hall the air of the imposter in this granite town. It rose scowling and unapologetic from the moors like an affront. Only the gothic arched windows and sandstone facings, carved with intricate coats and crests, tempered its oppressive face. The lopsided building leant against the east wing where its folly, a tourelle with a pepper pot slate roof, branched like new growth 20 feet above its grinning crenelated tower, and from this pinnacle a Union Flag slapped itself in a frenzy, maddened by the ceaseless wind. Three sharp arrow heads gave the central structure its great strength before it slunk unevenly into a shallow west wing.

A low-walled courtyard finally gave Gordon some respite from the gale that had beat against him since leaving town. Gordon crunched noisily over the loose gravel towards the hall, he felt as though eyes were watching him from every window. Up until that moment Gordon had not considered how he would explain his unexpected arrival, now doubts filled him with uncertainty. 'What question could possibly be so important for a man to march two miles through the wind and rain?' he wondered. His only reason for being there was a scrap of paper left by a drunken fisherman. He had no other excuse for visiting and suddenly felt ridiculous. Gordon rarely felt so nervous before a door knock but there was something oppressive about the ivy-infested walls and the dusty unlit windows which chattered in the wind like teeth. He fumbled through his pockets for a date but could only find loose change and tissue. The packet was back in the hotel, he could have really done with a date.

Even with Gordon's long legs the ten great stone steps were a stretch. They led to a pair of double oak doors. There was no bell only an iron knocker, cast in the form of a sheela-na-gig bearing her vulva and smiling maniacally back at the visitor. Gordon thought it an inappropriate ornament away from a mediaeval church, but gave it a sturdy blow and the dull thud echoed around the courtyard. There was no response so he tried again, then a third time, firmer to be sure. Still there was no answer. Gordon waited as the wind whipped through his wet clothes, the walk had warmed him, but he began to shiver. Still, nobody answered. Gordon decided to give one final knock, he could not wait any longer and a fruitless journey was better than frostbite. He beat the old iron against the wooden frame again. 'That was loud enough to wake the dead,' Gordon thought, but it was an unattractive prospect as he stood on that lonely step. The silence of the house was unnerving, to Gordon it felt like it was holding its breath at the presence of the stranger. Gordon could bear the cold and the creepiness no more and convinced himself the Colonel was out.

"Tell them I came," he said to the knocker.

Gordon trotted back down the steps eager to be gone. He turned to give the curious old Hall a final defeated glance and there in the bay window he saw the faintest shadow of form, distorted behind the intricate rose-stained glass. There was no mistake, a figure closed to the glass and the silhouette formed against the red and green panes. Gordon froze, locked for a moment in a spell of uncanny terror. Somebody was home and they had seen Gordon. At that moment a skinny, black cat leapt onto the sill. It hissed at Gordon with an arched back and puffed tail.

Gordon knew he could not leave now - he had been seen. Besides, after having tramped out all this way to speak to the Colonel, to skulk away would be defeat. Reluctantly Gordon made his way back up those Olympian steps a second time and knocked once more against the oak. This time he heard movement from within and then the sound of a key being turned. The heavy door pulled ajar but stopped short of a welcoming gape. Instead, a slim woman stepped out from within. She surprised Gordon, it was not what he had expected to see. She was in her 20s and wore a heavy layer of powdery foundation which stood in contrast with the oily, gloss red lipstick. She wore black wet-look leggings under leather boots and a white fur-lined jacket. Her blonde hair was pulled back into a tight ponytail, worn high at the crown. She was as tall as Gordon, even as she leaned with one crooked elbow against the door frame, she could meet him squarely with her glacial blue eyes which burned like a handful of snow down the neck.

"What is it?" she said with an eastern European accent.

"I'm very sorry to disturb you," said Gordon, who was always fawningly polite when he risked imposition. "My name is Gordon Athelney, I'm a reporter with the Associated News."

The woman shook her head in impatience and gave a slight shrug.

"Yeah?"

Her breath smelt of cigarettes and spearmint.

"I'm covering the dolphins beached in Penzance. I've reached a bit of a dead-end and I was hoping to speak to the Colonel Mortain."

The woman looked unimpressed. Gordon saw the hardness in her beautiful eyes melt to indifference, he knew she had decided to slam the door in his face.

"He's busy today," she said and slipped back fluidly behind the door.

Gordon put out a hand in desperate appeal.

"Please, I've walked all this way and I wouldn't need long. I just need to check a few facts. Won't you ask him if he'll see me, please?"

Her eyes wrinkled in frustration but her silence destroyed the hope of a credible excuse, so she agreed to ask. She fastened the door behind her as she went, leaving Gordon alone on the step once again. He hugged himself tightly but with little comfort from his rain-soaked jacket. The woman returned a few minutes later in no brighter mood but with news the Colonel would see him. She held open the door and Gordon gratefully entered.

She led Gordon hastily through a large entrance hall, he would have liked more time to take in his grand surroundings, they passed a marble staircase lined with a crimson carpet and flanked by an elaborate wooden bannister carved into a twisting serpent with painstaking perfection. On the wall hung muddy oil portraits of portly men. Gordon was hurried along every time he dallied, and he chased her heels that clicked satisfyingly across the black and white chequered tiles. His guide was laconic and brushed off Gordon's attempts at conversation but when they passed a large golden mirror that had blackened and cracked at the edges she admired her reflection with unashamed vanity.

They passed a snug, smoke-filled anteroom off the main hall and Gordon saw another young woman, equally as striking as his guide, with tousled pillar-box red hair. She peered back at him vaguely before returning to her magazine. They continued down a narrow corridor where once reeds had flickered but now electric bulbs glowed steadily. A small door formed itself from the darkness at the end of the corridor and Gordon was taken through to a warmer and more welcoming room. Inside it was oak panels, green leather and heavy, high-back armchairs. A great Samarkand rug covered most of the darkly stained wooden floorboards and a healthy fire blazed, casting a flickering golden light across the bay window. Leather-bound books lined two walls from floor to ceiling. At the far side of the room sat a man behind a large desk, he did not look up from his work as Gordon entered.

"He's here," said the woman. She turned and left the room without waiting for introductions.

The man had been concentrating hard on his papers but at the sight of his guest immediately sprang to his feet. The Colonel was entirely bald and looked younger than Gordon had expected. His face still had the puffiness of youth and his large, sparkling brown eyes beamed with a warm passion. His nose was proud and aquiline, and his large mouth fixed in a sincere smile. Those dark, expressive eyebrows gave him an actor's presence and he had a strength of gaze that fixed its recipient in dumb awe. Gordon was impressed.

"And so, you've enjoyed the warm welcome of fair Piret," the Colonel said.

He was good natured and seemed pleased to see Gordon as he shuffled out from behind his desk to greet his guest. The Colonel walked with a slight limp at the right knee but moved elegantly all the same, with a straight back and broad shoulders.

"Well let's see if I can't improve on her welcome. Randall Mortain, pleased to meet you."

The Colonel held out his large hand to Gordon. He wore a white shirt, untucked from the khaki herringbone trousers which were turned up over a pair of Edwardian fur-lined, leather slippers. His matching jacket still hung over the chair. Gordon thought he looked half-dressed but appreciated the warm welcome, the first that he had received since arriving in Selyvan. Gordon introduced himself in turn as he shook the Colonel's hand. His handshake was warm and lingering but facing this charm Gordon suddenly felt like a vagrant. He saw how the

Colonel had cast a deft eye over his shivering form and had spotted the damp patch on the rug where Gordon stood.

"My dear man, you're drenched," he said, ushering Gordon with a flat palm. "Take a seat by the fire."

Gordon happily assented and was soon much revived, all the more so after the Colonel presented him with a generous glass of red wine from the bottle on his desk. He offered it with humility and apologised if Gordon wasn't a "left bank man" but that "Margaux rather gets under the skin."

"My father believed the family had vines in Aquitaine up until the Hundred Years War," said the Colonel. "Of course, it's been out of our hands for centuries, but he had always rather regarded the Garonne, and any grape grown on its banks, as his birthright. I've a cellar full of the stuff now. But tell me what you think?"

Gordon had neither the money nor the inclination to develop a serious interest in wine, but he did have a keen nose and sharp recall for scents. He also knew that on the topic of wine you could never be too florid or poetic, and in this field, he revelled in a rare freedom of language, seldom granted to a news hack.

"Immediately I get the intense fruit, plums of course," said Gordon burying his nose deep in the glass of swirling Bordeaux. "But no, it's richer than plum. It's almost stewed. The sweet cherries you find on stodgy German desserts. Or the unpicked strawberry, the forgotten fruit discovered in September, that has somehow avoided hungry bugs and greedy human hands. Left as the plant's cherished son to swell and darkly ripen like arterial blood, now swollen with syrupy sweetness until on discovery it is gobbled down with all the lust for the dying summer."

The Colonel laughed.

"Is that enough?" Gordon said.

"More than enough, you've quite confused me now. I just need to know if it's any good," he said.

"It's excellent."
"Very good. I spotted the epicure in you at first sight. But I've lost my sense of smell; it all tastes like spiced tap water to me," said the Colonel. "Tonight I'm hosting and you've got to be so careful with these old vintages. It wouldn't be the first time I've served 60-year-old vinegar to a table of guests.

"But I'm told you're a journalist and not a sommelier, so how can I help?"

Gordon went to begin but his voice was hijacked by a spasm of shivers and his teeth chattered comically. The Colonel's face creased with concern and he prodded the cooling fire.

"It's dying. It burns too fast and you'll catch your death tonight. Let me get some more logs."

The Colonel twisted in his chair and called out for Piret but nobody answered. Instead, he called out for Iveta, Gordon supposed this must be the red-haired woman he had seen. The Colonel pricked an ear for a response but there was only silence. He admitted defeat and excused himself with a touch of embarrassment to fetch the logs, leaving Gordon alone.

Gordon went to stand closer to the fire, in its light he saw a fine steam rising from his jacket sleeve. He had gotten wetter on the walk than he had realised and he felt numb to the bones. A strong draught fed the fire's hunger and he was thankful the Colonel had proposed fetching more logs. Gordon paced the room to get his blood flowing. He admired the thick, leather-bound books stacked neatly on a shelf, twice his own height. He saw titles in German and Latin, some French, with schoolboy fluency, was able to translate several titles; Chaos Struggle; The Will of Man; Panbabylonism and the Flood Myth.

On the Colonel's desk Gordon spotted the bottle of Chateau Margaux he was drinking, the glass crusted in dust and mould. He knew Clara would be jealous of his afternoon swigging vintage wine, but he also knew she would demand proof - especially coming from a yarn-spinner like a Gordon. As evidence he took a grainy photograph on his old mobile. The Margaux was from 1953, older than Gordon had imagined, and an empty glass on the desk was evidence the Colonel had attempted a tasting of his own before Gordon had arrived. Beside his glass were scattered sheets of handwritten documents and a local naval chart with points of longitude scored across it. The papers were old and many had turned a rich amber over the years. Gordon's curiosity overcame him, and he thumbed the first few leaves but the handwriting was cramped and spidery making it difficult to read at a scan. Gordon supposed they were entries from various journals - many of the pages had dates written in the upper margin, he saw 'April 4th, 1939'.

Gordon's attention was distracted by an even stranger object on the desk. A small tablet of alabaster. It was cracked, fragile and housed within a glass case and arranged with care on green velvet. The rectangular tablet was just six inches long but across its surface had been scored tiny runes that Gordon recognised instantly as Anglo Saxon - long years with his father rarely provided such practical use. Across the lower runes, written as palimpsest, was another passage. It was shorter than the Anglo-Saxon text but seemingly carved by the same hand. To Gordon the second passage looked like Cuneiform, the Sumerian script, but he knew this was anachronistic with 1,500 years separating the two civilisations. The text was bordered by a crude depiction of a serpent swallowing its own tail. Gordon still had his mobile phone in hand and quickly snapped a photo, he knew the tablet would interest his father, if only to pooh-pooh.

"I don't know where those two are, I had to fetch the logs myself," said the Colonel who entered, burdened by his bundle. He addressed Gordon's empty chair. Gordon casually slid his phone back into his jacket pocket.

"I was just admiring the bottle," he said. "1953, you're spoiling me."

The Colonel looked surprised to see Gordon by his desk, but quickly recovered.

"I'm glad you appreciate it," said the Colonel. "Pour yourself another glass, please. No doubt it will find a better home on your discerning tongue than with my guests tonight."

Gordon was tempted but declined. The Colonel joined Gordon at the desk and nodded at the pile of papers.

"My father's diary," the Colonel told Gordon. "I'm editing it for a biography I'm writing. It's just a little amusement, nothing serious. But it's funny, I've learned more about my father through these old pages than I ever did in life. When I was 21, the evening before I went to Sandhurst, he took me for dinner at Rules. It was our only adult conversation. But these pages - piecing them together - well, it's made me see things quite differently.

"Do you know for all his years at sea, all the places he visited and all the people he met - the most interesting fact I've found about him is he never peeled his eggs. He had a hard-boiled egg every morning and ate it shell-and-all. He thought the shell improved his digestion. Can you imagine that?"

Gordon smiled, but unintentionally his eyes drifted back to the alabaster tablet. It fascinated Gordon and the Colonel had detected his interest.

"Now that is rather special. It's been with the family from the beginning. It's something of an heirloom, treasured for some long-forgotten superstition. These days we cherish it as a treasure in itself, much like the tatty teddy from childhood. You'll think it odd, but I prize that tablet more highly than everything within these walls."

The Colonel picked it up gently and held it out for Gordon to see.

"It's strange," said Gordon. "It looks like Saxon runes alongside Cuneiform."

Gordon saw the Colonel's surprise at his knowledge and felt a need to explain.

"My father is an Anglo-Saxon scholar. He'd be very interested to see it."

"He is?" said the Colonel. In a flash of recalculation, he put the tablet back on the desk where it had sat.

"Has it ever been looked at by a professional?" Gordon asked.

"Yes, yes," the Colonel said vaguely. "My grandfather had all that done. But it's really very precious, I don't like it out of my sight."

The Colonel returned to Gordon and smiled graciously, then with one elegant arm he led Gordon back to his seat by the fire.

"It's getting rather late and my curiosity is burning," said the Colonel. "What brings you out here? What's the story, sir?"

Gordon had become so distracted by the tablet it took a moment for him to recover. He had forgotten about the dolphins, about Clara and David, and about Associated News. He had even forgotten why he was sat in that strange room opposite this curious stranger. It was a rude awakening, but he snapped back into character seamlessly. He explained about the dolphin beachings and raised a few of the theories he had heard, with the exception of his interview with Guddy. The Colonel sat quietly and thoughtfully with his chin resting on his fist.

"Well, I'd heard a few had washed up - it's not uncommon I believe," said the Colonel. "I certainly had no idea that many had been found. What a shame, but I'm afraid it's a bit beyond my remit. Have you spoken to Ruben - that's to say Professor Burroughs - from the University? I know he's been down in Selyvan recently."

Gordon explained how the Professor had been curt and dismissive on the phone. The Colonel laughed and waved his hand breezily.

"I'll speak to Ruben. He was probably busy and he can be such a serious chap at times. I'll explain to him what you're doing, that you're a good sort. I'll get you some time. He'll have the answers you need - allow me to be your conduit."

The Colonel smiled and waved his hands like an orchestra conductor just as the fire hissed, popped and spat a smoking ember onto the Samarkand rug. Like a snake striking the Colonel pinched the glowing splinter and tossed it back onto the fire.

"The wood is too young and damp. I'll burn this place down one of these days," he said. He rubbed the soot from the ornate weave with a tongue-moistened hankie, it was already well-flecked with black scar singes.

Outside Gordon spotted the fierce black cat still sitting on the window ledge.

"Your cat frightened me earlier, it's got a temper."

The Colonel looked puzzled before he made sense of Gordon's tangent.

"Oh that, yes. It's a grumpy thing."
"What's it called?"

The Colonel shook his head slowly and drew his lips into a drooping bow.

"No name, I've had so many, I prefer not to sentimentalise them. The girls like it but it hisses like a swan at strangers."

"A guard cat, eh?" said Gordon, but the remark fell silent as falling snow.

A serenity descended on the room and both men stared aimlessly into the fire. It took a surge of will to break the lull but the Colonel was pressed for time.

"Well, I'm sorry to be rude," he said. "I have guests arriving shortly. Are you stopping the night in Selyvan?"

Gordon explained he was enjoying the pleasure of Lychgate's hospitality at the Cragg, rolling his eyes dramatically. The Colonel smiled. 'The solemn Mr Lychgate,' he told Gordon, 'was dining at the hall tonight.' Gordon cringed in case he had offended his host but a wry smile from the Colonel revealed the prickly hotelier was not his most welcome dinner guest.

"But that's perfect," said the Colonel. "I'll give you a ride back to the hotel and pick up old Lychgate – it will make his day and I can't let you walk back."

As the Colonel led him back to the entrance hall, Gordon looked out for Iveta and Piret, they fascinated him. The Colonel must have noticed Gordon peering furtively into the anteroom because he announced, only a moment later, that he expected the two girls would be getting ready for the evening ahead. He explained they were on the staff at his Mayfair members' club and that he takes them to Cornwall on occasion to help with hosting. The Colonel swung open the great oak door with a single effortless tug. Earlier Piret had strained to release it.

They crunched across the courtyard to an old barn serving as a garage. Gordon had expected to find something grander or more exotic to be parked in the Colonel's stable. Instead, there was an old Rover 75 which looked about as cold and sorry for itself as Gordon had felt earlier. The Colonel had to twist the key several times before the engine fired but when it did, he patted the wheel affectionately.

"My last little bit of England," he said with a wink.

The Colonel drove riotously and with a flagrant disregard for speed limits, road signals, the dark or potholes. Several times Gordon had to brace a hand above his head to stop it cracking the roof as they landed heavily from a hidden launchpad of a rut. The Colonel in cool contradiction did not appear to suffer any discomfort whatsoever during the ride and maintained breezy conversation with Gordon all the way to the car park at the foot of the Cragg. He pulled to a halt with a heavy-foot on the brake pedal and the long raking scrape of loose gravel.

"Tell old Lychgate I'm waiting for him; he'll be in a flap because I'm early."

Gordon thanked the Colonel once again and got out of the warm car. Outside an idea suddenly flashed and he turned back abruptly.

"I was just thinking. If I returned tomorrow with my photographer, could we get some shots of your old tablet?"

The Colonel was taken aback and momentarily dropped the guard of hospitality and his face darkened. A man crunched along the gravel down from the hotel carrying four heavy black bin bags. The stranger broke a tension that hung in the air and the three men exchanged a 'good evening'. Gordon and the Colonel waited in silence and watched the third man disappear into the darkness. When Gordon turned back the Colonel's face had recovered its natural brightness.

"I'm going to be a bit busy for the next day or so, but we'll try and make something work, eh? Good luck."

Gordon nodded and waved goodbye before he made the slow slog up to the Cragg. The winding route from the car park was certainly preferable to the perilous path that hugged the cliff's edge. When he finally returned to the hotel Gordon discovered some commotion at reception. Clara was in a heated discussion with Lychgate.

"This is the last thing I need tonight," said Lychgate.

"Yes, you've told me already. Your soiree at the manor with Lord Martin but there's no way we're going to pay for a new radiator, it was practically hanging off the wall."

"Mortain, it's Colonel Mortain," said Lychgate ruffled but imperious. "And I'm due any minute, so let's just get this matter settled quickly."

"It's OK, Randall said not to rush down," Gordon interrupted the conversation. "He said he's early and will wait in the car."

Lychgate tilted his head back at Gordon because it was the only way the tiny man could look down his nose at him.

"And how would you know, might I ask? And on such familiar terms."

"He just dropped me off. I was over at the hall," said Gordon, trying to sound blasé.

"You were invited?" said Lychgate and practically spat the words at Gordon.

"No, I knocked."

"Impertinence," he said, but his anger gave way to a victorious smile. "Well knocking doesn't count. I consider myself lucky to be one of Selyvan's most frequent visitors up at the Hall. I've had three invites this year alone. And I would never just knock."

He turned a snarling eye down to David, who was standing sheepishly behind Clara.

"Well, we'll deal with this mess in the morning," he said as he fastened up his binder of accounts before locking it behind reception. Then, without acknowledging his guests, he hurried with an impatient cantering step to the door and the waiting car.

"What time's breakfast?" Clara called out.

"It's on the board," Lychgate shouted back without a drop of courtesy.

"Shall we get a drink?" said Gordon.

Clara nodded.

"Ok, I'll meet you in the bar. I'm just going to change out of these, I'm soggy."

Clara grimaced when she remembered the radiator incident.

"Your clothes got a bit wet. Come to the bar," she said. "David can explain everything."

CHAPTER THIRTEEN

The snug bar at the Cragg was a welcome change from the rest of the hotel. It was one of the few rooms that had not been infected with Lychgate's fusty stuffiness. It was cosy without feeling cramped and nicely worn but not dog-eared. A toasty fire burned in the corner and the walls were filled with black and white photographs of Selyvan's happier days.

The bar was empty, all the locals drank at the Ship where they could smoke, and the beer was cheaper. The Cragg's bar was reserved for its guests and they were few and far between. Despite the dearth of customers, the barman flustered and fuddled at Clara's simple order. Clara had to repeat herself three times before making herself understood. Gordon was impatient and excused himself, he was anxious to speak to his father about the tablet he had seen on the Colonel's desk. There was no reception in the bar so Gordon braved the cold night air in search of a signal.

"Gordon, my boy," Dr Athelney said at the sound of Gordon's voice. "I've been trying to reach you all day but another man kept answering."

"I've had my phone on me all day, maybe I didn't have reception."

"Strange, a chap from the Malabar answered. He was very good about it but quite insistent he'd never heard of you."

"Are you sure you dialled the right number?"

"Anyway, it turns out he was from Kozhikode and we had the most fascinating conversation about the Vijayanagara Empire."

"What did you want?" said Gordon, and then it dawned on him. "Is my flat OK?"

"Yes, yes, all fine. I've resolved the problem. I couldn't find any cat food, so in the end I just gave it a can of tuna fish."

"Gave what?"

"Yes, yes. Well, I couldn't stand the poor thing mewing."

"Cat? What are you talking about?"

"Your cat."

"I don't have a cat."

"Well there was a cat in your flat this morning."

"I don't have a cat."

"I mean, it's possible it may have followed me home last night. I'm ashamed to admit I drank three glasses of red wine. Christian Schammer had put me in quite a grump. In Search of Penda's Ghost had just entered the non-fiction charts that week and he was strutting like a rooster - at my evening! I said to Professor Gideon, Penda's Ghost should be at number one in the fiction charts and he laughed so hard..."

"Where's the cat now?"

"In your flat. Don't worry, I made sure he had plenty of milk before I left."

"And you're back in East Anglia?"

"Of course."

Gordon gritted his teeth. He would return home to a flat stinking of
piss with a wild, half-starved cat bent on revenge against its gaoler. What was worse, he would have to phone his South African neighbour that evening to ask if Blute was missing. Vanderbeek was unlikely to be sympathetic, the cat had been a sore subject ever since Gordon had signed for a delivery to Vanderbeek. He had left the package on his neighbour's doorstep - where it was discovered by a ravenous Blute. "You've let me bloody cat eat me vleiss pakkies," he had screamed. 'He'll probably kick my door down,' Gordon thought.

With record efficiency, Dr Athelney had sunk Gordon's buoyant mood, so much so he almost forgot to ask about the tablet. On the subject of Anglo-Saxon runes his father was on firmer footing, a marked change from his bumbling alter-ego. Gordon wanted to send his father the photograph he had taken so he could assess it. Dr Athelney did not have a computer at home but promised to check his e-mail first thing in the morning at the museum. His father was sceptical and suspected Gordon had mistaken Cuneiform for Glagoltic.

"I waste my time with you," he said. "Do you not remember the summer I took you to see the Baska tablet?"

Gordon was unlikely to forget that summer in a hurry, but he thanked his father and they agreed to speak again the following day. It took five minutes to send the low-resolution photo from Gordon's phone because reception was so woeful. By the time Gordon returned, he found Clara sat at a table by the fire sipping her drink. David was still ignominious after his destruction of the radiator and subsequent soaking of Gordon's bag. He sat forlornly with a pint of Coke.

"What are you drinking?" Gordon asked Clara, eyeing her drink with suspicion.

"A cucumber martini."

"Is that even a thing?"

"That's what the bartender said, too."

For lack of inspiration Gordon had ordered a beer. He never drank much and had harboured a low-level fear of pubs ever since his 21st birthday at a soulless town centre bar in Wisbech. His head had been swimming so he had wandered off alone for air. By the time he returned his friends were gone and – although the precise course of events remained shrouded in the fog of war - at some point he was debagged and sick in the bar.

Clara related David's destructive adventures. Gordon was most annoyed about the fact his room would be cold that evening. They both supposed the bill for the damage could be comfortably sent to Associated News considering the perpetrator of the deed. David sat silently while he was being discussed, like the dog in the basket and a missing cake from the kitchen worktop. At one point he tried to explain but was silenced.

"That's enough from you, Keith Moon," said Clara. "It was the least rock and roll way to wreck a hotel room."

Clara then told Gordon about her unsettling encounter on the beach with Professor Burroughs. Gordon listened with genuine concern and suggested contacting the Police but Clara dismissed the idea. Gordon felt guilty as he remembered his conversation with the Colonel.

"I might have to interview the Professor again," Gordon said.

Clara rolled her eyes.

"Well, I'm not taking the photos."

Gordon nodded, he understood. He had no inclination to speak any further with the Ruben Burroughs, but the truth was he was running out of people to interview. There was no chance of filing any more copy that evening and the few leads he had uncovered proved to be dead ends. Defeat was looking increasingly inevitable and Croaker's victory over Gordon would be complete. There was simply no story, no matter how hard Gordon rummaged. Usually, he could find an angle or pick the seam for a bit of top-spin, but here he was grappling for a handhold.

"The high-heel shoe you found on the beach," said Gordon following a loose train of thought. "You don't think we should tell the police?"

"For a missing shoe?" Clara laughed. "Some girl probably lost it during late night hanky-panky on the beach."

'Clara's right,' he thought. His desperation was causing him to think erratically.

Clara had ordered some dinner at the bar. The kitchen was closed but the waiter had agreed to make some chips, it would never have been her first choice but was preferable to a frosty, trek into town. The waiter arrived with three bowls of anaemic looking chips and an armful of sauces. He was full of apologies and explanations as he laid each dish in front of the guests, only David looked satisfied and immediately started eating. The waiter solemnly placed the bottles of sauce on the table as though he was conducting a sacred ritual. He saved a red plastic bottle until last, this he placed directly in front of Gordon. The sauce bottle featured a cartoon drawing of a Polish flag being waved by a fat but happy tomato. It was called: 'Polanzski's Pomidor Pikantny'.

"This is my own, you can't get it here," said the waiter proudly. "It's really the best."

A flash, Gordon remembered the original clipping from the Cornish Chronicle he had been given by Croaker. He still had it in his jacket pocket and fished it, it was damp and torn but he could still read it. He found what he was looking for, the Polish waiter quoted in the article.

"Is that you," said Gordon with his finger hovering over the name. "Are you Tomasz Ludrinzki?"

The waiter was startled by Gordon's sudden intensity, but his reddened face revealed he could be nobody else. Tomasz backed away, impatient to leave. Gordon surprised Tomasz, and himself, by springing to his feet and grabbing the waiter's wrist.

"Please, it's important," he said.

Tomasz looked uneasily around the empty bar and then appealingly at Clara, who sat open-mouthed.

"Gordon!" she said.

Her tone shocked him, and he recovered his composure. Gordon released his grip with a sincere apology.

"I just need to check a couple of things with you," said Gordon. "Nothing big, only what you told Max Nash."

"I'm sorry," said Tomasz, who stared down at his feet in shame. "I can't say anything more. Mr Lychgate was unhappy. He was going to sack me. He said it was bad for the hotel, bad for business. He does not want me talking to the newspapers."
Gordon started to offer a counter argument, but Tomasz stopped him with a sincere appeal.

"Please, I need this job," he said. "Not for ever but for now. I told everything to the other reporter. There isn't much more, you should have asked your friend earlier."

"Which friend?"

"The soldier."

"The Colonel?" said Gordon in surprise.

"He could have told you more than I can. Why do you keep asking me questions?"

"What could he tell me? What does he have to do with the dolphins?" said Gordon, firing questions impatiently.

Tomasz resisted and Clara snapped Gordon back once again with a sharp reprimand. Gordon recognised the waiter's unwillingness to talk and had to respect it, despite his frustrations. Gordon thanked the beleaguered waiter and let him retreat back to the safety of the bar.

"Nice job," said Clara. "Is that how come we've got the Bevington Enquiry?"

Gordon chose not to respond and sipped his lager sullenly. He was stressed and failing. He felt Clara was not taking the assignment seriously and if she was ready to go down with the sinking ship there was no reason why she should carry him with her. 'I don't tell her how to take photographs,' Gordon brooded. 'Why do snappers always want to tell us how to do our job?'

But Gordon was wrong, Clara felt the same frustrations as he did. Luckily for them, she was less inclined to become morose. Clara knew there was nothing more either of them could do that evening and after half a cucumber martini and a plate of hot chips she was ready for some light relief. Clara saved Gordon from the argument he would have quickly regretted and changed the subject.

"Look," she said.

Her finger pointed over the fireplace at a painting. Gordon looked up and saw an accomplished portrait in oils of a morbidly obese man. The subject sat awkwardly, his legs facing away from the painter so that his head was turned to one side and rolls of fat spewed out above his ruff. He wore a black velvet jacket with one chubby hand perched effeminately on his hip. His other hand rested across his bulging stomach, and he wore a gold ring on his little finger, probably the only finger it still fitted. His proud eyes glistened and there was contempt beneath his high-brow. Above his cherubim lips a tufty moustache grew like cress in the dark and was combed carefully beneath the swollen, greasy cheeks. He wore a cavalier's wig which the artist had captured through intricate strokes, it even glistened from the fat man's oily pate and the subtlest brush strokes suggested a forehead which perspired even while its sitter sat motionless.

"Would you rather..." said Clara, slowly and thoughtfully, her voice already musical with mischief. "Would you rather, lick that fat man, every inch of his body with your tongue. You've got to bathe him like a mother cat, every night for the next year before he goes to bed... And then you've got to share a bed with him... And he's naked."

Gordon nodded, he watched Clara carefully. Her eyes were alive with thrill, this was her favourite game. She had a quiddity for the surreal and in Gordon she found a good sport. He too loved the ridiculous but did not have her knack for creativity in the field. However, Gordon's logical nature was the perfect foil for Clara.

"Or would you rather..." she continued, scanning the room for inspiration. "Have the head of that badger for a year."

She pointed to a stuffed badger in a glass case. Its pathetic head hung low and its tiny, sharp teeth poked out from a jutting bottom jaw. The glass eyes had been inexpertly placed so it was comically boss-eyed.

"Can I still talk?" said Gordon thoughtfully.

"Yes."

"Would the badger head be in proportion to the rest of my body?"

"Yes, if you like."

"Of course I'd like," said Gordon but then he was struck by another chain of thought. "Do I have to eat slugs?"

"Do badgers eat slugs?"

"Yes."

"Well, no, ok, no. You've got your brain. You still like the same food you like now."

"So the fat man... is he naked when I lick him?"

"Naturally," said Clara, unable to restrain her giggle.

"Is he naked when we share a bed?"

Clara raised her eyebrows and nodded.

"Do I have to lick orifices as well?"

She punched him and squealed.

"No! Just skin... no bums."

"What?" said Gordon in feigned shock. "I meant ear holes you mucky hussy. But while we're on the subject, does skin include his testiculies and penis?"

Clara pulled a face of disgust and pretended to wipe her tongue like the dog who ate a slice of cucumber.

"Well?" said Gordon. "I need to know, it's a deal breaker."

"No, penis... but yes to the, what did you call them, testiculies."
Gordon sat and mused with mock reflection. He pretended to smoke the pipe he dreamt of owning. He turned to Clara, shaking his imaginary pipe for maximum impact.

"Can I have my birthday off?" he said.

"Yes... but in return, I'm throwing in the penis."

Gordon sat back to consider, and Clara bent forward in anticipation, a broad smile across her face.

"I'm going for the badger," he said with conviction. "I could sell the story to the papers. 'The Day I Woke Up with a Badger's Head.' I'd make a fortune, like the man with the tree bark skin, only cuter. If I tried to sell a story about licking a big, fat naked man every night people would think I was sick."

"Yes but at least you'd be able to live a normal life during the day, with a badger's head you're a freak."

"True, but the nightly horrors would be hanging over me all day. I could be having the most amazing day of my life but all the while I'd be thinking about where my tongue will be in a few hours time. Besides, I think the ladies would love badger man."

"Seriously?"

"Of course," said Gordon. "Who wouldn't want to say they tamed the badger?"

"Me."

"You're kidding, right? You're mad for the badge. That's why you chose him. Your eyes met across this room. I think you wanted me to say the badger, I think it's your fantasy. Now give me a badger kiss."

Gordon started nuzzling her neck as Clara screamed with a laugh and tried to pull herself away.

"Go and lick a fat man's balls," she said.

David stood up suddenly, he knocked the table as he did so and the glasses chinked and chimed.

"I'm bored, I'm going to the room," he said.

Gordon and Clara were so lost in their game and laughter they had completely forgotten David. They both felt slightly foolish, and the silence of the bar jarred abruptly.

"I was bored today," David continued. "Tomorrow can I come out with you?"

Gordon and Clara could both have done without the inconvenience of babysitting him but neither was cruel enough to let on. David lacked the social awareness to realise he was burdensome. Gordon was searching for an excuse when Clara caught his eye, she did not even need to speak, her face plainly said: "He's the boss' son, we'd better be a bit nicer to him."

"Of course," said Gordon unconvincingly. "But I can't promise it will be any less boring."

"Right," said David and walked off silently to his room without saying goodbye.

Clara looked at Gordon with concern.

"Do you think he's OK?"

"Yeah, of course," said Gordon dismissively. "He's probably got withdrawal symptoms from Knight's Lore."

Clara broached the idea of Gordon going up to the room to talk to him, but it was firmly and decisively rebuked. The conversation reached an awkward silence with this firm conclusion, and they stared absently at one another. Gordon watched as her pupils flickered brightly, reflecting the fire beside her. 'Her eyes are burning', he thought. Her sealed lips unstuck with a smack and she bared the tips of her front teeth. She breathed through the mouth and Gordon could feel her breath. A strand of her hair fell across her cheek and tickled, she wrinkled her nose, laughed and brushed it away. She turned away. They sat in silence again but Gordon wanted to break it.
"How about I get us a couple of cognacs to take out onto the terrace?"

Clara agreed. Gordon was certain she would refuse and was already preparing his 'you're probably right' speech. It had dropped below freezing outside and the fire was like an addiction, but Gordon was pleased Clara had agreed and cheerily hurried to the bar before she changed her mind. Gordon was especially polite to Tomasz when he ordered the drinks and both pretended nothing had happened earlier in the night. Gordon wasn't sure why he suggested cognac, he hated it but he hated whisky more and he could hardly drink another pint of icy lager under a winter moon by the sea. Tomasz warmed the glasses with boiling water so the spicy aroma of the spirit could be inhaled as well as drunk.

It was cold on the terrace, but Clara was wrapped snugly beneath her chunky woollen scarf and Gordon was staying silent about his own chills. The Cragg had a remarkable clifftop location but little else to recommend it.

The terrace was poorly maintained and there were more weeds than mortar between the cracks in the flags. The cognac did well to warm Gordon and he clinked glasses with Clara.

"To a better day tomorrow," he said.

CHAPTER FOURTEEN

When Gordon blinked into consciousness the room oozed and shifted like a spirit level settling. He could taste cognac; it was trapped on the fur of his tongue. Last night he discovered he did not dislike cognac half so much as he had first imagined. Snuggled by the fire with Clara he had knocked back another three glasses before bed. He was drinking to prolong the happiness, but the following morning's misery was the predictable but equal and opposite reaction.

A tepid glass of tap water by his bedside was a source of little visible comfort. A milky suspension hung in the glass and his stomach turned. Gordon took a deep breath and lifted his heavy limbs off the bed with the little strength he had left. The strain brought on immediate nausea and he escaped to the bathroom where he stared at his grim reflection. 'Thirty years old and you look it,' he thought. The hangover made him maudlin.

Gordon wondered about another hour in bed. David was fast asleep and still clutched his mobile phone. He had fallen asleep playing Knight's Lore and the phone lit his face with a ghostly phosphorescence in the half-light of the room. No, a return to bed held little appeal. Gordon knew the jungle drums pounding in his head would never let him doze peacefully. The only remedy was paracetamol, icy water in the face and a long, steamy shower.

The plan almost worked, and Gordon emerged from the bathroom semi-restored with only sluggishness, anxiety and irritation as symptoms. Gordon dressed himself before rousing David. One shake and the teenager was bolt upright and raring to go, and his youthful cheeriness only exacerbated Gordon's wretchedness. Gordon would have appreciated a partner to suffer alongside him and wondered how Clara was faring. She had drunk the same as he had, only with a cucumber martini to complicate the mix.

"Right, breakfast and then we'd better do some work," Gordon said but David was already engrossed in his game, picking up where he had left off the previous night.

It was half past nine before they arrived at breakfast. It was served in a draughty, joyless room adjoining the bar. The room was painted a ghastly shade of turquoise and covered in chintz, Lladro and dry-brushed botanical watercolours which splashed their Latin genera like tabloid headlines. Lychgate was at his supercilious best, watching the entrance like a hawk and insisting on taking Gordon's name and crossing off his room number before seating him. The hotel's only other guest was a perma-permed femme malheureuse with a perpetual ill-temper, trumped only by her Yorkshire terrier called Pooky which only stopped whining when she stuffed it with smoked salmon. Oily old Lychgate fawned over her with an obsequiousness that soon brought back the sickness of

Gordon's hangover. Other than closely monitoring the whims and requests of his Madame d'honneur, Lychgate was happy to leave the task of serving breakfast to a joyless but reassuringly matronly waitress. She took Gordon and David's breakfast order. Gordon wasn't hungry, instead he opted for a few pieces of insipid fruit from the buffet and nudged the blackened bananas around in a bowl of yoghurt, he was really there for the coffee. David on the other hand ordered lavishly and commanded an ambitious mountain of sausages, eggs, bacon, hash browns with a reservoir of sticky beans overflowing from his white plate and onto the pristine tablecloth.

"You'll fur your arteries," said Gordon.

David looked up with a wounded expression and a slice of fatty bacon hanging from his mouth like a dog's lolling tongue. Gordon wondered where all the calories went, his tiny frame must hide a coal furnace. Gordon saw David as something like an imp, not quite human.

"There you are," said Clara as she plonked herself hurriedly next to Gordon at the table. "I knocked for you and I've been trying your mobile all morning."

Gordon hurriedly fished out his mobile from his trousers, it had run out of battery its overnight charge neglected from the cognac.

"I've been down at the beach this morning," she said. "It's all happening."

"Happening? Another beaching?" said Gordon with little enthusiasm.

"Yes, but this time human."

Gordon dropped his spoon into the yoghurt.

"There's another thing," said Clara gravely. "He was found wearing one red high-heeled shoe."
Clara explained the body of a middle-aged man lost overboard on a yachting trip had washed ashore. A report had already been phoned to the coastguard the previous night by his two friends. When the body was found that morning both friends were taken in for questioning. Clara had already spoken with the police, who described the interviews as routine but some of the details in their statements were at odds with the facts, most specifically the fact the body had been discovered decapitated by blunt trauma. But Gordon wasn't thinking rationally, a neurosis seized him and his heart pounded uncomfortably. He saw his end before him, he had missed his story and already Croaker's wrath was boring through to his nerve centre.

Without a moment's hesitation Gordon rushed back to his room and immediately plugged in his mobile phone to charge. As it slowly glowed back to life missed call after missed call began announcing themselves, each time with a double beep which made his heaving heart sink deeper and deeper. He pored over the call register for clues. The weekend editors had first called at half past six, when they failed to reach him they must have roused Clara - most probably by seven because he received his first call from her at five past the hour. He had missed 21 calls in total, it did not look good.

But Gordon was quick to salvage what he could and knew not all was lost. He rarely met defeat with despondency and reasoned that with some good fortune he could credibly claim to have been at the scene and hard at work only thwarted by a mobile reception blackspot. It was the sort of white lie the hungover reporter regularly relied upon. Gordon hoped Clara had not told the desk he had been hitting the cognac hard the night before. The faintest whiff of alcohol would rob his claims of all credibility.

Gordon's first call would be to the Police. He needed to stand up the facts, name, age, profession - all the basics. His luck was in, the Police already had a name for release: Quentin Frobisher. His brother and his only next of kin had been notified that morning after the two traumatised friends had identified the body. The conspiratorial constable who spoke to Gordon hinted there might be more to the story than he could report but suddenly changed tack. After this he became guarded and would not even speak off the record, not even 'for guidance'. Speaking in fluent police officialese - a language where it never 'rained' but rather 'precipitation was experienced' - "the gentlemen had been consuming a large quantity of alcohol on the evening in question leading to a state of inebriation. He had been on deck when the ship was struck by a sudden wave causing him to temporarily lose balance and alight the yacht permanently". It was an open and shut case for the station.

"And the decapitation?" Gordon said.

The constable paused and Gordon heard the click of a mic mute. A moment later the constable returned without announcement.

"The engine," he said with decisiveness. "He caught his neck in the propellor on the way down."

Gordon filed a few pars of copy, routine man overboard stuff. He was in no state to spin the story and, for once, was perfectly prepared to accept the police's version of events. Besides, there was no way he could satisfactorily link the dolphin beachings with the dead body - that would be far too sensationalist for Associated News. The police said the death was not being treated as suspicious and Gordon reasonably expected that was the end of the morning's excitement. He could be left to nurse his throbbing skull. More details might dribble out as the week unfolded but a drunk man drowning was not national news unless he was a politician or a celebrity.

No sooner had Gordon sent over his story for the news desk to taste than the picture editor was on the phone to Clara wondering about a collect for the drowned man. Half of an editor's job is covering bases. Nobody had any interest in the story or any expectation it would escalate but the base had to be covered all the same. Documentation becomes an obsession and a compulsion more akin to bureaucracy than the storytelling.

Clara knew her slim hope for a collect rested on a trip into Penzance and an awkward visit to the dead man's two friends. Trevellyan's bus was leaving in 15 minutes and she failed to persuade Gordon to join her. He was paranoid after the morning's events and struck with a paralysis made all the more acute by the hangover Clara had somehow dodged. She was desperate not to make the journey alone. She even tried to chivvy David out of his blinkered world of fantasy role playing but when he refused her mood soured irrecoverably. David's slight was an irritating sting to Clara, most particularly because it happened in front of Gordon who could not suppress a sly smirk at the rejection. However, his schadenfreude was short-lived. David had no intention of spending another day glued to Knight's Lore deciding instead to pal up with Gordon. Like a stray dog deadened to the kicks of rebuttal, David had taken a fancy to Gordon. He was insistent in joining him for a day's hard reporting. Gordon sighed long, sore and silently.

"Well since you two have grown so matey I'll go alone," said Clara, relishing the swiftness of justice. "I'll be glad of some peace."

Clara left in a hurry to catch the bus into Penzance. Gordon was alone with his young apprentice who stared wide-eyed and waiting for direction. The blunt edge of the hangover had made Gordon irascible and David's skulking presence was a further irritant. Alone together, the hotel felt cramped and crowded so he proposed a brisk walk down to the beach. Gordon invented an errand to divert the stream of David's continual questions and suppositions.

"Remember, Clara found a red shoe belonging to the drowned man on the beach?" he said. "Well, maybe other objects had washed ashore."

If anything, the plan had worked too well. The sense of a mission stoked David's fires of insatiable curiosity so that Gordon spent the walk down to the beach batting away wild suggestions and even wilder counter-proposals. David had the logic of a computer program, his brain worked well in the black-and-white binary code but was impervious to the tones, subtleties and shades in his periphery. Had Gordon humoured David's ambitious proposals then he would have chartered a speed boat and be well on his way to working out the best way to weld a semi-automatic harpoon gun to its bow.

The heavy lids of Gordon's hangover had not yet lightened and the sea spray was a welcome tonic to his puffy bags. He closed his eyes and rested a shoulder against the harbour wall. How Gordon envied the cool stone at that moment, he could have happily stood motionless for an aeon against the refreshing breeze and nothing but the gentle sound of rolling waves for company. An aeon was ambitious but five minutes like this and Gordon knew all would be right and well with the world once again.

"What would win in a fight out of a seagull and a chicken?" said David, shattering Gordon's peace like the 11am Friday fire alarm test.

"What?" said Gordon as he forced open a single eyelid to face his assailant.
"I mean like the sort of chicken they use for fighting, with the sharp claws."

"Talons, and it's a cockerel.

"So, which would win in a fight?"

"Oh, for a draught of Lethe waters," said Gordon. "Please, just give me five minutes of peace."

He closed his eyes again but once the question had been posed Gordon could not help re-enacting the unlikely combat in his head. This bloody battle to the death with all its squawks and feathers was not conducive to a cure. Despite himself, a victor emerged but it was a close-run thing, just edged by the cockerel's greater weight. Gordon was even prepared to announce the verdict to David when his mobile rang. It had saved him from hours of conjecture and debate about beak size and genetic viciousness. Gordon hurriedly retrieved the mobile from his breast pocket, he feared another call from the desk but was only mildly relieved to hear the voice of his father at the other end.

"Your tablet, it's very strange," said Dr Alfred Athelney. "A boustrophedon ..."

"You could read it?"

"Of course," said his father. "But it's nonsense. It reminds me of the Bramham Moor Ring. Magical gibberish. The Saxons were a superstitious lot and not immune to a bit of hocus pocus."

"So, what does it say?"

"Well it begins earnestly enough. 'This belongs to Ceolwulf the Dispossessed, captain of the Varangian Guard in Constantinople under Emperor Alexius.' The next section is fragmented. It starts 'At the horn of Holmstad follow - I assume it's a direction but it's barely legible. The next word is 'broken back fish'. The Roman numerals, of course you can read."

"Sure - and they are?"

"432," said Dr Athelney impatiently. "Then there's the cuneiform."
"Which you can't translate?"

"You know I served as dragoman for three summers running to pay my way through the near Orient during my undergraduate."

"So you can read it?" said Gordon hopefully.

"Well not with the accuracy required for academic publication perhaps... but is that your purpose?"

"No, of course not."

"No, of course not," Dr Athelney echoed with the barely concealed disappointment he had harboured ever since Gordon told him one bleak February morning that he would be reading English Literature and not Anglo-Saxon at Oxford. 'But look, Beowulf is on the syllabus,' he had pleaded with his father in vain.

"Well, this is where it gets particularly confused," Dr Athelney continued. "The cuneiform is sloppy and indelicate. It says: 'here is a lament for sunken Tiamat who sleeps deep beyond the far ocean.'"

"It's very old?"

"Relatively, no. In fact, I'm quite certain it was written by a Greek of the Eastern Empire. Tiamat is written with a clumsy literal of the beast from Thalassa - the sea."

"What does that mean?" asked Gordon, by now lost in his father's flow.

"I hope you're not taking all this too seriously, my boy, I'd hate to think of you looking foolish in professional eyes."

Gordon shrugged off the attack and asked his father to continue.

"Well, it's back to the runes and what looks like an incantation, but it's rather difficult to translate."

"Because of the language?"

"Because of the photograph you sent me," his father said, annoyed at the suggestion. "It's blurred beyond hope and the lack of definition introduces possibilities and uncertainties to the language. Is there a better photo?"

"No, but what's your verdict?"

"Hoax," said his father confidently. "It's implausible. But like all the best hoaxes I'm not saying there isn't a thread of plausibility."

"How do you mean, what's plausible?"

"The name was plausible. Ceolwulf the Dispossessed, I recognised it immediately.

"When I was a student, choked and asthmatic from dusty editions in the Bodleian, I had to make a cross reference with the Encyclopaedia Brittanica. There I found the entry for Ceolwulf. I remember it so well, between Ceorl and Cephalagia.

"His story was told in Aelfhere's chronicle - written in 1087. I had never heard of the chronicle or this Saxon lord who had continued the fight against the William the Bastard.

"I truly believe I had stumbled across some arcane branch of the history of this island. To find it hidden, of all places, in the humble Encyclopaedia. But it was an entirely fallacious entry. It had been inserted with great care. The malicious trickery of some wayward scholar, perhaps, seeking to deceive. And I was deceived and ridiculed.

"I presented the supposed discovery to my ill-tempered tutor who was very cruel and not in the least bit understanding of the trap I had unwittingly sprung.

"I never understood why the entry had been inserted and I never heard of Ceolwulf the Dispossessed again. In honesty, I wanted to forget about the whole episode - but this morning I see the same name again. Another hoax, I've no doubt."

"But what did the entry say?" Gordon asked.

"I tore the entry from the Encyclopaedia with the passion of academic fury. I was humiliated and wanted to destroy the lie. Perhaps a touch dramatically, I burnt the page."

"So, you don't remember?"

"Of course I remember. It said Ceolwulf was a housecarl with large estates in the extremity of Wessex. A century before, his ancestors had driven the Celts over the borders into the Welsh hills. The house remained loyal to Wessex and was highly regarded in kind. Ceolwulf fought as lieutenant on Harold's left flank at Hastings, one of the few loyal to the Saxon line left alive by nightfall. But loyalty was an offence punishable by death by the Bastard. Ceolwulf took flight East, to the welcoming embrace of the Emperor in Constantinople."

"Alexius recognised loyalty, bravery and martial prowess as attractive qualities in a mercenary army. You could say Ceolwulf's CV was a perfect fit. Ceolwulf rose through the ranks of the Varangian guard and served at the Emperor's side in ceremonial courtly matters but also on the battlefields of the near east. The entry stated he returned to England before his death."

"But what makes you so certain it's a hoax?"

"It's fantasy, I think you're teasing by asking. Cuneiform was the written language of whom?"

"Babylonian."

"And when would you date the height of influence?"

"The Uruk dynasty?"

"Good guess. And so how many years do you suppose separates the languages - Anglo Saxon and Cuneiform? You can round it up to the closest century."

"1,500," said Gordon doubtfully. "At a guess."

"1,800 years is a better guess," said his father. "You see, there's no logic to it. It's non sequitur. It's a hoax. A practical joke played by some loony Orientalist with a better imagination than his diligence to study even the rudiments of chronology."

110

"Right," said Gordon with a sigh of defeat - the bugle call his father had been waiting to hear.

"But of course, you know I have such an interest in the fantastic - fraudulent or otherwise. If you were to find me another photo - one taken with a steadier hand - then I'd be delighted to translate the hocus pocus."

"OK, it's a deal," said Gordon.

He said goodbye to his father in hurry. He had taken his eyes off David during the intensity of the conversation and looked up to find him teetering on the edge of the harbour wall 30 feet above, wobbling like the least sure-footed chamois in the herd.

CHAPTER FIFTEEN

The conversation with his father had given Gordon a furious, new energy. He had forgotten the morning's hangover. Even David's rambling musings could not derail him from his train of thought. Dr Athelney's story of the hoax encyclopaedia entry had increased Gordon's fascination with the tablet. He also had the name Ceolwulf the Dispossessed, that it should have appeared twice in such strange and distinct circumstances struck him as so unlikely as to be significant.

Gordon wished Clara had not gone to Penzance for the collect. He wanted her to photograph the tablet again so his father could translate the runes indistinguishable in Gordon's low-resolution photo. With Clara's camera, his father might even be able to learn more about the material or even, Gordon wondered, the hand that carved it. He was impatient and considering other options.

"I don't suppose you have a camera?" Gordon asked David.

"A what?" said David sulkily.

David was grumpy with Gordon. He felt he had been ordered down from the harbour wall a little too sternly.

"A camera," Gordon repeated with as much grace as he could muster.

"Yes, I do," said David with a sly glance up from his shoes.

"Can I borrow it?"

David realised he had been gifted a power over Gordon and he was not willing to relinquish it casually. The camera was back at the hotel, so the pair set off together to retrieve it. Gordon was keen to keep David on side. He asked him questions about Knight's Lore and listened with a patience that surprised even himself.

"There are seven different races in the Kingdom of Lu'ain - the humans, the elves - divided into the high-elves, forest elves, half-elves and night elves (they're the evil ones), the goblins, the ogres, the midjkins, and the beserkers - that's what I play as."

"And is there racism in Lu'ainia?" said Gordon earnestly.

David looked perplexed and continued unperturbed.

"The berserkers come from the Glaciasia - the cold kingdom in the far north. They have the powers of strength and weapon-craft. On a quest in Dannarken - on dungeon level 76 - I discovered the artefact Paranthrilla's Mace. It deals additional 4 10d of damage to evil or undead creatures and double impacts on demons. Paranthilla was a sacred paladin of the Holy Fire."

"Of course," Gordon nodded along.

"Well, yesterday, I found a set of gauntlets, discarded among the carcass of Radjuman the Unclean - one of the eight wizards of the Black Circle and the fourth I've slayed. Anyway, I nearly left the gloves on the dungeon floor because my bag was loaded, and I'd incur a minus two encumbrance penalty which results in a 20 per cent reduction in movement speed. I was deep in the dungeon and my scroll of recall had been burned by Radjuman's spell of hurricane fire - the most powerful spell from Kelek's Grimoire of Power and capable of inflicting a 300HP damage with a critical blow."

Gordon was forced to bite hard into his lip. David's sing-song nonsense was testing at the best of times but to listen and also maintain an air of interest was too much to bear. Gordon felt ready to snap as he thought about the amount of time David wasted on the pointless game.

"Did I tell you about Kelek's Grimoire of Power - well, it's the first of the seven sealed tomes of Harqun's Eldritch Library?"

"You know it's all bollocks? Everything you've said."

Gordon could not contain himself any longer and pulled up in his fury like a lamed horse. David turned slowly; his pride wounded but still sensing he had the upper hand while the camera remained in his possession. But Gordon was so annoyed he had forgotten about the camera.

"It's bollocks," he repeated. "This isn't how the world works. People don't just discover a magic sword, left strewn in a pile on the floor, and then head out to conquer the world. Power is the result of years of bullying, hard work, murder, dark intrigue, and irresistibility. This fantasy nonsense you clog your brain with is pointless. Nobody cares. Why not read the Odyssey instead? If you want heroes, monsters, magic weapons why not read the Classics."

"Are there midjkins in the classics?"

"No... in fact yes. And more besides. There are scorpion men who live in the desert, hyrdras and harpies, a snarling monstrous Minotaur and sea monsters who foam the brine; there are winged horses and magic shields, kingdoms forbidden to man and great Godly cities beyond the clouds. Knight's Lore is a waste of time and it's a waste of my time listening to you jabber on about it. I'm sorry David, but it's about time somebody told you."

David thought carefully and silently. His face was stung from Gordon's verbal assault, but it soon mellowed. He kicked moodily at the sandy soil on the winding path to the Cragg. Gordon waited for his mews of complaint and self-pity, but they never came. Instead, David walked on with a coolness and silent collection Gordon had never seen in him before.

"I think I'm going back to our room," said David when they reached the hotel. "I'm going to play some Knight's Lore. I'll have to see about the camera later, but I'd ask you not to disturb me please."

David marched away purposefully. His riposte was delivered so firmly and with such an unexpected authority that Gordon was stunned into immobility. He had just been silenced by a teenager he had hitherto assumed to be a fool of the highest order. He was also very grateful Clara had not been there to witness the scene. Gordon was weighing up whether his pride could ever recover from delivering a grovelling apology to David. It was a great relief when he spotted Clara trudging up the steep path to the Cragg.

"Hello," said Gordon. "What are you doing back so early?"

"The bus didn't turn up," she said. "No explanation. No apology. No notice. I stood there for 40 minutes and nothing."

"Never mind," said Gordon. "There's something else I need shooting."

Clara looked suspicious.

"What?"

Gordon explained on the way. He had lied and said the Colonel lived a short walk from town. Eventually, after ten minutes hiking up the steepening lane Gordon was forced to be more specific.

"Well, it's no more than 15 minutes," he said.

"15 minutes! You said it was a short walk."

"Well let me carry your camera then," said Gordon but Clara shot him a look that left him in no doubt his chivalry was too late and most unwelcome.

Gordon had also told Clara the Colonel was expecting their visit and had agreed that the tablet could be photographed. 'It was only a white lie,' Gordon told himself, but he knew full well that although the Colonel had not ruled it out completely, he certainly had not extended a specific invitation. Gordon remembered how the Colonel's pleasant face had soured so suddenly when he had asked to photograph the tablet, meeting the request with shifty reluctance. Gordon realised how difficult it would have been to persuade Clara to hike three miles on a bleak November on such a forlorn hope. Also, Gordon did not dare to call the Colonel directly to make an appointment for fear of rejection. He knew the element of surprise was his best hope.

Gordon remembered the few landmarks he had passed the previous day and knew it was not much further to the Hall. For Clara it was an unhappy journey. Gordon too was beginning to feel the cold. He promised himself in future he would pack too much, rather than too little. 'Layers are the secret' he said to himself as an icy wind found an entrance under his shirt. When they reached the stone wall that encompassed Selyvan Hall Gordon's mood lightened, he knew it was only another ten minutes. The wall rose steadily from the moors to a height even Gordon - at six foot two - could not crest. It was a sturdy wall constructed at considerable expense and as a statement of Lordly grandeur. Clara found little cheer in its formless face and cast a glum eye at its stretching expanse.

"Well, here we are," said Gordon as they reached the entrance. "The gates of Mordor."

"Thank God," said Clara, lifting her camera bag off her back to recover. "I'm ready for a sit down somewhere warm, I hope he makes us a cup of tea. He gave you wine, didn't he?"

Clara had mistaken the old gatehouse for Selyvan Hall and Gordon had to break the bad news to her very gently that it was still another half a mile away. The news was too much for Clara to bear and finally she told Gordon he would have to carry her camera the rest of the way. Clara was out of humour with her shoulder causing pain, but her spirits recovered when she saw Gordon struggling under the weight of the load that she had carried all the way from town. Gordon puffed and constantly shifted the weight of the bag from one shoulder to the other. When Gordon saw how Clara enjoyed his labours he exaggerated his suffering, and released pained sighs and deep, wheezy breaths - at one point he thought he had gone too far when he bent himself double against a fallen tree, but Clara was still enjoying it.

"It's heavier than I realised," Gordon said between gasps.

Clara smiled and marched ahead, urging Gordon along.

"What are you always chewing?" said Clara as Gordon sucked a date. "Have you got sweets and not offered me one? You could peel an orange in your pocket."

"No, I couldn't," said Gordon.

But he felt guilt. He had been sucking secretively, he only had four dates left and had already rationed them carefully, he needed to save at least one for long train journey back to London.

"They're just some old dates," he said. "Would you like one?"
"Ugh," said Clara pulling the horrid face of a little girl served olives for the first time. "Not likely."

They reached Selyvan Hall and although the weather had slightly improved since Gordon's last visit the house's grim aspect had not. It scowled back at the two visitors. Clara - who had been marching with purposeful strides - slowed her step and let Gordon take the lead.

"What do you make of it?" said Gordon.

Clara shook her head.

"It looks like Wuthering Heights."

The Colonel had been charming the previous day and Gordon was hoping for a similar reception. However, he felt an uncertainty about this second visit that had been increasing all the while he walked. The Hall was so uncanny, and the Colonel's character was so curious and unusual. In all his years as a journalist Gordon thought he'd met every variety of kook and nutter, rake and scallywag, fibber and exhibitionist the world had to offer but Colonel Mortain eluded him. The Colonel met all the criteria for the former specimens but married it with an air of the romantic, as though he belonged to a different age. An age of steam, an age of heroes, where Englishmen fastened the top button and strolled out under a baking sun plunging headlong into the heart of darkness without fear or a moment's consideration for consequence. The truth was Gordon admired the Colonel immensely and in him saw a reflection of all he longed for.

"Well, are you going to knock? We'll be late otherwise."

Gordon woke from his daydreaming and realised he'd stood poised at the door with the great knocker in his hand. He shook himself together and launched the Sheela na gig - with the dull clang of iron on old iron. Gordon waited. His breath was almost stolen from his lungs. Until then he hadn't considered what he was going to say. He could hardly say he was just passing. Besides, the matter was more complicated since he'd told Clara he had arranged a visit. He'd marched to Selyvan Hall with the blinkers of purpose but without the cool reason of logic. Gordon was usually confident the right words would find their way from his tongue but on that great stone step it deserted him and for a moment he was genuinely afraid the Colonel might get angry for an unannounced visit. Gordon was certain he was in, the old Rover sat by the garage coated with a brown skirt of mud.

Gordon waited a minute after the first knock before Clara encouraged him to try once again, but just as on his first visit there was no reply.

"It's a big, old house," Gordon said. "It probably takes five minutes to get from one wing to the next."

"Knock again," said Clara and he did.

They waited but Clara was losing faith and seized the knocker and sounded three mighty strikes.

"There," she said firmly and amused by her own decisiveness in the face of Gordon's dithering. "He can't have missed that."

Gordon agreed. There was a desperate impatience in her blows like the screams of a pained child that unsettled his guts and twisted his nerves taut until the sinews pinged and snapped. Gordon realised he was holding his breath as they stood in silence on the step, and he caught up with five hurried, shallow intakes. His breathing was so irregular that he even felt as if he might faint when the great oak door creaked back on heavy hinges to reveal a crack of warm light from within. The door opened just far enough for the Colonel to poke out his head, his face failed to conceal his surprise and muted alarm at the sight of Gordon - increased all the more when he spied Clara a step back and with her camera poised and ready to fire.

"Hello again," the Colonel said after some effort at recovery and with more than one furtive glance over his shoulder.

The Colonel wore a silk smoking jacket loosely tied about him, but his legs, feet and chest were bare. It was evident he hadn't expected to receive visitors.

"I'm sorry if I've caught you at a bad time," said Gordon, mustering his most casual tone. "You'd mentioned I might be able to take some pictures of the tablet today. This is my photographer Clara."

The Colonel gave her a pained smile before checking his civility and extending a limp hand in greeting. Clara returned the handshake with a smile as forced and unsteady as her unwitting host. The Colonel returned to Gordon.

"It's really a bit awkward today I'm afraid. If I had known you were coming I could have made provision but I'm really rather busy."

Gordon felt suddenly ridiculous and importunate and wanted to be gone. For appearance in front of Clara he attempted a few persuasive phrases but in each instance he provided the Colonel with an easy escape. Gordon wanted to be gone and regretted the impetuous streak that had overcome him. The Colonel shifted more uneasily and cast more glances back inside the house, as though he was being stalked by a tiger and expected it to pounce at any moment.

"Are you having a party?"

"Sort of," said the Colonel with a finality suggesting the matter was closed.

"On the day of the Lord," said Gordon, surprising even himself at his own response. The Colonel too looked puzzled before recovering.

"I'm not terribly religious I'm afraid," he said warmly. "It's all about prohibition and prohibition creates desire. Why not cut out the middleman?"

Gordon smiled bemused. He knew Clara would not be in a forgiving mood if the journey had been an entire waste so struck upon the idea of pressing the Colonel for a fixed interview with Professor Burroughs. Gordon had no particular need or desire to speak with the Professor - and he knew Clara certainly didn't want to see him again - but it would at least allow him to walk away from Selyvan Hall with a shred of professionalism. The Colonel appeared pleased to steer the conversation away from the tablet but slightly irked at the prospect of arranging the interview but after a moment of internal reasoning agreed to make a quick phone call to his friend. Gordon could sense he had annoyed the Colonel as he spun with martial impatience on his heels and hurried back to his study.

"He said he didn't know we were coming. I told you to phone ahead. And what's all this about 'my photographer'? I'm not your photographer any more than you're my journalist."

Gordon had reddened and didn't want to face Clara, so he nodded and waited for her anger evaporate away. He waited for a minute and traced the patterns in the old oak door, following the grain with a nail. The Colonel had gently pulled the door to as he left and had not invited the two journalists inside, marking a departure from the previous day's hospitality that wasn't lost on Gordon. Perhaps it was the strength of the wind eddying about the courtyard, or that Gordon had more strength in his index finger as he traced the pattern of the grain, but the oak door pushed ajar ever so slightly. Clara was still grumbling at Gordon. She bemoaned the Colonel's lack of common civility by not allowing them to wait in the warmth. Slowly and deliberately, Gordon leant towards the crack in the door and pushed a nose and his left eye to see within. He recoiled. Gordon had seen the red-haired Eastern European who had answered the door so brusquely the previous afternoon. The Colonel had called her Piret. She was marching across the entrance hall deliberately and with the preternatural airiness of a ballerina or phantom spirit. As she passed a draft from the door tickled her and she turned and faced Gordon, her eyes met his. She did not stop walking and turned away. Later Gordon would ask himself whether he had he recoiled so suddenly through uncanny terror or through embarrassment - Piret was nude. Her red hair was damp but wild and loose ringlets had formed at the sides and back but by the crown it flickered dry like flames. Her bones and veins appeared through her pale translucent skin, and it sparkled with a waxy perspiration as though she were half candle. But was it her face that frightened Gordon so deeply? Blackened, as though by soot from the chars and applied with great fat fingers, ten at a time. From behind that black face her two white eyes burnt the brighter for it. Gordon wished he could have maintained her gaze and watched her for just a second more. He wished he could have followed her with lustrous eyes across the hall and away. Without her eyes on his he could have appreciated her form the more and from the moment he turned away, he desired to see her once again.

Clara spotted Gordon's abruptness and looked shocked herself when she saw his ashen face and wild eyes. Seconds later the Colonel returned, and both were shaken when he thrust a scrap of paper with a time and telephone number into Gordon's hands. He clearly was in no mood for idle small talk. Instead, he apologised again that he was pressed by other business and that they could arrange another time for a visit shortly. The great door was closed before Gordon could even finish thanking the Colonel for his help.

"Worthwhile trip," said Clara sarcastically as she eyed the darkening clouds. "You're carrying the camera back; you know that right?"

"I know," said Gordon, and he looked ruefully down at his wet shoes. "These only just got dry, the leather will be ruined."

"Change the record," said Clara. "It's odd for a grown man to be so neurotic about a pair of shoes."

Gordon wanted to explain. He wanted to tell her they were not expendable. That they were hand-stitched in Northampton, not some distant sweat shop. That one pair would last him his entire life and that the leather would age as slowly and charmingly as his own weathered skin. But he didn't, he sulked.

"You're rather waspish today," he said eventually, but by then Clara had shrugged off her interest and was lost in her own thoughts.

Half-way back to Selyvan, Clara finally asked Gordon what he saw inside that had startled him so deeply. Gordon let the question hang until its reverberations were lost and it could have been forgotten but Clara was insistent.

"What did you see?" she repeated.

Gordon thought for a moment.

"A den of iniquity."

CHAPTER SIXTEEN

David returned to the room feeling smug, he felt confident he had bested Gordon. He turned the lock in the hope Gordon would follow ten paces behind and walk inelegantly into the locked door like a jilted lover. David threw himself onto his bed with a spring of satisfaction and let his gelled hair sink into the fresh pillow - crunching and cracking against the linen. David ceremoniously withdrew his mobile phone from the recesses of the inner breast pocket of his oversized grey suit. The phone's khaki rubber protective holster snagged against the silky pocket lining and its cheap stitching burst. And then something unexpected happened. As the phone lit into life and the title screen of Dragon's Lore appeared - with the Berserker Konig brandishing a burning sword to deflect the cyan flame of the Frost Wyrm - his passion dulled and a void of emptiness opened before him.

For several minutes David stared at his mobile phone and Dragon Lore stared right back at him like the emotion-drained couple facing one another at the final divorce hearing. Gordon's words echoed about the room and despite David's presumed victory he felt a lonely hollowness. Molitor - as David had christened his level 87 Beserker warrior 172 long days ago - was a stranger and his digital adventures seemed absurd to the point of pathos. Barely daring to breathe, David turned off his phone and slid it back inside the khaki rubber protective holster and with the air of an alcoholic returning an unopened bottle to the wine-rack, put it back inside his breast pocket, popping a few more stitches on the return.

David passed half an hour staring lugubriously at the cracked plaster ceiling, Gordon hadn't returned to find him as he'd expected. He might have lain there in that melancholy doze for hours if a text from his father hadn't woken him as though from a fairy-tale spell.

'Bagged a byline yet?' it read.

'No,' was his laconic reply.

Two minutes later his phone beeped again but it was several more minutes before David could bring himself to read it.

'Then go forth and gather - your mother is watching the wires for your name,' his father said.

David thought of his mother, mousey and meek avoiding his father in their detached house with its turning circle drive in Tunbridge Wells. It was a house purged of clutter and polished to a cleanliness that brought on allergies to all who spent time beneath its walls, so absent was the microbe and uninvited molecule. It was not home for David, who hated how the sun never fell evenly on its white walls and the thick weave in the lavender carpets seemed to soak up everything that touched them. It was a house where bedrooms appeared when there ought to be hallways and bathrooms where there ought to be cupboards. And it was never warm, David shivered at the memories of piano in the dining room with the smell of Pledge. And his mother was never warm but always distant, always avoiding his father - Sir Trevor. And his father would burst into rooms impatiently and expect amusement and action. He would turn off the radio mid-way through his mother's afternoon play and begin some poorly constructed diatribe or announce the commencement of some nascent project or other. She never complained anymore because he had an infantile petulance and little interest in matters in which he wasn't the subject of the sentence. So, she would listen as he waxed or ranted on a topic she knew would never come to fruition and would soon be forgotten.

His father lacked patience with David too and in 16 years had never once asked his only son a question; instead, he made statements with a raised inflection. "You're going to be a journalist like your old man?"; "You'll be captaining the first 15 next year like your old man?"; "Your Latin dictum will win the prize for Chads House like your old man?". David spent several long hours looking for his father's name on the lacquered wooden boards that lined the hallways of Sir Hareton's but never managed to find it. Of course, his father was thick with Mr Bartlett, David's headmaster, and widely praised as the most generous benefactor on the Old Haretonian Society social. Oily Bartlett would thank Sir Trevor before the cigars were lit as "the school's worthiest head boy". But David could never find his father's name on the long list of prominent pupils either. Once he thought he'd found it but it was just Terrence Starkey and his name was among the fallen from the Great War. David realised how glad he was to be away from home, and this despite his despondency with Dragon's Lore. No, he didn't want to return to Tunbridge Wells. In Gordon and Clara, he placed a cold pan of friendship of friendship, left on the hob to boil slowly - unguarded and insidious.

Friendship! It was a Eureka moment and David sat bolt up in bed, electrified with his sudden inspiration. He was going to be a journalist. He was going to work. He was going to find the story and he was going to present it to Gordon like the cat dropping a dead mouse on the doorstep. David scurried over to his sprawling suitcase and fished out his compact camera. Like everything David had a hand in choosing, the camera had a military theme with an infra-red night mode and gunsights in the viewfinder. David placed the camera in its holster and attached it to the exhausted brown belt his mother had drilled an extra hole into with a corkscrew, four inches from the last. David rushed from the room, down the spiral stairs and out of the Cragg's solemn front porch. He left the room unlocked, the door ajar and the key sitting on the desk by the kettle under the empty sachets of tea Gordon had polished off in the first few hours - but the shortbread biscuit crumbs were all David's doing.

David felt seized by an urge to see Gordon and his instinct drove him with a canter, only in completely the opposite direction. Despite David's martial pretensions he had little fieldcraft and so charged in manic pursuit neither down the narrow cliff path or the shallower service track but along the edge of the cliffs away from town. David's blind haste, his clumpy shoes and a squally wind made progress potentially treacherous and on more than one occasion he stumbled so that the breaking waves crashing against the jagged rocks beneath reared into dizzying sight.

After ten minutes of aimless charging, even David's malfunctioning radar sensed something was amiss. He scanned the horizon and saw vast ocean, gorse and rock. Where he had expected to find the town of Selyvan, he saw the end of the world. Where he'd hoped to find Gordon, he found solitude. David broke his canter into a limping trot which in turn gave way to a desolate stagger. David recognised then he was lost but lacked the apparatus of logic to rectify the situation. Rather than retrace his steps he pressed on in wild diagonals. Rather than stop, catch his breath and seek out landmarks he spun on the spot in giddy breathlessness without clear purpose. It was using this imprecise navigation that David picked up the scent of a stony trail that led down from the clifftop towards the sea. He followed it mechanically but even he knew Selyvan did not lie at the foot of this precipitous route.

David saw the path promised access to a secluded cove where the waves lapped lazily over large, twinkling pebbles and smooth, white driftwood stretched and arched like the ivory of an elephant's graveyard. David felt a desire to stand on this shore and toss stones into the foaming brine. He followed the path down, but it quickly became imprecise and at times he was forced to choose between two equally rugged alternatives and more than once had to retreat in search of sounder footing. At times, the path stepped up the cliff and David wondered if he would ever reach the secret cove. After he had traversed the cliff path for several exhausting minutes, he stopped and realised with disappointment he was further from the beach than when he'd first spied it from the top of the cliff, as if by some strange trick of perspective. David was already steeling himself for defeat when he reached a large flat granite face which blocked the path entirely. He had nearly turned back at sighting it but an odd compulsion to place two flat palms against the perfect rock overcame him and as he closed, he noticed a narrow passage hugging the cliff face bypassing the granite wall. Even with David's sparrowy frame it was a difficult passage to negotiate and seemed unnaturally dark, to the extent David was forced to fumble and feel for the route.

As David emerged blinking on the other side of the passage, he discovered with some disappointment that it hadn't led him to the cove but into a maze of similar granite passages and sharp, rocky obstructions but he continued, enthralled by the pillars and caverns that thrust and sunk in the cliff face. In fact, David had almost forgotten his cove as the path forked and looped back on itself. Progress was slower still; sometimes the path disappeared suddenly to the sea forty feet below and at other times it charged headlong into impassable rock or had crumbled away decades ago. But for every dead-end that presented itself, a new pathway appeared, sometimes requiring considerable searching and a hop or stretch. David had a casual disregard for personal safety, more a result of a deficit of common-sense than through a surfeit of bravery. After several minor stumbles the inevitable happened - David fell.

He had fingered his way through a dark corridor that led low into the cliff face towards a cave, whose yawning opening was fringed top and bottom by stumpy stone formations that gave the uncanny appearance of a sinister mouth gaping wide to swallow something whole. As David edged himself through, his right foot met air where he'd expected to find rock. He lost balance and lurched forwards, thrusting both hands before him and they were the first to feel solid ground as he slid headlong down an unseen slope, marble-smooth from centuries of gushing water. The smoothness of the stone, the shallow gradient of his tumble and David's lack of weight meant he avoided serious injury and - as he recovered from the shock in a pool of icy water at the bottom of the dark cavern, he considered himself fortunate.

David righted himself and wrung the worst of the water from his dripping jacket. His eyes quickly grew accustomed to the dim light, and the cavern appeared lighter than the passageway from where he'd fallen. The reason became apparent, around the corner David heard the crashing of waves and went to investigate. As he rounded a bend, the cavern widened into an atrium open to the sea. The cave lay only just above sea level, so the waves beat the walls and mopped the floors. Splashing through the brine, ankle deep in places, David made his way to the mouth and looked out over the sea. Occasionally a larger wave beat more furiously and sent a shower of cold water across David's legs and chest and caused him to start with a gasp.

There was something about the purple blue light in the dull sky and the hue it cast on the grey green sea that made David stop to think. Without understanding what the sensation was he unclipped his camera from his belt holster and started to take photographs. At first he wanted to capture the colours in the sky and the sea but was frustrated in his attempt; he could get the colours of the sky but then the sea looked like a black silhouette; or the colours of the sea but then the sky looked like a white light. In the end he settled for photographing each separately. Then his focus shifted to the dull light that fell into the cavern. He noticed how it touched parts and avoided others, which were cast in eternal 'shadow. He looked at the shape of the walls and how they altered and deformed as he changed his perspective and position. He saw how he could catch the drops of sea spray as they hung and floated through the light and how by placing the camera flat on the ground it created such a wider and more cavernous environment than when he shot from eye-level.

David noticed other things besides. He noticed a low, flat table-like rock in the centre of the space. He saw how this rock was not conjoined to the cave but stood as though it had been placed deliberately by man. His fingers felt the crude chisel blows that had shaped its edges and how smooth its centre had been worn. He snapped the table, long and low so its proportions were elongated and the chisel blows focused with perfect clarity. His eyes were now finely tuned and he noticed other things besides. How, in one wall, hollows had been hacked into the

124

rock and how green and brown bottles sat. David photographed these. He opened one of the bottles and a pungent herb vapour raced up his nostrils and dizzied him, as he screwed back the stopper, he noticed it was oily and slipped in his fingers. Next to the bottles were sticks of burnt wood and charcoal and David wiped his sooty hands on his wet trousers with all the concern of a baby eating its dinner. On the far wall David saw words carved. The first section looked like the language of the Doomahdills in Dragon's Lore and he couldn't read it but the second part - perhaps a translation - was in a strange English. He photographed both.

David was engrossed with his documentary and worked with a mania he had hitherto reserved for playing fantasy games; so engrossed that he failed to notice the water spilling into the cave mouth and puddling in a rapidly filling reservoir in the centre of the chamber. The first David noticed was when he kneeled in the puddle and it sent a chill across his thighs that stopped his breath and caused him to jump as though he'd received an electric shock.

David saw how his cave had transformed and how the sea now rushed openly through its mouth. He saw how quickly the cave was filling and recognised the danger. With a rare decisiveness David hurried back to the slope from where he'd fallen - already the seawater was flooding a channel down the corridor. Try as David could to find grip he couldn't pull himself up out of the cavern. The gradient was too steep and the blackness too thick to penetrate to help find suitable footholds. All saw him slide back and left him in a crumpled exhausted heap - David realised he needed to look for another exit. The water level inside the cave had already risen beyond his ankles and was increasing steadily. He made for the mouth and looked out over the sea - the idea to swim to safety had occurred but was swiftly forgotten when he looked out across the wild ocean and the waves that flung themselves with fury across the treacherous rocks.

David looked out across the sea; the coastline ran in a large sweeping arc that could be followed to its extremity at least two miles from where he stood. The low mists from morning were being tossed and tousled in the rising wind. The wind brought with it colder air from the far Atlantic and David shivered uncontrollably in his wet clothes. Half a mile out to sea, David caught sight of an object, distinct against the waves but yet impossible to trace with his eye. It stood upright like a tree, rising twelve feet from the sea. At first, David reasoned it might be a ship and even waved his arms in a vain appeal for help; then he supposed it could be a buoy to warn sailors of the perilous rocks around the coast but discounted this too. The object didn't bob and flinch with the swell of the sea - it stood so immobile and aloof that David began to question if it even existed and was not some trick of the light and the cold. He stared hard, but the harder he stared, the less distinct it became until, eventually, it grew vague through the mist and rising waves. However, from where he supposed it had been the waters seemed to thrash and bubble, as though from that point a great undersea volcano was erupting and giant bubbles of gas surged to the surface through an ear-shattering pressure. David was transfixed, not daring to turn away despite the danger he faced - a danger that increased with every moment of indecision. And yet despite the danger and the urgency of his situation David lifted his compact camera and looked down the viewfinder to photograph the phenomenon he witnessed but as he stared down the cross-hair viewfinder he could no longer find what he sought. He scanned the horizon but to no avail and pulled the camera from his eye, even without the encumbrance of a 16mm lens he could no longer see it. He fired a few snaps at the general area and pulled himself together. He remembered his mortal danger.

David remembered his mobile. He could phone for help, but when he went to retrieve it from his pocket the lining gave way as the final stitches broke and it dropped with an undignified plop into the knee-deep water. David quickly fished it from the brine but the dip in the deep affected the electronics. At first the screen froze blue, then the buttons stopped working before finally it died altogether. David thought of his camera and secured it fast on his belt, he suddenly felt strangely protective of it.

Panic seized David and he tried once again to clamber up the slope to safety, but this final attempt was enough to convince him of the futility. Alone in the dark cavern his fear turned to a mortification, and he wept at what he'd wasted. A great wave struck the cave and sent a surge of water rushing up the corridor and over his legs. He had seen the high-tide mark on the cave walls and knew it was well beyond his head height. David faced his own mortality for the first time and as the waters swirled about his thighs he thought of Molitor.

CHAPTER SEVENTEEN

Clara was still bitter as she trudged back to Selyvan with Gordon. He pretended the Colonel must have forgotten their pre-arranged appointment but Clara didn't believe him. She was sore because she'd yet to tell her picture editor about failing to find a collect and she knew he could never be made to sympathise with the irregular scheduling of Trevellyan of Selyvan's timetable. But when she received a text message from the picture desk telling her Gordon's story had been spiked and not to worry about the collect of the dead man her mood improved considerably.

"They've spiked your story," she said, spinning around and walking backwards as she spoke.

Gordon was labouring under the weight of the camera and had fallen several metres back.

"What?"

"They said it was littered with factual errors and unfit for human consumption."

For a moment her words had a ring of truth and Gordon nearly bit before catching himself. Clara's face lit up with a grin she couldn't suppress so she turned back to the road to enjoy her mischief. When Gordon saw her mood had improved and he was once again fair game he hurried to catch her.

"I'm sorry to have dragged you out here," he said. "I really believed there was a story at the end of it."

"Don't worry about it, these things happen. It's been a nice walk."

Gordon felt comfortable again. He had been worrying how grumpy he'd made her and was concocting explanations for the mission of increasing implausibility. Clara's early forgiveness had saved him from himself.

"It's my fault, I shouldn't listen to a word my father says. You know, he's locked the neighbour's cat in my flat."

Clara burst into laughter and Gordon retold the story. He'd always been slightly shy about his father. People unused to academic types would recoil in horror when his father ventured his clumsy introductions and Gordon got to notice, in his childhood he caught whispers and snippets spoken in conspiratorial tongues behind his father's back. Mothers at school, mothers at private parties, the words of classmates, even teachers - the general consensus was that Dr Athelney might be very brilliant at whatever it is he does, but as a single-parent raising an introspective child he's entirely unsuitable. Gordon was pleased Clara took an interest in his father, and happy his quirks caused amusement rather than alarm.

"Do your family know you're in Cornwall for the weekend?" Gordon asked.

Clara shook her head.

"I've not posted anything on Facebook either."

"Because of Zara?"

"Yes, she's already convinced we're having an affair."

Gordon was shocked, Clara hadn't mentioned this before. He pressed Clara but she grew a little pale and brushed it away. Gordon was tenacious and quizzed and quizzed until sick of the constant hammering, she relented.

"I told her I thought you were handsome."

Gordon was surprised, this wasn't the answer he'd expected and reacted clumsily. Now Clara quickened the pace and Gordon dropped behind slightly breathless.

In town, they went downhill towards the harbour. Gordon had long suspected there was a shorter route to the Cragg but burdened with camera gear as he was, decided then was not the time for experimentation. The Colonel had arranged an interview with the Professor for four in the afternoon. There was no danger of being late, but Gordon had hoped for a bit of time to prepare, he hadn't really intended to interview the Professor and needed to dream up some questions.

By the harbour Gordon saw a face from the day before; it was Guddy. Gordon recognised him instantly, there was something so alien about him, even down to the way he moved. He belonged to another world and yet there he existed among the beer and barnacles in Selyvan. Gordon couldn't help feeling sorry for Guddy - of all the ports in all the world he washes up here. Guddy was heaving at a blue net on board his boat. It was a black boat with a smaller mizzen mast, a much taller main mast and a bowsprit jutting out like a narwhale. It had a small wooden cabin just off centre. A sun-bleached orange life ring hung by a loose nail off the wall. Mjöllnir was painted in white against the black on the port side in Guddy's own cursive hand.

Gordon felt an inclination to impress Clara as the fisherman's friend. He called to Guddy who blinked back, his eyes steadying themselves. For a moment Gordon feared the old drunk had forgotten his guest but Guddy quickly returned the greeting and - after spotting Clara - extended a more formal welcome that took Gordon by surprise. Gordon asked if he was busy and had time to give a tour of the ship. This amused Guddy and he agreed. Gordon and Clara boarded unsteadily, with a predictable lack of proficiency.

"I sailed from Iceland on this boat," he said. "Before that it was my father's boat. When I was a child, we would heave it along on whale bones on the black shores back home.

"It would have been my eldest brother's but he was lost at sea. Two others I lost to the ocean. A wife I lost to the ocean. And yet here I am, heaving at nets."

The tour was perfunctory and Guddy seemed embarrassed in Clara's company, but she was thrilled at the adventure and longed to photograph the fisherman, his knickknacks and his boat. It was the first thing that had truly inspired her since she'd arrived in Selyvan. It was the first thing that had truly inspired her in many months. Mjöllnir was unmistakably a working vessel, it was small, around 30ft. It had a small deck and below Guddy kept his tools, his catch and at least one misty bottle of his home made Brennivín. Decades of fish blood had stained the wet decks a muddy brown and everything Gordon touched left the silvery trace of scales on his fingertips.

Guddy invited them into his small cabin to escape a wind that was just beginning to bite. The cabin had two chairs bolted to the floor and Guddy offered these to his guests. The plastic had cracked and splintered, and the foam was escaping from within. The chair Clara took was positioned in front of the ship's steering wheel and she sat with her legs either side to face the party. Gordon took the second chair while Guddy lit a camping stove, screwed tight to a small wooden table. He took a black kettle from the cupboard and a couple of chipped mugs.

"We've just been to see the Colonel," said Gordon, who stared hard at Guddy to judge his reaction. He hadn't forgotten what Guddy had written on the scrap of paper in his house. He would have liked to see the old fisherman's weathered face, but Guddy kept his back to his guests as he unclogged the instant coffee from the jar.

"Oh yes," said Guddy without inflection.

Guddy remained attentive of the gas stove as the water boiled. Gordon let the silence hang in the air for a minute and casually flicked through a yellowing, mildewy copy of the South Cornwall Chronicle discarded in the cabin window. Guddy was wearing the same clothes he'd been wearing the day before, only with the addition of a pair of fingerless gloves which glistened like glitter as the multi-hued scales caught the blue light of the burner. His whiskery white stubble also glittered. Has he been gnawing raw fish, Gordon wondered?

"How is he?" Guddy said after a minute of silence and also without inflection.

"Rather pre-occupied," Gordon said and Clara readily agreed. "But yesterday he was more hospitable, and we shared a glass of vintage Bordeaux."

"I'm afraid all I can offer is coffee."

Guddy poured for Gordon and Clara. The mugs were tannin-stained like museum teeth, they were rinsed only in the brine but never washed. Guddy's milk had turned to cottage cheese so they drank it black. Gordon cast a rueful glance into his filthy cup and decided if he drank his it meant Clara wouldn't feel compelled to do the same. He took a gulp as though it had been a shot of tequila but when he opened his eyes again he saw Clara sipping her coffee as happily and gracefully as if she'd been at a royal garden party. Gordon sensed Clara was inspired.

"I think she'd like to take some photographs," he said to Guddy.

Guddy looked at Clara, who in turn looked at Gordon as if to scold him.

"Do as you please," said Guddy. "Don't let me stop you but I'll doubt there's little beautiful to see here."

"I just saw the wet nets with the shells and the old wood," she said.

Guddy extended an open palm to show her the way and she rushed out with an eagerness that made the old fisherman smile.

"I've been working on this boat for 30 years and never saw anything I wanted to photograph on it," he said. "But then I suppose I wasn't looking."

Gordon was left alone with Guddy and sensed the opportunity was right to ask about the Colonel. He was still unsure why Guddy had written his name. Gordon asked him directly, but Guddy shrugged and walked heavily to the second chair Clara had vacated, as he passed Gordon could smell drink on him. Guddy was looking past Gordon, wondering about all the jobs, bodges and fixes that needed doing on Mjöllnir. In several places, weathered holes had been plugged by plastic bags and water found its way into the cabin through more than one leak - in stormy seas it was like sailing a teabag Guddy joked as took a great gulp of coffee like a Biblical whale. But Gordon refused to let Guddy derail him and he tried again, even more forthright this time.

"Does Colonel Mortain have anything to do with the beached dolphins?"

This time Guddy returned Gordon's gaze. He looked bemused, but with just the slightest flicker of an emotion behind his cool eyes that Gordon couldn't place. After a minute of silence that Gordon found excruciating, Guddy laughed.

"You're the journalist, Whiting. It's not my job to invent the fantastic. But surely you asked him yourself?"

"I only asked you what you've seen, what you've heard. I don't want you to invent."

"But you didn't," said Guddy firmly. "You asked me what I thought, and the answer is it's none of my business."

Guddy stood, looking vacantly over the ship's wheel, past the middle-distance of the harbour and at the darkening sky; even at anchor Guddy couldn't take his mind off it. It was long years of staring at the clouds, watching the swells, a wet cheek to the wind. The capricious heart of the weather and its temperamental moods were stitched inside Guddy like an extra organ. Guddy would sense a storm before anybody else had even heard an inkling of one on the shipping forecasts and like the cow sitting in the field announcing the onset of rain, the local fishermen used Guddy as their barometer. If he was mending his nets at anchor with a bottle of Brennevin then they didn't set sail. Guddy turned back to face Gordon and startled him with the impulse.

"Now, if you ask me: have I ever seen Mortain naked on the rocks like a lizard, sometimes in the dead of night? I have. And on those nights the sea swelled and those within sought to be without, those were the nights I saw him. Those nights when a man who's sailed these seas for longer than you've lived can't predict the patterns in the swells or understand the currents pulling with magnetic force below the surface. Those nights terrify me. My business is reading the sea and when it is so mysterious, I am terrified. That's why I take to my little boat when I sense the changes. Out alone and silent, listening and looking. That's when I have seen him, naked and weird, arms stretched to the sky or on his knees, flailing or flapping on his back like a fish hauled from the waters, or screaming, even screaming I've heard. He's quite insane you know."

"And have you told anybody about what you saw?"

Guddy shook his head, Gordon didn't understand.

"They say the Mortain's power and wealth was never from the land. What is there? Some sheep to graze, some orchards, the harbour with its little catch? You can't sustain power on this little empire. The Mortain's power has always been their knowledge. There is nothing they haven't known, through favour and through condescension they have a power over everybody in town. If the name of Mortain is ever spoken in the Ship Inn, the room dulls to a murmur, and everybody shifts in their seats without ever declaring the sudden drop in temperature of a once happy room. Everybody is in his debt in one way or another - some deeper than others, too. It's the legacy he bequeathed from his father, and his grandfather and so on."

"But not you? You're not afraid of him? He has nothing on you."

Guddy smiled.

"Whiting, catch up, you're smarter than this. It's wrong to ask if I am afraid or if I'm not. My life ended long ago when my wife Catherine died. That's why Mortain has nothing on me. I ceased to exist. But I never forgave him."

"You're suggesting he was involved in Catherine's death."

"He was."

"He told me not to trust you," said Gordon revealing a sudden intimacy. "He said Catherine was engaged to him."

The Colonel had never mentioned this to Gordon so he was being dishonest with Guddy. It was Max who had told Gordon about the sad history both men shared.

"It's true," said Guddy with a shrug. "There's no secret there. But one fact doesn't change another truth. I'm not one to play tricks.

"Before I knew Catherine, she was close to the Colonel. She was the prize catch in town and he was young, rich and handsome. They shared a passion too, with their myths and folklore and magic.

"He hadn't yet left for the military. It was natural they should join. Catherine was an anthropologist, with all the passion of the student mind. She was comparing fishing folklore around the world, superstitions, rituals and that kind of thing or as she would call it sympathetic magic. Mortain was her patron, he funded her PhD.

"You should have heard her talk, she could tele-transport you around the world in a sentence. One minute you were on the shores of Sumatra, the next sailing on the icy Baltic, then again off the Peruvian coast. She was really quite brilliant. She studied these seas with mad hunger.

"I remember thinking, years later, how strange she should be engaged to Mortain - a man who cannot bring himself to even stand in a boat and who looks at the sea with animal fear. It was Mortain too who paid for her field studies in Iceland, that's where we met. She was studying the wind cult. The fishermen would pay certain old women for

132

the wind, can you believe that? The old women - witches if you're feeling romantic - would set traps for the black-headed guillemots and drain their blood on a sacred stone at the top of the first volcano to see the morning sun. They would throw the dead bird over their shoulder and tie them to a tree facing the direction the fisherman wished the wind to blow. Sometimes you'd find these poor birds with their beaks staked open with a stick. I was never superstitious, but most were. You could pay for clear skies, smooth waters and when the seas were stormy it was a vengeful witch who wished you harm. Quite silly really.

"I think because I didn't believe I found her amusing. I couldn't believe clever people were paid to study nonsense. She couldn't believe clever people would waste a life hauling cod - but we all have our passions.

"Quite unexpectedly, we fell in love. Love, what a thing for a grizzled old cynic like me to be talking about. But it was love and I would have done anything for her.
"I followed her back to England. Of course, she'd told me about her engagement to Mortain before I came - there were no secrets, but we reasoned that none of it mattered. My family thought I was crazy and I left them with great hardship, I suspect. At the time I blocked it from my mind, but I've thought about it a lot since.

"At the time it was difficult for Catherine too and I wanted to support her. She had her family to confront. And Mortain. I can imagine he was very unhappy when she returned home from a trip he'd funded with me on the end of her hook.
"I don't think he believed it at first, or chose not to accept it. Either way, it was the same result, a great black cloud over us and we just sat waiting for it to break. I suppose this is the first time I understood what a man of influence was. Little things became big barriers of bureaucracy. People would not return greetings. She felt it more than I did, of course, because these were her people. Then one night she said she had to leave and she went to Selyvan Hall and told him she wished to marry me. I'm not sure what she'd said to him, but he accepted it and let us be, by and large. Of course, it took a long time for the local people to accept me - with or without Mortain's blessing. But in time they did, and we married at the Methodist chapel as was her family's wish. Her family wasn't rich and had no expectations of wealth and for a few years we were truly happy. The fishes bit, her dissertation was creating interest in those academic circles and I can say life was as good as I've known it.

"She never spoke about the night she went to see Mortain but I could see it was painful to her and she carried it like a burden. Now, I believe, she was in some way indebted to him. I believe this because that is how he works, he sows generously in times of desperation and then reaps at his leisure, and reaps and reaps again. It was never money - she paid him back everything he had loaned for the studies. We struggled penniless for many years, but I hoped it would clear her conscience. But even then, there was still something more.

"There is something dark about Mortain, something that is so hard for me to be precise about. He is everything we're warned about "perfidious Albion", everything we were taught about you English. Charming, but double-headed hydras, buttoned-up and full of politeness but overspilling with dark bile inside. But you understand better than me, right?"

Gordon wasn't sure that he did and guessed it was easier to see from the outside looking in. Gordon knew he'd been charmed and that the Colonel's graces would only extend as long as it profited him, he saw this but never questioned it. To him it felt as natural as buying a loaf of bread and wishing the shopkeeper a good day. Gordon shook his head and Guddy shrugged.

"Be careful, Gordon," Guddy said sternly. "Selyvan will carry on just as it did when you leave. I think the people here would rather that was sooner than later. Get the train to London tomorrow morning. Forget about it here. You could be searching and never find. Just be careful."

Something dropped noisily to the deck outside and Gordon leapt to the window to check Clara was safe. Her tripod had rolled from the side, and she was cursing as she gathered it. Guddy smiled when he saw Gordon's concern.

"You like her, right?"

Gordon shook his head awkwardly and then corrected himself shyly.

"Well of course... as a colleague."

"I never thought I could marry Catherine," said Guddy. "The fish were biting but I'd have needed to land a bass the size of this boat to afford the ring. Back in the early days I would leave her the best of my catch before returning to work. Brain food, she called it. She must have lived off fish soup. One day I caught this big mackerel, it shone in the morning sun and was one of the finest fish I've ever pulled from the sea. I was so proud of it. I dropped it at Catherine's door, she was busy, so I just left it hanging with a little note. When I returned home that evening, she was waiting for me with a big hug and smile. Did you enjoy the fish? I asked, I guessed she must have liked the present. Of course, I will, she said. I was so confused. She told me not to play any more tricks, but my confusion was genuine. As she cut open the fish to make her lunch, inside was the most beautiful emerald ring, shining like a star in the night in that wet belly. How it got there I'll never know, but there it was. We married six weeks later."

Clara came in with her kit banging against the narrow door frame.

"Please could I just get a quick portrait?" she asked Guddy.

He smiled at Gordon and then turned to Clara.

"Why not?" he said. "I'm feeling adventurous today." And he lifted his heavy limbs with both hands and followed Clara out of the cabin.

CHAPTER EIGHTEEN

"I liked Guddy," said Clara as they hurried back to the Cragg. The interview with Professor Burroughs was in 15 minutes and Gordon walked with an urgent stride. He deplored lateness and had a neurotic fear of it in himself. He hadn't had time to plan for the interview as he'd hoped but was confident he could wing it. Clara had reluctantly agreed to photograph the creepy Professor but hadn't forgotten how he'd curdled her blood on the beach the day before.

"Guddy has a rare honesty," said Gordon. "But he knows more than he's letting on. The longer I spend here, the more convinced I am there's a story."

Clara scoffed, she was ready to return to London and Gordon could sense it. He realised then he didn't want to leave, he wanted to stay another day away from town with Clara. He felt a contentment in the chill air with the gentle roll of waves and the brine in his nostrils. He was even prepared to forgive Lychgate and the Cragg - if for one more night away. He resolved then to call Plummers on the weekend desk and see if he could square another night.

The Cragg was empty, as always, but the front door was wide open. Tomasz was red-faced and glistening, resting on a mountain of industrial-sized baked bean tins in the lobby; the armpits of his grey shirt were five shades darker from exertion.

"Afternoon," he said, and leapt to his aching feet.

"Thirsty work," said Gordon and headed through to the bar to wait for Professor Burroughs.

Tomasz failed to understand and supposed Gordon wanted a drink and chased after him to the bar. By the time Gordon had explained his intended meaning twice it was less awkward just to ask for a tonic water and lemon; Clara had a vervain tea.

"Busy day?" Gordon asked.

"Yes, busy day," Tomasz replied.

"But the weather wasn't so cold this morning. Did you get a walk on the beach?"

"No, I don't like to look at the sea," said Tomasz, Gordon puzzled over this but the hissing, steaming tap from the espresso machine that spluttered hot water interrupted his thoughts.

Gordon sat in silence with Clara while they waited for the Professor to arrive. Clara felt particularly uncomfortable and had twice asked Gordon if a headshot was really necessary. It wasn't but Gordon wanted some support. He wasn't relishing the interview any more than she was. When the professor finally arrived, he was 20 minutes late. He breezed into the bar without explanation or apology and pulled up a chair and sat at the same time that Gordon stood to greet his guest. The professor ignored Gordon's handshake and looked annoyed it had even been offered. When he spotted Clara - who had edged herself to the furthest corner of the table - his face dropped for a fraction of a second, but he quickly recovered himself and met her with a sickly smile and his hand, offered with some affectation at the end of a long, limp wrist. Clara gave a curt smile and returned to her camera, she was rejecting and deleting images to save time at the laptop later. There was very little worth keeping and that did not improve her mood at the table.

Gordon made a clumsy start by incorrectly assuming the Professor's field-of-expertise lay in Cetaceans. The professor corrected him bad-temperedly and it gave him the opportunity to suggest the entire interview was likely to be a waste of everybody's time.

"Of course, not without its charms," said the Professor with his eyes lingering for too long on Clara's décolletage.

Gordon was in an unforgiving mood too and made little effort to exercise his own, not inconsiderable, charms. When the Professor chose to answer Gordon's questions he nodded and made little impatient "mmms" when the cadence permitted but he made scant effort to jot down the words and his shorthand degenerated into illegible squiggles and swirls. Whenever Gordon asked about the dolphins beached in Selyvan the Professor deftly parried like a career politician and Gordon wondered how much bluff and bluster masked an academic ignorance. The Professor liked to steer every question to the subject of falling sea temperature and the effect on the microscopic organisms that support the entire food chain. Gordon realised he was going to get nothing of any use from this tedious interview. The Professor saw Gordon's waning interest and took the opportunity to best him.
"Would you like me to repeat that last sentence?" he said. "I spoke quickly and I'm not sure you quite got it all down."

"No, I got it thanks," said Gordon.

"What a language you have," said the Professor peering at Gordon's shorthand nonsense. "I'd be keen to see how interdisciplinary biological oceanography looks like written down in... how is it called?"

"T-line," said Gordon and pointed at one of the last squiggles he'd scrawled.

"Fascinating, really. A system of writing capable not only of matching and recording human speech but even of pre-empting it. Interdisciplinary biological oceanography doesn't exist. I'm wasting my time as I suspected. Gossip and contumely."

The Professor thrust back his chair petulantly but to Gordon's surprise did not leave the bar.

"Where did you want to do the portrait?" he said to Clara. She was as surprised and Gordon and turned to him for an indication if it was still necessary, but he offered no definitive.

"Outside on the balcony, I guess," she said with an uncertainty which robbed her of any authority.

"Lead the way," said the Professor, who extended a gracious arm and followed at ten steps distance, so Clara felt his eyes boring into her behind the whole way. Gordon followed; he'd promised not to leave Clara alone with the Professor. With bold assurance the Professor strode over to the stone balcony with the sea and cliffs as a backdrop and announced it to be the best spot. He waited with impatience and Clara studied the light – ideally, she'd have liked him two feet to the left but was in no mood to extend or complicate the shoot.

"Which is my best side would you say?"

"Just look down the lens please," she said.

Clara fired six or seven shots, took a cursory glance at her LCD screen, nodded vague approval and signalled she was done. The Professor shot Gordon a wicked glare before he bounded over to Clara playfully, eager to see his portrait. He closed behind and stuck a chin over her shoulder and her flesh crept.

"So, let's see the magic," he said, and Clara smelled his sour breath like milk in the sun.

Clara lifted the camera and tried to wriggle herself free, but the Professor kept a magnetic attraction to her. He reached around and pressed the magnification button on the camera and admired himself.

"What do you think?" he said, and once again she winced at his breath.

"It's OK, sharp enough."

"I didn't mean technically, I meant of the subject."

Gordon had been wrestling whether he ought to rescue Clara while this was happening. She wouldn't like him to presume and she hadn't asked him to, on the other hand she might ask him later why he'd allowed it to happen. He was torn but this was the final straw and he took a decisive step forward and was just forming the word "Enough" when Clara herself was struck with a sudden repulsion and she leapt free as though she'd been pricked by some burning needle. She spun and faced the Professor with a combative look in her eyes, Gordon took a step back - he could see she didn't need rescuing.

"Gordon, I know what you forgot to ask the Professor," she said turning to him.

"What?" Gordon was puzzled.

"What would you like to know?" said the Professor performing a bow of mock courtesy but then with a sick smile added, "My vital statistics."

"Why did you put the red shoe in your pocket yesterday on the beach?"

"What shoe?"

"The red high-heeled shoe on the beach, I think you'll remember, it was the only one."

"Did I? Well, how absent-minded of me," said the Professor wobbling like a boxer in the tenth round, but maintaining his composure and relaxed smile. "I'm certain it's nothing."

"It's just the Police found that body wearing one red high-heeled shoe. It's rather a coincidence and the more I think about it the more I wonder if I shouldn't say something."

"It's not our habit in Cornwall to leave litter on our beautiful beaches - these aren't the streets of London."

"So where's the shoe?"

"In a bin most probably. If you want to waste the Police's precious time, go ahead and call. We can start a county-wide bin search immediately."

Clara said nothing more but maintained the Professor's sneering gaze for so long that, for the first time, he turned away.

"Well, I've got to go and file," said Clara. "Goodbye."

After Clara had gone the Professor was keen to leave also. He was more civil than usual to Gordon and asked if he had everything he needed. Gordon noticed his right hand was trembling as he fastened the buttons on his trench coat with some difficulty. The Professor walked with long strides as he left the Cragg and ignored Lychgate at reception who wished him a good day.

Gordon went back to the room. He had planned to go to see Clara to digest the interview with the Professor but had a sudden crisis of self-confidence. He worried if the mixture of the warm bar and the cold air had given him a red and runny nose. He wanted a mirror and some solitude to give himself a quick once over. At these times Gordon couldn't help feeling awkward in Clara's company. Mostly he was confident and strident but occasionally she seemed so otherworldly he felt debased. Clara's eyes had tightened and twinkled when she confronted the Professor and her pale skin had flushed such a pastel rose, Gordon had never seen anything so beautiful. Even as he hurried along the dim and ugly corridors of the Cragg he wrestled to recall this vision, which was already fading from distinction into impression.

But Gordon was snapped from dreaming to discover his room door ajar. He called to David as he entered and tapped a firm and precautionary warning knock, the sort necessary when sharing a room with a teenage boy too long in bedroom pent; but the room was empty. Gordon noticed the bathroom door was fastened. Again, Gordon gave a warning knock, just in case an unwitting David strolled robeless and dripping from a shower. There was no reply and Gordon pressed an ear to the door but only heard silence. Delicately he edged the door open, the light was off and the bathroom was quite empty. David was missing, the realisation grounded Gordon. David was missing and Gordon was responsible.

His first logical action, after a moment of flustered panic, was to call David's mobile but this went straight to answerphone. This heightened Gordon's panic once again and so it was another minute before he carried out his second logical action, to find Clara. Gordon rushed back down the corridor to her room and knocked four times on her door, the international language of panic. Clara muttered from behind the door. 'Hang on,' she'd said. 'Come in,' Gordon heard, and he did. Clara screamed and span away as Gordon entered. He faced her bare back with her hands poking like prisoners in the stocks from the sleeves of her jumper, halfway over her neck. Gordon had seen the briefest flash of her bra as she'd spun to safety but at that moment all thoughts were overcome with mortal embarrassment. He closed the door behind him, uttering a thousand apologies as he fastened it. He stood in the solitary darkness of the corridor cursing himself but even before Clara had opened the door a minute later he had already reimagined the arch of her white back and the contours that spread softly into her hips.

"What the fuck?" said Clara. "Don't you knock?"

"I did."

"No, knocking like a nutter and then barging straight in does not count as knocking. It's the same as barging straight in with the added spice of making me shit myself at the same time."

Clara's tongue was barbed. She felt humiliated. She felt embarrassed herself. She believed Gordon had seen more than he had. She was wearing her cheap bra, the bra she wore at work. It didn't match her knickers. God, she suddenly thought, had he seen those too? They rode high over her skinny jeans. He must have seen them, she reasoned.

"Well, what is it?"

Gordon apologised again and then told her David was missing. At first Clara was relaxed and failed to share Gordon's alarm. Call his mobile, was her first suggestion. Gordon confirmed he wasn't an idiot.

"You could fool me," said Clara. "Well perhaps he's gone for a walk along the cliffs then?"

No sooner had the words left Clara's mouth than the vision had formed in her head. It started with a teeter, the dramatic arc was a topple and it ended like a government information film with a pair of broken glasses lying on the jagged rocks for a moment, before a silent wave sweeps with a foaming caress and they're lost forever.

"Ok, let me get my boots back on," she said. "We'll go and find him."

Clara now shared Gordon's sense of panic and in her haste laced all the wrong eyes in her Dr Marten's, cursing as she fumbled with the knot. In frustration she gave up and left with Gordon, her loose boots flopping clumsily like first day at big school.

Lychgate was still at the reception desk when Clara and Gordon headed out. They asked if he had seen David but received such a pained expression borne of the utmost inconvenience that they decided to cut short his impending ire and leave. Gordon felt he should follow the script and suggested they split up but was glad when Clara rejected the idea. Instead, they trudged the lonely precipitous path away from town as the waves battered hundreds of feet below. When Gordon thought Clara wasn't looking, he cast a surreptitious glance down at the deadly rocks. Once or twice, he mistook a piece of flotsam for David's ragged, sea-battered corpse. Clara spotted Gordon and joined him in an unspoken and insidious mutual paranoia.

It was half in relief and half in horror when Clara spotted a bedraggled figure on the horizon, stumbling animalistically like a fatally wounded soldier returning from some ill-considered raid.

"What the hell is that?" Gordon asked.

"David?"

The figure neared and in the fading light Gordon recognised his unwanted charge. David was sopping wet, and his baggy suit stuck to his limbs and exaggerated his skinny frame; like the shaggy dog fresh from the pond. David's body swung heavily from side-to-side but, all the while, his head stared straight ahead, bobbing slightly in fatigue. In his hand he clung onto his camera. His glasses were bent and fell to the left leaving his right eye uncovered and it appeared half the size of its magnified twin. David's vacant expression changed when he recognised Gordon and Clara and his stagger quickened, nearly causing him to lose balance. Gordon decided to quicken his own pace but didn't want to appear too dramatic. Clara had no such qualms and ran to David.

"What happened?"

"I found a sea cave," said David breezily, belying his pitiful state. "It was amazing. I'll show you."

"Not now, I don't think," said Clara in a motherly tone. "You're soaked to the skin."

"I fell in the sea," said David.

Gordon arrived shaking his head but relieved. Being sacked for upsetting Croaker was one thing; being sacked for killing the Chief Executive's only son was quite another. This is how Gordon cynically explained the relief to himself, and later to Clara, but against his better judgment he had begun to feel a fraternal bond, reminiscent of his boarding house days when even the most odious little toad in the bunk beside you became a brother of sorts.

"Let's get you back to the hotel, I don't know what you were thinking running off?"

"I didn't run off," David said, holding his camera aloft in evidence. "I was taking photos of the cave. Can I show you?"

"Not now," said Gordon, who had to feign a gruff voice through his relief. "I don't want to hear anything more about this bloody cave."

CHAPTER NINETEEN

Back at the hotel, the inquisition began in earnest. Gordon was failing to impress on David the sense of responsibility he felt for his welfare, and the dire consequences any misfortune might have to his own stuttering career. David, in his defence, was quite deaf to Gordon's appeals and smiling contentedly and steaming as Clara blasted him with her hairdryer. He occasionally released puppy yelps of pain if the dryer remained static for a fraction too long.

David needed constant mothering and would have happily remained in his clinging, wet suit had it not been for Clara's insistence. Instead, he was dressed in his tartan pyjamas with his soggy suit slumped over the chair by the radiator. Clara was having to discover a nature for nurture she'd never previously experienced, it was nascent but not entirely unwelcome. She remained firm but friendly with David, this was in stark contrast to Gordon's fractiousness. While Clara got on with the practical task of drying David, Gordon paced the room maddeningly. Clara shot him little glances of annoyance - which he missed - until eventually she was driven to switch off the hairdryer and warn him to desist or decamp.

"Why couldn't you have just stayed in your room and played your bloody game?" said Gordon eventually.

"Molitor's dead," said David with the sudden sombreness of an old man reflecting on his carefree youth. "And my phone fell in the sea and now it doesn't work."

Gordon considered whether he could be held accountable for David's broken phone. His father might start asking how it got broken. What he was doing in a sea cave on his own. Where was the responsible adult? Gordon dipped a toe in the water.

"What will your father say about your phone?"
"Nothing," said David breezily. "I'll just get a new one. It happens a lot."

David fished through his soggy jacket pocket and retrieved his camouflage print wallet and from within revealed an American Express card with Associated News written across the name strip.

"He said to put anything I need on this."

Gordon choked on a dry cough and his eyes bulged at the sight. It was as if David had casually retrieved the Holy Grail from the depths of his suitcase.

"How long have you had that?" said Clara, as Gordon regained composure.

"Since I left, Dad says expenses are there to be used but not abused."

Gordon looked at Clara, suddenly reinvigorated with a journalist's natural instinct for the blag and the freebie. Clara had the same look in her eyes. If anything, photographers had an even more finely honed blag radar.

"I'm rather tired of Selyvan," said Gordon merrily. "I think we should get a cab into Penzance and treat ourselves. Poor David's had a shock and a cold, what he needs is a chicken madras, a bowl of pilau rice and a garlic naan. It's good for what ails you."

Clara   smiled.

"That's if we can get a cab to rescue us," she said.

Gordon snatched the card from David's fingers and held it aloft with a dramatic flair.

"Then we shall pay them double."

Even offering a double fare was not enough to convince the first three numbers he tried from the Yellow Pages. He was told abruptly and without apology that no driver would come out "all that way" on a Sunday evening. Eventually a firm towards the bottom of the list accepted. Gordon couldn't help detecting a note of hesitation from the operator when he gave his address as the Cragg Hotel. Gordon asked when to expect the taxi and was told the driver would leave immediately and be with them in forty minutes. Gordon was surprised it would take so long to arrive.

"Well, he's not going to take the old drover's road," she said. "Not at night with a storm closing in. He'll have to loop around and return with the coast road."

Once Clara had finished drying David, so he was fluffy and frizzy like a groomed parlour pooch, they had another problem to contend with. David had failed to pack a change of clothes, only his suit and his tartan pyjamas. Clara hectored Gordon into loaning him a jacket but there was no way a pair of trousers fitted for Gordon's long legs could ever fit David. Instead, Clara had to call once more on the over-worked hairdryer and give his soggy suit bottoms an airing, the legs of the light cotton billowed like an airport windsock.

After twenty minutes of arm-achingly tedious drying, David squelched back into his trousers as Gordon and Clara turned to the wall for modesty. "A bit damp when I sit down," was David's verdict and all the thanks Clara received for her efforts. She rushed back to her room to change, and Gordon sat sipping a cup of weak black tea. He'd run out of complimentary tea bags that morning and was recycling an older bag. David had quickly become engrossed in a film on the flickering television about a talking dog with burgeoning career as a rap artist, and so it was with some crowbarring that Gordon had to convince him to leave. In the end, Gordon was forced to pull the plug from the wall. When David eventually lifted himself off the bed with a sigh of resignation he left a dark, wet shadow on the white sheets where he'd been reclining.

"Come along wet arse or we'll miss the last chopper out of Saigon."

Gordon, Clara and David arrived five minutes early, but they found the cab driver already waiting and with his engine running. The doors of his taxi were locked. The driver failed to notice his passengers, instead he kept both eyes fixed on his rear-view mirror. The doors were locked and Gordon had to knock on the driver's window. It was a gentle rap but the driver almost leapt into the passenger's seat in shock. Ruffled and without courtesy the driver unlocked the four doors as his heart attempted to recover its broken stride.

Even with his passengers boarded the driver's mood did not improve. He had the clammy fidgetiness of 40-a-day man on long haul to Bangkok. Gordon supposed it must be his last job of the day because he refused to entertain small talk and pulled away so impatiently Clara had yet to locate, let alone fasten, her belt. However, his mood improved as they chugged laboriously in second gear up the steep coast road from Selyvan and all the more so when the last lights of town had disappeared behind the crest. So, by the time they passed the 'Welcome to Penzance' sign the driver was merrily bestowing the merits and vices of the four Indian restaurants in town. Two he could "rule out for starters"; the first on account of its miserly consideration for complementary poppadoms and the second because it had given his wife a bout of food poisoning so violent he refused to rule out the possibility of canid meat. He favoured the Bombay Brasserie from the remaining brace, chiefly on account of its all-you-can-eat buffet, now serving every night of the week. When friends from Solihull came to stay for the week they had dined there three out of the five nights. It was enough evidence for Gordon to opt for the Punjab Palace - slightly to the driver's chagrin.

As they entered the empty restaurant the manager, who had been sipping whisky on a far table, leapt to attention and greeted his diners warmly. After the hospitality they had become accustomed to at the Cragg it was a breath of fresh, but boozy, air. With no little ceremony the manager directed them to the best table in the house. It was hard to distinguish it from the other tables in the house and sat rather too central for Gordon's personal preference, but he accepted. The manager had literary pretensions and took great pleasure in discovering Gordon was a writer by profession. Throughout the course of the evening, he threw him little scraps of Kipling, always shooting a ready eye in Gordon's direction waiting for a nod of mutual recognition. The frequency of his recitations was in direct correlation with whisky consumption, which he continued to sip in stolen, surreptitious trips below the counter at the bar. The manager, with an earnestness that touched Clara, informed them his wife was the best cook in the entire world and they would not regret their decision to dine.

With two greedy eyes scouring the extensive menu Gordon's appetite had conquered his rational mind. He ordered impulsively and with a gluttony he repressed well but that overcame him when tiredness and a company credit card were his will's opponents. David was not overawed by Gordon's Bacchanalian menu and added an extra two garlic naans for himself. Clara was content with a lamb balti and a glass of house white, which she declared passable and - by the third glass - actually surprisingly good for a Bulgarian. The meal arrived on a silver trolley, and it didn't take Gordon long to realise how misguided he'd been. So ambitious was his appetite that the manager was forced to drag over a second table to accommodate the steaming plates, breads and booze.

"At least we're not paying," said Gordon, once the manager had retired for another crafty chug.

Clara was in good spirits and had settled upon the idea of getting David a pint of lager. Gordon instinctively recognised this was a bad idea, particularly since David had not expressed any desire to drink. However, once the proposal had been aired David struck upon it with a determination he'd previously reserved for fantasy role-play. Asserting his new-found authority, he countered Gordon's reservations with the awkward and unavoidable truth that the entire meal was going on the credit card belonging to his father; the threat was veiled but as subtle as a bludgeoning. Clara clapped in delight when Gordon accepted the idea of "just a half" but when the manager arrived the order twisted itself into a bottle, and when the bottle arrived it was export strength and 500ml. Gordon shot Clara a look of warning, but she was already well into her third wine and enjoying the prospect of David's first drink. "You've drunk before?" Gordon said sternly.

"Of course," said David. "Three times. Once at my father's 50th, the other time in Venice when the waiter made a mistake and one time, I drank three beers at a barbecue and was sick in the swimming pool so we had to drain it."

"You see," said Gordon, turning to Clara. "This is on your head."

"Yeah, yeah, yeah," she said.

They made a valiant attempt at the feast, flying out of the blocks with great bites into the moist naan and liberal scoops of the rich gravies, applied over white mounds of fluffy rice. But after the initial pangs of hunger were satisfied the manager's promises of the best cooking in all of India were losing credibility. Although the six different dishes varied in hue, from brick red to a creamy orange, they had a consistency of flavour that suggested a shared parentage. What was more, the parent gravy was insipid and heavily reliant on sunflower oil and onion. With less than a quarter of the meal demolished, the three had to concede defeat and watch guiltily as the manager cleared the heavy plates. He suggested bagging the leftovers but all three returned a no with such synchronicity that the wound would have been fatal to a sober sensibility. Fortunately, the manager was too wobbly from the whisky to take offence.

As the loaded silver trolley creaked sadly back to the kitchen, Clara began partitioning the table into three and inspecting the white cloth, she tutted and sucked her teeth as she did so.

"So, you've lost the Mess Olympics," she said to Gordon.

"What?"

"Look," she said and counted three orange oil stains, a white blob of raita, a dozen grain of basmati and a scattering of naan crumbs. "I win of course."

Gordon deftly flicked a few grains of rice from David's sector across the demilitarised zone and onto Clara's previously impeccable cloth. Clara glared at him and attempted a return flick but misjudged her power and aim and sent it flying diagonally across the restaurant where it stuck against the red velvet curtains. Clara looked mortified for a moment but was soon laughing. Gordon silenced her with a subtle shake of the head.

"What is it?" she said.

"The manager saw," he whispered. "He looks angry."

"No, he didn't." said Clara, her face whitening and looking for assurance.

"He's coming over, just apologise."

Clara looked appealingly at Gordon for support, but he shook his head. She straightened and turned to face the manager, who was half dozing in the corner after the exertion of his single table of customers and half a bottle of Johnnie Walker.

"Bastard," she said and turned to David, who always rose with a smile when attention came his way. "I'd like you to report Gordon Athelney to your father. I'd like you to witness the level of unprofessionalism he has reduced this great agency to. Where once was truth, now there is only mendacity. And instead of doing interviews and whatever it is journalists are supposed to do, he's squandering company money on lavish suppers and cheap wine."

"If I'm going down," said Gordon, also addressing David, "I'm taking her with me. David, I'd like you to make an official statement on the conduct of the Associated News' most junior photographer. Well, I say photographer, but I can't seem to remember her taking many photographs, certainly relative to the number of drinks she's consumed at the expense of this illustrious news organisation."

"Really?" said David, looking from Gordon to Clara to work out if there was a joke, and if so, who was it on.

"Yes really," said Clara. "Although the tribunals can probably save their time since we're both getting sacked this week anyway."

"You are?" said David with sudden pain.

"We're storytellers," said Gordon. "Where's the story? We've produced nothing. There's nothing here, there never was. It was a wild-goose chase."

"But what about the cave I found," said David.

"A cave isn't really front-page news I'm afraid."

"But there were things in it."

"What?" said Gordon with more snap than he'd intended. "A hundred dead dolphins? Elvis' ghost?"

"No, other things. I've got photos."

Gordon smiled but without interest and his attention turned to Clara.

"Shall I ask for the bill?"

She nodded. David rummaged into his trouser pockets and pulled out his compact camera.

"Look," he said showing it to Clara.

"Do you think I should leave him a tip?" said Gordon.

"Did you take this?" said Clara and David nodded proudly. Clara said nothing more and continued cycling through his images from the cave.

Gordon gave the manager the company credit card and watched in frustration as the manager fumbled with the card reader, twice cancelling the transaction. When Gordon was eventually handed the receipt he had to point out he'd been charged £9.40 for dinner and not the £94 on the bill. This caused considerable confusion as the manager wrestled first with comprehension of the problem and then with the subtraction required to rectify it. By the time Gordon had successfully completed payment, and left a £10 tip against his better judgement, he found Clara quite engrossed with David.

"You should see these," she said to Gordon handing him David's camera. "He's a snapper in the making."

"They're black and white," said Gordon.

"Obviously. He's experimenting with high-contrast tones and the low light noise."

David didn't have the heart to say he'd chosen Covert Ops mode on his camera. Gordon cycled through the images and was impressed despite his unwillingness to acknowledge any talent. He carefully examined the bottles on the shelves cut into the cave walls but even more carefully the graffiti hewn in the wall beneath. The photograph was low resolution and the lack of light made it difficult to read but Gordon believed he could make out the same cuneiform he'd seen on the Colonel's tablet.

"David, this writing, did you recognise it?"

David shook his head and confessed he hadn't noticed it specifically, aside from looking like the writing in his game. Gordon sat thinking for so long that Clara eventually shook him out of his brooding.

"Come on, it's nearly eleven - we should phone the cab company before we're stranded again."

But there was a problem. The woman who'd taken their call earlier that evening was no longer working, instead the phone was answered by a man with a thick and gruff Cornish accent. He informed Clara in no uncertain terms that there's no way Margaret would have agreed to a cab back to Selyvan at eleven on a Sunday night and even if she had it didn't matter because he wasn't going to drive out there even for triple fare. Clara prickled, outraged and helpless. She had considered offering him four times the fare but instead chose to ask if he could recommend a more professional taxi service in Penzance. The man laughed, apologised, and hung up. Gordon volunteered to make a conciliatory call back and try to reach a compromise, but the line just rang and rang. The manager was starting to nod off in the corner of the restaurant and from the depths of the kitchen they heard the loud crash of pans being thrown into the dishwasher. With the slow and patchy connection Clara managed to find the numbers of three other firms, the first declined without explanation and the other two rang for minutes without response.

"What are we going to do?" said Clara, nodding at David who had fallen asleep in his chair - exhausted from a day's adventure, a bellyful of Balti and a pint of Indian lager.

"There might be a firm on the high-street," said Gordon. "Or we could try our luck at the station if we wave some notes."

They roused David and thanked the snoozy manager, who murmured a goodbye with half-closed eyes. Outside, the temperature had dropped and the wind had strengthened, it was obvious even to the three city folk a storm was blowing in. Already the fine spray from the sea was suspended in the biting wind and Clara tied her scarf tight around her head. They were out of luck on the high street, the only cab firm they found was closed for the night. They fared no better at the station, the rank was empty and with no more trains expected in that night there was little hope the situation might change.

"What now?"

Gordon shrugged. He was generally optimistic and typically phlegmatic in adversity.

"Well, we've got the company credit card," he said. "Worst comes to the worst we'll just check into the Travel Inn over the road."

Clara looked troubled and Gordon couldn't fail to spot it.

"It's just I've got some medication I need to take," she said with reluctance. "It's at the Cragg."

Gordon didn't ask any more but understood Clara would not have mentioned it if it was not important. He nodded in silent thought but was interrupted by a gust of wind so icy and severe it took his breath away and made Clara scream.

A car pulled up on the pavement beside them.

"What does he want?" said Gordon impatiently.

"It's a taxi," said Clara.

The driver wound down the passenger's window with slow, steady turns.

"Are you chaps looking for a lift?" he said in a gentle Scouse accent.

Gordon and Clara looked at one another with mild suspicion. A generation of stranger danger had embedded itself in their subconsciousness.

"I'm about to knock off for the night so speak now or forever hold your peace," said the driver and chuckled.

"Will you take us to Selyvan?" said Clara.

"Sure, gal, why not? Hop in."

Clara was inside the taxi and rubbing her hands warm on the hot air of the car's fan before Gordon could even hesitate caution. He jumped in the back with David and the driver pulled slowly away.

CHAPTER TWENTY

Gordon sat in the back of the taxi with a feeling of uneasiness. There was nothing overtly sinister in the driver's manner, but the cumulative cup of creepiness was brimmed to overflowing. David, on the other hand, drifted in and out of sleep without a moment's disquiet and at increasingly annoying intervals his head slumped against Gordon's shoulder before righting itself in an instant of confusion. Clara too, riding shotgun, was perfectly relaxed and made breezy conversation with the driver who was as responsive as the earlier driver had been intractable.

The driver was a thin man with long, skinny frog-like fingers that turned the wheel and shifted gears with a true artist's delicacy. His face was gaunt, which only served to exacerbate his sandy eyebrows, which crept like wild ivy towards a straggly head of hair. The man wore a faded denim shirt and even more faded jeans which, if he'd been standing, would have revealed a smooth sheen around the buttocks from years of sitting. His Liverpudlian accent was soft but incongruous. Early in his conversation with Clara, he'd hinted at his father's background in military service and a transitory childhood spent between bases. Once he'd lived in Germany, near Hamburg, they learned. For reasons less satisfactorily explained, he'd settled as a young man in Penzance, never left and he had driven a taxi ever since. He spoke with a piped musicality and turned - when the road conditions on the dark and stormy night permitted - to face his passengers with a gentle movement of his long head on his long neck with the grace of the giraffe stretching to the boughs.

"Call me Kevin," he said, and Clara did.

Kevin took the direct route to Selyvan using the old drover's road. He was oblivious to the potholes and ruts and rode the shocks as if his entire body was one great spring. In the back, Gordon was thrown from his seat on several occasions as the suspension bottomed out with unnerving crunches. David too bounced and rattled but never once woke. Kevin was indifferent to his rear passengers' discomfort and far too engrossed in his conversation with Clara to notice.

"So, you must see some things in this job," said Clara.

The driver turned to her with an impulse, as though he'd been waiting for her to ask him that very question from the moment she took her seat in his cab. He answered with a promptness of a clairvoyant.

"Well, it's mostly humdrum," he said with a bard's flourish. "But this one time..."

Kevin stretched back a little in his seat and Clara, in a subconscious equilibrium, leaned forward in her own to listen.

"I'd just finished an airport run and was driving home. It must have been about four in the morning and I knew I'd wake my wife if I came crashing and banging through the front door. Besides, I was wide awake from all the coffee I'd been drinking so I thought I'd pull in by Tredegarrah Craggs and watch the morning sun come up over the sea. I always keep a few Penguins and bananas in the car so I figured I could have a happy, little picnic at dawn.

Very delicious it was too, but I don't like to leave the banana skins in the car on account of the smell - some passengers have the noses of a bloodhound and it's on account of this that I never eat onions.

I know the skins will biodegrade and fertilise the soil and what have you but all the same I can never quite bring myself to toss them from the window and so I trotted over to the bin. I remember it was a chilly morning and I'd left my jacket in the cab, but then I hadn't expected to be out for long. I say "expected" because it was some time before I got back in the car.

Well, here you have it. Over by the bin something caught my eye, rising from the sea I saw a great, dark shape. It was so enormous that I admit a fear came over me and all sorts of strange things entered my mind."

Gordon - who until that point had been irritable and tossed in the back - suddenly leaned forward, ears pricked, to listen to the driver's story. At the same time a dull wave of horror passed through him like the cool pump of anaesthetic that paralyses muscles before an operation.

"Of course, I can laugh about it now," Kevin said. "But my first thought was of a sea monster. I probably sound crackers, right? Well in the cold light of day I'd dare say so. But alone in the half-light of dawn it's a different story. Your eyes see it and your brain does the rest."

Kevin chuckled to himself at the absurdity of his recollections, but Gordon was impatient and, losing control, interrupted.

"So, what was it?"

Kevin turned slowly in his seat and gave Gordon a half-smile, he was delighted to discover a new and unexpected member in his audience.

155

"Well, this black object rose up out of the sea, maybe half a mile from Selyvan harbour. My eyes were better then, and the early morning sun lined the silhouette in silver. I could see it was a submarine."

"A submarine?" said Clara in subtle mocking, detected by Gordon but fuelling Kevin's narrative.

"Oh yes, a great submarine, like the sort you'd see in images of the Cold War. I knew it was military, but I suppose what other type of submarine is there?

"Out of a hatch, three men appeared. I could see them fishing around and working busily at something. They were putting together a rubber dingy and had fitted it with an outboard motor. I tell you, when they fired that thing up it buzzed and howled like all hell had been kicked in the gonads. I thought it would wake the whole town. Well, I watched this dingy skip across the waves like a dolphin and I was very impressed by its speed. I can't say I envied them the cold sea.

"I was so fascinated by this little boat that I admit I hadn't paid a blind bit of notice to where it was heading. Only when it arrived in Selyvan cove - just half a mile from the harbour - did I think anything of it. It was difficult to see because the Craggs look down from the east and the view in August is obscured by the leaves on the trees. Anyway, I had to stand right on the cliff's edge to keep them in sight, and even then on my tiptoes. I saw the men from the dingy hop out and drag their little boat to the shore. Somebody was waiting for them. I couldn't see where they'd come from because the cliffs are steep backed, but there they were all the same. Now it wasn't a long rendezvous because, within seconds, the men were dragging their boat back out of the shallows and racing back to the submarine. No sooner had they hauled their boat back on board than it sank beneath the waves as though it didn't want to be spied a minute longer. I never saw it again.

"I looked back to the shore to see if I could see the person that they'd met but it was deserted. It was only later it occurred to me that perhaps they were picking somebody up. I wished I'd counted the heads more precisely because then I could be sure. You know with these things it's all so sudden and unexpected your brain doesn't always think it through rationally. It's only later when you start turning it over that you realise just how curious it all had been."

"And did you ever report it?" said Gordon.

"I did indeed. At that time. I was learning to sail and part of the Penzance Sailing Club. We used to have drinks every Thursday evening - a boisterous little crowd we were, and never far from mickey taking. Well, I suppose it was the wrong venue to raise the subject, but I happened to mention it to the club captain; he's the harbour master over in Penzance so I thought the story might amuse him. I don't think he took me very seriously and I got a fair ribbing about drink-driving and seeing an optician. You know, when I went to sleep that night, I'd half convinced myself perhaps I'd dreamt the whole thing.

"Perhaps I'd have thought nothing more of it, but the next morning the club captain phones me up with nothing but gravity in his voice. He asked me if I'd remember what the submarine looked like and I said I wasn't sure. He said he had some photographs and would I come to look at them. Of course I would.

"And you know what? The moment I saw his pictures I recognised it immediately and pointed it out like I was fingering the thief in an identity parade. I remember, it was as if he'd second guessed me, and he snapped the book closed like a crocodile's jaws; I nearly lost a finger.

"He said it was an American nuclear submarine and he was almost purring like a cat with cream. You see, he was due a share in harbour duties for the landing and with a vessel that size I think he'd estimated all his Christmases had come at once and he was already spending the cash. Bold he was too. He went straight to the US Navy and claimed his harbour fees."

"And they paid?"

Kevin laughed.

"No chance. Denied all knowledge. He didn't have a leg to stand on, they just dismissed him like a horse swats a summer fly. Now that I think on, it wasn't far from here that I'd seen it."

Kevin pointed out through the passenger window and Gordon and Clara turned to look, half expecting to see a submarine in the bay. Instead, they saw the navy-blue storm sky with its wind-whipped clouds black against the rising moon. Where the little light caught the ocean, great waves were unfurling and thrashing and the churned foam was caught and tossed in their grasping throes. With Kevin's story completed a silence entered the taxi, the first since he'd pulled away from Penzance. The wind howled and snarled around the car's contours and in the bouncing beam of the headlights Gordon saw twisted, back-broken trees forced to stand the gale for long years and he pitied them. Suddenly, like the sticks of a military drummer, rain beat against the car's shell and the potholes filled, spilled over flooded the road in moments. Everybody in the vehicle cast a nervous eye at one another.

"I'm glad this is my last job of the evening," said Kevin, breaking the tension.

By the time they reached Selyvan the storm had broken with its full force. Water gushed down the steep central street into town and down to the harbour. As he stepped from the taxi Gordon's brogues created dams which the volume of eddying rainwater spilled over, soaking the leather through to the socks. Gordon cast a rueful glance down, but the ferocity of the storm didn't permit a more sustained period of mourning. Kevin had parked as close to the hotel as possible and even offered to accompany them to the door since not one member of their hapless party had thought to pack an umbrella; and Kevin always kept one handy in the boot. Clara declined his chivalry on compassionate grounds, the gale would have torn the umbrella's limbs asunder.

The three ran in a pathetic half-stagger to the unlikely sanctuary of the Cragg. The rain had plastered Gordon's trousers to his thighs which restricted his stride and deprived him of a more graceful gait. Clara ran blind with her leather jacket hoisted over her head. The jacket had more than proven its practical shortcomings and unsuitability for a stormy winter weekend in Cornwall. David was the least distressed by the weather's violence and, without the impatient encouragement of his senior partners, would have preferred a more leisurely pace, allowing ample time for counting the gaps between the deafening thunder and lightning and watching how the rain ran like fire hoses from the outmatched guttering of the Cragg. It was David who turned, before diving like the others through the Cragg's great portal, for a final look at the turbulent sea. It was David who spotted a figure, robed like a monk and with a great hood that flapped furiously in the gale, taking the rocky path he'd taken himself to discover the mysterious cave.

"Look at that man," said David, calling to Gordon.

Whether the wind carried David's voice with unnatural speed, or the robed figure had an even more preternatural sense that he was being spoken about, he turned just as Gordon did the same. For a moment both men, at a distance of over 100 metres and through the midst of the lashing rain, faced one another. Despite the distance and despite the elements Gordon knew instantly who he saw. It was Colonel Mortain. The Colonel's face despite the distance, or perhaps exacerbated by it, had a wild and pale look to it and Gordon felt dread. Without acknowledgement and displaying no outward reaction, the Colonel turned with an avian swoop that shook wide his cloak and stooped his head to face the storm and marched away.

"That was the Colonel," said Gordon.

Clara was uninterested and was already within the Cragg's shelter, holding the door open and encouraging Gordon to hurry inside. She dismissed the idea and threatened to leave if he didn't hurry in.

"Let's chase him," said David.

The sight of the Colonel had frozen Gordon like an old lap-top but David's suggestion struck him with a sudden inspiration. 'Of course,' he thought. 'It's obvious, let's chase him.'

"I'm going to follow the Colonel," said Gordon to Clara who pulled a face of great pain, already aware there was nothing she could say to make him change his mind.

"I want you to fetch your camera but stay with David, he knows the way to his cave. I'm certain that's where he's heading. Meet me there."
"Are you drunk? This is crazy," said Clara. "I'm going to bed... and so is David. And so are you."

But Gordon didn't hear her protests, he ran off in the direction of the Colonel. His leather-soled shoes slipping on the mud and wet stones, the wind inflating his suit and his eyes stinging from the pellets of rain. Gordon didn't notice these discomforts; the drink and a long-dormant determination drove him forward. Something important was happening, Gordon felt it with a clarity as though it was the defining moment in his life. Something was happening and it gave strength to his stride and breath to his raw, chilled lungs.

CHAPTER TWENTY ONE

Gordon stood breathless at the top of the path. He had charged like an assault to its summit, determined not to lose sight of the Colonel, whose black robes made the task even more difficult. But there was no sign. Gordon strained his eyes through the biting elements, forcing them wider open as the rain stung them closed again. Away from town, away from the lights of the Cragg, the world darkened. The storm clouds obscured any little moonlight, and the perilous path was no longer visible. Gordon could navigate only by the dark forms of the cliff and the lighter, thrashing water below. The wind howled so wild he could no longer hear the ocean's tumult. The wind howled with a madness Gordon couldn't escape, no matter where he turned his head.

But there was no trace of the Colonel and Gordon was alone on the cliffs, exposed and hopeless. He stumbled on for another minute before turning back. David and Clara would arrive soon, Gordon thought. David might remember the path he had taken down to the cave, because Gordon was certain that was where the Colonel was heading. But waiting for David was logical and instead Gordon was thinking frantically. He retraced his steps and discovered a narrow path that ran steeply down the cliff wall. Half on his bottom and hands, Gordon fumbled a way down. He was still aware of the dangers he faced but was compelled to continue. He hoped Clara would not follow him, he told himself she would not, he promised himself she was too sensible to attempt this. He wondered if he should return the way he had come and tell her not to follow him. Clara wouldn't let David do this, Gordon reasoned. There was no way Clara would attempt it, he convinced himself.

The first descent was steep and on several occasions, Gordon had to perform a controlled slide using his outstretched fingers as weak brakes and all the while feeling for roots and rocks in case an anchor was required. Sometimes the rocks broke loose and Gordon's heart skipped a beat as he slid momentarily out of control. The steep path plateaued and hugged close to the cliff wall, about halfway down its face. Gordon walked carefully with both hands groping the rock face with flat palms.

Gordon had set off in such wild pursuit he hadn't stopped to ask himself what to do if he finally faced the Colonel. Now, alone in the dark on the very edge of England, he began to wonder. Firstly, the distance at which he'd seen the Colonel was extreme. Gordon supposed perhaps he had made a mistake, he asked himself why he'd been so certain the man he sought was indeed the man he saw. Secondly, the circumstances in which they might meet could hardly be described as everyday. It was one thing knocking on a man's door, but quite another to surprise them on a stormy night in a remote and wild location. It was quite possible, whatever the Colonel's reasons for being out late and alone, he would prefer to keep them secret and would not welcome intrusion. Finally, Gordon wondered about the strange clothing. He saw the robed figure only fleetingly but there was something weirdly esoteric about the attire. If it was the Colonel, then why was he wearing such a cloistral cut of cloth? Gordon's mind stirred these thoughts like thickening porridge until a wave lashed the rock below and revived him with a cold draught of brine.

Gordon had hurried in his pursuit and become lost in his thoughts. He was not aware just how far he'd descended until the wave broke his spiralling train of thought. Gordon saw he stood just metres above water level and that each wave - even the relatively minor ones - would send spray crashing against the cliff face. Larger waves broke at waist height. Gordon's eyes had grown more accustomed to the darkness and he watched the swell of the sea, picking his moment to advance along the path to avoid being battered by the breaking waves.

Still the path descended until Gordon was splashing through rocky pools.

The lightning flashed in great sheets that backlit the clouds and froze the fractured sea. It stuck in great purple triangles in a way Gordon had never seen before. It cracked and burst with the fury of war and refused to exhaust itself. Every burst only enraged it further and the clouds churned and spat and rubbed themselves like lovers' passion. The sea, too, rose to meet the challenge from above and tossed tempestuous waves to the skies. The waves which had been mauling Gordon's legs now stopped and instead retreated to meet the lightning strikes in a way that defied the order of the natural world; instead of breaking against the shore they broke against one another in the centre of the sea. Gordon watched a great spiral of water fired from the ocean as though it had been blown by some Titanic whale. The jet hung in the air, frozen in the strobing flashes of the storm. The cold air became chilled to the point that Gordon thought his heart might stop beating and every breath stung the lungs like mustard gas.

Clara didn't believe David when he ran inside to tell her Gordon had bolted, lost into the night. She was tired, tipsy, damp and cold. Gordon might have been able to persuade her to take another brandy in the bar, but there was no chance she would have ever agreed to fetch her camera for a midnight chase along the cliffs. David's earnestness and unquenchable appeals finally swayed her. She waited a moment for Gordon to burst through the door, laughing and admit it was all a wind up, but he never came.

"Has he lost his mind?" Clara said to David, who needlessly chose to answer her question and defend Gordon.

David felt anxious with the shuffling lack of ease of a child whose parents are going through an acrimonious divorce. He had been caught in two minds when Gordon ran out into the night. His natural instinct was for adventure and to tear off in pursuit. However, he felt a curious protectiveness towards Clara and Gordon's final words had ultimately convinced him to stay by her side.

"Well I suppose we'd better go and find him," she said. "But there's no way I'm taking my camera out tonight."

David back to his room to fetch his torch and jacket leaving Clara mooching impatiently in reception. She started. In the reflection of the great gold frame mirror she saw the face of a man behind her right shoulder. Lychgate. He was stood behind the reception desk; she was certain he hadn't been there a minute ago.

"You frightened me," she said, to explain her gasp.

Clara wondered how much he had heard. There was a dark disapproval written across his face, but this was hardly novel. He laid down his clipboard with grave purpose and kept his eyes fixed on her. Lychgate emitted this silent anger as impotently and impalpably as radio waves. He burned inside but could never make the world fear his wrath, which only aggravated the sense of injustice he'd harboured since childhood and now itched raw like a shameful rash. Wrath without respect smoulders like the acrid yellow smoke from fresh mown grass dumped carelessly on a bonfire.

"What's going on?" he said, after a long pause to heighten its impact. "You've let all the heat out leaving the door open like that. It's late and you'll disturb my other guests with this racket."

Clara knew well he had no other guests, his grand dame from breakfast had checked out that morning, but she had no intention of entering into an argument. Instead, she gave a cool smile and apologised before turning to David who came thudding along the corridor lacking any of the nimbleness his slight frame suggested. Lychgate winced at every step and was charging his batteries for another barbed lash but Clara, sensing trouble, refused to give him the opportunity.

"Let's go and see where he's got to," she said and together they left the Cragg. She sent a tornado of leaves and rain into the entrance hall as they left.

Lychgate leaned over his desk and watched them disappear into the night. He picked up his telephone and began to dial, his face white.

The noise of the storm was maddening and assaulted Gordon from every direction, with no hope for respite. It howled and roared like jet engines, it screamed at a pitch to wrinkle the eyes then sunk to a boom that sent waves of stacked pressure barging down his ear canals like opened sluices. Worse still, nestled above in the nooks of the cliff, great gulls squawked in berserk union with a cadence to match the churn and swell of the ocean. Their calls quickened with an almost premonitious anticipation of each lightning strike. The sea outmatched the gull's chorus and shook, shattered and showered thousands of tonnes of water which crashed and destroyed itself in a rumbling

162

anger. But when the thunder clapped as the heavens tore like ripped card, all else paid reverential silence to its authority. Each member in this cacophonous orchestra could have threatened the sanity of those subjected to it, but as an ensemble it was almost unbearable and Gordon - shocked, shivering and plastered like a limpet to the cliff wall - fastened his eyes, as though one sensory organ felt such pity for the other that it was striking on sympathy.

Gordon drove himself forward, he was dragging himself along the rock face, one hand over the other, forcing himself on into the heart of the storm. Gordon saw how the cliff stepped out sharply into the sea and how the path disappeared from sight around a sharp corner. He made for this promontory with the last of his strength and will. He knew that from this vantage point he would get a clear view of the entire Selyvan coast. The waves now crashed closer and, in his fear, Gordon crushed his chest into the rocky face. Still he kept his eyes on the promontory and still his arms hauled him forward; it wasn't even necessary to look back along the path from which he'd come, he already knew there was no return.

Every muscle in Gordon's wiry body burned, but his core felt more alive than he'd known, as though his heart glowed brassy red and pumped as if driven by the pistons of a steam train. He felt the hot blood surge through his body and the seawater hiss and sizzle against his burning skin. With the exertion and will he had transcended the physical and saw his struggle against the elements from the third person. He was a spectator willing his body forward, whipping it into action when it flagged and urging it to take one more step with an outstretched hand when he saw the shoulders sag in the resignation of defeat. By this slow and agonising progress Gordon rounded the headland and stood on the edge of what might have been the last crag of England amid the raging storm. Broken, bruised and battered by waves Gordon looked out across the coast. Nearing the point of total and exhaustion and collapse, somehow his heart fired with red heat once again.

The coastline curved as a great amphitheatre. In the centre the lights of Selyvan blinked dimly through the stormy night. Gordon saw all along the coast the great white explosions of broken waves plume and shatter. The vista made him feel suddenly tiny and insignificant. He saw the absolute power and nature of the storm and felt afraid of its indiscriminate brutality, but nature's brutal strength was nothing for the cruel contrast which sat calm and cross-legged on a cool, flat rock just thirty feet before him. The robed-figure had his back to Gordon and about him the waves dashed and smashed, but never once threatened his meditation. The man's voice was stolen by the gale but Gordon could be certain he spoke, he clearly saw the muscles in the back of his bald head tighten and contract. His outstretched arms had the appearance of longing, like the mother summoning a lost child, but the twitching fingers gave the simultaneous impression of a conductor, directing the vast orchestra of the storm. Every slight twitch of the man's slender fingers sounded the gull's maddening cries, but now they barked with the rage and fear of a cornered dog. The man raised his arms above his head, bringing both palms together. Above, the sky

163

crackled and charged with energy. He flung both arms down to the rock on which he sat and the thunder clapped and a bolt of purple fire punched from the black clouds into the sea, sinking beneath a swirling vortex.

Gordon flinched at the strike as though it had passed through his own body. He watched the man again raise his hands and a powerful dread came over him. His muscles atrophied and his grip on the cliff face loosened. The waves no longer beat against the cliff and the sea became calm. Gordon feared another strike, but he did not know why. There was something unnatural about the purple lightning and the way it responded to the robed man's will. Gordon wanted to rush forward and seize him, to shake him, to slap him, to wake him from his hypnotic swaying and chanting, but he had no energy, his own will was nullified by the intense will of the strange figure. But was he strange? Gordon knew him, he had known it when he saw him at such a distance outside the Cragg. He knew it was the colonel, there was no doubt in his mind, and yet he refused to acknowledge the fact.

The Colonel lifted from his robe the body of the skinny black cat Gordon recognised from the hall. The animal must have been drugged, Gordon reasoned, because it did not claw and spit at the sight of the raging sea. The Colonel held the animal facing the waves, gripping it beneath the forearms so the body swung beneath pendulously. The Colonel tossed the creature into the sea, Gordon watched helplessly. The ablution released the cat from whatever doping spell it had been held under and it flailed in the foam. A wave broke over the animal's head and it was lost under the water. A minute later it bobbed back to the surface, flailing all the more frantically. Another wave broke, this time shattering the cat's body against the sharp granite.

With his muscles weak and his will broken, Gordon surprised himself. Without having made the conscious decision to do so he called out, with the last grains of energy left in his chest and with a forcefulness that made his ribs ache sharp with the strain. He called out the Colonel's name, two strong syllables carried on the wind. It silenced the seagull's cawing and the ocean stilled to listen, even the sky stopped growling for that instant. Two long syllables. Mor-tain.

Slowly and deliberately, betraying neither panic nor surprise, the Colonel twisted his neck without shifting a shoulder blade. His head seemed to turn half a degree than Gordon had expected it to reach and there was something darkly uncanny about its unnatural position. But more unnerving still for Gordon was the hollow look in the Colonel's one eye that stared unblinkingly back at him, the black pupil fast against its westward edge. He was automatic and emotionless; Gordon could not even be certain the Colonel recognised him. At that moment he wasn't quite human, he wasn't quite God.

Clara hurried David along. He had been urging her to take the coastal path that led away behind the hotel but Clara's instinct drove her down towards the lights of Selyvan and the harbour. David's torch, gifted to Clara as the pack leader, quickly flickered, dimmed and died. Clara cursed as the path disappeared ahead.

"Stick close," she said. "It's dangerous in the dark."

Her words were perfectly timed. David lost his footing and slid forward on loose gravel and into Clara's arms. In his grasping desperation he'd caught hold of Clara's breast and he withdrew his hand shamefully, he was pleased for the darkness.

"Be careful," Clara hissed.

After his stumble progress was slower. Clara picked the path with great care and together they fumbled down the narrow path. Now lightning appeared in the storm and Clara was thankful for its flashes of light to guide them, at the same time she recognised their vulnerability on the cliffs. Clara looked out over the raging bay and her anger rose, Gordon had endangered them. But her anger evaporated when she considered the danger he might be in. Behind her David grumbled. They were heading in the wrong direction, he protested, but Clara remained obstinate. Twice she slipped during the descent and grazed her skin through the her jeans. Her rain-soaked hair had stuck in thick, damp stands across her eyes, blinding her more effectively than the night.

Ahead Clara saw the single streetlamp by the harbour wall. She waited for David as he stumbled down the last steep bank of the Cragg's path and hurried him along. The town was silent. There were no lights in any of the houses and the chimneys chuffed lazily, exhaling the last reluctant puffs of stinking smoke into the frosty night. The orange glow of the light offered a small beacon in the darkness. Clara made for it without logic or reason, its pull was magnetic. She had some buried notion that if she could climb those granite steps of the harbour wall and look out across the black bay she would see Gordon, glowing like a firefly and she would call to him, and he would awake from his madness and return to her. She saw him then in her mind, encircled with a green phosphorescence like a nuclear halo. She yearned for him at that moment, desperately and felt a terrible fear for his well-being. Clara hurried David along with an impatient arm.

From the darkness the silhouette of a man emerged and stood directly in their path. He was tall, powerfully built and with a forward stoop that saw him tower menacingly over Clara and David. Clara recognised immediate danger and panic seized her, she screamed violently. She willed herself to turn and grab David, to run, but her weightless legs refused. She tottered, her head grew unbearably heavy, and darkness overcame her.

The sky burnt with the heat of purple flame and the clouds bubbled like an unwatched pan. Everywhere was noise, disturbing and weird. But the sensory world ceased to exist for Gordon. He was locked as truly as a manacled prisoner hanging from a dungeon wall, the red-hot poker approaching and hissing in the damp air. Gordon was locked in the gaze of the Colonel's hollow eye, a gaze that neither demanded or expected, it only saw and that was the worst.

The Colonel lifted both hands back above his head and held them there with insidious menace. The Colonel's movement lessened some of the hypnotic power he held over Gordon, who now felt strength returning to his muscles which had been paralysed by fear, exertion and cold. Gordon knew then he could turn and run, that he had broken the trance. He wished he had never fled the Cragg and felt his foolish exposure. His thoughts in those fleeting seconds were for fire, for brandy, for laughter, and for Clara. It was a plunge pool of regret. Gordon gripped tight the cliff face with both hands and steeled his body for action. He was ready to break the bond and fling himself in one powerful movement away and return back along the path he'd taken. But he never did.

The sky crackled once again and the air grew heavy and impatient with the energy it contained. The gulls, whose screams had reached an unholy crescendo, ceased with an abruptness that only heightened, rather than relieved, the unbearable tension. The Colonel turned his head back to the sea, sharply and impatiently, and fixed his gaze to where the purple bolt had struck. With his gaze broken, Gordon now dared himself to look out onto the water and saw with horror how the sea was turning in on itself in a weird vortex. The black gulf that opened was visible even in the night and even from Gordon's low elevation. From the depths of the sea's chasm came air so cold and stagnant that even the frozen night felt like a warming fireside in comparison. The mix of air created a backdraught that blew Gordon's black hair like storm barley and strangled his billowing shirt around his neck. Suddenly the Colonel dropped both hands to the rock and the great static charge of the sky unleashed and burst in a white and violet explosion into the ocean vortex. The blast was deafening, blinding and so compressed and inflated the lungs so that they burst hard against the ribs. Gordon was flung into the cliff and struck his head hard against the rock, immediately he tasted the salt of blood in his mouth. Two visions of the world were now before him, one twenty degrees off the horizontal plane of the other and Gordon lost all balance. He slumped to his knees, then to all fours before collapsing his heavy head down into the cool rock. There he could sleep.

The sea was churning. Millions of gallons of water rushed to close the great chasm that had opened and the movement shook the earth. Gordon watched as a dream as the vast bodies of water met and slammed shut this unnatural portal. He watched without a breath as the aftershock rumbled and a towering wall of water sped towards him. For a moment, he tried to pull himself to his feet but as if he'd shot himself with a dozen dull opiates, he remained calm and unmoving until the water seized him with a powerful but gentle grasp and plucked him from the cliff. He felt the great pressure of its weight above him and the irresistible but peaceful pull of its current. Peaceful was what he felt. The dull but sinister peace of piped music. Spirited away along the trod, the ancient fairy song on the foam. Peaceful and evil. Peaceful and evil it pulled him towards that black chasm. The black hole was the evil. Terror rescued Gordon and he thrashed and fought and pulled himself to the surface and every muscle fought the current. Every last ounce of strength fought back; fear gave power to his stroke but his body had nothing more to give. A voice called to him, the voice of the past and he called back dumbly, there was nothing left in his lungs. Gordon let himself go willingly and peacefully.

CHAPTER TWENTY TWO

Darkness. From darkness a pinprick of light. First one, then another and another until the sky was spattered with star seeds, all pulsing in weird syncopation. Yanked. Weighless. The bubbling clouds had boiled clear until the night sky settled vast and eternal. The matted twinkle of stars, the milky way yawned with outstretched arms. Arms. The arms and the hand, the elbow, the armpit. All around the stars wheeled dizzily, drunkenly and looped in giant arcs, quickening at each rotation. Sick from the merry-go-round some of the stars began to break from the dance and drop exhausted into the sea, hissing, fizzing then carbonising into wrinkled grey hearts like forgotten garlic. One by way, they extinguished themselves until the cold, inky sea bubbled like a tar pit from their fire. The sky was black except for the bloody moon that dripped like seared cheese flesh into the steaming ocean. Crimson fog, death fog. The sky is black.

"The stars are dead," said Gordon. "The stars are dead."

"Gordon."

"The stars are dead."

"He's talking."

"Dead, dead. Gotterdammerung."

"Whiting? Drink this."

Gordon's lips burned, his tongue burned, his throat burned, his stomach burned. He vomited three times; a thin, foamy, burning bile. He rolled back onto his back and saw Clara. She kissed him, right on his vomit lips. Behind Clara stood Guddy, he gave a smile of satisfaction when Gordon's eyes met his. He turned and disappeared. Gordon tried to speak but his stomach turned, he caught himself, steadied the nausea and tried again. He vomited.

Guddy rowed hard back to where Mjöllnir lay at anchor. With Clara and David's help they hauled Gordon on board, but it was Guddy who really sweated despite the cold night. Gordon was taken through to the cabin and Guddy flicked on his gas heater. Next, he found Gordon some dry clothes. A thick knit jumper greased with layers of Vaseline and a pair of heavy rubber trousers. Gordon sat still as his body absorbed the warmth, his hair steaming in the low light. His body began to shake, and Clara was concerned but Guddy recognised this was a good sign.

Gordon's mind, dulled by trauma began to wake, and he became aware of his surroundings. He felt too weak to remember and let his eyes fall on Clara. David stood in the corner, white and afraid, unable to help, unable to speak. Guddy handed Gordon a mug of hot Brennivin. He sipped it gratefully and his burning blood coursed to the extremities.

"We call it burn wine in Iceland," Guddy said tapping his chest with an open palm. "You feel it here, right?"

Gordon nodded and took another sip. It warmed him faster and more completely than the pathetic gas fire.

"You pick a storm for a swim?" said Guddy when he was satisfied Gordon was out of danger. "You're lucky we found you, Whiting."

Gordon looked up with a heavy neck and heavier eyes.

"If I hadn't met Clara and the little Whiting down by the harbour, you'd be six fathoms deep by now."

"Thank you," said Gordon, the first words croaked and gurgled out.

Guddy laughed, nodded and poured himself a measure of Brennivin and knocked it back. He shuddered, bared his teeth and sucked the air.

"Cheers," he said, holding up his empty mug. "Next month, I have promised myself I will stop drinking this. I have shelves full of the stuff. Each month my aunt Eydis sends me a bottle and a stockfish. She's in her 80s but she never forgets. She's done it since I moved away. She doesn't want me to forget, I think. She's been doing it for so many years and for so many years she's been sending it for six króna, that wouldn't send a postcard from me to you. So, each month I get a card through my door to say if I want my parcel, I owe £16.80. My bottle of Brennivin and my fish are getting expensive."

"Can't you just tell her to stop sending it?" said Clara.

"I like that she sends it," he said. "It's my connection with home. Every month I worry the parcel will be her last."

Guddy went to pour another drink but after a rueful glance into the empty mug he thought better of it. Gordon gasped and all eyes turned to him, he grasped down at his feet in a sudden panic.

"What is it?" said Guddy. "Don't worry your feet are still attached."

168

"My Church's?" said Gordon with sad eyes.

Guddy shook his head and laughed with breathy exhalations. He nodded to the top of his gas heater to where the sodden brogues sat steaming. Gordon's face dropped so visibly and with such sorrow that everybody laughed, from relief that the trivial once more dominated the significant.

"You might want to give them a polish in the morning," said Guddy.

Gordon was overcome by a fit of shivers and his bones, numb like monumental marble, tried to shake some life into the muscles which wrapped them.

"You need a bath and bed," said Clara. "You'll catch pneumonia out here."

"Don't be so dramatic," Gordon slurred like a drunk through his blue lips.

"If you're good," Guddy said. "I'll pour you another glass of Brennivin."

"Please. I won't be good."

The storm had settled by the time Guddy moored Mjöllnir back in Selyvan harbour. The town still slept and the last of the smoking chimneys had dampened. The stars were bright and the air chill. Gordon was determined not to make a fuss and made a brave attempt to work his frozen bones. The small step from the boat onto land required concentration and determination, Gordon's thighs had tightened and his knees locked. Everybody was pleased when Guddy signalled the battered old car by the harbour belonged to him. He kept the keys above the mirror and it coughed into life with the reluctance and glum resignation of an old dog preparing for his daily walk. Guddy's car spared them the arduous climb up the narrow coastal path to the Cragg, but not the longer route, the same they'd taken hours earlier shortly before Gordon ran off into the night.

The door to the Cragg was locked and Clara rang the bell impatiently, she no longer cared what Lychgate's reactions might be. She was ready to leave Selyvan and Cornwall for good. The story had lost what little charm it ever held with her. Back in London, days earlier, the idea of the misty mystic West had twinkled like a chest of buried jewels. Cold, tired and wearing the damp and musty robes of failure, Clara was ready for London. Lychgate, still dressed, opened the door with some surprise when he saw the bedraggled guests. His shock at the sight robbed him of his moment's initiative and Clara was able to lead Gordon safely past this final obstacle. Lychgate rued the missed opportunity the moment it passed and dreamed, with comforting pleasures, of leaving the three "dirty stop outs" shivering on the porch.

Clara turned to the sorry sight of Gordon, who stood blue-lipped and dripping.

"Is this enough now?" she said. "Can we go back to London tomorrow."

Gordon nodded glumly.

David was tired of adventure and ready to sleep. To not disturb David, Gordon readily assented to Clara's suggestion that he ought to bathe in her room. There was no chance of sleep for her, she explained, and besides she wanted to make sure Gordon didn't pass out in the bath. The proposal suited David too, but he met it with apathy, it was all the same to him. He lacked Clara's concern for Gordon and refused to acknowledge the subtleties of suffering. In his mind, Gordon was either alive or dead, sick or well. Gordon's stoicism and brave face more than met David's sketchy medical judgments for wellbeing and so he was perfectly content to discharge the patient. Gordon on the other hand was less certain of his own health. He had swallowed a lot of seawater, faced death, and frozen his limbs to temporary atrophy. A hot bath and a cup of strong, black tea were his best hopes for recovery. But something else lurked in the back of his mind like a shadow behind the curtain. Gordon had not addressed his memory of the Colonel. The very recollection of that strange, robed figure on the rocks chilled him. The hollow eyes, the command of the storm, how could he explain this to Clara? Gordon wondered, was it not likely the Colonel too had been washed out to sea by the same great wave that plucked him from the rocks? The thought of phoning the coast guard occurred to him while he sat on Clara's bed as she drew the bath next door. But what would he say? The truth he supposed. But then the cold crept back down his spine and he felt the rot at his heart, the sharpness of guilt but with the acuteness of fear.

"Ok, it's ready," Clara called from next door. "The bubble bath smells a bit funky but at least it's hot. What's verbena?"

Gordon was still distracted with the colonel and answered absently. Instead of asking Clara if she wanted the bath water after him, he asked if she wanted it with him. He hadn't realised his mistake and his innocent expression and the directness with which he met Clara's eyes only enforced the error. Despite his vacancy Gordon eventually recognised the shocked expression Clara bore and corrected himself but he lacked the energy to present a convincing case.

"Remember, MY flatmate is YOUR ex," she said.

Gordon tried to explain and wanted to blame the cold and the burn wine he'd been force-fed on the boat but Clara was nursing her own guilt and the mention of the boat reminded her of the kiss and she misunderstood Gordon's meaning.

"I was happy to see you," she said.

It was Gordon's turn to look puzzled, he hadn't formed the association between the boat and the kiss.

"I thought you were dead," Clara continued. "I was happy."

Both Gordon and Clara let their embarrassment continue. Clara stood in the doorway to the bathroom, Gordon by the bed. The room suddenly felt much too small and the sticky heat of the bathwater made the atmosphere even more uncomfortable. Sheepishly Gordon squeezed past Clara and into the bathroom. He locked the door and slowly began to undress, his bones still aching from the chill.

Gordon was surprised at breakfast by a familiar voice and a stinging slap on the back.

"The famous Gordon Athelney."

Max Nash sat opposite him at the table without invitation, but he wasn't unwelcome. In his hand, he held a bottle of Brennevin and Gordon guessed the sequence of events. Max spotted Gordon's eyes on the burn wine and laughed.

"I can see you eyeing it up," he said. "A present from Guddy. I bumped into him down in the harbour. He told me about your adventures last night and I came to make sure you're well, I'd tried to reach you on your mobile."

Gordon looked around to be certain Lychgate wasn't still hovering. Gordon wanted a clean break from Selyvan and was exhausted by the hotelier's interferences. Gordon graciously accepted the Brennevin.

"My mobile was a casualty of last night's adventures, but at least I'm not."

It quickly became clear that Guddy had told Max what had happened the night before. However, he kept the vision of the Colonel to himself. Only David had asked him about it, and his question was delivered so clumsily and with so little conviction that Gordon easily batted it away. Clara, he suspected, guessed there had been some incident but had no intention of poking it. She recognised some shame or guilt in Gordon's silence, and it sat exposed and ugly like the beached jellyfish she'd stabbed at with a stick in Aldeburgh as a child.

"It was quite a storm last night," said Max cheerfully. "I slept through it somehow, but the chaps down in the harbour said it was one of the worst they've seen in decades. Guddy too, and he's ridden a few tempests in his time."

"I'm leaving today," said Gordon with finality.

Max looked disappointed and made no attempt to disguise it. Gordon poured a drop of milk into his tea with a gentle hand, but a spasm of last night's chill returned and issued a creamy glug, instant anaemia. Gordon settled the cup back in the saucer never to touch it again.

"Well, I'm sorry to hear that," said Max eventually. "Is the great dolphin debate settled?"

Gordon looked thoughtfully at Max, perhaps a moment too long because for once Max sensed an awkwardness and retreated.

"Of course, I'm not asking for insider secrets. Naturally it's your story."

"Don't be silly," said Gordon, recognising the slight he'd unwittingly delivered. "It's not my story, there is no story. I tried and failed. If there's anything to write, it's you who should write it. I was out of my depth, last night should be evidence of that."

"You were onto a scent, you trusted your nose, you shouldn't fault that. I'm lucky, I have the time. Our lead times are long and our circulation is low. Where's the pressure. But I must say I'm sorry you're leaving. It's been refreshing having another hound on the patch. Together I think we'd have stitched this one up in no time. You've got a keener nose than I have but there's not many people in these parts who I don't know. If you'd needed anything, numbers, names, addresses, I'd have given you them in a flash."

Gordon knew he would. For a moment he felt sorry to be leaving, he wondered about phoning the desk and retracting what he'd said. Concocting some elaborate excuse, one more ripping yarn they couldn't resist but to bite. Then the memories of the previous night seeped out like the first suspended swirls of the dunked teabag, but not just that - Clara's words, David's pestering, Lychgate's officiousness and Selyvan. Selyvan, Gordon had forgotten how he loathed the town with its impenetrable stone, sea-blown sullenness and hostility.

"It's best I go," he said eventually. "I'm expected back."

His words went largely unregistered because at that moment Max overturned the sugar bowl with which he'd been fiddling and sent granules spilling across the table and into the lace tablecloth. Max attempted to return the sugar, but his trials were ineffective and only served to dislodge Gordon's jam-covered spoon from the porridge bowl on which it rested and so added a berry red splodge to the cloth.

"You like a story, don't you?" said Max.

"Certainly, but I'm a bit pressed."

"It won't take long. In 1815 Napoleon lost the battle of Waterloo."

"This is about Selyvan? Are you sure it won't take long?"

Max ignored the interruption and continued without losing rhythm.

"Rather than fall on his sword or surrender himself to Wellington, Napoleon fled across France. There was no grand army to defend him, it was a rout. He had nowhere to run. He surrendered to the British and was brought on board HMS Bellerephon. Nobody quite knew what to do with the richest prize in military history, certainly not to poor Captain Maitland, on blockade duty off Rochefort, who suddenly found himself in possession of this charge. He sailed to England and dropped anchor at the first port he could get a messenger with a horse ashore. And so that's how he ended up in these unlikely waters, bobbing patiently just off the coast while word was sent to London for further orders. It's unlikely anybody in the Admiralty had heard of a sleepy fishing port called Selyvan before that moment - the harbour is shallow and unsuitable for anything but the smallest fishing fleets. If the sailors knew nothing of Selyvan then it's doubly true of the politicians who had to decide the great man's fate. Their biggest fear was having England's bête noir bobbing like a buoy within swimming distance of the prize he'd sought for so long. So Napoleon was duly despatched to St Helena and there he died, but that wasn't the end of Selyvan's part in the saga.

"Half of the admiralty, senior politicians and a good many more tourists were camped out in Selyvan for the spectacle. It was a town that hadn't expected, or ever welcomed, such an invasion. It sent the locals scurrying and scattering like the insects beneath an old stone in the garden. You know that sudden disgust you feel when you wonder how these lowly crawlies have lived away from the sun in such rot?

"Of course, everything I tell you is more local legend than historic fact, but it's fun all the same. Well, chief among the beetles and lice was Admiral Mortain - that's the Colonel's great, great, great, great grandfather – who was largely retired after a wound he received at Trafalgar. He'd spent ten long years with a musket ball slowly working its way out of his leg. It had quite shattered the bone so he drank heavily to kill the pain. On account of his years of daring service, the Navy gave him an honorary command of home waters. He had to patrol and protect the coasts of Selyvan. I suppose the Naval command had hoped for a pleasant week in Mortain's pile, enjoying his well-stocked cellar, drinking to Napoleon's final defeat. Instead, they found a crotchety old crank, withered and unhinged. He was unrecognisable from his 1804 portrait, which then hung in the Admiralty but has since been mothballed. His cheeks were hollow - so I've read in several contemporary diary entries - his eyes were sunken but yet strangely bulbous at the same time and his complexion was yellow green like a stagnant pond. His mood

173

too flitted between impatience, distraction, anger and bouts of odious charm. Needless to say, his fellow Admirals had little desire to prolong their visit unnecessarily, but most were prepared to forgive the old war hero for his dilapidation. A few of his former friends perhaps pried a little too deeply, doubtless out of concern and in respect of the closeness of the bond military men maintain right to the end. Well, whatever they discovered snapped the bonds and this set about the chain of events which led to Admiral Mortain's most infamous hour, and which would overshadow all the recklessly brave heroics associated with his earlier years.

"One of Mortain's duties had been the maintenance and care of a large prison hulk moored just off the coast. It was mostly filled to the rafters with French prisoners who were awaiting release after the end of the war. Come to think of it, there are two engravings of the hulks in the Ship Inn, but I doubt you'll have time to see them before you leave. Creaking, rickety old hulks they were and apparently when the wind blew in from the sea the whole town stank to high heaven. It's fair to say, the welfare of the prisoners hadn't been the Admiral's primary concern. You'd hear some tales in the Ship if you ever do go to see those engravings and start asking around the bar, but you'd leave none the wiser. The truth is nobody now knows exactly what had been discovered and why Admiral Mortain hobbled down to his 16-gun brig leading an ashen faced First Naval Lord before him with a carbine trained at his lower spine. Mortain sailed his old Brig out to the harmless old prison hulk. The twitchy but helpless Naval command, who watched the affair from the shore, thought the mad Admiral was going to release the French prisoners and launch a daring escape attempt for Napoleon himself. But it didn't go like that. Instead, Mortain ordered the motley powder monkey he'd pressed into service to fire three shots into the hulk; two rounds of grapeshot and finally roundshot to hole the hull. The ship went down with 300 hands - 297 to be precise.

"Of course there was a court-martial, there had to be. I've seen the papers. But they're sketchy and incomplete. I once tried to write a book on this curious chapter of Selyvan's history but only met conjecture and censure. Despite my early enthusiasm I became side-tracked and disappointed by dead-end after dead-end and put the project to pasture. Well, the Admiral was certified and the whole affair was rather inconclusively swept under the carpet. It's rather a juicy tale though, don't you think?"

Gordon nodded but was dissatisfied.

"But what do the locals say? What's their version?"

Max drummed the breakfast table in delight.

"I knew you'd want to know. Well, catch them after a few drinks and they'll condemn with the freest tongues. They claim ever since that hulk went down there's been no fish within five miles of the submerged wreck. In three cannon shots Mortain emptied their hunting grounds of prey."

"But why did he do it?" Gordon was persistent. "How do they explain it?"

"They say it was a blood sacrifice," said Max, all levity had left his voice and he spoke gravely, quietly and with a conspiratorial tone that Gordon could not help but miss. "They say the admiral sacrificed those 300 double-ironed men."

"To who?" said Gordon.

"To Magog."

CHAPTER TWENTY THREE

Clara woke badly but so she had slept badly. She only dozed off into uneasy sleep sometime after the green lights of the alarm clock had flashed 4am. She'd watched the numbers turning since 2am, when Gordon had left her to go back to his own room. She tried to distract herself by working out what letters could be spelled using the alarm clock's crude numbering system. She was trying to distract herself from thinking about Gordon. She was certain he was interested in her, but then as soon as the idea formed a thick churning rose in her stomach and she convinced herself it was not true. At first she thought she did not want it to be true and that she was lying to herself. After an hour of broken meditation, she realised it was the opposite, that she wanted it to be true but was telling herself it wasn't. By 4am her brain had turned over so many of the possibilities and permutations that she was so sick and exhausted that even thinking about his name triggered the grasping panic of a sudden fall that occurs seconds after sleep.

It was Monday morning and the dull regret that the adventure was over dawned on Clara. She thought about the long train journey home. She remembered she'd forgotten to pack her Kindle charger and so would either spend seven hours listening to David lecturing on the penetrative strength of Soviet assault rifles versus the accuracy of the US equivalents or would be forced to buy a real-life magazine; a habit she'd hoped she had well and truly kicked into the long grass. There was no possibility of spending seven hours with Gordon. She had to sit as far from him as possible, without making it look as if she was deliberately avoiding him since that would provoke his interest. She thought of the bag to pack and unpack. Order appealed to Clara and this single train of thought saved her from the paralysis of introspection any longer. She rose, made her bed, and began laying out her clothes and kit onto the sheets. She unzipped her suitcase and almost sighed in satisfaction at the prospect of the job in hand.

David awoke in saturnine temperament. His first action of the day was to stub his toe painfully against the desk of drawers as he made his way sleepily to the bathroom. He'd slept soundly but woken with a fit of sneezes and a streaming cold. David was frequently sick and knew the signs and symptoms well enough. As a child he'd been kept from school for so many weeks as he nursed ear and throat infections, that textbooks and exercises were packaged in brown A4 envelopes and sent to his house by the school. David had a frustrating knack of absorbing knowledge without the critical process. Facts clung to him like iron filings leaping to the embrace of a horseshoe magnet. When David was asked to order, arrange and analyse the clinging chaos he struggled, lost interest and retreated to his world of more facts. He was a messy librarian but always managed to pluck the information he needed from the mad jumble inside his cluttered brain. Since an early age his father had singled out his profession and convinced himself his son's shortcomings could be overcome with practice. He refused to acknowledge his disappointments and became lost in a fantasy world even more tangled than his son's. David's mother wasn't a practical ally and entirely unable to steer him down a more suitable career path. She had never worked and allowed herself to become befuddled and hoodwinked by the modern education system, trusting entirely in her husband's shaky judgement.

David looked at himself in the toothpaste smeared mirror. He ran the tepid tap water and splashed it on his face. His thin, black hair stuck upright like a mohawk where he'd slept, snapping the rigid gel and fixing it in an even more ridiculous pose. Without his glasses David looked even more like the baby bird, kicked from its own nest by a cuckoo chick; blinking and bawling at a world ready to gobble him up without compunction. David didn't see a baby bird in the reflection, partly because the mirror was grimy, and his eyesight was atrocious. David saw everything he wanted to see and believed it too. He saw an action hero, a chiselled officer who stood unmoved by hissing bullets and mortar fire that sent others cowering for cover. He'd seen this reflection for so long he believed it to be true and it gave him a self-confidence and bravery that made his fellow pupils and teachers scratch their heads.

David called through to Gordon from the bathroom to complain he was ill but got no response. Disappointed by silence he stumbled back into the bedroom and realised Gordon's bed was empty. David felt suddenly hollow.

Gordon had slept as badly as Clara but, unlike her, he'd risen early and had already eaten. Talking to the famous Max Nash over breakfast had been refreshing and amusing. It was with sincerity and warmth that Gordon shook his hand goodbye for the final time. Gordon recognised Max's love of folklore and local rumour and saw a faint reflection in his own character. He envied Max in many ways. Max with his patch and his friends and his contacts and his smoky storm-washed pubs full of salty characters ready to pour forth great glugs of unverifiable gossip. Dark hints of blood sacrifice and legendary Goemagot who took an offering of one in every ten fish caught. Goemagot who was tossed from England's shores by Corin, and where he now sulks in his watery tomb waiting for revenge. Gordon's lips were whetted by Max's tale of unhinged admirals and naval conspiracies and would have loved to help research, write and stir up popular fancies.

Gordon had also spoken to the desk, or more specifically to Croaker. Without a mobile he'd been forced to use payphone in reception where he'd stuffed a finger in an ear to make-out the faint and tinny voice of Croaker at the other end. Gordon had hoped he had found the magic hour as the night editor was signing off and just before Croaker arrived. The night editor would be impatient, exhausted and compliant, he would agree to write in his handover notes whatever Gordon steered him towards. Unfortunately for Gordon, Croaker was in the office early because his motorcycle needed servicing that afternoon. Although Croaker hadn't taken a dip in the icy sea the night before, his mood suggested otherwise. He'd been forced to stand from Croydon after begrudgingly offering his seat to a pregnant commuter. To make the journey worse he'd picked up, with much self-righteousness, a screwed-up newspaper that had been tossed on the train floor. As he attempted to stuff the litter into the tiny train bin a pair of shitty pants fell out. Croaker's day hadn't started well but a phone call from Gordon, who he was expecting in the office that morning, was just the tonic.

"No, I haven't read the handover," said Croaker, gleeful in his officiousness. "My first priority isn't to track your comings and goings, but I shouldn't mind fitting an ASBO tracking device to your ankle."

Gordon explained how he had delayed his return by 24 hours when he'd heard the news of the drowned man. Gordon stressed the decision had been made by the weekend editor Richard Woodward, but that the story had quickly petered out and failed to excite any national interest. Croaker sniffed cautiously but Gordon's story sounded plausible enough. Gordon promised to return on the afternoon train and be ready for work first thing the next day, Croaker agreed cheerlessly.

"What of the dolphins?" said Croaker, with a curiosity that surprised Gordon. "Did you uncover anything juicy?"

Gordon had believed Croaker had exiled him to the land's ends in wrath and retribution. The dolphins, he had supposed, were a Herculean task designed to expose Gordon's inefficiency and bungling. Suddenly, Gordon saw things differently. He wondered if Croaker had believed in him all along, and had sent Gordon on a special mission, beyond the orthodox capabilities of the rest of his editorial team. Unfortunately, Gordon had nothing to report and so felt as though he was rather pricking the balloon of optimism he'd just inflated. His words, when he found them, sounded like a confirmation of his own inadequacy and he lacked his typical bluff and bluster.

"There's no story," said Gordon. "I tried, but there's nothing."

Croaker sighed with a resignation Gordon knew well. He could see him hunched over his keyboard with his telephone headset on, already stressed and reddening before he'd taken even his first sugary tea of the day. His broad shoulders and square jaw and deep-set eyes, it made Gordon shudder. Occasionally the entire office would sit up at the noise of Croaker banging crumbs out of his keyboard with anger. Crumbs the weekend editor had dropped inside. Banging his keyboard with such force his slash key had fallen out so many times it was no longer capable of complete depression. The reporters would exchange nervous glances and wonder whose turn it was next. Who would be sent to a tribunal hearing in Norbury, a joyless inquest in Walthamstow or whose copy would be torn apart in earshot of the entire floor? Gordon repeated himself for emphasis, aware of his failure.

"I tried, but there's nothing."

Croaker hung up without a goodbye and, slightly abashed, Gordon hung up the receiver and hoped not too much of his conversation had been heard by Lychgate who lingered in the breakfast room nearby. Gordon turned and jumped back in horror. Stood less than two feet behind him was the Cragg's Polish waiter, Tomasz. He looked flustered and nervous and could not speak. Tomasz motioned for Gordon to follow him and he obeyed in confusion and surprise. He led Gordon away from reception and into an empty function room. He closed the door softly behind them, first checking they hadn't been followed. Gordon noticed dark patches under the arms of Tomasz's shirt and his forehead, above two bulging eyes, looked like hot wax. Powerful waves of stress radiated from him in pulses that echoed with the unsettling alarm of a dropped tray of glasses in a restaurant. Tomasz faced Gordon with a sudden intensity; he looked as though he might grab Gordon's collar and pull him closer such was the manic expression he wore.

"What is it?" said Gordon, mustering up his most unaffected voice.

"Delfin," said Tomasz. "It's delfin."

"Who's Delfin?"

"Hundreds of delfin, and other fish too, thousands of fish."

"Dolphin?"

"Yes delfin, I've seen them," said Tomasz impatiently. "You ask me yesterday about the beach, now I see it. It's very bad."

Gordon began to understand but already Tomasz was keen to leave and eyeing the door nervously. Tomasz's narrative was moving at a pace Gordon could not match, he had to keep interrupting him to clarify points but Tomasz, in his haste, just nodded and hurried Gordon along with a "yes, yes."

"There's thousands of fish. On the beach. I see them just now. Go with the photographer lady, go now."

"Where?" said Gordon. "In Selyvan."

"No, there," said Tomasz and jabbed his hand like spear thrusts in the direction behind the hotel. A shiver ran through Gordon, it was the direction he'd taken the night before.

"Can you show me?"

Tomasz shook his head and pointed back to the closed door with an implication Gordon missed.

"My family," said Tomasz. "He doesn't like me to talk. He pays me well. My family, you see."

Gordon nodded; he wasn't going to press a reluctant man - although he felt just as much the reluctant man himself.

"Ok, tell me where. Tell me how to find the dolphins."

"Take this road," said Tomasz jabbing again with his arm. "It's five minutes. I see it when I smoke."

"The coast path?" said Gordon. "The coast path behind the hotel?"

There was a creak, a floorboard perhaps, Tomasz started and immediately reached for the door handle to leave but Gordon stayed his hand.

"Tell me," he said. "Do I take the coast path behind the hotel?"

Tomasz nodded.

"I don't remember hiring out the conference room for a morning meeting," said a voice from the far side of the room, Lychgate stepped from the shadows and Tomasz instinctively reached for the door.

"Shouldn't you be in the kitchen with the breakfast pans?" Lychgate said, addressing Tomasz who apologised and scurried from the room.

"I was just getting directions for the bus back into Penzance," said Gordon. "I'd forgotten the timetable."

Lychgate paced towards Gordon with a resolute bravery he rarely displayed, such was his conviction that Gordon took a nervous step back against the wall. Lychgate closed until he was inches away from Gordon and his proximity broke social convention. Gordon wondered if he should run or strike first. Lychgate stood poised but then suddenly broke, he reached out, behind Gordon's back and leaning closer as he did so, before fastening the door shut behind them. Lychgate reached into his pocket and held up a large iron key, he showed it to Gordon without speaking a word. He turned the key in the lock and the mechanism clanked shut. Lychgate stared into Gordon's eyes with a burning intensity, but Gordon maintained his calm.

"This door isn't for guests," said Lychgate eventually. "You can follow me out. And I'll expect you all to be checked out and gone by eleven. You'll want to be in town for half past."

"Why?" said Gordon unsteadily.

"For your bus to Penzance, of course... or didn't Tomasz tell you?"

"Of course," said Gordon. "We'll be gone by then."

Lychgate raised a palm to indicate Gordon should leave. Gordon could sense Lychgate just half a step behind him but he didn't slow his pace or turn back. Gordon continued walking until he reached the top of the stairs before turning back to check he hadn't been followed. He was alone. He strode to Clara's room at the bottom of the corridor at such a pace it could have been mistaken for a jog.

"What do you mean get my camera?" said Clara, who looked seen surprised to see Gordon when she opened her door.

Gordon's garbled explanation did little to satisfy her or to quash her most pressing concern that the only bus out of town would be leaving in just over an hour's time. The thought of trekking back to scene of last night's drama held little appeal.

"Last night, you promised we would be leaving in the morning," said Clara. "I've spoken to the desk; they're expecting me back. I want to go back. There's no story, you said so yourself."

Gordon persisted and Clara adopted a different line of argument, but it was non sequitur alongside her former and weakened the defence.

"You nearly drowned yourself chasing this," she said. "Just let it go. Whatever it is - and I'm not saying there is anything - whatever it is, isn't worth it. It isn't our story."

"Fifteen minutes," said Gordon. "That's all it will take, and you're already packed. We'll just go and look. If there's nothing there we come back and take the bus. We'll be in London for dinner, I promise. I'll even buy you a large white at the Jugged Hare."

Clara could hardly refuse. She had filed so little over the weekend she was harbouring secret guilt. She remembered the insecurity of the job she loved to do. Besides, she had a journalist's instinct for storytelling. She wanted her photos on the front of every newspaper as badly as Gordon wanted his by-line below the headline. She agreed on the proviso it was a fifteen-minute venture and darted back inside to fetch her camera.

"What about David?" Gordon asked, remembering his charge as they paced down the corridor.

"He's sick," said Clara. "I knocked at your door ten minutes ago when I couldn't find you at breakfast. He looks like death warmed up. Let him stay."

The pair of them strode past Lychgate in reception who eyed them with the suspicion they'd come to recognise as his default position. Gordon held the heavy oak door open for Clara and together they sucked in the chill November air of a cloudless morning, swept clear by last night's raging storm.

CHAPTER TWENTY FOUR

Gordon raced with wild purpose, he had been dissuaded by the previous night's events and quickly rediscovered his hunger. Clara too showed alacrity in the task and hurried half-a-step behind Gordon with her warm breath misting the morning air. She breathed heavier than Gordon, but she also heaved the camera. A rare haw frost had settled on the ground, and it had yet to be broken by the warmth of day.

Clara was still feeling ill-at-ease in Gordon's company and didn't like it. She wondered if his silence was born from an embarrassment he felt from the previous night. She jogged to catch him and then struggled to match the stride of his long legs and had to jog once again to re-join, quickly she was panting. Gordon noticed and turned to wait for her.

"Is everything OK?" he said.

"Sure, you walk too fast."

"Sorry it's habit. Besides, I promised we'd be back in 15 minutes."

Gordon slowed to pace for a few steps but quickly reverted to type and led Clara on another forced march.

"You said you'd slow down."

Gordon turned and waited once more, this time with a face of pained expression. This gave Clara the opportunity to ask if everything was fine.

"Why wouldn't it be?" he said unhelpfully.

"Last night," Clara started but lost the train she'd played out in her head moments earlier. "I just thought you might be upset with me, that's all."

"Why would I be? Did something happen."
"No reason," said Clara awkwardly and annoyed that Gordon wasn't offering her a chivalrous hand. "If you say everything is fine, it's fine."

Gordon shrugged and returned to the path. Clara could tell he had turned his mind from her all too quickly and was thinking of what Tomasz had said to him. Gordon quickly re-established his distance ahead and it grew with every step. Clara knew he was not going to stop to wait for her again so resigned herself to a more comfortable pace and watched him disappear ahead over the crest of the hill. She wondered what she felt about him. She found him intriguing despite herself. He seemed so assured and yet racked with a self-consciousness that often left him isolated and open to criticism. His sense of humour never failed to make her laugh when he employed it, but he so rarely did. She supposed he was handsome in an unkempt sort-of-way, but too skinny and she thought he would not age well. She imagined when his black hair whitened - and there were already the first grey hairs sprouting from the temples - and his eyebrows grew bushy and curled in on themselves like ringlets. She thought of his father when she met him at Paddington Station, he had made her laugh and she liked him instantly. But she knew Gordon was prone to stress and could become silent and introvert, she witnessed it then and she hated it. Clara never liked things unsaid, she deplored reticence and liked to confront the fallacies of social convention. Then she thought about Zara. What a pain she was. How she complained about Gordon and the things he'd done. But why had Gordon even dated Zara? She couldn't have ever appealed, she was the sort of person Gordon would sneer at with his cruel tongue, which he employed as rarely as his sense-of-humour but with similar effectiveness. Of course, Zara was attractive, Clara knew that, but did Gordon? She thought not. He seemed to transcend the physical. She had never once caught him making sly glances like so many other men. When Gordon had stared, he did so in earnest, open-mouthed and awestruck like a child gazing upon a shire horse. She had liked this. It was the closest she'd ever felt to being worshipped, closer ever than the soppy lovers who'd thrown themselves gushingly at her feet with sentimental, purple poetry and misspelled declarations made by text. Clara asked herself, as her cheeks reddened about the white earth like the Robin of winter, whether she was falling in love. She asked herself the question, but she had already guessed the answer.

Gordon's head bobbed back from behind the crest of the hill. He looked panicked and called out for Clara. She stopped dead in her tracks to try to hear what he shouted, but the wind blew in the opposite direction and all she heard was the mad flap and crack of her camera's leather strap in the wind. Stopping had made Gordon wave all the more furiously so she guessed he wanted her to follow him quickly, so she made a valiant effort to jog up the final and steepest climb. She crested the summit and Gordon held out a supportive hand to embrace her.

"So, what is it?" she said panting.

Gordon took a step to the side and Clara saw what he'd seen.

"Holy..." said Clara but words seemed inadequate once her mouth had started forming then.

"Moley?" Gordon added helpfully.

"Exactly."

Clara stared where the cliff dropped steeply away and down into a shallow cove, just 40 metres wide and ripening to a gentle embrace of the calm sea. Clara wished the sea had been turbulent, it would have made the stark contrast more bearable. The smell was the first assault, the stormtroopers of the nightmare vision. It wasn't a smell of decomposition but the sour, faecal smell of writhing bacteria thrashing in warm lactose, a salty sexual smell. The beach of the cove was a silver litter, glittering eerily but beautifully in the strong morning sun. Sometimes it twitched like the pulse of one single serpent, at others it stared back still and lifeless with black dead eyes. Tomasz was right. The sea for miles around was barren and dead. Its contents strewn like flotsam on the pebbles. The hardest part for Clara to see was the noble resignation of the fish, the patient fatalism of the dolphins who would rather crisp under a dry sun than return to the waters.

"What are we going to do?" she said eventually.

"Call the police? The coastguard?"

Clara shrugged, half in acceptance but without any motivation.

"I've got down there to take the pictures. This is our story, Gordon. This could be huge. We have to file first. We'll report it afterwards."

"How many fish would you say are down there?"

Gordon was writing copy in his head.

"10,000, 100,000, a million? It's impossible." said Clara distracted as she considered angles and the best way to frame. "I need to get down there."

Both stood in a vacant hypnosis, both measuring the possibilities of success, both calculating the size of the story before them.

"Ok, you go," said Gordon eventually. "But lend me your phone, I need to file copy and mine went swimming last night."

"I don't have it," Clara shrugged. "It's in the room."

"Why did you come out without it?"

"Why did you take yours swimming? Don't blame me."

Gordon was annoyed at the sudden inconvenience and obstacle in the way of his immediate and impatient plans.

"Well I need to jog back to the hotel to make a call to the desk."

"Not until you've seen me down there safely. I can't waste any time, Gordon. If the tide comes in, we've lost it all, right?"

"Of course," said Gordon, the gentlemen returning. "The path leads down that way. It looks well used but I'll watch you from here. Once you're down there give me a wave and I'll run back to the Cragg. I'll be back again in less than 20 minutes, I promise."

Gordon watched as Clara picked her way slowly down the path. He was right, it wasn't steep, but Clara was unsteady and cautious compared to his own reckless ride the night before. Gordon gave little account for the camera she carried, shielding the uncapped lens as it swung about her shoulder. When Clara reached the bottom, she gave Gordon a wave of recognition and he returned it with a nod she had no chance of seeing. He stood and waited a moment, watching how quickly she became absorbed in her task. He watched how she picked her way carefully among the silver flesh and crouched and framed and shook her head and moved on. He was happy for her. She had seemed lost to him, her cynicism bubbling and distilling like a blinding spirit. Snappers are always cynics, he told himself, it was inevitable. And journalists aren't? Another voice returned. He often played out conversations with himself in this manner, like Phaedrus he would explain it to himself. But he had been too harsh, he saw that now. How focused he'd been on arriving at the cove, how intent he'd been as he marched ahead. Now he had arrived and all he wanted to do was to stare down at Clara, to make sure she was happy and working.

At close quarters, the smell of the fish was overpowering, but Clara realised she was lucky - once decomposition set in, she knew the smell would quickly become intolerable. She worked in short gasps with air sucked through her woollen scarf. Even this was little protection against the stench and soon she was unable to differentiate smells, as if fish was all she had ever known in her nostrils. Movement too was difficult in the cove. So thickly carpeted were the fish that she could not help but occasionally step on a few stranded bodies. At first Clara felt enormous pity and half wondered about mounting a solo rescue operation but the sheer scale of the disaster and the sorry state of the twitching fish revealed the futility. Many of the fish were tiny sprats flapped and slapped more frantically than the larger mackerel and herring, who foundered breathlessly and with a glassy resigned stare.

In among the fish Clara saw twelve or so dolphins. She recognised two factors were crucial for a successful image. The first was the sheer scale. She needed to find an angle which best illustrated the thousands of fish washed up on the cove. Secondly, was the dolphin. The dolphins would evoke the necessary sympathy and came bundled with a bag of visual connotations tailor-made for tugging the heartstrings of the British press. What's more, the reason she had been sent to Cornwall in the first place was to record the dolphin beachings. This lucky find - and lucky she felt despite the desolation around - more than met her brief.

The last few fish convulsed in violent throes, but the dolphins were all clearly dead. Clara placed a tentative hand on the body of one of the dolphins closest to her. She did not know what she was expecting, a pulse, warmth, cold? As their naked skin met, she recoiled in sudden horror, as though some spark of connection had been made between the two. She felt a sudden uneasiness and the dolphins wet skin filled her with uncanny terror. She stood up and found an angle to photograph the scene, she had no intention of remaining down there any longer than necessary.

Clara fired a few shots. The light was tricky. Despite an early sun it had not yet reached the cove and the scene looked flat and without energy. She experimented with her flash but she was dissatisfied, although it brought out the dolphin in the foreground with a sharper outline and better clarity, it rendered the silvery mass of fish in the background dull and formless. She spun around looking for inspiration and cast a forlorn but hopeful eye towards the sun behind the cliff tops above, wondering if it would suddenly break in brilliance like deus ex machina. It was then she saw Gordon, he was still there, he had waited for her. A giddy shot of happiness bubbled through her, and she felt a sudden guilt at her early grumbling in his name as she bounced and slid down the path to the cove. There could be no mistake, Gordon was looking down at her. Watching over her and making sure she was safe. He was waiting for her. But then Clara spotted another figure. Approaching slowly along the path. A black figure, she could not make out anything more, but she was certain it was a man. The man approached from behind and it was clear from the way Gordon stood so firm and unflinching that he wasn't aware of his arrival. The man stood within a foot of Gordon and Clara wanted to shout a warning up to him, but her voice would never carry as the wind whipped about the cove. She felt a sudden fear for Gordon's safety and knew she had to leave immediately.

CHAPTER TWENTY FIVE

"Quite a sight," said a voice from behind. Gordon nearly jumped from the cliff in fright. He turned and saw the Colonel, sallow-eyed and pale. He wore a black Crombie, pulled tight against the wind. He shot Gordon a quiet smirk of recognition with just a flicker of malice.

"We found them this morning," said Gordon dumbly. "It's odd."

"The water was no place to be last night," said the Colonel. "Perhaps you heard the storm blow in."

"I did."

"It doesn't howl like that in London, does it?"

"Rarely."

The Colonel took a step forward and looked down at Clara who was busy taking photos below, she was oblivious to everything but her viewfinder.

"She's doing a fine job down there," said the Colonel but Gordon felt uneasy and protective over Clara and changed the subject.

"What brings you out here?"

"A morning constitutional. And yourself?"

"The same."

The Colonel took another step forward, drawing level with Gordon, and together they stood side-by-side staring out over the whale grey sea. Gordon became aware of the cold and wished he had a coat like the Colonel; he felt at a disadvantage in his company and wanted to be gone. His disadvantage wasn't purely his attire, there was something so charming and familiar about the Colonel that Gordon knew he could not ask him about the previous night. The Colonel radiated a soothing calm, like gentle motherly strokes on a burning convalescent brow. His words came unexpected and gentle with orchestral richness of tone but with a crisp and reassuring meter. His face, despite the evident exhaustion, maintained a youthful vitality and glow, only a few light creases had found a home across the forehead and around the eyes and there were no broken veins or pigmentations. But his eyes were the most alluring. Dark and liquid, never quite the same twice so that they demanded examination. Gordon was drawn to them quite hopelessly and sought to avoid meeting them because he could never quite be certain of breaking their spell.

Eventually the Colonel turned to face him.

"So, I hear you leave today."

"That's right," said Gordon.

"Shame, shame. The weather might just pick up tomorrow. And did you find what you were looking for?"

"It's hard to say," Gordon said in a gruff and guarded tone he hadn't intended to betray.

"Keep those cards close to your chest," said the Colonel. "I might be up in London in a week or so - depending on how things go down here - the girls are eager to get back to town."

Gordon remembered the Colonel's strange companions with their cold, languid beauty and hostile charm. The Colonel's mind also turned to the girls and both stood silent in thought.

"I must indulge them from time to time," said the Colonel breaking their contemplations. "You know you should come to the club back in town and we'll take a drink."

"I'm not sure," said Gordon.

"I insist," said the Colonel. "I might have some news for you."

"News you can't share now?"
The Colonel's genuine smile disarmed Gordon and made him feel boorish and rough. The Colonel placed a gentle hand on his shoulder.

"I like you Gordon, it's a shame you can't stay because I think you'd have found my work very interesting."

Gordon recognised the dangled carrot but knew how important it was to remain aloof, a molecule of eagerness in the Colonel's nostrils would see its reach extended.

"But perhaps I can stay," said Gordon casually, but then lacking subtlety. "Just tell me what it is."

The Colonel gripped Gordon's shoulder tenderly and gave it a shake of affection, he smiled, and broke into a laugh.

"It's awfully cold this morning and I'm exhausted from last night's excesses but do keep in touch."

The Colonel turned and walked away.

"Wait," Gordon called to him. "The tablet."

The words were like a bell to toll the Colonel back to his reality. He looked puzzled for a moment, his guard was dropped and the unexpected question - delivered so boldly - stole his firm footing. The Colonel's reassurance soon returned, and he paced towards Gordon in measured steps.

"You're very interested in that aren't you," he said, the slightest hint at malefic anger smouldered behind his eyes,

"Can I photograph it?" said Gordon, who by then had lost all reserve, risking all his heaped chips on a single spin. "It's for my father."

The Colonel thought for a moment. He was making assessments and evaluations like a chess master. His brain rushed down so many canals of thought, but eventually they all met at the same delta and his conclusion was settled.

"No, I think not, I'm afraid." he said sadly, but then his voice warmed in confession. "It's a red herring, Gordon. Forget about it."

The finality of the answer robbed Gordon of his momentum, but he was determined not to back down.

"Have you ever heard of Goëmagot?" he asked with the same crashing brutality.

"Of course, everybody around here knows the legend."

190

The Colonel was in control once more. His self-possession astonished Gordon and his words dripped like sweet opiate.

"He was a giant flung into the sea by Corineus. Very entertaining. I'm guessing you've read Monmouth's Historia Regum Britanniae?"

Gordon hadn't read it and felt foolish. His father would no doubt have had a cutting revisionist comment to parry the blow, but he was dumb and flailing. Eventually the Colonel saved him.

"Another red herring, Gordon, but you're a smart man. I already said it's a shame you're leaving, I'm certain you could have been useful. Dr Athelney too."

Gordon's eyes narrowed and his brow wrinkled. He hadn't expected the Colonel to mention his father, the words sounded alien from his lips and threatening. Gordon shook from the chill and the Colonel turned apologetic.

"You see, I'm wrestling with something deep, Gordon. I've been hauling at it from the depths for more years than I can even remember. Hauling and dragging with chapped, calloused fingers. But it's close and I shan't stop hauling. It's close and now I can almost grasp its cold, slimy body in my hands. I've been hauling at it all my life and now it's nearly mine."

The Colonel paused deliberately, he had the air of an orator. His eloquence made his sentences sound rehearsed but they were spontaneous. The Colonel felt a curious warmth towards Gordon, it was clear he wanted to explain something - to make a gift of his knowledge. He also recognised in Gordon's profession gifts were lightly received and rarely repaid. The silence revealed the uneasy stand-off in his mind. Gordon too wanted more but could not think of a way to extract it delicately and was cautious not to blunder. The long silence proved the best serum and the Colonel let out a long sigh and began.

"The truth is I've been plagued by a dream all my life," he said. "At first it sounded like a distant ship's horn somewhere through the fog. I heard echoes but could never penetrate the mists. First came the smells, they provided my first fragile footing. Salts, and sulphurs, and honeys, and the iron tang of hot blood on my lips. Then I saw phantom faces, they appeared as vague and fleeting as forms in the clouds. It maddened me. The harder I tried to crystallise the images the more fractured they became. But still they persisted, this was evidence enough of their importance. Eventually I learned to be patient, not to force them. I learned tricks and methods to prolong the dreams and even bring them about. I spent years perfecting the disciplines and followed a lot of fallacious advice before arriving at more effective methods. Now I have the dream in my mind complete and brutal. What's more, I understand it."

191

"But what has a dream got to do with any of this?"

"It has everything to do with this? It brought you here for example."

Gordon looked doubtful. The Colonel's words were confusing rather than clarifying and Gordon was disappointed.

"You shake your head but it's true," said the Colonel. "My dream brought you here. It is one great flywheel in the centre of the steam engine around which the rest revolves. It is the sun, and when it rises the truth can be seen. It's the gravity, its magnitude, it's boundless."

"What is the dream?" said Gordon. "Can you share it with me?"

The Colonel stopped himself once again. He had come seeking Gordon on that lonely cliff-top but he was giving more than he'd expected. He had come to Gordon to dip a tentative toe in the water. He wanted to know the journalist's intentions, he wanted to assess the level of his understanding. Now he saw Gordon defeated and on the verge of retreat and he regretted it. The Colonel knew every great endeavour deserved posterity. His vanity and the strains of his labours were overwhelming. He thought of Max Nash and a hot wave of disgust surged through his body. Gordon could be taught to understand, the Colonel believed, just as others had been manipulated before him. The Colonel would retreat within himself at moments like this and remember with misty romance the baking desert of esotericism he had crossed, blind and alone. The clues he'd found, the riddles he'd solved, the dark pacts he had made with himself. But those seedy back rooms, how many had he entered and what a sapling he'd been at first. In those grubby rooms that stunk of cigarettes on stale thin curtains that only half shut out the sickly amber light. The grubby rooms that stunk of bacterial sex and where he had enlightened his mind. These grim memories he stored with overwhelming pride. Women and men with glistening thighs and wet backs stuck to threadbare sheets rubbed raw. The flesh he had used and consumed, half-delirious and swaying. The black eyes of the brothel madam who made her quick, amoral calculations as he appeared at her door. That stinking sex hung over him and she would wonder what dark corners he had arrived to exorcise with the spell of viscid, tarry lust. She would nod silently and sullenly at some skinny Chinese girl nursing the scars of a recent bronchial infection or, once, a plump, half-drunk Albanian who smelt his poison but submitted all the same. Lower and lower he had sought for the truth in ever more vile and ridiculous employment of the sex magic. What then had he to lose with this journalist? What danger was in the truth, spoken proudly and unexpurgated. The story was nearing its conclusion and the climax was foreseen and assured.

"It starts with twenty men-at-arms," the Colonel began suddenly, catching Gordon unawares. "Always I sought clues. Their weapons, their armour, the braids in their bleached hair, even their sunburnt skin. Everything was a clue. One of the first things I saw was their pain, their humiliation, and their fear. It shocked me. They were running through the thick mists that blow in from the sea. I thought the mist was the cloudy fogginess in which lost memories shroud themselves, but it never cleared, and I recognised it as reality.

The warriors run, stumbling through the wet sand, encumbered by great axes, shields and swords - all of which I had traced in my mind and then put to paper. I have consulted with authorities and the verifications impressed me. This was around the time I first heard the name Athelney. That's right Gordon, but don't look alarmed. That was the first time I heard the name Dr Alfred Athelney, your father.

All of the men are bloodied and bear scars of recent defeat. One has lost an eye and it's been crudely bandaged in haste, it has blackened and congealed to the empty socket. Several have broken arrow heads snapped at the shaft sticking from their bodies, but the wounds aren't being tended. The wild panic drives them on, their eyes are like war stallions in the final charge. The berserk madness of death is in their eyes. Always one figure revealed himself the strongest. His was the first face I saw, and I recognised the significance of this very early. This one man is encouraging the others, driving them on and baring his yellow teeth streaked and stained with blood. I know now he is Ceolwulf.

I see him so clearly now it is as though I'm holding a photograph before me. Ceolwulf is tall and his braided sandy hair has lightened gold from a sun more intense than has ever shone on England. His complexion too is darker than his companions. Ceolwulf calls to his men in a language so beautiful when it is transposed from beyond the dark mirror of time that I have wept at its echo.

Ceolwulf winces in a pain and notices for the first time the thick bolt sticking from his stomach at an obscene angle. A thick black blood runs from his bottom lip and mats his golden beard. He spits more bloody bile onto the ground with fierce defiance. He turns to his men with a look I can only describe as demonic lust, a grin with all the ferocity of primordial creation. He stares out death, his own death and the death of all who stand between him and his ambition; death pulsing from his body as palpably as the lifeblood trickling from his mouth. His men are afraid no longer of their own mortality, today they are fighting alongside a devil of a man. A warrior of such wild hate his name is vengeance and the earth bends to his will. If you could see his face Gordon, if you could feel what I feel when I stand on that shore facing him. The clouds crackle with his charge and the waves are afraid to break at his feet. He is the master of the universe. I became fascinated by the power he wielded.

Ceolwulf orders a defensive arc, shield locks to shield. In the surf they knit tight. This is the stand, and it is beautiful in its grim resolve. Already shapes form from the fog on the horizon. The warriors grit their teeth, panting from fear and rage and wondering how their death will come - all know their deaths are inevitable now as a host approaches. From the fog I see a second army, unbloodied and gleaming. Striding arrogantly on horseback or with trained crossbows, their sinews taut like Olympian muscles. They are beautiful too, magnanimous, and wielding death with a grace and majesty of a reluctant God.

Fearlessly, Ceolwulf turns his back to the advancing army and falls to his knees in the shallow water. He removes a tablet from a leather strap beneath his breast plate and holds it out to the grey sea. I saw it in his hands and I woke shivering and sweating. For the first time the significance dawns. I had to hold it in my own hands, the same object he held. It has passed through generations and it is my link, the key through the portal. After I had seen our tablet there in his hands my search became obsessive and I had to possess the knowledge. Everything else became secondary. However, the irony was - in those early days of feverish search - that the visions had never been so impenetrable. Then I believed if I sought, I could find; if I looked, I could see. It was later I came to realise that understand came through an emptiness of thought and not the promotion of it. That vision came through blindness and not the telescope.

But all of this is aside, you've come to dine for the steak and not the gravy. So Ceolwulf begins to speak lowly and slowly in that beautiful tongue from that ugly mangled jaw. He is reading from the tablet. A few of his men in the defensive wall hear him and look at one another in confusion before turning back to snarl at the enemy who advances in pace by measured pace. I smell the brine and the shit that streaks their leg, and the piss and with death so close it brushes their cheeks with feathery black wings.

Ceolwulf is kneeling and his voice becomes louder and more distinct. His eyes are closed, I remember, as if in prayer and his outstretched arms in vain appeal. He is aware of nothing but his own ancient voice and the dusty mantra he repeats over and over again.

The opposing army closes. I see them clearly, the whites of their eyes. Again, everything became a clue. Their cropped hair, their plate metal, their weapons, their horses, their standard. At their head rides a stately figure on a white stallion that snorts and froths in fear but is driven on by its master's will. I recognise the horseman as plainly as my own reflection. I see myself. That is my blood which courses through his veins. I can smell it like a dog smells his own. He is Earl Mortain, the first Lord of Selyvan. What a sight, wrapped in heavy brown furs and without armour. I come to recognise his aloofness but also, I sensed a determination behind his unblinking eyes that I know in myself. His slender but steady outstretched arm holds an ornate sword, he points its gleaming blade directly at the men surrounded on the shore. The sword channels his will of destruction and those at his flanks march on with heavy steps driven on by that steel compass. Thirty paces from the enemy the Earl raises his hand and the army stops with hive mind. Both sides stand on the lonely beach in silence, as a wind whistles about the steel and whips the sodden standard while the waves gently break. Still, I hear Ceolwulf's words regardless of all else.

The Earl calls out to Ceolwulf, he addresses him directly. The words took the longest to crystallise and for many years I thought I would never understand them. Every time I pricked an ear to decipher meaning they would distort into a drugged blur; it was like tuning a broken radio. With much dedication they came to me, this was only last year. So, you understand now how contemporary we are in the tale?

I remember the first time I understood those words. When the visions were over I remembered nothing of them but it was enough to know I'd understood them once. The second and the third time I could recite snatches. Now I have the whole speech transcribed and translated. It is very powerful and if you could have heard it spoken it would chill and impress in equal measure with its vast sublimity.

Come forward Ceolwulf. You have sinned against God with black heresy. You have corrupted and perverted nature with your crimes. Come forward now and you heal some of the wounds you have opened. You are the dispossessed, but these men still have homes and families to return to. If you come forward now and bring to me what you possess then I will spare their lives. I will spare the lives of those loyal to you despite the suffering and death they have brought under your misguidance. Come forward now and they live. Stay where you are if you prefer their deaths on your already bloody hands. Stay where you and they die, and their wives die, and their children die and their animals die and their homes are burnt and anybody who weeps for the death will also die. All of this death is on you, I am absolved. I swear now to God I want no more death, only justice for the sins you have committed.

Those are his words, you hear them now only as an echo from the axe age. Of course, I fail to do them justice, but you would shiver as I did if you could hear them from the mouth of the Earl.

But back to the narrative. Ceolwulf does not respond to my ancestor's commands. The Earl holds out a hand in appeal, he is asking for the tablet, but Ceolwulf is unmoved and continues his mantra. Perhaps he does not hear the Earl's words or instead chooses to ignore them. Again, the Earl orders him to hand over the tablet or else his loyal English will die in that wet grave. He tells Ceolwulf the lives of his men are not his to throw away, that only God has the right to decide who lives and dies. Ceolwulf continues reciting his mantra and still his men stand firm, growling and resolved.

A long roll of thunder rumbles a low salvo and a sudden wind blows in from the sea, it sweeps away the fog with one majestic swoop. Now my vision is alive with a blinding clarity and every woollen fibre, every bow string, each hair is defined as though it was inspected under a magnifying glass. With the thunder comes rain and it pounds with dull thuds on the leather armour and tinkles on plate metal. The Earl pulls the furs tighter around his neck and looks impatiently at the darkening sky as a great bolt of lightning strikes the cliff top above, a tree is rent asunder in an anguished crack. The storm has unnerved several of the Earl's Norman knights, the fresher faced who hadn't had their mettle tested at Hastings. Their young eyes flicker for support from the wavering ranks. The Earl meets their wild eyes with a magnetic glare and a greater fear grips them still. They turn once again to face the enemy and the lashing rain. Still Ceolwulf continues.

I can see the Earl's cool, rational mind as he estimates Ceolwulf's loyal housecarls who have formed a protective ring about their former thane. He sees their bloody faces and their muscles tense and quivering. He sees their rage and the strength contained in their rage, the beauty of this trapped energy and the power of industry. He knows they are humiliated, that they are proud men, but he knows they are men with families. They are men that can help him to build, to sow, to toil and to bring prosperity and security. I recognise in his eyes that he doesn't wish for death, and he stalls to avoid a bloody conclusion. So he appeals for them to leave, once again his words are measured and each syllable has the weight of gold.

This is not a question of honour. This is not a question of cowardice or disloyalty. You have stood beside your thane to the point of death, you have proven your bond. Look now at who you pledge your lives to, who you die for. Consider carefully the sacrifice he asks you to make. Consider well the lives of your women and children, of the homes you've built and the hours you've toiled tilling this acid land. Consider almighty God and the heresy you are being ordered to defend. Is loyalty worth damnation because that is what he asks of you. Consider loyalty, what is a bond of blood compared to the bond of life everlasting. The bond that joins all men as one and the bond he would snap with his witchcraft. Leave the field now and return to your homes. With God as witness you shall not face punishment for the death and destruction you have already wrought. In proof of my clemency your lands shall be extended, and your lives enriched. I swear this oath. Do not stand now for death and damnation. His mind and soul were sold to the devil and Turc in the east. His heresy is wicked, his turpitude incurable, his madness complete. Go. I release you.

The speech is impressive, once again I fail to do it justice but how those men stood firm after hearing his words astonishes. They choose their own death, the death of their families and the promise of damnation and all for a man kneeling in the sea clutching a tablet and chanting like a mad monk. They straighten themselves and tighten the shield-wall.

The storm agitates the sea. Minutes before the waves lapped but now they break and batter the legs of the English. The Earl dismounts his white horse, slipping from the saddle in one fluid movement. He slaps its hind legs as a signal of release and it bolts, running from the beach at full gallop.

The Earl turns to his knights. It is decided, he says, and as one they encircle the Saxons. From the shieldwall a housecarl breaks rank and jostles himself free. With his head held high he walks away from his comrades and into the Norman lines. He walks slowly, with the measured steps of a wedding march, towards the Earl and with the exaggerated gestures of symbolism he drops his axe into the surf. He continues and several of the Normans twitch and raise their weapons, but the Earl orders them to lower arms with a wave of his hand. The Saxon has shame in his eyes but is resolved, behind him the shield-wall reforms more compact as though he had never stood in the ranks. The man now faces the Earl and drops onto his knee in submission. The Earl places a hand on his head and utters an absolution and frees him. From within the Saxon removes a dagger and lunges in one powerful thrust at the Earl's throat but he is too quick, perhaps suspecting deceit, he steps aside, and the Saxon loses balance and falls to the ground. Instantly five of the Normans fall on him, hacking and stabbing. The Saxon is left chopped and bloody - a sickening pitiful sight that I never cared to witness but which always held me in dark fascination at its raw viscerality. The Earl is given the honour to administer the final blow in revenge for the assassination attempt but after casting a disgusted look at the groaning flesh he refuses. Instead, he screams command in a petrifying voice he had until that moment kept hidden and his army flies at the shield wall behind a flurry of bolts and arrows.

Several of the Saxons drop instantly from the missiles and the wall struggles to tighten as the first wave of Norman swords fall upon it. The fight is brutal but quickly resolved. Once the shield wall broke the defenders lost their unity and fell into the sea foaming bloody phlegm from ruptured lungs and the quick, dark blood of deep head blows. All that is left is Ceolwulf, still kneeling with water up to his waist and facing the growing storm - unaware of the massacre behind him and chanting his same mantra with its hard syllables thumping a beat to the gentle music of the Germanic tongue.

It was many years before the conclusion of the dream came to me. In the earliest years the violence and brutality would shock me, and I would awake wild eyed and sweat-soaked. At first, I would feel the force of the blows and the wounds suffered by the men on the beach. With familiarity, the shock of violence lessens and its mangling impact deadens. Later I could steel myself for the blows and even began to enjoy the sensation and suffering. Only through familiarity could I progress to the conclusion, it was necessary to undergo the gruelling pilgrimage to arrive.

So, the Earl waves back his men and they retreat to the shore. One nurses a grave cut down from the shoulder to the armpit. His friends support him but when he reaches the beach he collapses, and they can only watch him choke in splintered pain on his own arterial blood. The Earl is alone in the sea with Ceolwulf. With the violence of humanity settled it is nature's turn to demonstrate its wrath and the storm has broken with all its almighty fury. The waves become stronger and its with great difficulty that the Earl strides deeper to meet Ceolwulf. Strangely the waves break before reaching the Saxon thane and their power is lost. He holds out the tablet to the heavens and with every verse he recites the brewing storm crackles in return. My impression began to form that the tablet and the words it contained were a formula of control, an invocation. Its words were cracked and distorted, and the very fabric of reality blurred and warped around its sound with the power of enormous gravity.

197

From the sea, great spouts of water gush and spout, thrown with violent anger towards the churning storm clouds. Thrown with a fury and to a height impossible to fathom. Something is thrashing beneath the waves, and I can see the cool lines of the Earl's face crack under the revelation. Suddenly the touch of the water is both sickening and chilling. The icy depths have been blown to the warmth of the surface and gnashes with sharp Jurassic teeth. The men on the beach are afraid and retreat further. A noise like giant wheels whirring is deafening, it pulses like radiation. It can barely be described as sound, it's more sensation. It has no fixed location but exists within the air like a gas. The Earl keeps a steady head and wades closer to Ceolwulf.

The final part of my vision I have seen only once. I have gone to great pains and lengths to recreate the circumstances that permitted this moment but never with success. The resistance within my mind is too strong. Even the spark of recollection causes it to flinch and retract. I forced myself to confront that which I saw but my memory refuses to permit it. However, it is my memory - conscious or unconscious - and it remains within me like some insoluble drug. I saw the thrashing waves, the black sea like some churning primordial soup flecked with white foam like the jaws of a rabid dog. I remember the Earl's face as he witnessed the horror and Ceolfwulf's red unblinking eyes as his victory rises from below. I see a form, impossible to distinguish but emerging. It is a hand and an arm and then, from within the tormented ocean, I see something else. A face. The Earl recoils in horror but recognises the gravity and danger. He removes a knife from beneath his soaked furs and - from behind - cuts the Saxon's throat in one deep gutting slice. I see Ceolwullf's face, without pain or fear, staring with those wild eyes in vain appeal to the ocean, his tongue clucking automatically through guttural, bubbling clacks. The Earl seizes the tablet from his hand and wades back to shore. With Ceolwulf dead the storm subsides and the sea calms.

That is my vision. That is my legacy, it's bound in my blood with the irresistibility of atavism. It is the Mortain curse."

Gordon could think of nothing to say, he had no opening or introduction. Questions formed but popped like bubbles in the air before he could vocalise them, his mouth goldfished mutely.

"You photographed the tablet, didn't you?" said the Colonel eventually.

Gordon had no reply, he could not assess if the Colonel, there was something oddly conspiratorial about it all. The Colonel rightly understood silence as affirmation.

"And of course, you showed your father."

Gordon was still unable to speak.

"It's OK," the Colonel reassured him. "What did he say?"

The Colonel's voice was calm and soothing and earned Gordon's absolute truth. Nevertheless, it was reluctantly and with some difficulty that his mouth formed a reply.

"My father said it was bunk, gibberish. He said it was a hoax. He said it was an anachronism, that it was impossible."

The Colonel smiled at Gordon's unabashed response.

"My father and my grandfather have caused me a lot of problems," he said. "They too shared my passion but were less patient in the pursuit of a final truth. They saw the destination but when they lost the path, they simply paved new ones, that is to say they were not prepared to take the journey. You can't fly over the jungle and parachute into its heart of darkness. No, you need to take out the machete and hack your way through. You need to embrace the weeks of malarial sweats, you might lose your helmsman to a spear in the flank, or your hull to the rapids. Their purpose was the same, and they wanted to convert and enlist and so much of their work and study was downright fiction, sometimes even malicious. It has been a considerable nuisance to separate the truth from the propaganda."

Gordon remembered his father's story about the fallacious encyclopaedia entry in the Ashmolean and wondered about recounting it, but the Colonel's flow swept him along regardless.

"Honestly, it's never been about power for me. I am pure-hearted in study. You should not undertake a PhD for riches, no good can come from that. It is the same for me. I am not ashamed of my travels. I am not ashamed of the sacrifices or debasements. I want to be honest with you, Gordon. Do you trust me?"

The question was left hanging in the chilly air. A great seagull squawked manically from the pained and twisted branches of a nearby tree, the only tree along the entire clifftop. Both men turned, startled to face the bird which flapped away desultorily, lazily riding the low thermals.

"It's called the Damned's Eyrie," said the Colonel nodding at the lonely tree. "A few hundred men have probably seen the world for the last time hanging from that stout branch. It's not a bad view I suppose, if you're ignorant."

Gordon disregarded the Colonel's aside and was still turning over his words.

"I trust you," he said. "I don't know why, but I trust you."
The Colonel smiled with the faint echo of warmth of a midnight fire.

"Come to the hall at five, miss your train. But don't bring the photographer - or the boy. Come alone. Bring a camera if you have to, it's not important any more."

The Colonel clasped Gordon on his upper arm and squeezed it, an acknowledgement of initiation. The Colonel turned, without another word, and left. Gordon watched as he strode away with one arm half raised in farewell. Gordon stood and waited until the Colonel was out of sight.

CHAPTER TWENTY SIX

Clara came puffing, Gordon heard her before he saw her. Loaded with camera gear, her strong legs alone dug their holds and her thighs and calves burned their way up the steep path. She was surprised to see Gordon standing precisely where she'd left him half an hour ago and wore a quizzical look as she approached - her lungs too raw for speech. Gordon, too, was surprised to find himself rooted to the spot where he'd been stood with the Colonel, fixed like the storm-struck trunk.

"You were quick," said Clara. "I thought you'd be back at the hotel filing."

Gordon had to shake himself from a dreamy daze in order to respond.

"I haven't filed yet," he said vaguely. "I was waiting for you."

Clara looked surprised but a hot breath of warmth melted her face like frosted glass. Gordon realised at that moment he was going to keep a secret from Clara. He had already and quite deliberately concealed certain aspects of the previous night's events but, even to himself, he could not explain his reasons. Either through fear of not being believed or in protection of - even collusion with - the Colonel, Gordon would not discuss what he'd heard and seen with Clara. He wasn't inclined to venality and there had been no suggestion of compromising his professional ethics, but he recognised it would be impossible to make Clara understand; not the intrigue - that would come naturally - but the dull terror that lurked beneath the respectability. Even Gordon refused to acknowledge what his mind hinted at, the security blanket of self-deception.

"Come on," she said. "Let's head back to the hotel and see just how slow Lychgate's internet connection is. I'll wind him up one last time before we leave."

She stopped dead in her tracks to emphasise the blinding flash of inspiration that had struck her.

"We'll probably need to order a taxi to take us to the station soon if we're going to make the train."

"Yes," said Gordon absently, disappointed at the mundanity of her practicality. He knew he had no intention of making the train back to London, but he also felt a desire that David and Clara should. He wanted to be alone now; their company would hinder his own progress down the shady path the Colonel was steering him.

In sharp contrast with Gordon's brooding, Clara was in good spirits on the walk back to the hotel. Her photos had been a success and she knew it, her stars had aligned - a miracle rarer in photography than astronomy. The low sun had broken from behind the billowing cumulus at just the precise moment and caught glints from the foaming crests of the waves in perfect contrasts with the shades of marine greens, blue and greys providing a gluttonously rich depth to the background in her photographs.

"Look at this buttery bokeh blur," said Clara in high spirits as she cycled through thumbnails, magnifying her efforts for Gordon's approval.

"It's out of focus," he said, and Clara hung her bottom lip theatrically before resuming in her happy sing-song, self-absorption.

The promise of the bright morning was quickly collapsing, and banks of dull clouds stacked to the horizon like folded sheets. The precious, saturated blue green of the sea had slunk in silent depression to a faded film, blue-grey, only just escaping a misty monochrome. But Clara was immune to any change and her brightness bounced along with the same skip as her step.

"I wonder how young master David is feeling," she said, hoping for some sport from Gordon - but he shrugged with a blanked face.

"That's not very kind," she said lightly.

"I don't care. He was making such a fuss, it's only a touch of cold."

His low simmering frustration had been carelessly guarded and spilled with a steaming hiss over its sides. Gordon was focusing elsewhere and had let his words ring with the harshness of clanging steel, Clara looked shocked.

"You're an insensitive prick, aren't you?" she said, her mood transformed.

"No," said Gordon defensively. "I just thought he was milking it a bit."

"You're so right wing," said Clara, smirking irresistibly as she walked on - it was Gordon now who stopped dead in his tracks with a face like the garden toad suddenly revealed in the sunlight with its stone lifted.

"I'm not," Gordon shouted after her. "I'm apolitical."

202

"Yeah, yeah," said Clara, dancing a jig in her happy head with the reaction she'd provoked.

Gordon's spell was broken, and he spent the rest of the walk home listing reasons why, if anything, he was centre-left and a naturally inclined liberal. Clara nodded along, her silence was the perfect and prolonging foil.

Gordon and Clara arrived warm and glowing at the Cragg. She was impatient to file her photos. So long as they remained on the flash card of her camera, they were worthless, only once they'd been received back in the office could they begin to resurrect her tattered career. Gordon was pleased for Clara but once more diverted by the distraction of his strange conversation with the Colonel. Within, he was steeling himself to a course of action he instinctively felt was wrong, the inexorable and accelerating pull of gravity to the deadly core. The plan was Clara would file her images with a note to the desk alerting them of impending copy, which Gordon would provide. Clara knew her photos carried their maximum impact alongside the text and was confident Gordon would deliver. But Gordon wasn't typing, his chest was tightening, and a warm, sickly stew churned within.

It took less than five minutes before Clara was cursing the upload speed in the Cragg. She sat on the wooden floor of the lobby with her back jammed against the wall and her laptop perched precariously on knees bent double. She had selected a dozen of the best photos in her lightbox from the hundreds of frames she'd taken. At first the wi-fi crawled, then it became patchy and eventually died altogether. Clara's impatience bubbled over, hissing, spitting and steaming. She banged at the reception bell and Lychgate duly slithered out from behind his office door rather than bothering to open it. His face was wrinkled like a perishing vegetable and expressed both disgust and a supercilious shock at the low affrontery of having been summoned.

"Your wi-fi's down," said Clara, who had forsaken all civility with him.

"I don't think so," Lychgate said, dismissing her with the hand that bats away the persistent fly around the cream cake.

"Well it is, I've got no bars."

Lychgate cast the slightest glance at the laptop she thrust before him.

"It's working perfectly fine in my office. I know because I changed the password just two minutes ago."

"Well that's it then," said Clara with a sense of relief. "What's the new password please?"

"I change the password everyday at 11am for the benefit of my patrons. Although I notice you've not checked out yet - and it's already five past the hour - the wi-fi is for my paying guests, not for tardy stragglers."

"I just need to file some pictures - it will take ten minutes. Charge me for another hour on the room if you like?"

"I can charge you a late check-out fee, but since I'm not a sleazy roadside motel I'm not in the business of renting out my rooms for the hour."

"Look whatever," said Clara. "Just charge me the late checkout fee and tell me the new password, please."

"I could show you the business brunch package I offer," said Lychgate. "You get use of the function room, coffee, biscuits and a sandwich platter. Of course, you get access to the wi-fi and telephone too."

"Fine," said Clara. "I'll take that. What's the password please?"

"Certainly," said Lychgate baring his crooked teeth behind his curled-lip smile. "I'll just need a credit card, your business VAT number and two forms of ID. That's £149, please."

Clara coughed, looked to the heavens, and collapsed her exhausted head onto the reception desk.

"Forget it," she said. "I'll use the wi-fi in Penzance, yours crawls. Can you order us a taxi please, we'll just go and collect our bags so we don't delay our checkout any longer."

Clara marched off.

"Of course, Madam." Lychgate called after her with mock courtesy.

"Come on," said Clara huffily as she passed Gordon, who still sat with glazed eyes at his laptop - barely registering her appearance. "Get your stuff together and check out; and give the sick man of Europe a prod to make sure he's still breathing."

Gordon watched her stomp away. She'd left her camera and laptop by the reception desk. A taxi would be arriving shortly, and they'd be on a train back to London. It wasn't a dead loss; he had his story about the beached dolphins - and dramatic photos of the fish washed ashore. He could probably cobble together an environmental story if he strung together a few loose facts and quoted selectively. But there was the Colonel, Gordon could not stop his mind straying back to his stirring words. Barking mad or not, the weird world the Colonel showed through the narrow crack in the door, held ajar by his delicate foot, shattered a path for Gordon like blasted rock - splintering those jaded press conferences, the Whitehall grip-and-grin drudgery and "knock out six pars" from some unlikely and crudely engineered survey.

"I'm still charging you for late check out," Lychate shouted from behind the reception desk, Gordon stared back with eyes resolved to their purpose and, for a moment, Lychgate shrank away from their intensity.

CHAPTER TWENTY SEVEN

Gordon left the Cragg at a half canter and cast furtive glances back for any sign of Clara. He had escaped Lychgate's notice, too. Gordon wanted to leave like the thief and as his feet crunched the gravel outside the hotel it was like alarm sirens ringing for an escaped prisoner. He kept up the pace all the way down the long and winding cart path. He chose the less precipitous route into town so he could maintain his long strides, also the longer path concealed him from the views out across the bay from Clara's window. He felt the great weight around his neck of Clara's camera, it pinched with all the weight of sickening guilt. It had been necessary, he told himself, he had to photograph the tablet, he had to photograph what he saw.

A low thunder churned over the sea and the blue grey had blackened. It was not yet midday, but a premature dusk had fallen over Selyvan. Gordon knew even at his impatient pace he was twenty minutes from the Hall and had no desire to be caught out in the open under those apocalyptic clouds. Gordon wondered too if the Colonel was expecting him. There had been such a cool assurance about his words, they were almost premonitious. But how would Gordon explain his arrival? Was his very appearance at Selyvan Hall not tantamount to conspiracy? These are the questions that tortured his mind, entangled as it was in the barbed wire of no-man's land. For a minute at least he was granted respite when the rain began to fall - at first a patter but rapidly growing heavier. Gordon tucked the camera within his suit jacket, he had no idea if it was waterproof or not but played it safe.

The rain running hard from the hillsides had found a collective path and created a gushing stream across the sandy path. The channel stopped Gordon mid-stride, just sparing his sorry Church's a second soaking of the day. He paused before the channel, it was fordable or a springing hop for Gordon's long legs but a memory of Clara held his step. He thought of her back at the Cragg, suitcase at her side, irritable to be leaving and impatient for Gordon and David. By now, he thought, she would have knocked on their door and a bleary-eyed David would have answered. Clara may have discovered Gordon was missing, Lychgate might have spotted him leaving. She would have discovered her camera was missing, this wouldn't go down well. But he would take good care of it and return it to her with all her photographs intact. He was just delaying rather than scuppering the mission. There would be another train back to London, Gordon would be ignominious for the long journey home but by Paddington it would be quite forgotten. Clara was forgiving, she would understand and besides, if his hunch proved true, they would all have the story of their lives.

Gordon took a step back, rocked in his brogues, and flung himself over the obstructive stream. Alea Jacta Est.

The low amber lights of Selyvan Hall burnt softly as Gordon trotted along the long elm tree-lined avenue. There was a strange comfort in their warm glow despite his increasing chill at arrival. The rain had slackened but the damage had already been done, rain bled with sweat and baubled on his nose, chin and fringe. His heart was pumping uncomfortably, and the pressure of his discomfort spat with the angry hiss of steam.

The great oak door of Selyvan Hall now felt familiar and Gordon let the weird iron knocker fall with more authority than on his previous visits. Nervous, he was, but there was a furious determination driving his actions and the resolve, that so frequently evaded him, was lit with all its blinding luminosity. Piret saw it too as she heaved back the Hall's main portal to the visitor. She saw Gordon cast anew and smiled at him with half laughter at the transformation - she approved. On 'any other day' Gordon might have reeled at the sight of such a welcome, but he had transcended 'another day'. Piret slouched nonchalantly against the timber frame and met Gordon squarely in the eyes, her smile had not yet melted. She wore a black silk evening dress that sparkled kaleidoscopically as oil where the weightless material caught the breeze. She might have been part of some elegant function was it not for a slit sliced in her dress from ankle to pelvis or the backless cut which exposed both flanks of her breasts.

"He said you'd come," she said. "I'm pleased."

Gordon did not respond. His black hair had jewelled in the rain until the beads formed one single mass and, with the weight, glued his fringe across his forehead in glossy strands. His brown eyes licked with the dead intensity of a serpent and water dripped from his chin.

"I need to see him."

"Surely," she said. "He will be down soon, he's changing now. We're having a party."

Gordon looked at her as though to verify her words. She curled her lip baring her front teeth, it was enough to shock the reaction her first appearance had failed to stir and he took a clumsy step away from the door. She laughed again and Gordon was forced to rediscover his composure.

"Don't stand there in the rain," she said, stepping aside. "Come in."

Gordon took an uneasy step across the threshold onto the cold, chessboard tiles. Piret strained against the door and it fastened with a firm clunk that echoed many times around the stone entrance hall. The little light of the dark day was snuffed and they stood together in a gloom that strained the eyes and where only dull shapes existed. Gordon felt Piret's cold fingers seeking his own, she squeezed gently.

"You're not afraid of the dark?" she said. "We must make our steps carefully."

Piret led Gordon and he followed obediently. Her eyes had adjusted to the low light more quickly than his own and she steered him safely across the entrance hall. The satisfying click of marble under his feet gave way to the creak of wooden boards and the warmth of confinement indicated he was being led down one of the many corridors that ran south, east, and west to the three wings.

"Wait a second," said Piret and she drew them to soft halt. She placed one hand against his chest and stood in silence as though she was listening.

"It's ok," she said after half a minute, and once more led him by the hand, twice veering left as the corridor truncated. Gordon had felt certain of himself on the march to the hall, nervous certainly, but certain. Now all that certainty had vanished and he saw with new clarity the absurdity of his position, walking hand in hand with such a glamorous stranger through this ancestral warren. And for what purpose, he wondered. Was it still the truth he sought? Gordon felt less certain of this too.

"OK?" she said.

Gordon nodded mutely in the dark and beside him the rushing whispered roar of a struck match flared painfully. Piret lit a small candle she'd plucked from a holder on the wall and held it out before her.

"We can light this now," she said. "This is the oldest part of the house. I don't come here often."

Gordon once again followed her and about them the candle cast low and eerie shadows which lengthened and snapped as they pressed on. At the end of the corridor, they came to a low wooden door, shafts of light at its base indicated a brighter society within.

David opened the door at Clara's sixth rap. He stood blinking back in a pair of Y-fronts and his great grey shirt so large it was almost a dress and with the buttons all askew.

"Oh dear God," said Clara, averting her eyes. "You're not at all ready? Where's Gordon?"

David blinked back.

"Gordon? The taxi's here" she shouted through David. "Thanks for rescuing my camera, but you might have taken the laptop too."

David blinked.

"Gordon?"

"He's not here."

"What do you mean he's not here?"

David blinked. Clara pushed past him and strode into the room, she spun on her heels and marched into the bathroom.

"The bloody shit," she said. "I'll kill him."

"What's happening?" said David wiping his snotty nose with the billowing sleeve.

Clara was white with rage and even through the fog of his cold David recognised a danger. She was distracted by the betrayal and operating by a different code of convention. David backed from the door, he wanted to lie on his bed, to smother himself under the covers and fasten his eyes to the sickness but he couldn't. He couldn't even bring himself to sit. Instead, he edged nervously around the bed, his eyes on Clara waiting for her fury to subside. It was a minute before she broke the ice of her frozen rage. She laughed and it melted the paralysing frost in the room.

"What is it?" said David.

Clara looked at David, suddenly aware of his presence.

"You can stay here by yourself," she said to David, but addressing Gordon. "We'll get the train back to London and you can stay. You can hang yourself, but I won't be part of your suicide pact."

And then to David.

"Pack your things. Our train leaves in forty minutes."

The door swung open and painful light came churning down the dark corridor like a burst dam. Gordon covered his eyes and was led squinting into the room. The dank, cool was replaced just as dramatically by the roaring fire in the far corner of the room – even at the extremity Gordon could still feel it licking his cold cheeks. He tried to blink some sight back into his eyes, feeling blind and vulnerable. Gordon was able to prise his lids apart by sheer force of will. The room he stood was roughly pentagonal in shape. It had the look of a castle keep with great grey stone locked fast by its own weight. But the room had a softer edge to temper those first forbidding fortress impressions, reproduction tapestries of hunting scenes hung twenty feet high broken by five great arched windows. In the centre of the room was a thick wooden table, bearing the detritus of a night of revelry. Several wine bottles lay prone like drunks, dribbling the last soft spots of themselves from exhausted lips. Several more bottles remained standing, uncorked, half-drunk and destined for the sink. The twenty or so wine glasses were an equally sorry sight, distributed across the board like a scattered flock. One bore a jagged wound and contained the parts of its own shattered body where its clumsy owner had stored them for safe-keeping. Empty plates with congealing syrupy desserts which coagulated like blood completed the picture.

Only two guests remained seated at the demolished banquet and Gordon started at the sight. On a high-backed chair close to the fire Professor Burroughs sat, a glass with the dregs of a heavy red swung gently in his swaying hand. On his knee sat Iveta in a silk nightdress. Her bottom lip hung open, her hair tousled wild, and her dark make-up ran like the first stab at watercolours. She fixed her vacant eyes on Gordon as he stood shivering at Piret's side. The Professor's free hand rubbed with greedy strokes her inner thigh, across her stomach and then cupping and pecking her exposed breasts with loveless, lusty gropes. Iveta sat in hollow numbness, still she kept her eyes locked on Gordon who could do nothing more than maintain her gaze.

"You're cold," said Piret. "Sit by the fire."

She led Gordon by his wrist towards the fire. At first, he resisted, not wishing to take another step in the Professor's direction, but Piret pulled him along firmly. The Professor finally noticed the intrusion, sitting himself more upright as though startled during some secret act. He followed Gordon suspiciously with dark drunken eyes. Gordon shifted awkwardly while Piret pulled a heavy chair from the table, its legs wailed painfully against the stone floor. The Professor bore a grim, toothy smile and met Gordon's eyes with filthy malice. Iveta sat staring at the door, where Gordon had been stood a moment ago. The Professor did not say a word, Gordon stood in silence.

"Sit," Piret ordered and breaking some of the tension. "Dry yourself."

Gordon reacted hypnotically and eased himself into the chair. He sat steaming by the fire, his prickled lungs burning from the exertion, cold and tension. Still the Professor met his gaze, looking at every second as though he was about to speak but never allowing the weight of momentum escape his lips. Still the Professor bore the same lascivious smile, aimed squarely at Gordon. Then he moved and Gordon flinched, and his smile grew wider still, almost breaking into a snort of a laugh. His hands slowly and precisely resumed their lurid massage. The resumption awakened Iveta from her trance and she made to stand but, dropping his wine glass with a piercing smash, the Professor seized her with both strong hands about the waist and pulled her tightly back into his lap. She resisted for the spark of a second but quickly slunk back into her vacancy. Gordon shocked went to stand, looking at Piret in support, but she shook her head and motioned for him to remain seated. Instead, she sat, curling her body like a cat around the legs of his chair and his legs. She rested a lazy head and arm across his thigh. Gordon backed further into the chair and his entire body burnt with the mixture of an exotic cocktail whose spirits fired his heart in gushing spurts.

The door burst open and the fire roared a welcome with the sudden breath of air. The Colonel strode into the room purposefully and without a trace of surprise at Gordon's presence. Gordon felt a sudden shame and rose quickly, shaking off Piret clutches as he did so.

"Good, you came," said the Colonel naturally, walking straight to Gordon to shake his hands. "Forgive the mess, we were celebrating late into the night."

Gordon smiled weakly but words would not form.

"Are you warm enough?"

Gordon nodded.

"Good. I rarely use the central hall – the vault my father used to call it. It takes an age to warm up and then once the fire is burning strong enough it rather sucks all the air and life from the place. Not last night though. And I suppose you're glad for a bit of a toasting, it looks like you swam to see us again."
Gordon looked wretchedly at his sodden clothes, he felt like the naughty wet dog.

"Sit, sit," said the Colonel. "Wine?"

The Colonel didn't wait for a reply and instead located a clean glass from the array and hunted for a bottle.

"Would you take a sniff of this and tell me if it's drinkable."

The Colonel thrust the bottle under Gordon's nose. Still Gordon could not speak, let alone smell the distinctions of a vintage wine, instead he smiled and nodded. The Colonel poured a mighty measure and then, rescuing a second glass, one for himself. With a single strong arm, he pulled a chair opposite Gordon.

"To our adventure," said the Colonel raising a toast and drinking. Gordon mimicked his host robotically.

"But it feels a bit claustrophobic in here yet," said the Colonel turning to the Professor.

"Burroughs, are you still here?"

The Professor steadied himself and looked with tired eyes and a swaying neck.

"Unlock Iveta, the poor girl's exhausted and get yourself back to Penzance and to bed. You're too old for this."

The Professor stood suddenly to attention. His movement caught Iveta by surprise and he nearly toppled her as he rose. He gave a wallowing bow to the Colonel and lost his footing, causing him to lurch forward indecorously.

"Goodnight, old friend," said the Colonel in a bid to hurry the Professor along, then turning to Iveta who had begun to gather glasses with clumsy lethargy. "Don't worry about those, they don't matter now. There's a taxi waiting outside, make sure he gets in. Then go and shower and get some rest, I'll need you later."

Iveta followed the Professor, who was making uncertain progress across the room. When he sensed her presence, he latched onto her waist with childish fawning. Iveta, who seemed suddenly recovered, led him authoritatively and with evident strength out of the room, fastening the door behind her.

"That's better," said the Colonel. "He's a bore but a useful ally. His weaknesses are so exploitable it's pathetic. A night here and there at the Hall and he'll be sober sorry and pliable for a few months. The University has useful authority along the coasts. There aren't many people who can close entire stretches of the Coastal path to the public. The Professor claims to have discovered the fledgling nest of some endangered coastal bird, for example, fills out the forms and I have the peace and quiet my studies require. Even the police can't breach the cordon without permission from the University."

The Colonel smiled to himself.

"I abhor a bore and a boar, but I know when to make exceptions."

Gordon coughed, clearing his throat. His voice felt cracked and parched. The wine soothed it and staved off the chill he felt creeping its way up his spine.

"I'm sorry," he said eventually. "I'm a little cold and not very good company. Another bore."

The Colonel shook his head forcefully, annoyed at the suggestion.

"No, you're different. I like you. You are to be initiated."

"Initiated into what?"

"Don't worry, I'm not asking for a pound of flesh or a bond of blood. But you will be rewarded. Today we will see the fruits of my preparation, you and I, provisions over long decades, and that of others before me. Victorian pioneers, piecing together esoteric knowledge that had gathered dust through the dark ages and even a Renaissance overlooked. Scattered ancient fragments, seeds which had pollinated in Dionysian wood cults, Sumerian sea gods, even within the Bible. These splinters, hints at a thing greater than our minds could comprehend – bent crooked as they are by the Mistral of egos. But in some primordial soup, in the black emptiness of our subconsciousness, it lurks and chimes in curious harmony, a resonance with the past. Such were the sights man saw in his infancy that the shadows of their greatness were seared within us. Vague silhouettes that could haunt us all the way to insanity. Why the shape of the serpent disgusts, or the eerie creep of the spider. They are the fragments. They are in possession of the dreadful image. The man who tells you he does not fear the spider is lying. He has suppressed fear and yet it exists. He has allowed his social environment to deaden instinct to the point that now we are all dull beasts, like the cows in the field chewing cud until the moment of slaughter."

Gordon took another heavy swig of his wine. Was this what he had come for, he wondered. The Colonel's words always rang with such conviction and his speeches with eloquent fluency that even psychobabble assumed authority. Psychobabble or was this Gordon's own crippling ego damming the flow of truth, he asked himself these questions as he drained his glass without even realising wine was passing his lips.

"Forgive me," said the Colonel. "You're cold. You should have changed your clothes; I should have offered. You can probably fit into something of mine, it might be a bit loose."

Gordon's clinging clothes would take another hour to dry, even by the fireside, so he accepted gladly. Whatever the Colonel had in store he would rather face it toasty than the soggy squelch he was then.

"Piret, find Gordon some clothes and help him dress."

Piret, who had resumed her seat by his chair, lifted her light bones and held out her hand to Gordon. Gordon looked uneasily at the Colonel and back at Piret who motioned for him to follow.

"Don't be such a miserable Anglo Saxon, she's beautiful." the Colonel said. "We're liberating ourselves from these repressions today."

Gordon saw that Piret was beautiful. She stood before him so naturally poised, alabaster and Junoesque. The previous day she had seemed modern and shop-worn, frayed at the edges, but she was transformed. Gordon saw strange faces in her own, it twisted and distorted like an image held in water. For a moment he saw Clara, only blinking shattered the mirage. Piret seemed to coo like a siren and – through the black silk – Gordon saw every contour and curve of her body. Miserable Anglo Saxon. Wood builder. Walking in the footsteps of giants. The unworthy conqueror. The bastard inheritor. Miserable Anglo Saxon. Gordon seized himself, shaking action into his bones. He stood, swayed, caught his step and steadied himself. He smiled at Piret who lent forward and kissed him. Miserable Anglo Saxon, he said to himself. Miserable Anglo Saxon. Piret led Gordon from the room, who followed with uneasy footsteps. The Colonel took an uncertain sniff of his wine and threw the dregs onto the fire.

CHAPTER TWENTY EIGHT

"Evil is only good perverted," said the Colonel.

Gordon's head rocked like a sinking ship, his gums were numb, and his teeth bobbed in empty space as though he could spit them all into his hand. He groaned in an aching weight, but his mouth stuck dry. The colours he saw bled and ran, the reds pumped luridly, and the blacks of the shadows pulsed and oozed. His clarity increased, as though every figure and form were traced in sharp ink. The sharpest of all was the Colonel, who stood before Gordon weird and stately as some alien emperor. He held a strip light in one hand, and it cast a blue white light across half his face. Gordon's head bowed as though under a great burden. He realised he was still wearing Clara's chunky camera around his neck, this was some relief to him, it was a totem, a key back to the world he'd betrayed.

"Good is only the suppression of evil. Evil is a flickering concept ascribed by transient morality."

"Where am I?"

"Morality and immorality are for religion. We revel in amorality."

The Colonel's words were sickening, and Gordon stopped trying to follow them, he let them flow into one consecutive stream of noise. From these meaningless syllables patterns began to emerge, insidiously but becoming clearer. Gordon realised he was communicating with himself. The words were his own and they were distorted and confusing. He felt himself slouching in his chair with a great weight pulling him into himself and he laboured to sit but his arms were both frail and heavy.

"You've drugged me," said Gordon in a low slur. "The wine."

"Drug?" the Colonel laughed. "That sounds so pejorative. You drank too quickly on an empty stomach. You'll recover. We're cresting a new age, Gordon. The drug is the breath in our lungs and the blood in our veins. Bliss is it this dawn to be alive, but to be young, Gordon, is very heaven."

The Colonel's words came to Gordon in a hard rhythm and added an unsettling percussion to the soft music he heard. Once Gordon was aware of the music its volume seemed to increase and the gentle piped tones resonated but whenever melody threatened to impact on those discordant notes it retreated back into its own sickening drone, lost in its own thoughts. Note landed on top of note, creating infectious frequencies that broke inside the organs like disease and choked Gordon's brain like a fist down the throat.

"Please make the music stop," Gordon said weakly but the Colonel ignored his pleas.

"Listen, Gordon. 432Hz. The very frequency of this universe. Every rock, stone, plant and animal resonate at this frequency, it is nature itself. You must restore your own balance. 432Hz was recognised as harmony by emperor and mathematician. For so many centuries the greatest orchestras of Europe tuned themselves to this frequency as Europe lived through the great Renaissance. Turn on the radio today, listen to the television, play a CD and you hear 440Hz – a subtle change, so slight our ears can barely detect the shift but discordant and alien; 440Hz is monstrous, unnatural. The change occurred in 1933. The Nazis changed the frequency of their broadcasts to 440hz under the order of Goebbels. Overnight, the Reich resonated with a chaos more powerful and infectious than any of the steel hammered into weapons of war in the smoking factories. The world adopted 440hz. It is all you have ever heard. Sound is reverberation and now our bodies are resonating at 440hz. This discordant pollution is piped malevolence, it pits man against nature and we lose the final faithful hair of our essence. This is an acquisitive, shrink-wrapped age and 440hz is the dirty, great engine powering this smoking hulk into meaningless oblivion. The essence of our understanding is lost, or - more accurately – it will never be awoken. But, today, let the sound enter you as it did in the Ming courts, as it did on a lonely beach with the twang of a 'Jew's harp, as it reverberated around the bold Andean Ziggurats of the Inca. 432Hz, let it guide you, Gordon. Close your eyes and follow it."

Gordon's vision was dim, and reality was filtered through the grime-crusted porthole of a submerged wreck but despite this the Colonel's mysticism sounded incongruous and odd. He had seemed a figure of formality, with the exception of his occasional martial quirk and eccentricity, he was an authority. Now, in his words, Gordon detected the faint squawk of madness and it rang with the unsettling air of an unanswered phone. For the first time Gordon saw the Colonel bare and brutal and those bloody sinews beneath the epidermis were twisted and writhing.

"432, it's always the same," the Colonel continued. "That's how I found it. 43.2 degrees. Written with an inevitability that makes the weary pilgrim weep at its ever-present obviousness. But why should I not expect to discover it on my own doorstep? I understood then it was my birthright. My genetic destiny. The first foundations of Selyvan Hall were laid in 1099, the year Jerusalem fell to the Crusader armies. The Mortain standard flew over the liberated city. The snarling jaws, the flickering tongue, the scaled coils. The serpent flew beside the cross, side-by-side. Forty-three years and two months later, at the fateful Horns of Hattin the serpent fell, trampled in the rout; 432 years after the serpent fell a new standard was raised as a new dynasty entered Westminster Abbey for coronation; 432 years on and the serpent flew beside Nelson as the French fleet was splintered into the storm-brewed sea. Throughout history my family – my blood – has shaped the course of this island. And so, 43.2 degrees west from the Greenwich Meridian this ancestral hall was built. An accident? It could only be. Here, in the very spot where you sit, the first block of hewn granite was dragged by the stringy sinews of the conquered. Here, it was raised. The Earl of Mortain raised his eternal home here as a monument for the truth he had discovered. It was his legacy for those who bore his name. A millennium has passed but now I am ready to claim our inheritance."

Gordon looked about him and, for the first time, realised his surroundings were new. He had the impression of a dungeon. The sound of dripping water. A smell like leaf mould was in his nostrils. The fog from which he'd awoken was burning away and he saw the room was indeed foundations. An earthy floor, which bore the jagged grin of ancient rock. Clearly, the later red-brick additions to the hall had been built to encompass this still heart with considerable care – leaving space for these ancient bones. But little remained of that Norman hall except for the circular central foundations, and evidence of two linear walls which led away from the nucleus. In the middle of the room, excavations had uncovered an old well, plumbed to its source at a depth the darkness would not reveal. Gordon looked over at this black chasm uneasily, from within an unhealthy, mephitic air blew with sour, wheezy breaths. The Colonel caught Gordon's nervous glances at the pit and smiled to himself in thought. He walked over to Gordon, clasping his two great hands about his aching shoulders.

"Our old well, my favourite part of the house," said the Colonel. "When I uncovered the well only then was I certain the hall had been deliberately built on this inhospitable plot for no other reason."

Gordon shuddered, even talk of the well chilled him. He wanted it covered in sheets to stifle its breath. It seemed to pant all the more eagerly at mention of its name.

"Let me show you something you'll like," said the Colonel. "A demonstration of Norman ingenuity... or bloody-minded willpower. This hall is built on a granite base so impenetrable we could erect a second Manhattan on its back. A granite that deadens the kisses of sharp iron and callouses the cartilage in the arms that strike it. Even the diamond-tipped tools of modern industry laboured to impress when I had the west wing re-inforced. But through this stone, a thousand years before, men chipped with dull blows – an inch a day – until they reached water."

The Colonel lifted the camera from around Gordon's neck. He let it dangle before his eyes, examining it carefully as a poacher might a snared rabbit. He walked over to the well and Gordon groaned, his words lost again in the medicinal fog and fear.

"Allow me," said the Colonel, and let loose the camera from his grasp. It disappeared, down into the darkness. Gordon cast his head back in despair.

"Listen," said the Colonel, rallying Gordon from his dejection. The Colonel was counting the seconds on his fingers and then came the dull splash as the camera found the water table. The sound echoed around the room, reinforcing Gordon's misery each time.

"One-hundred and seventeen feet," the Colonel said with childish excitement. "They tunneled nearly 120 feet just so he could build his hall on this precise spot. There's water half a mile down the valley. Three streams meet, you could power a mill. The soil is better too than this rocky scrubland. It wasn't accident he built here; it was design. When I discovered this well, I knew."

Gordon wasn't listening, the horror of losing Clara's camera had numbed him but at the same time liberated him, like the gambler who has lost his last hand.

"My ancestral home," the Colonel said, opening his palms in welcome. "Ancestry, the very word was once a poison. I did everything I could to avoid what I now see was always inevitable. It's funny, I once believed the sea was the poison. I defied centuries of family tradition and joined the army out of spite."

Gordon's head sagged with a heaviness accumulated by his efforts, and he was surprised to feel a trickle of saliva gather and drip from his lower lip. He caught himself and shook with his remaining strength to restore some vitality. The Colonel watched Gordon carefully and then a smile broke across his lips.

218

"My own recipe," he said. "I'd like to say it's purely organic, but the NHS has supplied the slow burning bottom-end."

Gordon was angry and frustrated. He rarely felt rage but then it surged to the surface from the depths of a sunken volcano. The fury at the destruction of the camera – suppressed by shock - was now beginning to recognise itself. His brain was somersaulting with the cocktail of emotion and drug. He had difficulty gathering coherent thoughts and felt as though he might spin himself backwards with the confusion, come thumping to the ground like a winged gull. Gordon stood from his chair, summoning all his reserves. He went to speak but the exertion rocked the ship perilously and he was forced to steady himself with a thrust hand against the cold stone wall. He took a deep breath and began again.

"You said you would share. You said you would show me, then show me."

Gordon was firm now. He had nothing left, there was no need to charm and flatter, his regular tricks, they were shadowed by this looming directness.

"Be clear and be precise. My head is swimming, and I can't follow these vague dates or riddles. Whatever you've done is done. Now explain."

"Explain? You already know. I'm gently nudging you towards the edge, but you have to take the plunge yourself. The shock of the icy waters could stop your heart. Explain. You know it. You can feel it. We all sup from the same shared vessel, we all drink the same thick primordial soup. It's all there, sloshing about in our bellies – yours and mine – it's molten lava beneath the sleeping mountain waiting to vomit forth in violent splutters of our own, shared vicious essence."

"Riddles!" Gordon shouted but the Colonel ignored the interjection and continued apace.

"A thousand names have been given to it, and by those with the far sight and nature to sense its presence. Dagon… Leviathan… Goe'magot... Kraken… Neptune… Tiamat; it is one and the same. It is alien and idiot. Of a nature and scale we cannot understand. Once a thousand of its kind thrashed their great and meaningless wars of power across the sprawling chaos of an infant universe. Flailing and consuming as galaxies blasted themselves apart. Its nature is not of our reality. It both exists physically beneath those waves and yet ceases to exist. Its dimension is not of our own, its dimension is not of the proportions our minds can calculate or comprehend. It is through the absolute levelling of all hindering perceptions that I have begun to visualise this perfect nature. Through this levelling, I have been able to stir life into its slumbering body. To antagonise but not command. Unlike those before me I am seeking neither service nor servant, I am not looking for alliances for the pale purpose of earthly power. I am a student, and understanding is my only reward. I have only ever sought the knowledge and my will is unbending to that goal. Only I can slip the bonds of this modern disease – infected, the whole of humanity. Itching its infected skin with consumer fancy, alcohol, the friction of one another's scabby skin in the dark because we can't bear its own sight in the light. I have slipped these bonds of the human condition; I have become holy. Devout, but not in service to some false god our primitive understandings warped and perverted into some self-serving state of religion. Tonight, it will wake. It will rise and you will see for yourself. Our minds will be blasted together. The god-seed sown, before this planet even began to form itself from the chaos, will return."

Gordon vomited, covering his shoes with the curdling acid foam of returning wine that tightens the throat and stings the nose.

"The sex act is the closest we can get to the enlightenment, those milliseconds of orgasm. I am not talking about the lust – because that is only narcissism. Or the fucking itself, thrown together as we are like the shameful tangle of some clumsy accident. Not then, it is ourselves we are fucking, our own ego, hardened like diamond and just as brittle. So not the action, not the sensory, not the nerve endings tingling but that one critical moment of orgasm. For those brief moments we slip the shackles of the human bondage and float away. Gordon, we touch it. A million poets and artists have attempted to understand the condition as they speak of the 'earth moving', but their experience has failed to recognise itself, its true purpose and, more importantly, its potency. Of course, this shallow species has failed to understand the act, ascribing it to love, or even a reproductive trigger for our survival. But I do, I do understand. In those brief moments of ecstasy, I channel my will, and never does it radiate through the voids with such clarity or with such primal force. It sends out a shock wave of will."

The Colonel was ranting. His madness was evident in the very certainty of his speech, spoken without flaw or pause. It was a speech he had spoken to himself for long years, refined and distilled. The Colonel twitched and paced, stressed each syllable with a weird emphasis and spat unapologetically. There was nothing chemical about his madness, no drink or drugs could have produced such a powerful effect. It was as if his core was burning, super heating and thrashing out with death-throe fury. Then, instantly, the Colonel's mood turned again, and he became silent, he turned away, he paced with slow distracted steps. Eventually he switched off the strip light he'd been carrying and the pair were plunged into total darkness. Gordon listened intently. The soft drip of water, the breath of the well.

"There is something chilling about the sea," the Colonel began softly and suddenly. His voice was behind Gordon now and he turned to face the sound. It was melancholy and without the vigour it had seemed to be accumulating.

"I'm not saying the natural order does not exist, just that the rules are of its game are played differently. It is alien, more so than any other environment on this planet. I love to look out over it with a sort of dark fascination. It was the backdrop to my childhood; for most of my life I've lived within earshot of its low roar. I imagine it's the same stirring that draws men to the peaks of mountains; the awesome sublimity. But the foot of the mountain to its summit is a less treacherous journey than the depths I would plunge. From a religious perspective it's easy to understand. The mountaineer has the light of God in his eyes for the duration of his ascent. His very action is allegorical as he reaches to heaven. But believe me when I say there are no benign gods where my gaze has been cast these long years. Prey on prey like so many Russian dolls until great, hulking monsters form from the fat of the weak. Monsters that fascinated early mariners, whose tales and legends swelled their proportions to the fantastic. But there was always the low current of dread within this fiction. Even today when I see those mythical images of sea monsters – crude misconceptions of the whale, the walrus, or the shark, twisted beyond all modern recognition – even in those do I see him; the eternal within us. These are misted reflections of the shadow print on our soul. In them his likeness was mirrored – although with the satisfaction of a solar eclipse viewed through shades."

The Colonel's sad voice trailed away and at the point of total silence he flicked on his strip light, Gordon cowered from the painful brightness. When he opened his eyes again the Colonel was stood just a foot away, staring back at him with a terrible intensity. Both stood without speaking, Gordon fighting to maintain the gaze, too afraid to look away.

"It's time," said the Colonel. "We must go."

CHAPTER TWENTY NINE

The Colonel led Gordon along a dark corridor, steering him with a firm grasp. Gordon's footsteps were heavy, and a queasy sickness was brewing. He felt half a second slower than the world as it moved around him and stumbled frequently along the gentle incline. Eventually they reached a heavy wooden door and the Colonel released Gordon to bear his full force against it. It swung open against his strain and from the smell of polished wood, Gordon could tell they had returned to the main chambers of the Hall. The Colonel once more seized Gordon's wrist and pulled him along, now with greater speed as the course became easier.

They arrived at the entrance hall, and here there was enough light for the Colonel to extinguish his torch. Piret and Iveta sat side-by-side, nestled on the steps of the great stone staircase, and peering down like birds through the ornate banister.

"We wondered where you'd gone," said Piret with the hint of cat call, Gordon stared back at her as the Colonel dragged him along, he ignored them. Piret gave Gordon a coquettish wave that sent a slice of sharp memory through him, but left no trace of its presence. Gordon wanted suddenly to leave the Colonel to his insanity and curl up beside Piret and Iveta, who seemed like the complete picture of homely love. But the Colonel dragged him to the door.

"Play nicely," said Piret as the oak door of Selyvan Hall slammed behind them.

The day had been dark when Gordon arrived but now it was clearly night. The low clouds had broken, and above thousands of stars shone brightly. The clear sky had brought with it a bitter cold and already frost was forming in the most exposed areas. The sharp air helped to enliven Gordon, but it also irritated his raw chest. He realised he was still wearing the same wet suit he'd arrived in, although it had dried slightly in the lost hours and was cloying and moist. Gordon now followed the Colonel without question, his will was absent and only a desire to see this through to its end sustained his actions and so it was without argument that Gordon seated himself beside the Colonel in his old Rover. The Colonel reached into the blackness of the rear and retrieved an old tartan rug, handing it to Gordon who gratefully and silently accepted. It was a scant act of kindness that carried greater weight with Gordon than its small measure should have allowed. It impressed on Gordon a renewed sense of the Colonel's sanity and the collusion he'd felt earlier in the day returned. But not for long.

The Colonel sped along the avenue away from the Hall at such pace that on several occasions all four wheels seemed to leave the ground as they hit unseen bumps in the old road. Gordon looked across at the Colonel whose large eyes stared unblinking into the night, picking a way through the insufficient light of a single headlight. The Colonel felt Gordon's eyes on his own and turned to face him. There was something so alien and insane in the shadowy face of the Colonel that Gordon turned away in shock and horror. For the first time since he'd arrived in Selyvan, Gordon felt a sense of mortal danger. Even facing the Colonel alone on the rocks the previous night, battered by the ferocity of the storm, the adversity and his pumping adrenaline had sustained a sense of action and adventurousness. Now he felt bound and gagged, a prisoner of another's dark will, unable to resist or appeal. His thoughts turned black and, with uncanny sense, the Colonel looked at him curiously.

"What's wrong?" he said.

Gordon refused to answer and maintained his blind gaze from the side window.

"What is it?" he repeated.

Still Gordon could not respond, afraid to answer and unsure of his own swirling emotions. The Colonel crunched the brakes and they jerked to an inelegant stop at the crossroads to Selyvan.

"You'd better tell me."

"It's nothing," said Gordon dreamily. "Only I have to leave now. I should never have come."

Gordon grabbed the door handle with a sudden mania but it swung uselessly in its hinge. He looked for the lock and pulled it free, still the handle would not open. He tried once more, frantically and desperately yanking but to no avail. Eventually he gave up and turned back to the Colonel, who sat all the while in cool observation.

"It's broken," he said smiling. "I've been meaning to get it fixed for some time, just never got around to it."

Gordon looked back in silent horror, the Colonel's face was twisted and vulgar. Gordon did not recognise him, he was a stranger.

"And besides," the Colonel continued. "You can't leave now. I should have to have a little pig hunt if you went running off into the night. I should have to stick you where I caught you."

Without another word the Colonel restarted the car from where it had stalled in the road, put it into gear and drove on. Soon he was chatting garrulously to Gordon about his army days in Cyprus and the time he had to oversee the court-martial execution of a Greek sentry who had been caught napping on duty. Gordon sat listening uneasily.

Before they arrived into Selyvan, where the low amber lights already spread like sickness through the low squall, the Colonel took a narrow road off to the right. Gordon had walked the road from Selyvan to the Hall several times, but this was the first time he'd noticed this new track. It began from the opening of a crumbled drystone wall and led across a boulder strewn field where only ugly, stalky grasses flourished. Gordon's head still pulsed with numb pressure and he wondered how far he would get if he tried to run when the Colonel finally released him. He felt his legs, they tickled with pins and needles and his muscles felt limp and distant. The drug was still coursing and in full effect. To attempt an escape felt futile and Gordon's fear was evoking that hidden anger in the Colonel that he sensed bubbled below the surface. The idea of smashing his head from behind with a suitable rock had begun to formulate. Had the Colonel's actions already warranted the use of such extreme force. Still Gordon was thinking rationally. He had been drugged that was certain, and a vague threat of violence had been stated against Gordon's escape. Or had it? Gordon's head could not maintain a train of thought without derailing itself with indecision.

"Welly, welly, welly, well," said the Colonel. Gordon started at his outburst, a silence had descended in the car as the Colonel concentrated on the uneven road and his exclamation rang out with exaggerated volume. Gordon followed the Colonel's eyes and in the road ahead the silhouette of a figure walked, shielding its eyes against the incoming light.

"It's a bleak night for a stroll across a heath," said the Colonel to Gordon with a conspiratorial wink. The Colonel pulled alongside the figure and wound his window down. Gordon looked but could not see the face, hidden by the Colonel. He slunk back in his chair in resignation of whatever twist the Colonel had prepared.

"It's a bleak night for a stroll across a heath," said the Colonel.

"Yes."

Gordon recognised the voice immediately, it was Clara.

"Jump in," said the Colonel. "Gordon and I are just taking a little drive down to the coast."

Clara opened the rear door and climbed in, scooting herself over to take the seat behind Gordon. He suddenly felt a great concern for Clara. He accepted his own danger with resignation, the foolishness of his own curiosity, but now he had endangered Clara. But was there danger? He still wasn't certain. With Clara beside him once again he received the warmth of reassurance.

"What are you doing out here?" said Gordon to her.

"I could ask you the same thing?"

The Colonel laughed.

"You're a pair of journalists, no mistake" he said. "Always questions, questions. No room for the pleasantries."

"Where's David," said Gordon, ignoring the Colonel.

"On the train back to London," said Clara after a moment, Gordon felt her seething.

"Have you got my camera?" she asked as they bounced along the road.

"It's back at the Hall," the Colonel said, talking over Gordon who let his own words die away.

Clara hummed in annoyance but said nothing more.

From the field the road's incline increased steeply and the car's wheels slipped and slid as they struggled to find traction in the mud. Always as Gordon thought the fight was lost and they would slide powerlessly back down the hill it found grip and laboured painfully on. The Colonel drove with abandon and total disregard for terrain or condition. Eventually the steepness plateaued and looking out Gordon sensed they were nearing the same cliffs he had made the strange and fateful interview with the Colonel, just that morning. How long ago that felt to Gordon then, as he stared ruefully at the low glare from Penzance in the distance. He envied David, on the warm train back to London, away from the madness.

The Colonel pulled to an unannounced stop that sent Clara tumbling and grumbling in the back. He got out of the car without a word and walked around to open Gordon and Clara's doors. They emerged shivering into the cold night. The Colonel had stopped at the top of a high cliff and the wind blew icy blasts up from the black sea. The Colonel gathered several items from the boot including the torch, which shone with a solid beam against the night.

"Follow me," said the Colonel.

He led them along the high path until they reached the stump of a fallen tree, this served as a marker for the Colonel who immediately veered over to the cliffs. Leading down to the sea was a path. To compensate for the steepness a thick rope had been secured into the cliff face which, with considerable daring, could be used to reach the rocky bay below.

"You don't expect us to go down there?" said Clara.

"You first," said the Colonel to Gordon, then turning to Clara. "You follow at the rear. And watch your step, tumble and you'll take us all with you."

"How about you go on your own and then you don't need to worry about me tumbling?"

The Colonel's stony face collapsed with the rumbling fury of a landslide and his eyes flickered with white heat. Clara stepped back in fear, the realisation that had dawned so gradually for Gordon illuminated like a light switch. Gordon saw her pale face in the torchlight and his sympathy flooded.

"It will be fine," he said to her. "I'll be going first. If I can get down there without breaking my neck, you can."

Clara nodded nervously in return and the Colonel smiled in satisfaction.

Gordon would have been unable to make the descent by himself. His left arm pawed the cliff senselessly and his legs folded weakly beneath him in the footholds. The Colonel, with great reserves of strength, clung to Gordon's right arm just below the shoulder and lowered them both steadily down the cliff. Clara, unburdened by another, progressed behind them. Once on the cliff she found the footholds were firm and numerous and provided she kept a constant grip on the rope, never felt in any real danger once she'd learnt not to look down.

The bottom of the descent landed on a small ledge which led into the shelter of a cave mouth. Inside the sea cave the ledge widened and sloped gently into the lapping waves. A wooden platform had been built into the sea, fastened against the cave mouth by crude brackets. A small boat bobbed at the side of this hidden port. The Colonel once again switched on his torch and entered the cave.

Gordon slumped exhaustedly against the entrance of the cave wall, panting with irregular gasps. Clara pounced from the cliff beside him, her own bravery had empowered her. Her vitality in contrast with Gordon's near collapse was marked and she looked with concern at his pale and pained face.

"Are you OK?" she said. "You look ill."

"I'm fine," said Gordon, noticing the Colonel's attention was diverted. "We're in danger."

Clara nodded quickly.

"Do you have your phone?"

Clara felt inside the shoulder bag she'd lugged down the cliff. She scrabbled furiously in search of it, past pens, and receipts and lens caps and long-forgotten lipsticks. She found it.

"Let's begin," said the Colonel's voice from behind. Clara jumped and let her phone fall back into the bag. She turned to face the Colonel but he showed little interest in her. Instead, he seized Gordon once more by the wrist and led him into the cave, Clara followed. The Colonel stepped onto the boat and guided Gordon beside him. Clara was unsure what to do, or what she could do if a crisis was provoked. The Colonel ignored her repeated questions and continued on his tasks with the duty of an automaton. Gordon was seated in the front of the boat and before he or Clara could protest or resist, the Colonel tightly bound his wrist with twine and fastened the other end to a mooring loop at the stern.

"A Gordian knot," said the Colonel.

The blood in Gordon's hand pumped hot against the tourniquet.

"What the hell are you doing?" said Clara.

Still the Colonel ignored her and instead headed to the outboard motor at the rear, he pulled once, twice against its cord and it spluttered into life and filled the cave in oily smoke. The sound of its buzzing engine reverberated around the solid rock and the noise grew unbearable. Clara had to shout to make herself heard. Gordon began to emerge from the fog of his drugs and a panic seized him. He pulled hard against the cord to free himself, but it only bit hard into his wrist, bruising bone against the skin. He appealed to Clara for help, who appealed to the Colonel. He did not listen to her pleas, he was calmly adjusting the rudder at the back of the boat and tied it into position once he was satisfied.

"You are going to get something of a scoop," said the Colonel to Gordon, raising his voice against the din. "I am sending you out into the ocean for a closer view of our golden dawn. There's just enough vapours in that tank to get you the perfect spot."

The Colonel kicked free the boat from its mooring, and it strained its way against the current out from the cave.

"You can't be serious," said Clara. "Stop this."

The Colonel as though suddenly spotting the circling fly that pestered his summer snooze turned to her.

227

"You can scream like Andromeda on the rocks," he said. "I rather like that image."

The Colonel pushed her aside and slung himself up the cliff in one bound. With three great tugs from his strong arms, he had already climbed twenty feet. He stopped and reached for his kukree, with one ringing blow that blunted its blade against the rock, he cut the rope beneath him and left Clara stranded below, who called up to him in futile appeal.

Clara turned her attention back to Gordon, who called out to her. His boat was heading from the cave and into the open sea. Clara seized a piece of driftwood and, at full stretch, was able to ram the stern of the boat. It was enough to steer the boat into the side of the cave where it nestled in a nook. The motor snarled maddeningly to free the boat, churning water white in the struggle.

"Well done," said Gordon, who was busy working on the second part of his escape. In the boat the Colonel had left a length of rope. It was out of the reach of Gordon's free hand, no matter how hard he strained against the cuff, but his long leg had just managed to tickle the end loose from the coil. With the leather sole of his Church's gripping against the twine, Gordon slowly pulled the rope towards him. His stretch upset the balance of the boat and it shook, freeing itself from the nook that saved him from the hostile waters. The boat began to creep beyond the safety of the cave, Gordon had to double his efforts. Soon the rope was within reach and his hungry hand grasped the cord as though it were bound in priceless gems. The Colonel, had bound Gordon's right arm to the boat, his weaker hand. Only with his left could Gordon manage to hurl the rope to Clara, already twenty feet away at the mouth of the cave. To his relief Clara caught the rope.

"Now tie it firm, quickly there's not much rope left."

Clara looked around for somewhere to tie it and saw only solid, faceless rock. She ran into the cave, already she could feel the rope tightening in her grasp, soon it would pull taut and she would not have the strength to hold. She jumped onto the wooden pier, which cracked and creaked as she landed. The rope pulled tight, and she leapt forward and to the ground to slacken it. At the base of the mooring she spotted a bracket, this was her chance. Her fingers worked dexterously despite the pressure, and she'd just completed the knot when the rope tightened and the weight and momentum of the boat tightened what she had begun. Her fingers caught inside the loop and her ring finger caught. It was slammed hard against the wooden bracket, and she felt her bone crack with a cool, shooting pain that surged from her head to her toes. Instinctively, she pulled her hand free and cradled her throbbing finger.

"It's done," she called out to Gordon, who now bobbed at safe anchor thirty feet out into the sea.

228

Gordon had been straining into the darkness to look for Clara and her voice was a great relief; a greater relief still was confirmation she'd secured him. He let his head rock back from the exhaustion of the drama. After catching his breath, he called back to her.

"Well done. Now we just need to wait for the fuel to run out and you can try hauling the boat back to the cave. Can you..."

A splitting crack silenced him.

"I hope the fuel runs out soon," he shouted back once the echoes had subsided. "Did you hear the thunder? A storm is coming."

But Clara knew otherwise, a storm might be coming but the loud crack was not thunder, it was the brackets that held the mooring fast against the cliff shattering. The sudden jolt knocked her off her feet and by the time she'd righted herself she was floating on board the pier out to the open sea, towed behind Gordon's pilotless ship.

CHAPTER THIRTY

"Clara, I'm moving again," Gordon called unseen to Clara who clung with hands and knees to her floating raft. Gordon was less than 30 feet from her but the night, the mists, the spray from breaking waves and the din of the outboard motor made it feel more like 100 feet. Clara didn't know quite how to break the news to Gordon.

"Yes," she called back eventually.

"Why?"

"The mooring broke, I'm floating behind you."

Silence. Clara looked down at her uncertain vessel. Essentially it was a scout's raft – oil drums fastened by twine and sea-sodden planks. It was no ocean-goer and she recognised the danger as the weight of the waves caused its extremities to sag heavily in the sea.

"I think I'm sinking," Clara shouted to Gordon.

"What do you want me to do?" said Gordon, yanking at his bound arm and waspish with the stress. "Any more bad news?"

"Yes, there's another thing," Clara shouted, her voice straining. "David isn't on the train to London, I left him in Selyvan."

"Well, when we're both drowned," Gordon called in slow, defined syllables. "Sir Trevor can't hurt us."

His final word rang loud and clear to Clara. The wind turned and dropped away and even the waves calmed, the only sound was the increasingly irregular buzz of the engine. Both Gordon and Clara looked about them to see what had caused the eerie tranquility but everywhere was the impenetrable black. Along the coast Gordon saw the darker outline of the cliffs and, as his eyes grew accustomed to the low light, he was able to pick out its shapes with greater definition. He traced the coastline and, with some certainty, was able to identify the fallen tree where they had made their descent to the boat. Further along Gordon's eye was attracted by a blue light that flickered with the timidity of a dying flame. His eyes strained to define it until they became pained, but he resisted the temptation to relax the muscles and let the picture slip into blur. For seconds the light extinguished or burned so lowly it lacked the power to illuminate at such a distance. Then it flared once more cast long silhouettes about the white halo of its penumbra with bold contrast, it was in these brief flashes of intensity that Gordon first began to define the figure of a man.

"On the cliff," shouted Gordon back to Clara. "Do you see, a man?"

Clara didn't even turn to look but sensibly began shouting into the dark for help. At the precise moment Clara began her cries for help, Gordon realised it would not come. The light flared once again and against the outline of the starry night Gordon recognised the figure on the cliff, it was unmistakably the Colonel. It was the same uncanny shapes in which his twisted limbs writhed themselves that Gordon had seen the previous night. Suddenly Clara's calls were answered from the cliffs by a chilling series of screams that bore the pattern of strange language. The cries silenced her immediately and she listened in breathless terror as the sounds swept low over the still sea. They came alien, tuneless and pained but with the authoritative cadence of calls to prayer. As suddenly as they began, they stopped.

"What was that?" Clara shouted.

"It was the Colonel," Gordon returned. "We have to get out of the sea. It's not safe."

"Agreed."

No sooner had Clara spoken than the outboard motor coughed, choked on its fuel and burbled into a low death.

"Well, that's one problem solved," said Gordon, able to speak more easily without the competition of the engine.

He stared out from the boat, tracing the line of the rope back, and could just make out Clara's shape kneeling on the raft. What Gordon couldn't see was her frantic efforts to stay clear the water, which had already submerged a quarter of its surface. She balanced her weight to try to reduce its inevitable advance. The engine burbled in its death throes before issuing a throaty cough and jet of black smoke that Gordon believed to be its last inhalation of vapours igniting themselves before expiration. But instead of silencing itself it rallied with the deathbed patient's burning will to prolong and fired a few final strokes. The sudden jolt pulled the rope taut with force and Clara was thrown flat to the decking. Even from thirty feet away Gordon heard the ping, crack and snap. Clara, much closer to the crisis, saw the wood splinter and the rope break free. She made an athletic lunge to catch the rope but fell an inch short, instead she could only watch as it slithered out into the sea behind Gordon's boat with the joy of an escaped eel.

Gordon called out to Clara, unable to affect any attempt at rescue while his hand remained locked to the stern. He redoubled his efforts to free himself, using his legs as levers to strain at the rope. The bolts fixing the mooring hook to the boat were rusted and the wood into which they were fastened had softened and crumbled. Gordon saw how it wobbled and attempted to loosen it further, rocking and teasing it free. The engine finally died but its final spurt had already driven Gordon away from Clara and her calls came fainter and fainter until he could no longer hear her voice.

All about the storm had arrived. Great purple clouds, backlit by the electricity, churned and ripped through one another with anger. Rain fell hissing into the sea and puddles formed in the little boat. The loud music of the sky was deafening and maddening, and the sympathetic sea responded to its cataclysmic tune. Gordon felt woefully insecure alone in the raging sea and thought of Clara with dread. He knew she would be afraid and his inability to even comfort her shot waves of frustration radiating from his core. The anger restored his muscles and with wild strength he tore at the binding, snapping it free and sending himself sprawling into the slimy pool that had puddled at the bottom of his boat. But he was free.

Gordon sprang to his feet and clambered to the back of the boat in search of petrol. If he could get the engine started, he would be able to rescue Clara and himself. He was oblivious now to the rain that lashed his face and did not hear the thunder cracks. Lit by the blinding strobes of lightning, Gordon tossed aside the tarpaulin at the back of the boat and found the can of fuel with which the Colonel had so precisely filled the tank. Gordon shook the can, the little petrol within sloshed at the bottom – there might be just enough to get them back to shore. Gordon was inexpert with engines and had never controlled any sort of boat, so his efforts were clumsy and traumatic. He spilled precious drops of petrol as the sway overcame his legs and fumbled half-blind with the filler cap on the motor. But his efforts were in vain. A powerful wave he'd failed to spot approaching crashed hard into the side of the boat and the can, balanced in Gordon's uncertain grip, was lost to the sea.

Gordon sank back into the boat in a dejection and anger at his clumsy haste. He let his head sink back and had the curious sensation of fainting, as though his legs were somersaulting over his body. He opened his eyes and the stars above him were reeling, as though in motion. He sat up, suddenly alert and once more felt himself falling backwards. The boat was rising, its stern pointing to the stars as though the sea had become a great hillside. Gordon waited for the thump as the wave broke but it never came, instead the stern rose higher to the heavens until he thought it might overturn at the vertical. Fear gripped him and he supposed he must be cresting a freak tidal wave set to break with fury on the shore, the result of some colossal seismic shift in the ocean floor. Just before the boat reached a tipping point the great wave plateaued and, at the same angle at which he'd ascended, the boat suddenly plummeted toward the black ocean.

The rise had unnerved Gordon, but the fall gripped him with terror and he clung to the side of the boat as it plunged. The cold night air chilled rapidly with the descent, the ocean expelled an icy belch from its sunless guts. With the cold came a dank sulfurous stink that stung Gordon's nostrils and made him retch with disgust. It was fetid and chemical and yet with an organic decay, like dead flesh on the living and all coated an iodine brown. Gordon braced his legs against the stern and waited for the inevitable destruction as his tiny wooden dinghy slammed into the water below, but the crash never came. Instead, the boat continued its path down, spiraling in a great vortex to depths Gordon dared not consider, the reassuring, black silhouette of the cliffs had long since been lost to sight. Gordon's survival instinct had departed, and he accepted in dumb horror the certainty of his own death. The fear was so overwhelming in the clutch of the sea's sublime power that he could not even spare a thought for Clara – who endured a fate equally as terrifying.

Without warning, and without the destructive impact Gordon feared, the small boat levelled itself; the vortex was closing, and the great rush of water surged into the empty space. Gordon was driven back to surface level with a powerful up-thrust but without the violence of the descent. The vortex fastened and, for a second, all was silent. Gordon lay back in his boat breathless, waiting for the next surprise. Above the lightning lit the sky and in its burning flash Gordon saw Clara, alone and afraid. He saw her only in his feverish mind because when he looked out across the sea there was only emptiness. He called out to her several times, straining an ear in the direction of the shoreline to catch her response. His chill-tightened chest wheezed heavily so he tried to hold his breath to better distinguish sounds, but there was only the lap of the waves against the boat and the roll of thunder. Then, from the shore he heard a voice. Not Clara's, it was the same alien screech he'd recognised earlier. It was the Colonel's voice; the second stage of his incantation was beginning. The words caught on a swirling wind and carried out across the sea. They came to Gordon's ears weird and ancient. In earlier incantations he had heard the guttural hardness of Anglo-Saxon, but these flowed faintly with a gentle music, a strange poetry. Gordon recognised a few words, eighteen long years with Dr Athelney made it impossible not to mop up at least some of the trivia from his overspilling tap. It was ancient, pre-Roman, the language of the Celts and it sounded eerily beautiful.

The boat shook as though a great eruption was blasting below the surface. About, great bubbles filled with hot, sulphurous air, foamed and frothed the surface. A low mist quickly formed, white and soupy and the air dropped cooler still; the sleeve of Gordon's jacket now stuck rigid in a fine frost and his lips turned a deathly shade of blue, as though he had become his own spectral self. The Colonel's chant was now drowned in the violence of the hissing and fizzing of the gas. Gordon dipped a hand into the water, and it burned with cold. The mist thickened, beading a dew on everything it touched with a sickening sulphurous odour. Gordon felt a great pressure rising, something was moving, and he felt the low rumble in his bowels, he sensed the vibrations through his brittle and frozen bones. Like the passing of a freight train through a station, he sensed something colossal was stirring.

A great jet of water fired from the ocean, just feet from where Gordon's unsteady boat bobbed. The force of the expulsion rocked it powerfully and only Gordon's rapid redistribution of his weight prevented it capsizing into the poisonous sea. Thousands of tonnes of water rocketed to the heavens, reaching heights Gordon's eyes could not pierce. More water gushed forth in a deafening roar, a solid stream like a great pillar of salt. Gordon could not bear to look; he knew that when the water fell back into the sea he would be crushed beneath its great weight. He rushed to the tarpaulin at the back of the boat, hiding beneath it. It was a forlorn hope, but it was the only protection the boat afforded. But the water did not come with thundering destruction. It froze in the winter air, fell like fat white blossom and melted into the steaming sea.

The lightning flashed and the sea began to bubble more furiously, spitting over the side of the boat. There was a deafening crack and the ocean split, parting itself. Gordon was thrown down hard, hitting his head against the wooden decking. His head reeled but he sensed danger and forced himself prone.

From the darkness a mass emerged. Gordon strained to see but it was formless, but he felt the maddening oppression of some great presence. A blackness, darker than the pitch sky, was rising from the ocean. He could not distinguish form or feature, but still it rose, towering and colossal. The cool shadow fell on him, frozen by the awe, it was the size of a cathedral, hulking and splitting. The noises, like the trunks of a vast forest snapping under irresistible gravity, splintering and rending themselves in terrifying bursts. It was as though a sunken Titanic was slowly re-emerging from the bottom of the sea, with all its fossilised horrors suddenly breathing the same oxygen as humanity once more. The sensation was ineffable, it was too alien, too primordial. Gordon tried to scream; the gravity of this rising planet stole his breath. But form began to grow, he looked in horror as limbs began to shape themselves, blotting the stars. The terror rose fewer than 100 feet from Gordon's boat and his proximity to this great entity created about the surreality of insanity. Gordon even considered jumping into the ocean to escape but the thought of sharing the same water as this insidious terror was too great to bear.

The black form moved, slowly and with the rigid tension of atrophy. Were they wings that spread themselves or arms? Gordon was compelled, he thought of nothing else but a sight at this strange creature – he was certain now it was organic. Thoughts of danger, thoughts of Clara, thoughts of returning to England, his career, they had all evaporated in the presence of a deity. Gordon felt miniscule in its awesome, infinite presence.

Still, in the darkness, there was no definition. Its outline could only be traced by the stars which suddenly disappeared when its great, lumbering limbs passed over them. The mist began to clear and the boiling sea cooled rapidly. The faint cries of the Colonel still carried over the waves and the great presence Gordon faced seemed to respond to their intensity in kind. The cries became more frantic and were losing their gentle cadence. Even language was indistinguishable now, but Gordon felt as if in those bold, staccato calls commands were being given.

A sheet of lightning made day of night and then, in those fractions of illumination, Gordon saw it in all its horrific majesty. A face, human but twisted, turned monstrous by millennia of cankerous decay. Skin, white as ocean foam, crusted by a thousand layers of death. Was it hair that grew in great spines, segmented like the trunks of palms or some snaking prehistoric parasite? Its entire body was sores and wounds that oozed a shimmering blue-black blood. The eyes nestled where ears ought to have been, heavy-lidded and black as antinomy, dead as the eyes of an octopus. There was no definable body, just one oozing mass, where only the web of sharp ribs, that stuck through the flesh, indicated any sort of internal structure. Flailing and etiolated, its crawling cancerous limbs branched and flourished like fungus. They snapped and broke under the weight of the water and the waxy skin bubbled with living blisters in the burning air, it appeared to be melting, and sliding from its body. What cold heat powered this titan with such nuclear power? Even in its death-throes, Gordon could feel its intensity but also its raging pain.

Darkness returned and Gordon could only trace the movements of the creature once more against the night sky. It was shifting and threw great waves that buffeted the boat and forced Gordon to break his trance-like gaze and take action to avoid capsizing. But even as he wrestled to balance the boat, he shot nervous glances towards the awesome creature. The Colonel's words once again came to him, with the same wild passion as earlier, and in that ancient tongue that once spoke the rites of Druidic sacrifices. The sky answered the Colonel's call and the clouds bubbled in anger and gruff rumblings.

From the blackness came a scream of terrible potency. It was dying, Gordon knew it. A scream of fury fattened on the sudden agonies brought on by its rude awakening. In the long ululating howl Gordon thought he detected pattern. It was vicious and raging, with the explosive anger of a collapsing star. Gordon was forced to stop his ears forcing his fingers deep to silence the sound, but it was futile. The lightning briefly illuminated it and Gordon saw its face once again. Already it had lost the few definable features it possessed. The image was alive and writhing, dissolving and reshaping in flash of the storm. Its great tentacular limbs thrashed at the water and it toppled in collapse. The vision was lost as the curtain of night drew once more. A second later Gordon heard its body crash back into the sea.

For a moment everything was calm and Gordon caught his breath, his brain racing for comprehension. There was no time for considered inquiry, Gordon heard the rolling thunder of the wave it had sent in its fall and crouched low in the boat to brace for the impact. A fraction of a second later he was stuck by this powerful blow and the boat was immediately toppled. Gordon had just enough time to wrap the loose cord about his wrist and only this crude harness had saved him from being swept away to his death. The boat was overturned, and the cold water had driven the air from his lungs. He could make no attempt to right the boat and instead clambered to safety on his upturned craft. On this uncertain platform he finally lay, back to the deck, face to the stars, breathless, exhausted and afraid. For the first time in his life, he looked into sprawling chaos of spattered stars and knew humanity was not alone. In the distance he heard the choked phut of a diesel motor. At once, he knew Guddy had arrived and that he was saved.

Guddy's old boat pulled cautiously alongside stricken Gordon on his raft, the old fisherman was careful not to overturn Gordon from his already perilous position. Gordon was relieved when he saw the old man's face peering down from Mjöllnir. Guddy threw a rope to Gordon and with his last remaining vapours of strength he pulled himself up and to safety.

"That's twice now," said Gordon as he lay flat on the deck.

"I'm not counting," said Guddy. "You need to get inside, you're frozen."

"Clara!" said Gordon with a heart-stopping rush.

"She's safe," said Guddy with a smile. "She's in the cabin keeping warm. She pointed us in your direction. Now get inside."

"But how did you know where we were?"

Now that he was safe Gordon's head was suddenly brimming with questions.

"Thanks to the little man," said Guddy, nodding a head in the direction of the David who stood dutifully at Mjollnir's helm, one hand on the wheel. When he caught Gordon's gaze he stood to attention and saluted. Gordon weakly returned the gesture.

"Now get inside," said Guddy. "I've got a mug of hot Brennivin waiting for you."

Gordon groaned.

CHAPTER THIRTY ONE

Clara was pleased to see Gordon when he stumbled heavily into the cabin. She had her feet up against the gas fire and both hands wrapped around a hot mug of Brennivin. Gordon was even more pleased to see Clara, he felt his recklessness had endangered her. He had been convinced she'd drowned. Clara shot to her feet, making space for Gordon by the fire. She helped him into the plastic chair. The adrenaline was dissipating, and uncontrollable shivers overtook Gordon, he'd not been properly warm since stepping off the train in Penzance but the two soakings on consecutive nights had iced his marrow.

"Here," said Guddy handing Gordon the Brennivin. "I want to see you drink it. I'm going to steer us home before our young captain sails us to the New World."

Guddy left Gordon and Clara alone and for a minute both sat in contented silence, staring deeply into the blue gas flame that was slowly thawing their frozen vitality.

"I'm quite relieved to see you're OK," said Gordon eventually, Clara smiled. "I was worried about you."

"I was fine," said Clara. "Guddy arrived just in time, I was taking on water. I was more worried for you. When the storm broke, I was onboard Guddy's boat but you were out there."

"Did you see anything?" said Gordon, his tone changing.

"I think we heard something. It was so dark and we were looking for you. We saw the storm and then thought we saw something on the horizon. That's how we found you. I didn't have my camera, but I borrowed David's. I don't think anything came out."

"Can I see?" said Gordon.

Clara handed Gordon the camera. He cycled through the images. They were black frames, nothing.

"Too dark," said Gordon.

"Keep going," she said. "It's got a night vision mode. I was trying to work out how to turn it on."

Gordon continued clicking through the black frames. He suddenly recoiled at a green close-up portrait of David's leering nose.

"There," said Clara. "David turned it on."

Gordon looked closely at the next image, then the next. Was that a silhouette he could make out? The vaguest shape, perhaps even his own boat was visible? Or was his mind playing tricks on him? The image of what he'd seen was seared in his memory, but already he was beginning to doubt it and was desperately seeking for digital confirmation.

"Can you make these any clearer?"

"Maybe I could level it out a bit, pump the brightness, but look how grainy it is already, you won't get any more definition."

The next few images were shaky and blurred beyond comprehension. An unexpected wave had struck the side of the boat and Clara had nearly dropped David's camera into the drink. Gordon continued.

"Here," said Gordon, thrusting the camera at Clara. "It's the great jet of water. Look you can see it. Thousands of feet high."

Clara strained at the viewfinder, squinting and turning her head to try to see what Gordon saw.

"I can't see it," she said. "Isn't just another wave?"

Gordon shook his head impatiently and checked the next image, his eyes were greedy and gobbled through the photos. He stopped dead, he found what he had been looking for. The flash of the lightning outlined what had been the vague silhouette. It was still at a great distance but by magnifying the image he saw it again, captured with the lens. He even saw his boat, just a few pixels wide, tiny in the frame but recognisable. His heart beat with painful thuds against his chest at the excitement.

"You've done it, Clara," he said looking up at her with wild, elated eyes. "You photographed it."

"Photographed what?" Clara peered curiously over his shoulder, as Gordon traced the outline of what he saw.

"What is it?" she said. "It looks like a tree. I don't remember that?"

"You took it, Clara. You must have seen it?" Gordon's words hung heavily in the air, but he felt the need to reinforce, he needed confirmation. "Clara, you saw it?"

"Saw what, Gordon?" she said, stressing his name in return.

"This," he said, holding the camera to Clara's eyes and jabbing at the tiny screen. "This."

Clara shook her head; she was uncertain of Gordon's behaviour. His pupils were dilated and shivers overtook him so the camera wobbled in his hand. He had taken two dips in the sea and his behaviour was becoming increasingly erratic. Clara was a little scared and looked at him closely, she noticed a trickle of blood mingling with the brine on his brow.

"You're bleeding," she said. "You've cut your head."

Gordon touched where he'd smacked his head against the boat and saw red blood on his wrinkled, white fingers. He felt no pain and did not want to derail the conversation.

"It's nothing," he said dismissively.

"It's not," Clara retorted firmly. "I need to look at it."

"You saw it," said Gordon, just as firmly as he batted away her probing fingers. "You saw it, didn't you?"

Clara shook her head, there was pity in her eyes. She wanted to help her colleague, she saw him at that moment as shipwrecked and desperate. He was bloodied, bruised and beaten, she saw it, why could he not accept it. After the adventures of the night Clara was keen to restore some normality. She could not follow the savage tracks Gordon was bolting along with abandon. She shook her head again as Gordon's disbelieving eyes begged her for some slight acknowledgement. She knew she could not help him.

"I'm sorry," she said. "Let me dress your wound."

David, with Guddy's ever present corrective hand, steered Mjöllnir back to a private harbour just half a mile up the coast from Selyvan. Guddy knew another late arrival into town would only provoke more whispers. There had been an awkward scene in the Ship earlier in the day. The local fishermen were experiencing difficulties, the fish weren't biting and they were no longer blaming the Spanish. Suspicious, superstitious and jealous, the fishing community twitches its curtains at the merest cough from the harbour. They had watched Guddy come and go on his late-night jaunts. They had seen him trudging a weary route back to his lonely cottage. They had wondered what his purpose had been, why he never returned with fish, what he was looking for. Old Yomus, who was gruff and argumentative when sober, cornered Guddy after an afternoon sloshing back his treacly beer. The rest of the Ship watched on, all burning with the same curiosity that only Yomus had been brazen enough to voice. Guddy, who always drank alone, did not respond despite the eyes of the Ship pinning him into submission. He finished his drink, rose casually and stood eye-to-eye with his adversary. Yomus shrank back. Everybody in Selyvan maintained a secret but respectful fear of Guddy, he was taciturn and mysterious and although his smile was warm there was sometimes that black flicker crackling behind his eyes.

"You're fishing in dead waters, Yomus."

Guddy left the pub as casually as if it had been his own home. Yomus stood staring at the wall where Guddy had been standing, burning with shame and embarrassment and suddenly feeling quite sober. But Guddy knew he was under observation and could not afford to arouse any further suspicions.

When Mjöllnir was secured, Guddy helped Gordon and Clara back onto dry land. The firm earth felt good beneath her feet, but Gordon was too preoccupied to sense any relief. He cast secret glances back out to sea, a nervous chill swept across him as he did so. After the swells and storm, a tranquility had descended across the water. Gordon would have preferred a raging sea; the calm had an eeriness about it.

They followed the old coastal path back to town. Selyvan was not far and Gordon reassured the party he was strong enough for the short hike. All the same, Guddy paid him close attention. The path was dark but David lit the way proudly, sweeping away the darkness in broad strokes with his SAS-issue torch.

"It's got a Morse Code feature," David explained. "I just press this button once and it will flash S.O.S. Press it again and it requests aerial support. Press it again and it brings down an artillery bombardment on the enemy line."

Clara tripped on a rock.
"Can you just shine your weapon of mass destruction on the path, please," she snapped at David.

David obeyed and his beam caught the legs of a figure darting across the path. They stopped as one. Slowly David lifted his torchlight to meet the stranger.

"Oh my God," said Clara.

The Colonel stood before them naked except for a black robe draped carelessly over his shoulders. His eyes were red and overflowing with tears. David, who was leading the troop, sniggered and Clara grabbed him by his shoulders and moved him to the rear. The Colonel's face was sunken and petrified to an open-mouthed gape. His body shook violently with the cold or fever. It took the Colonel a moment to recognise who he was facing but when he did, he lifted a long, bony finger towards Gordon. Clara stood protectively in front of him, she felt afraid and was glad for Guddy's presence. Gordon was still shaky and needed the support of Guddy, he could barely see he was so mummified in towels. Gordon felt a sudden shame at the sight of the Colonel before him, especially in such a state of lunacy, like Lear on the heath.

"You saw him," the Colonel said to Gordon, ignoring the others. "You saw him."

"We saw you try to bloody kill us," said Clara.

The Colonel ignored her.

"You saw him, didn't you?"

"Yes," said Gordon blankly, under a dull hypnosis.

"He's half-mad with hypothermia thanks to you," Clara interrupted again. "He's not speaking right."

"You have to tell them," said the Colonel. "You have to tell them, we're not alone."

"We have to tell the police," said Clara. "You nearly killed us both."

The Colonel stepped forward with an aggressive start that made Clara back away. Clara need not have feared him, his only concern was Gordon, every ounce of his will was channelled at Gordon and the pull was irresistible. "You have to tell them Gordon," repeated the Colonel. "It's your duty."

"He has to do nothing," said Guddy suddenly. "I haven't cleaned behind my fridge for 20 years. I am not going to shine a light behind that, no matter what I hear scratching in the darkness. We have to learn to share our space. There are things that are better not to know."

Guddy's unexpected speech rocked the Colonel's assurance, and he was dumb to respond. His words restored a rationality that blew the foundations away from the Colonel's overshadowing tower. He slunk back, his eyes still rolling in their madness. Guddy urged Gordon along with a gentle nudge and Clara and David followed behind.

They stepped around the Colonel who stood petrified in Pompeian horror and continued along the road to Selyvan without looking back. From the darkness behind them came heavy, soul-drenched sobs.

They returned to Guddy's cottage cold and exhausted. It didn't take Guddy long to have a warm fire burning. He rarely lit it for himself and had stacks of wood ready to burn. Gordon changed into dry clothes and let his wet suit steam by the fire. He stuffed his sodden Church's with newspaper and resisted Clara's plans to place these close to the warmth of the fire.

"You'll crack the leather," were his final words before drifting into a deep sleep from which he would not awake until afternoon the next day, when the sun was already sinking in the sky. Gordon felt refreshed from the sleep but with a slight grogginess from whatever had been in his system the day before. Clara and David were already packed and ready to leave. Clara had booked them tickets on the overnight train back to London that was leaving in a few hours time. She, too, had spent most of the day asleep. It had been a later night than either of them had realised. Only Guddy had risen at dawn and continued his usual routine. He had returned from the Ship with a bag of fresh fish which he was frying for a late lunch.

The four of them ate with little conversation around Guddy's small table. Gordon and David sat on suitcases in lieu of chairs. Gordon's mind was preoccupied. The strange events of the previous night were troubling him. At the table Gordon caught Guddy shooting him thoughtful looks, as though he was trying to read his mind. The fish at least was restorative and when a horn outside signalled the taxi was waiting to take them to the station, Gordon felt braced for the long journey home. Clara and David thanked Guddy for everything and rushed out to meet the taxi, keen not to get stranded in Selyvan for an extra night. Gordon lingered, he wanted to speak with Guddy. Somehow, he had the feeling the old fisherman from those black volcanic shores would understand better than anybody else. Guddy sensed Gordon's intentions and headed him off.
"You must let it go," he said.

"I can't, it's consuming me. Do you know what it was I saw?"

Guddy shrugged.

"I've seen this passion before. I lost my dearest possession to the ocean. Whatever it is, let it go. It's not yours, it's not Mortain's, and it was not Catherine's."

"But there's something there," said Gordon.

"What if there is? I fish these seas and as long as what I pull up fetches a price at market then I'm not going to cast my line any deeper. Go back to London, take Clara to dinner. Forget about what has happened here."

Gordon could say nothing more and Guddy would never have let him. They stood in silence, neither certain how to make the farewell. Eventually Clara interrupted, hurrying Gordon along. She was the most impatient to leave Selyvan. Gordon shook Guddy's hand. The single word, thanks, was all he could say.

In Penzance, Clara hurried to the ticket office to confirm their booking. Gordon sat with David who was steadily working his way through a bag of jelly sweets, exclaiming the flavour of each one. Gordon's mind was elsewhere. His conversation with Guddy had unsettled him and doubts were spread like haw frost, but always his self-belief thawed them.

"I got you these," said Clara as she thrust a green plastic bag into his hands, almost with a hint of shame. Gordon looked inside, a pack of fresh dates. He could have wept.

"From Mark's?" he said.

"Yeah, I thought they might bring some colour back to you."

Gordon inspected the pack with great ceremony.

"They're 'Special Heritage' range," he said, nodding.

"Yeah, they're infused with orange blossom syrup. Hope that's OK?"

"Sure, thanks again," said Gordon. He wasn't sure if he should kiss Clara's cheek to thank her and she lingered for a moment, unsettled by his indecision. He paused just a moment too long and the opportunity passed.

"Right, I'm going to try to grab a coffee from somewhere that doesn't look like it will serve me hot dishwater."

Gordon strolled to the platform to wait for Clara by the train. He was always nervous at stations and airports and liked to board at the earliest opportunity. There was still ten minutes before the train left, but he could not help shooting anxious glances at the station clock every few seconds. Gordon felt a hand on his shoulder.

"Time for a quick cup of tea with a famous friend?"

He turned to see Max Nash holding a little tartan flask. He was pleased to see him, sorry that he'd not had the chance to say goodbye in town.

"I'd love to," he said. "But my train leaves soon."

Unperturbed Max fished through his bag and withdrew a couple of plastic cups.

"I've not been a journalist for nearly four decades without learning a thing or two. The number of times this old flask has saved me. Mind you, it doesn't keep the tea so hot as it used but then right now, when you've only got five minutes, a tepid cup is just the ticket."

Gordon smiled and took a cup as Max poured out the tea delicately, still managing to spill his milky brew at the conclusion.

"Quite a night, was it?"

Gordon nodded. He liked Max but was too engrossed with his own internal monologue to allow small talk to intervene. His mind was turning over the events of the past few days and the things he had seen. He was returning to London without a story to tell, and yet within him he held one of the most fantastic tales ever told.
"I can imagine it was," Max continued fluidly. "I've been there myself. I was a bit younger than you, and probably the more headstrong for it."

Max's words caught Gordon's attention and he looked deeply into the old man's eyes.

"How do you mean?"

"I mean just that. I saw it too."

"What? What did you see?"

"I don't suppose I'm in any better position to answer that now than I was 25 years ago. I don't reckon you could say what either, am I right? That's probably the reason you're looking so preoccupied now."

"Why didn't you say anything before?"

"Why don't you say anything now? Tell me what you saw. Explain it to me. Make me understand."

"I can't," said Gordon. "It's impossible."

"Not such a pair of newshounds now are we. How quickly we lose the scent, with the quarry at bay we turn our backs. It's hard to accept, isn't it?"

"Tell me what you saw, Max?"

"A lot of people around this town think I'm the story-teller, the great bard. I'll spin yarns about the day Merton Brandy's German Shepherd scored the winning goal at Runedown Park when old Merton let loose the lead after the bottom fell out of his piping hot pipe. I remember in 1976 when thirteen American tourists got lost inside Rook Hole caverns for the whole night and when they were discovered the next morning they'd elected themselves a President and were working on the foundations of a new subterranean civilisation."

Gordon laughed.

"But if you ask me to tell that tale, I can't. I never have done."

"Why not?"

"It's not our tale to tell, Gordon."

"My tale to tell is the truth. An accurate account of that which I've seen and that which I've heard and believe to be true from reliable sources."

"Well I'd meditate hard on that mantra on the long train back to civilisation. Don't do anything hasty."

"You doubt what I saw?"

"I know what you saw. I know what I saw. The world is too young, Gordon. I'm not saying there's not a story to tell, just take care how you tell it. If you still want to tell it in ten years time..."

"In ten years!"

"If you still want to tell it then, we'll be waiting for you. Don't be hasty. Come back to Selyvan, rent a cottage, grow a beard and write yourself a novel."

"I will not write a novel. Facts are my medium," Gordon protested, but Max shook his head with a paternal smile.

"I left Cornwall once. I'm not much of a traveller. My wife's folks had rented us all a cottage up in the Peak District over the Christmas of 1981. I wasn't keen to go, but you know how it is. It wasn't a busy period on the desk, and I'd been putting in lots of weekend shifts, my news editor practically frogmarched me out of the office. The next day the Penlee lifeboat sank with 16 hands lost. My fellow reporter was a chap named Simon Starr, a famous one he turned out to be. Fleet Street descended on our little community and he won himself a lot of favours. He toadied up like a courtier to a king. He earned himself a regular shift on the Daily Express, the "Great British paper". I heard on the radio two days later. It wasn't exactly the age of the interweb and mobile telephone. I got back to Cornwall as Fleet Street were clearing out, leaving their dirt and detritus behind.

"I missed the biggest story of my career by a day and I couldn't have been more relieved. For the only time in my life, I thought about quitting the profession. I didn't see what good I could serve the community. I was a lost soul, Gordon. I saw Simon Starr packing his belongings for a famous life in London and I only felt pity for him.
"I carried on, as you do, but it took me a decade to resolve it. On the tenth anniversary of the disaster, I put together a memorial edition. Long after the rest of the world had forgotten, I gave the local people a voice and a chance to tell their stories, to remember. I filled 27 pages. It's the proudest moment of my career.

"Sometimes the best time to tell your story isn't in the aftermath when it's too raw and unformed. Never forget, we're only storytellers, Gordon. We're nothing but a pair of old yarn spinners."

The guard blew the whistle for the night train to Paddington. Max nodded at Gordon, whose passions were too roused to notice the departure signal.

"Jump on or you'll be spending another night in Cornwall," Clara shouted from the train. "And you'll be spending it alone this time."

Gordon handed back the tea and shook Max's hand warmly but without a word of goodbye. He boarded the train but before the guard could fasten the door behind him, he turned back to Max.

"I'm going to write it," he said. "It's all true and I'm going to write it."

Max smiled and waved a final goodbye. The guard, who had lost his good humour, slammed the door to and hopped on the next carriage as the train creaked and lumbered into motion.

"Good luck, Gordon," Max called. "It's your story now. If it makes you famous, don't you go forgetting your famous friend."

As the train rolled out of Penzance, Gordon opened his notepad. The paper was damp and his pencil tore at the leaves without impression. He found a discarded edition of the Cornish Chronicle and unfolded it in his lap. The front page was a story by Max Nash. It was a fluffy story about a parking warden from Penzance who was claiming disability benefits for stress and depression after a dive-bombing seagull had terrorised him for six long months. There was a large photograph of the parking warden looking deliberately glum for the camera. Max had even included a CCTV screengrab of one of the attacks. Gordon smiled, he knew what he had to do. If Max Nash couldn't tell the story, then he could. In the narrow margin between the newsprint of the Cornish Chronicle Gordon began to write and he didn't stop until he'd finished.

"Clara, I need you to e-mail the desk that photo you showed me earlier."
"The out of focus one of the tree?"

"Yes, that's the one."

"Really?"

"Really. It's going with the story I'm about to file."

"OK," she said with little assurance. "What do you want me to call it?"

Gordon paused; he hadn't thought about this. He needed a topic and a keyword.

"How about SEA?" he said. "SEA Monster."

CHAPTER THIRTY TWO

Gordon emerged from the night train's belly, bleary and blinking into the perma-day of Paddington. Already the station was mercilessly flowing with the churning current of commuters who poured into the drains of the Tube station. Gordon's head was clearing, and the fogginess of the previous day had mostly lifted. He didn't feel any better for the clarity, instead it was replaced by a vague paranoia and disassociation with reality. Clara was more chirpy and very pleased to be back in London. Her first thought turned to coffee and she left Gordon with her bag while she sniffed out a Morrocochino. David, too, was in better spirits, he'd slept for the entire journey and that rest had all but cured his aches and sniffles. Gordon, at least, was relieved for this small mercy, since it lessened the possibility of his father finding out about his icy dip in the sea cave. Gordon looked around him, trying to readjust to metropolitan life but felt as if he was inhabiting two worlds without truly belonging in either of them.

Gordon remembered the copy he had filed with such determination the night before. He cringed, the memory was painful, but he couldn't stop himself from picking at it like an itching scab. In London, his decision to file seemed unstable. There was a griminess about everything like the white shirts under a night club's UV strobing. Away from the spray of the thrashing sea, it was all too unreal. Where was the spirit among the Moroccochino, the overspilling waste bins, the inexorable march of the departure boards, the dust of the Circle Line, the buy-one-get-one-free tie, the remains of an all-day breakfast bun in a brown paper bag with dark grease spots, the adverts for shampoo which were written like your closest friend confiding the nature of their soul and with the expectation you should know what jojoba oil is... Gordon suddenly felt like he was going to be sick.

"Look," said David. "It's Chip Steel."

"Who?" said Gordon, his brain spinning like the blurred reels of a fruit machine.

"Chip Steel. The WBW wrestler."

"Who?"

"No, it's not," said David. "It's just a fat bloke."

At this point the no-neck Goliath turned around bearing the wrath of his thunderous face at Gordon. Gordon flustered and fussed, and the man slumped away. Gordon had to get some air; the sickness was welling. He ordered David to watch the bags and set off in a directionless trot. He found the toilets but needed 50 pence to get in. He wondered about hurdling the low barrier but couldn't bring himself to carry it through. By the time he'd reasoned his alternatives, precisely criminality or throwing up in one of London's busiest stations, the sickness had passed and he was content for air and solitude.

"What have I done?" Gordon said quietly to himself. He could see all of the general reporters reading through his copy, forwarding it by e-mail with nothing but several exclamation marks as comment, they would not be not be sure whether to laugh out loud or feel prickly and uncomfortable staring at their colleagues frayed ends of sanity.

Clara caught up with Gordon, she was clutching her Morocochino and wearing a look of vague disappointment.

"Not a single word in any of the nationals," she said. "I can't believe it."

Gordon's sickness returned twofold.

"Please, not now," he pleaded meekly.

"I'd have thought somebody might have picked it up. I'd half thought it might make the centre spread in the Guardian. It ticks all the boxes. Especially with your copy to go alongside it."
Clara had not read the copy Gordon had filed. She assumed he had spun a nice environmental angle to go alongside her photos of the fish-covered cove. Only Gordon knew he had worked late into the night editing and honing his first-hand account of what he'd seen out in the sea. What he alone had seen? Cold, drugged, concussed, afraid and through the screen of impenetrable night. What had he been thinking? Hot waves of shame tickled his skin like nettle stings.

"Don't talk about my copy, not now," he said.

Clara had been talking to herself, but Gordon's protests snapped her out of her gloomy analysis and she turned to him.

"Gosh, you're white as a sheet. You're catching cold."

"No, I'm fine, I just need to sleep."

Clara looked uncomfortable, as though she wanted to say something but then thought better of it, but Gordon had already spotted her internal dilemma.

"What is it?" he said pleadingly.

"You're not going to like it," said Clara with stern gravity. "I had a call from Croaker, he wants to see you in the office first thing."

Gordon's eyes performed a wheeling death roll, and his agony was evident. Clara felt a responsibility for his sufferings and pitied him.

"I told him you were tired and needed to sleep, I told him, but he insisted. I didn't know what to say."

Gordon's fatalism kicked in, he saw Clara's guilty face and didn't want her to feel bad on his account. He managed to produce an unconvincing half smile for her benefit

"I wouldn't be able to sleep if I went home anyway," he lied. "It makes sense to head straight to the office."

Clara was feeling especially guilty because the photo editor had given her the rest of the day off and had hinted that she wasn't needed the following day unless something "huge broke". She wanted to give Gordon a consolation hug, but it might have seemed insincere with the relief she was feeling with freedom in sight. She gave him an ironic punch on the arm, it was a tap but nearly sent Gordon reeling as he swayed and swam in sickness.

"So, I guess I'll see you later in the week," said Clara.

"Sure," said Gordon. "I'd better go and find David. Take care."

Clara watched as Gordon trudged with heavy steps back to David. She gave them both a wave and lifted her bags to leave but something prevented her. Gordon and David waved back at her and she waved once more. She watched Gordon wearily swing his sports bag over his shoulder and lead David away towards the Underground. She wanted to rush after them both and follow. It felt as if a bond was breaking, and her heart ached to fix it. She was surprised as a tear welled in the corner of her eye, she wiped it clear and steeled herself with an order to pull herself together. She prayed Zara wouldn't be at the flat when she got home. It was possible she'd bagged another "duvet day" because her boss was "such a sweetie". Clara left Paddington less certain of herself.

**

Gordon could barely return an exchange with avian Debbie on reception who greeted him cheerily as she sipped her morning camomile leaving greasy, red stains around the mug. His head had fogged over on the Tube and his heart ticked weak and erratically every time he thought of facing Croaker, which was most of the time. For once he'd welcomed David's musings, hypothetical questions and dubious nuggets of information.

"If I was Al-Qaeda I'd blow up a Northern Line train between Bank and London Bridge and flood the entire network. Why didn't they do that? They're stupid. Or I'd have got thirty suicide bombers in one carriage and..."

Gordon pushed himself forward, back bent to the wind, with grim determination. He did not know the source of his will as he pushed the button on the lift for the second floor. He operated in an opium daze; his actions did not feel his own. It might be the tiredness, he reasoned to himself, or something more chronic. He felt a disassociation not just with Associated News but with everything in London and all its teeming millions. David looked up at him with mild concern as the lift doors slowly fastened themselves. Gordon just wanted to see an end. He wanted to face Croaker, he wanted to acknowledge the consequences of his actions and leave free of responsibility and burden. It would be an honourable discharge or, more precisely, facing the firing squad with chin aloft.

With a diabolic sixth sense Croaker was waiting as the lift doors slid apart. For a moment the two adversaries stared at one another, each mustering the strength for civility. Gordon found it particularly difficult to remain diffident and the strain of biting his lip often became unbearable. Croaker was well aware of Gordon's insubordination - a vice he claimed, with a certain martial pretension, to deplore above all others. The silent face-off was eventually interrupted by the lift doors closing and it was only a speedy stab at the buttons that stopped Gordon heading back from whence he'd come. Croaker gave a grim smile.

"My office please," he said in a sinister monotone.

"I'll just check my e-mails..."

"Now," said Croaker firmly.

David scampered off to the sixth floor in search of his father. Gordon had given him a strict briefing of what truths could and couldn't be related, as well as a few lines which must be related. David had enjoyed a mischievous half hour with an out-of-humour Gordon deliberately misunderstanding the directions. Gordon eventually caught on, but with no less humour at the jape. He was beginning to recognise in David a dry sense of humour, nascent and budding but with the prospect of unfurling into an overpowering flower like some stinking Amazonian lily.

Gordon followed Croaker into his office. It felt as though no clock had ticked since he had been stood there last. Time sighed wearily and the adventures in Cornwall seemed as non-existent as they had done the previous week.

Croaker was quick to burst this bubble of unreality and recovered with some ceremony two A4 sheets from his rickety old printer.

"For a minute I thought one of our general reporters had accidentally filed the next chapter of Harry Potter," Croaker began with a refined air that betrayed rehearsal. "But I realised this couldn't be the case, especially when the author in question has the sword of fucking Demosthenes hanging over his fucking head."

"Damocles, Damocles, Damocles," Gordon screamed in silent agony.

"I realised I must have been dreaming when I came to the lines about shadowy cabals practising some esoteric Eastern fish god quackery. Sadly, I woke right up, right fucking up when I came to the vague first-hand description of a sea monster - are we calling it a monster? Or should we go with something vaguer? After all we wouldn't want to get taken to court for libel by fucking Nessie, would we? Or perhaps we should be worrying about more pressing concerns... like the whole of Fleet Street getting your latest penny dreadful landing on their desks with the Cornflakes. You do realise Associated News has been fast, fair and accurate since 1871. Were you hoping to undo the reputation built up over nearly a century and a half with one-and-a-half minutes of madness?"

Gordon's squirmed inwardly. He had no response. He no longer cared about his job, his reputation or Croaker. He wanted to get up and walk out of the door, to never look back. To forget his final salary and move to a distant island, grow a beard, befriend a native, and never think about a newspaper ever again. What had he been thinking? He was kidding himself, his entire life felt like a great sham.

"Well, are you going to explain? Because I'm going to have some explanations to make and it would be nice to hear the sorry tale straight from the horse's sorry mouth. I'd like to know what to tell the editor of the Times when he calls to ask why we're sending Harry Potter and the..."

Croaker's brain whirred like a dusty hard-drive but inspiration was slow to strike robbing the snipe of all its barbs by the time it arrived.

"...Load of old Bollocks."

Gordon smiled and nodded in ironic appreciation. Croaker's mood boiled over and his face flushed rotten berry red in rage, but Gordon was saved from the outburst by the shrill ring of the phone. Croaker answered hastily and grumpily but his tone quickly changed to an oily lightness so Gordon guessed it must be Sir Trevor.

"Of course, Sir Trevor," said Croaker. "Right away. Of course. No, I understand. OK. In one minute."

His face drained of its bubbling blood, and it was with ashen fear that he turned to face Gordon. Croaker was unsure of his words and speaking mechanically.

"He wants to see me," said Croaker. "You, too. He read the article."

Croaker picked up the sheets of paper he'd just printed and reread Gordon's words, hoping to convince himself that the situation wasn't so dire as he feared but it had the opposite effect and he slumped back in his chair in desperation.

"Oh Jesus Christ, it's a disaster. Why did we have to send his fucking son with you. What was I thinking?" Croaker's composure and control were well measured when his authority was insurmountable but the moment the balance of power shifted, he crumbled. It was pathetic for Gordon to watch and gave his own confidence - born from his mental severing of ties - a boost.

"Let's not keep Sir Trevor waiting," said Gordon firmly and Croaker stared back with disbelief as though Gordon had just spoken in fluent Mandarin. A dark frown formed like a gathering storm across his brow. Croaker's paranoia always imagined crosshairs training on him. He was suspicious of anybody above or below him and contemptuous of those on his level.

"Ready?" said Gordon.

****

When Croaker arrived outside Sir Trevor's office, his nerve failed him at the last and so it was Gordon who gave the gentle rap at the frosted-glass door. His PA opened the door to them and asked them to take a seat. Gordon and Croaker had only just chosen a seat - one awkward figure facing the other - when the PA reappeared to say he would see them immediately. The pair shot one another a final glance, and both were surprised by the sudden bond of camaraderie, like the two scrapping schoolboys, sworn enemies until they face the headmaster's cane together the warring tribes united against a common enemy. Gordon supposed Croaker's nerve was still shaking and made to enter the office first, but Croaker - reasserting his shaken authority - headed Gordon off and walked upright to meet his maker.

Sir Trevor's office was the antithesis of Croaker's murky dungeon four floors below. It was light, spartan and with a few elegant touches of chrome and leather - the gold leaf and marble of executive power. They stood level with the tower of Westminster Cathedral as it poked over the red-brick mansion blocks of SW1. Sir Trevor looked up cheerfully enough from some missive and welcomed them with an outstretched arm. Gordon and Croaker found their places, somewhat awkwardly and in silence, on the opposite side of his large desk.

"Right, your trip to Cornwall," Sir Trevor began and fished about in his pile of papers for the copy Gordon had filed. Croaker guessed his intention and produced his only print out.

"No need, no need," said Sir Trevor with a dismissive wave. "I've already read it a couple of times."

Then turning to Gordon, "You know David is my son, right? I'm sure they all told you this."

Gordon nodded and a silence descended which filled Croaker with horror and his whirring brain lost the composure it had wrestled to maintain.

"I'd never have sent him Sir Trevor had I known," Croaker was burbling. "I thought a trip from London would be good for him to see how the reporters work in the field. I just didn't know..."

"Know what?" said Sir Trevor with an amused smile.

"It's just, I had no idea it would turn out like this."

"Like what?" said Sir Trevor just as good naturedly with a smile almost breaking into laughter.

Croaker looked uncertain and flustered and fluffed a couple of lines. Sir Trevor interrupted.

"Have a look at these," he said to Gordon and Croaker, handing them a sheet of A4 paper loaded with baffling figures. "Do you know what they mean?"

Gordon eyed them casually - like a dog's interest in the television - but Croaker's face hung with a more serious aspect, however, his interpretation of the figures drew a blank. He suspected they were the number of clients and subscription revenue Gordon's copy had cost the Associated News. So blind was his prejudice he failed to recognise the situation.

"All I can say is how sorry we are," Croaker began. "I will put in place an extra security buffer between the editor and the subs to ensure something like this never happens again."

"Why wouldn't we want it to happen again?" said Sir Trevor with a troubled brow.

254

Croaker sat in confused silence.

"What do you think?" said Sir Trevor turning once again to Gordon, the patronising concern he adopted with Croaker effaced. "You know a good story when you see one, clearly?"

It was Gordon's turn to look puzzled.

"I've had the editor of the MailOnline on the phone. He loves the new direction; he was very interested in what we're doing. An overnight sub posted your story with the photo and the response nearly crashed their servers. Within hours it was all over the social networks, redirecting links, creating speculation - there's even a series of monster memes doing the rounds."

Sir Trevor spun his monitor around to face them. Gordon saw Clara's blurred photograph with its dark trunk and sea spray and a sudden chill ran down his spine with the recollection. In capital letters somebody had written "OMG!!! RIDICULOUSLY PHOTOGENIC MONSTER".

"What does it mean?" said Gordon.

"Buggered if I know," said Sir Trevor. "But I know what 12 million clicks in less than six hours means for us. It means the MailOnline is looking to subscribe to a premium service for another three years. And that's just the tip of the iceberg. The Telegraph, the Guardian, the Sun... they all ran it online and they all had similar responses - 7 million clicks between them."

"19 million," said Croaker numbly. "There's barely 15 million literate people in the UK."

"You're a flat earther," said Sir Trevor bad temperedly. "Maybe a quarter of these hits came from a British IP. The rest is America, Australia, Canada, South America, even Japan. We're talking to the world now. I'm glad somebody was listening when I made my "band of brothers" speech."

Sir Trevor smiled at Gordon who felt uncomfortable once more. He still wasn't certain this wasn't all some warped good cop bad cap ruse to trick a confession.

"This is what the Click News initiative is all about. This sums it all up. It's storytelling, it's back to basics, it's working closely with the photographer to tell the story that people can't help but click on. It's compulsive, it's riveting, it's unbelievable, it's everything journalism 2.1 is all about. You are our Killer App."

Gordon squirmed.

"And where's your photographer?" said Sir Trevor.

"Sleeping, I suppose," Gordon said.

"Well, I want to see her too. The pair of you, you're my dream team. I'm not going to let you separate. From now on, you work together or not at all."

A silence returned. Croaker dumb-founded, Gordon only just less so, and Sir Trevor steeling himself for his next question.

"Was young David a help?" he said eventually once he'd mustered the nerve to vocalise his pride.

Gordon turned to Croaker, it was a mechanical response as he fought with himself and truth. Croaker performed Gordon a rare service and the glare in his eyes snapped him from indecision and allowed him to respond with confidence and conviction.

"He was a star," said Gordon, and then in the language Sir Trevor recognised from his Citizen Journalism lecture tour. "Perhaps he brought something new to the table. Some blue-sky thinking."

Sir Trevor banged the table with flat palms in delight.

"I knew," he said. "It's the young who are teaching the old in this new age. It's second nature to them. I'm thinking of a permanent understudy for the desk. Somebody to give our wire copy the once over, maybe inject a bit of spunk into the dusty words."

Croaker felt his innards shrivelling and the pumping hot rage of blood swelling his ears.

"Listen," said Sir Trevor conspiratorially. "How do you fancy a little peripatetic tour of East Anglia."

Gordon looked puzzled.

"It might be nothing, but I found this little article in the Eastern Eye and I reckon it's got you written all over it."

Sir Trevor thrust a clipping into Gordon's hands, he read: "THREE WALKERS DIE IN BOG HORROR."

"You've been working hard, so I don't propose anything too strenuous but why not check it out, spend a few days in the Fens. Just see what you think. And you'd take your photographer too of course."

"Clara?" said Gordon, betraying too much delight.

"Yes precisely. Clara."

Gordon weighed it up. Wisbech wasn't far from his father, and he always felt a strange sense of service to the old man. He had rather fancied a few days off, but the prospect of seeing Clara again awoke a spark of life that had not long ago been extinguished.

"Sure," said Gordon. "It's a great idea."

Croaker bit his lip.

"Give it the Gordon Athelney treatment," said Sir Trevor. "But naturally I trust your judgment every time. Do what you think is right. And take as long as you think it needs. We can spare you in London this week, right Percy?"

The bones in Croaker's clenched fists nearly snapped at the sound of his first name, particularly spoken in front a junior.

'So that's his name," thought Gordon. 'Gotcha."

"Of course," said Croaker. "We won't miss him."

"Then it's decided," said Sir Trevor delighted at the smoothness and speed of his will. "Get travel Alan to book your tickets and I'll look forward to reading what you've got for us."

Gordon stood in triumph. He felt like giving Sir Trevor a little bow.

"And of course, you'll be wanting me to spare David, right?" said Sir Trevor.

Gordon looked blank. It took a moment for him to process what was happening.

"Permission granted," said Sir Trevor. "His mother will no doubt chew my ear for letting him go again but it's good for the lad. I'm just pleased he's found his feet."

Gordon smiled and left; the words BOG HORROR stamped across his brain in indelible ink.

Printed in Great Britain
by Amazon